CHARLOTTE'S WEB

with STUART LITTLE *and* THE TRUMPET OF THE SWAN

E. B. WHITE

HarperTrophy®
An Imprint of HarperCollins*Publishers*

Library of Congress Cataloging-in-Publication Data is available.
ISBN-10: 0-06-112557-1 (pbk. bdg.)
ISBN-13: 978-0-06-112557-7 (pbk. bdg.)

1 2 3 4 5 6 7 8 9 10
❖
First Edition

Charlotte's Web
with Stuart Little
and The Trumpet of the Swan

Contents

Charlotte's Web

Contents

I

Before Breakfast

"WHERE'S PAPA GOING WITH THAT AX?" SAID Fern to her mother as they were setting the table for breakfast.

"Out to the hoghouse," replied Mrs. Arable. "Some pigs were born last night."

"I don't see why he needs an ax," continued Fern, who was only eight.

"Well," said her mother, "one of the pigs is a runt. It's very small and weak, and it will never amount to anything. So your father has decided to do away with it."

"Do *away* with it?" shrieked Fern. "You mean *kill* it? Just because it's smaller than the others?"

Mrs. Arable put a pitcher of cream on the table. "Don't yell, Fern!" she said. "Your father is right. The pig would probably die anyway."

Fern pushed a chair out of the way and ran outdoors. The grass was wet and the earth smelled of springtime. Fern's sneakers were sopping by the time she caught up with her father.

"Please don't kill it!" she sobbed. "It's unfair."

Mr. Arable stopped walking.

"Fern," he said gently, "you will have to learn to control yourself."

"Control myself?" yelled Fern. "This is a matter of life and death, and you talk about *controlling* myself." Tears ran down her cheeks and she took hold of the ax and tried to pull it out of her father's hand.

"Fern," said Mr. Arable, "I know more about raising a litter of pigs than you do. A weakling makes trouble. Now run along!"

"But it's unfair," cried Fern. "The pig couldn't help being born small, could it? If *I* had been very small at birth, would you have killed *me*?"

Mr. Arable smiled. "Certainly not," he said, looking down at his daughter with love. "But this is different. A little girl is one thing, a little runty pig is another."

"I see no difference," replied Fern, still hanging on to the ax. "This is the most terrible case of injustice I ever heard of."

A queer look came over John Arable's face. He seemed almost ready to cry himself.

"All right," he said. "You go back to the house and I will bring the runt when I come in. I'll let you start it on a bottle, like a baby. Then you'll see what trouble a pig can be."

When Mr. Arable returned to the house half an hour later, he carried a carton under his arm. Fern was upstairs changing her sneakers. The kitchen table was set for breakfast, and the room smelled of coffee, bacon, damp plaster, and wood smoke from the stove.

"Put it on her chair!" said Mrs. Arable. Mr. Arable set the carton down at Fern's place. Then he walked to the sink and washed his hands and dried them on the roller towel.

Fern came slowly down the stairs. Her eyes were red from crying. As she approached her chair, the carton wobbled, and there was a scratching noise. Fern looked at her father. Then she lifted the lid of the carton. There, inside, looking up at her, was the newborn pig. It was a white one. The morning light shone through its ears, turning them pink.

"He's yours," said Mr. Arable. "Saved from an untimely death. And may the good Lord forgive me for this foolishness."

Fern couldn't take her eyes off the tiny pig. "Oh," she whispered. "Oh, *look* at him! He's absolutely perfect."

She closed the carton carefully. First she kissed her father, then she kissed her mother. Then she opened the lid again, lifted the pig out, and held it against her cheek. At this moment her brother Avery came into the room. Avery was ten. He was heavily armed—an air rifle in one hand, a wooden dagger in the other.

"What's that?" he demanded. "What's Fern got?"

"She's got a guest for breakfast," said Mrs. Arable. "Wash your hands and face, Avery!"

"Let's see it!" said Avery, setting his gun down. "You call that miserable thing a pig? That's a *fine* specimen of a pig—it's no bigger than a white rat."

"Wash up and eat your breakfast, Avery!" said his mother. "The school bus will be along in half an hour."

"Can I have a pig, too, Pop?" asked Avery.

"No, I only distribute pigs to early risers," said Mr. Arable. "Fern was up at daylight, trying to rid the world of injustice. As a result, she now has a pig. A small one, to be sure, but nevertheless a pig. It just shows what can happen if a person gets out of bed promptly. Let's eat!"

But Fern couldn't eat until her pig had had a drink

of milk. Mrs. Arable found a baby's nursing bottle and a rubber nipple. She poured warm milk into the bottle, fitted the nipple over the top, and handed it to Fern. "Give him his breakfast!" she said.

A minute later, Fern was seated on the floor in the corner of the kitchen with her infant between her knees, teaching it to suck from the bottle. The pig, although tiny, had a good appetite and caught on quickly.

The school bus honked from the road.

"Run!" commanded Mrs. Arable, taking the pig from Fern and slipping a doughnut into her hand. Avery grabbed his gun and another doughnut.

The children ran out to the road and climbed into the bus. Fern took no notice of the others in the bus. She just sat and stared out of the window, thinking what a blissful world it was and how lucky she was to have entire charge of a pig. By the time the bus reached school, Fern had named her pet, selecting the most beautiful name she could think of.

"Its name is Wilbur," she whispered to herself.

She was still thinking about the pig when the teacher said: "Fern, what is the capital of Pennsylvania?"

"Wilbur," replied Fern, dreamily. The pupils giggled. Fern blushed.

II

Wilbur

FERN LOVED WILBUR MORE THAN ANYTHING. She loved to stroke him, to feed him, to put him to bed. Every morning, as soon as she got up, she warmed his milk, tied his bib on, and held the bottle for him. Every afternoon, when the school bus stopped in front of her house, she jumped out and ran to the kitchen to fix another bottle for him. She fed him again at suppertime, and again just before going to bed. Mrs. Arable gave him a feeding around noontime each day, when Fern was away in school. Wilbur loved his milk, and he was never happier than when Fern was warming up a bottle for him. He would stand and gaze up at her with adoring eyes.

For the first few days of his life, Wilbur was allowed to live in a box near the stove in the kitchen. Then, when Mrs. Arable complained, he was moved to a bigger box in the woodshed. At two weeks of age, he was moved outdoors. It was apple-blossom time, and the days were getting warmer. Mr. Arable fixed a small yard specially for Wilbur under an apple tree, and gave him a large wooden box full of straw, with a doorway cut in it so he could walk in and out as he pleased.

"Won't he be cold at night?" asked Fern.

"No," said her father. "You watch and see what he does."

Carrying a bottle of milk, Fern sat down under the apple tree inside the yard. Wilbur ran to her and she held the bottle for him while he sucked. When he had finished the last drop, he grunted and walked sleepily into the box. Fern peered through the door. Wilbur was poking the straw with his snout. In a short time he had dug a tunnel in the straw. He crawled into the tunnel and disappeared from sight, completely covered with straw. Fern was enchanted. It relieved her mind to know that her baby would sleep covered up, and would stay warm.

Every morning after breakfast, Wilbur walked out to the road with Fern and waited with her till the bus came. She would wave good-bye to him, and he would stand and watch the bus until it vanished around a turn. While Fern was in school, Wilbur was shut up inside his yard. But as soon as she got home in the afternoon, she would take him out and he would follow her around the place. If she went into the house, Wilbur went, too. If she went upstairs, Wilbur would wait at the bottom step until she came down again. If she took her doll for a walk in the doll carriage, Wilbur followed along. Sometimes, on these journeys, Wilbur would get tired, and Fern would pick him up and put him in the carriage alongside the doll. He liked this. And if he was *very* tired, he would close his eyes and go to sleep under the doll's blanket. He looked cute when his eyes were closed, because his lashes were so long. The doll would close her eyes, too, and Fern would wheel the carriage very slowly and smoothly so as not to wake her infants.

One warm afternoon, Fern and Avery put on bathing suits and went down to the brook for a swim. Wilbur tagged along at Fern's heels. When she waded into the brook, Wilbur waded in with her. He found the water quite cold—too cold for his liking. So while the children swam and played and splashed water at each other, Wilbur amused himself in the mud along the edge of the brook, where it was warm and moist and delightfully sticky and oozy.

Every day was a happy day, and every night was peaceful.

Wilbur was what farmers call a spring pig, which simply means that he was born in springtime. When he was five weeks old, Mr. Arable said he was now big enough to sell, and would have to be sold. Fern broke down and wept. But her father was firm about it. Wilbur's appetite had increased; he was beginning to eat scraps of food in addition to milk. Mr. Arable was not willing to provide for him any longer. He had already sold Wilbur's ten brothers and sisters.

"He's got to go, Fern," he said. "You have had your fun raising a baby pig, but Wilbur is not a baby any longer and he has got to be sold."

"Call up the Zuckermans," suggested Mrs. Arable to Fern. "Your Uncle Homer sometimes raises a pig. And if Wilbur goes there to live, you can walk down the road and visit him as often as you like."

"How much money should I ask for him?" Fern wanted to know.

"Well," said her father, "he's a runt. Tell your Uncle Homer you've got a pig you'll sell for six dollars, and see what he says."

It was soon arranged. Fern phoned and got her Aunt Edith, and her Aunt Edith hollered for Uncle Homer, and Uncle Homer came in from the barn and talked to Fern. When he heard that the price was only six dollars, he said he would buy the pig. Next day Wilbur was taken from his home under the apple tree and went to live in a manure pile in the cellar of Zuckerman's barn.

III

Escape

THE BARN WAS VERY LARGE. IT WAS VERY old. It smelled of hay and it smelled of manure. It smelled of the perspiration of tired horses and the wonderful sweet breath of patient cows. It often had a sort of peaceful smell—as though nothing bad could happen ever again in the world. It smelled of grain and of harness dressing and of axle grease and of rubber boots and of new rope. And whenever the cat was given a fish-head to eat, the barn would smell of fish. But mostly it smelled of hay, for there was always hay in the great loft up overhead. And there was always hay being pitched down to the cows and the horses and the sheep.

The barn was pleasantly warm in winter when the animals spent most of their time indoors, and it was pleasantly cool in summer when the big doors stood wide open to the breeze. The barn had stalls on the main floor for the work horses, tie-ups on the main floor for the cows, a sheepfold down below for the sheep, a pigpen down below for Wilbur, and it was full of all sorts of things that you find in barns: ladders, grindstones, pitchforks, monkey wrenches, scythes, lawn mowers, snow shovels, ax handles, milk pails, water buckets, empty grain sacks, and rusty rat traps. It was the kind of barn that swallows like to build their nests in. It was the kind of barn that children like to play in. And the whole thing was owned by Fern's uncle, Mr. Homer L. Zuckerman.

Wilbur's new home was in the lower part of the barn, directly underneath the cows. Mr. Zuckerman knew that a manure pile is a good place to keep a young pig. Pigs need warmth, and it was warm and comfortable down there in the barn cellar on the south side.

Fern came almost every day to visit him. She found an old milking stool that had been discarded, and she placed the stool in the sheepfold next to Wilbur's pen. Here she sat quietly during the long afternoons, thinking and listening and watching Wilbur. The sheep soon got to know her and trust her. So did the geese, who lived with the sheep. All the animals trusted her, she was so quiet and friendly. Mr. Zuckerman did not allow her to take Wilbur out, and he did not allow her to get into the pigpen. But he told Fern that she could sit on the stool and watch Wilbur as long as she wanted to. It made her happy just to be near the pig, and it made Wilbur happy to know that she was sitting there, right outside his pen. But he never had any fun—no walks, no rides, no swims.

One afternoon in June, when Wilbur was almost two months old, he wandered out into his small yard outside the barn. Fern had not arrived for her usual visit. Wilbur stood in the sun feeling lonely and bored.

"There's never anything to do around here," he thought. He walked slowly to his food trough and sniffed to see if anything had been overlooked at lunch. He found a small strip of potato skin and ate it. His back itched, so he leaned against the fence and rubbed against the boards. When he tired of this, he walked indoors, climbed to the top of the manure pile, and sat down. He didn't feel like going to sleep, he didn't feel like digging, he was tired of standing still, tired of lying down. "I'm less than two months old and I'm tired of living," he said. He walked out to the yard again.

"When I'm out here," he said, "there's no place to go but in. When I'm indoors, there's no place to go but out in the yard."

"That's where you're wrong, my friend, my friend," said a voice.

Wilbur looked through the fence and saw the goose standing there.

"You don't have to stay in that dirty-little dirty-little dirty-little yard," said the goose, who talked rather fast. "One of the boards is loose. Push on it, push-push-push on it, and come on out!"

"What?" said Wilbur. "Say it slower!"

"At-at-at, at the risk of repeating myself," said the goose, "I suggest that you come on out. It's wonderful out here."

"Did you say a board was loose?"

"That I did, that I did," said the goose.

Wilbur walked up to the fence and saw that the goose was right—one board was loose. He put his head down, shut his eyes, and pushed. The board gave way. In a minute he had squeezed through the fence and was standing in the long grass outside his yard. The goose chuckled.

"How does it feel to be free?" she asked.

"I like it," said Wilbur. "That is, I *guess* I like it." Actually, Wilbur felt queer to be outside his fence, with nothing between him and the big world.

"Where do you think I'd better go?"

"Anywhere you like, anywhere you like," said the goose. "Go down through the orchard, root up the sod! Go down through the garden, dig up the radishes! Root up everything! Eat grass! Look for corn! Look for oats! Run all over! Skip and dance, jump and prance! Go down through the orchard and stroll in the woods! The world is a wonderful place when you're young."

"I can see that," replied Wilbur. He gave a jump in the air, twirled, ran a few steps, stopped, looked all around, sniffed the smells of afternoon, and then set off walking down through the orchard. Pausing in the shade of an apple tree, he put his strong snout into the ground and began pushing, digging, and rooting. He felt very happy. He had plowed up quite a piece of ground before anyone noticed him. Mrs. Zuckerman was the first to see him. She saw him from the kitchen window, and she immediately shouted for the men.

"Ho-*mer*!" she cried. "Pig's out! Lurvy! Pig's out! Homer! Lurvy! Pig's out. He's down there under that apple tree."

"Now the trouble starts," thought Wilbur. "Now I'll catch it."

The goose heard the racket and she, too, started hollering. "Run-run-run downhill, make for the woods, the woods!" she shouted to Wilbur. "They'll never-never-never catch you in the woods."

The cocker spaniel heard the commotion and he ran out from the barn to join the chase. Mr. Zuckerman heard, and he came out of the machine shed where he was mending a tool. Lurvy, the hired man, heard the noise and came up from the asparagus patch where he was pulling weeds. Everybody walked toward Wilbur and Wilbur didn't know what to do. The woods seemed a long way off, and anyway, he had never been down there in the woods and wasn't sure he would like it.

"Get around behind him, Lurvy," said Mr. Zuckerman, "and drive him toward the barn! And take it easy—don't rush him! I'll go and get a bucket of slops."

The news of Wilbur's escape spread rapidly among the animals on the place. Whenever any creature broke loose on Zuckerman's farm, the event was of great interest to the others. The goose shouted to the nearest cow that Wilbur was free, and soon all the cows knew. Then one of the cows told one of the sheep, and soon all the sheep knew. The lambs learned about it from their mothers. The horses, in their stalls in the barn, pricked up their ears when they heard the goose hollering; and soon the horses had caught on to what was happening. "Wilbur's out," they said. Every animal stirred and lifted its head and became excited to know that one of his friends had got free and was no longer penned up or tied fast.

Wilbur didn't know what to do or which way to run. It seemed as though everybody was after him. "If this is what it's like to be free," he thought, "I believe I'd rather be penned up in my own yard."

The cocker spaniel was sneaking up on him from one side, Lurvy the hired man was sneaking up on him from the other side. Mrs. Zuckerman stood ready to head him off if he started for the garden, and now Mr. Zuckerman was coming down toward him carrying a pail. "This is really awful," thought Wilbur. "Why doesn't Fern come?" He began to cry.

The goose took command and began to give orders.

"Don't just stand there, Wilbur! Dodge about, dodge about!" cried the goose. "Skip around, run toward me, slip in and out, in and out, in and out! Make for the woods! Twist and turn!"

The cocker spaniel sprang for Wilbur's hind leg. Wilbur jumped and ran. Lurvy reached out and grabbed. Mrs. Zuckerman screamed at Lurvy. The goose cheered for Wilbur. Wilbur dodged between Lurvy's legs. Lurvy missed Wilbur and grabbed the spaniel instead. "Nicely done, nicely done!" cried the goose. "Try it again, try it again!"

"Run downhill!" suggested the cows.

"Run toward me!" yelled the gander.

"Run uphill!" cried the sheep.

"Turn and twist!" honked the goose.

"Jump and dance!" said the rooster.

"Look out for Lurvy!" called the cows.

"Look out for Zuckerman!" yelled the gander.

"Watch out for the dog!" cried the sheep.

"Listen to me, listen to me!" screamed the goose.

Poor Wilbur was dazed and frightened by this hullabaloo. He didn't like being the center of all this fuss. He tried to follow the instructions his friends were giving him, but he couldn't run downhill and uphill at the same time, and he couldn't turn and twist when he was jumping and dancing, and he was crying so hard he could barely see anything that was happening. After all, Wilbur was a very young pig—not much more than a baby, really. He wished Fern were there to take him in her arms and comfort him. When he looked up and saw Mr. Zuckerman standing quite close to him, holding a pail of warm slops, he felt relieved. He lifted his nose and sniffed. The smell was delicious—warm milk, potato skins, wheat middlings, Kellogg's Corn Flakes, and a popover left from the Zuckermans' breakfast.

"Come, pig!" said Mr. Zuckerman, tapping the pail. "Come pig!"

Wilbur took a step toward the pail.

"No-no-no!" said the goose. "It's the old pail trick, Wilbur. Don't fall for it, don't fall for it! He's trying to lure you back into captivity-ivity. He's appealing to your stomach."

Wilbur didn't care. The food smelled appetizing. He took another step toward the pail.

"Pig, pig!" said Mr. Zuckerman in a kind voice, and began walking slowly toward the barnyard, looking all about him innocently, as if he didn't know that a little white pig was following along behind him.

"You'll be sorry-sorry-sorry," called the goose.

Wilbur didn't care. He kept walking toward the pail of slops.

"You'll miss your freedom," honked the goose. "An hour of freedom is worth a barrel of slops."

Wilbur didn't care.

When Mr. Zuckerman reached the pigpen, he climbed over the fence and poured the slops into the trough. Then he pulled the loose board away from the fence, so that there was a wide hole for Wilbur to walk through.

"Reconsider, reconsider!" cried the goose.

Wilbur paid no attention. He stepped through the fence into his yard. He walked to the trough and took a long drink of slops, sucking in the milk hungrily and chewing the popover. It was good to be home again.

While Wilbur ate, Lurvy fetched a hammer and some 8-penny nails and nailed the board in place. Then he and Mr. Zuckerman leaned lazily on the fence and Mr. Zuckerman scratched Wilbur's back with a stick.

"He's quite a pig," said Lurvy.

"Yes, he'll make a good pig," said Mr. Zuckerman.

Wilbur heard the words of praise. He felt the warm milk inside his stomach. He felt the pleasant rubbing of the stick along his itchy back. He felt peaceful and happy and sleepy. This had been a tiring afternoon. It was still only about four o'clock but Wilbur was ready for bed.

"I'm really too young to go out into the world alone," he thought as he lay down.

IV

Loneliness

THE NEXT DAY WAS RAINY AND DARK. RAIN fell on the roof of the barn and dripped steadily from the eaves. Rain fell in the barnyard and ran in crooked courses down into the lane where thistles and pigweed grew. Rain spattered against Mrs. Zuckerman's kitchen windows and came gushing out of the downspouts. Rain fell on the backs of the sheep as they grazed in the meadow. When the sheep tired of standing in the rain, they walked slowly up the lane and into the fold.

Rain upset Wilbur's plans. Wilbur had planned to go out, this day, and dig a new hole in his yard. He had other plans, too. His plans for the day went something like this:

Breakfast at six-thirty. Skim milk, crusts, middlings, bits of doughnuts, wheat cakes with drops of maple syrup sticking to them, potato skins, leftover custard pudding with raisins, and bits of Shredded Wheat.

Breakfast would be finished at seven.

From seven to eight, Wilbur planned to have a talk with Templeton, the rat that lived under his trough. Talking with Templeton was not the most interesting occupation in the world but it was better than nothing.

From eight to nine, Wilbur planned to take a nap outdoors in the sun.

From nine to eleven he planned to dig a hole, or trench, and possibly find something good to eat buried in the dirt.

From eleven to twelve he planned to stand still and watch flies on the boards, watch bees in the clover, and watch swallows in the air.

Twelve o'clock—lunchtime. Middlings, warm water, apple parings, meat gravy, carrot scrapings, meat scraps, stale hominy, and the wrapper off a package of cheese. Lunch would be over at one.

From one to two, Wilbur planned to sleep.

From two to three, he planned to scratch itchy places by rubbing against the fence.

From three to four, he planned to stand perfectly

still and think of what it was like to be alive, and to wait for Fern.

At four would come supper. Skim milk, provender, leftover sandwich from Lurvy's lunchbox, prune skins, a morsel of this, a bit of that, fried potatoes, marmalade drippings, a little more of this, a little more of that, a piece of baked apple, a scrap of upsidedown cake.

Wilbur had gone to sleep thinking about these plans. He awoke at six and saw the rain, and it seemed as though he couldn't bear it.

"I get everything all beautifully planned out and it has to go and rain," he said.

For a while he stood gloomily indoors. Then he walked to the door and looked out. Drops of rain struck his face. His yard was cold and wet. His trough had an inch of rainwater in it. Templeton was nowhere to be seen.

"Are you out there, Templeton?" called Wilbur. There was no answer. Suddenly Wilbur felt lonely and friendless.

"One day just like another," he groaned. "I'm very young, I have no real friend here in the barn, it's going to rain all morning and all afternoon, and Fern won't come in such bad weather. Oh, *honestly*!" And Wilbur was crying again, for the second time in two days.

At six-thirty Wilbur heard the banging of a pail. Lurvy was standing outside in the rain, stirring up breakfast.

"C'mon, pig!" said Lurvy.

Wilbur did not budge. Lurvy dumped the slops, scraped the pail, and walked away. He noticed that something was wrong with the pig.

Wilbur didn't want food, he wanted love. He wanted a friend—someone who would play with him. He mentioned this to the goose, who was sitting quietly in a corner of the sheepfold.

"Will you come over and play with me?" he asked.

"Sorry, sonny, sorry," said the goose. "I'm sitting-sitting on my eggs. Eight of them. Got to keep them toasty-oasty-oasty warm. I have to stay right here, I'm no flibberty-ibberty-gibbet. I do not play when there are eggs to hatch. I'm expecting goslings."

"Well, I didn't think you were expecting woodpeckers," said Wilbur, bitterly.

Wilbur next tried one of the lambs.

"Will you please play with me?" he asked.

"Certainly not," said the lamb. "In the first place, I cannot get into your pen, as I am not old enough to jump over the fence. In the second place, I am not interested in pigs. Pigs mean less than nothing to me."

"What do you mean, *less* than nothing?" replied Wilbur. "I don't think there is any such thing as *less* than nothing. Nothing is absolutely the limit of nothingness. It's the lowest you can go. It's the end of the line. How can something be less than nothing? If there were something that was less than nothing, then nothing would not be nothing, it would be something—even though it's just a very little bit of something. But if nothing is *nothing*, then nothing has nothing that is less than *it* is."

"Oh, be quiet!" said the lamb. "Go play by yourself! I don't play with pigs."

Sadly, Wilbur lay down and listened to the rain. Soon he saw the rat climbing down a slanting board that he used as a stairway.

"Will you play with me, Templeton?" asked Wilbur.

"Play?" said Templeton, twirling his whiskers. "Play? I hardly know the meaning of the word."

"Well," said Wilbur, "it means to have fun, to frolic, to run and skip and make merry."

"I never do those things if I can avoid them," replied the rat, sourly. "I prefer to spend my time eating, gnawing, spying, and hiding. I am a glutton but not a merrymaker. Right now I am on my way to your trough to eat your breakfast, since you haven't got sense enough to eat it yourself." And Templeton, the rat, crept stealthily along the wall and disappeared into a private tunnel that he had dug between the door and the trough in Wilbur's yard. Templeton was a crafty rat, and he had things pretty much his own way. The tunnel was an example of his skill and cunning. The tunnel enabled him to get from the barn to his hiding place under the pig trough without coming out into the open. He had tunnels and runways all over Mr. Zuckerman's farm and could get from one place to another without being seen. Usually he slept during the daytime and was abroad only after dark.

Wilbur watched him disappear into his tunnel. In a moment he saw the rat's sharp nose poke out from underneath the wooden trough. Cautiously Templeton pulled himself up over the edge of the trough. This was almost more than Wilbur could stand: on this dreary, rainy day to see his breakfast being eaten by somebody else. He knew Templeton was getting soaked, out there in the pouring rain, but even that didn't comfort him. Friendless, dejected, and hungry, he threw himself down in the manure and sobbed.

Late that afternoon, Lurvy went to Mr. Zuckerman. "I think there's something wrong with that pig of yours. He hasn't touched his food."

"Give him two spoonfuls of sulphur and a little molasses," said Mr. Zuckerman.

Wilbur couldn't believe what was happening to him when Lurvy caught him and forced the medicine down his throat. This was certainly the worst day of his life. He didn't know whether he could endure the awful loneliness any more.

Darkness settled over everything. Soon there were only shadows and the noises of the sheep chewing their cuds, and occasionally the rattle of a cow-chain up overhead. You can imagine Wilbur's surprise when, out of the darkness, came a small voice he had never heard before. It sounded rather thin, but pleasant. "Do you want a friend, Wilbur?" it said. "I'll be a friend to you. I've watched you all day and I like you."

"But I can't see you," said Wilbur, jumping to his feet. "Where are you? And *who* are you?"

"I'm right up here," said the voice. "Go to sleep. You'll see me in the morning."

V

Charlotte

THE NIGHT SEEMED LONG. WILBUR'S stomach was empty and his mind was full. And when your stomach is empty and your mind is full, it's always hard to sleep.

A dozen times during the night Wilbur woke and stared into the blackness, listening to the sounds and trying to figure out what time it was. A barn is never perfectly quiet. Even at midnight there is usually something stirring.

The first time he woke, he heard Templeton gnawing a hole in the grain bin. Templeton's teeth scraped loudly against the wood and made quite a racket. "That crazy rat!" thought Wilbur. "Why does he have to stay up all night, grinding his clashers and destroying people's property? Why can't he go to sleep, like any decent animal?"

The second time Wilbur woke, he heard the goose turning on her nest and chuckling to herself.

"What time is it?" whispered Wilbur to the goose.

"Probably-obably-obably about half-past eleven," said the goose. "Why aren't you asleep, Wilbur?"

"Too many things on my mind," said Wilbur.

"Well," said the goose, "that's not *my* trouble. I have nothing at all on my mind, but I've too many things under my behind. Have you ever tried to sleep while sitting on eight eggs?"

"No," replied Wilbur. "I suppose it *is* uncomfortable. How long does it take a goose egg to hatch?"

"Approximately-oximately thirty days, all told," answered the goose. "But I cheat a little. On warm afternoons, I just pull a little straw over the eggs and go out for a walk."

Wilbur yawned and went back to sleep. In his dreams he heard again the voice saying, "I'll be a friend to you. Go to sleep—you'll see me in the morning."

About half an hour before dawn, Wilbur woke and listened. The barn was still dark. The sheep lay motionless. Even the goose was quiet. Overhead, on the main floor, nothing stirred: the cows were resting, the horses dozed. Templeton had quit work and gone off somewhere on an errand. The only sound was a slight scraping noise from the rooftop, where the weather-vane swung back and forth. Wilbur loved the barn when it was like this—calm and quiet, waiting for light.

"Day is almost here," he thought.

Through a small window, a faint gleam appeared. One by one the stars went out. Wilbur could see the goose a few feet away. She sat with head tucked under a wing. Then he could see the sheep and the lambs. The sky lightened.

"Oh, beautiful day, it is here at last! Today I shall find my friend."

Wilbur looked everywhere. He searched his pen thoroughly. He examined the window ledge, stared up at the ceiling. But he saw nothing new. Finally he decided he would have to speak up. He hated to break the lovely stillness of dawn by using his voice, but he couldn't think of any other way to locate the mysterious new friend who was nowhere to be seen. So Wilbur cleared his throat.

"Attention, please!" he said in a loud, firm voice. "Will the party who addressed me at bedtime last night kindly make himself or herself known by giving an appropriate sign or signal!"

Wilbur paused and listened. All the other animals lifted their heads and stared at him. Wilbur blushed.

But he was determined to get in touch with his unknown friend.

"Attention, please!" he said. "I will repeat the message. Will the party who addressed me at bedtime last night kindly speak up. Please tell me where you are, if you are my friend!"

The sheep looked at each other in disgust.

"Stop your nonsense, Wilbur!" said the oldest sheep. "If you have a new friend here, you are probably disturbing his rest; and the quickest way to spoil a friendship is to wake somebody up in the morning before he is ready. How can you be sure your friend is an early riser?"

"I beg everyone's pardon," whispered Wilbur. "I didn't mean to be objectionable."

He lay down meekly in the manure, facing the door. He did not know it, but his friend was very near. And the old sheep was right—the friend was still asleep.

Soon Lurvy appeared with slops for breakfast. Wilbur rushed out, ate everything in a hurry, and licked the trough. The sheep moved off down the lane, the gander waddled along behind them, pulling grass. And then, just as Wilbur was settling down for his morning nap, he heard again the thin voice that had addressed him the night before.

"Salutations!" said the voice.

Wilbur jumped to his feet. "Salu-*what?*" he cried.

"Salutations!" repeated the voice.

"What are *they*, and where are *you?*" screamed Wilbur. "Please, *please*, tell me where you are. And what are salutations?"

"Salutations are greetings," said the voice. "When I say 'salutations,' it's just my fancy way of saying hello or good morning. Actually, it's a silly expression, and I am surprised that I used it at all. As for my whereabouts, that's easy. Look up here in the corner of the doorway! Here I am. Look, I'm waving!"

At last Wilbur saw the creature that had spoken to him in such a kindly way. Stretched across the upper part of the doorway was a big spider's web, and hanging from the top of the web, head down, was a large grey spider. She was about the size of a gumdrop. She had eight legs, and she was waving one of them at Wilbur in friendly greeting. "See me now?" she asked.

"Oh, yes indeed," said Wilbur. "Yes indeed! How are you? Good morning! Salutations! Very pleased to meet you. What is your name, please? May I have your name?"

"My name," said the spider, "is Charlotte."

"Charlotte what?" asked Wilbur, eagerly.

"Charlotte A. Cavatica. But just call me Charlotte."

"I think you're beautiful," said Wilbur.

"Well, I *am* pretty," replied Charlotte. "There's no denying that. Almost all spiders are rather nice-looking. I'm not as flashy as some, but I'll do. I wish I could see you, Wilbur, as clearly as you can see me."

"Why can't you?" asked the pig. "I'm right here."

"Yes, but I'm near-sighted," replied Charlotte. "I've always been dreadfully near-sighted. It's good in some ways, not so good in others. Watch me wrap up this fly."

A fly that had been crawling along Wilbur's trough had flown up and blundered into the lower part of Charlotte's web and was tangled in the sticky threads. The fly was beating its wings furiously, trying to break loose and free itself.

"First," said Charlotte, "I dive at him." She plunged headfirst toward the fly. As she dropped, a tiny silken thread unwound from her rear end.

"Next, I wrap him up." She grabbed the fly, threw a few jets of silk around it, and rolled it over and over, wrapping it so that it couldn't move. Wilbur watched in horror. He could hardly believe what he was seeing, and although he detested flies, he was sorry for this one.

"There!" said Charlotte. "Now I knock him out, so he'll be more comfortable." She bit the fly. "He can't feel a thing now," she remarked. "He'll make a perfect breakfast for me."

"You mean you *eat* flies?" gasped Wilbur.

"Certainly. Flies, bugs, grasshoppers, choice beetles, moths, butterflies, tasty cockroaches, gnats, midges, daddy longlegs, centipedes, mosquitoes, crickets—anything that is careless enough to get caught in my web. I have to live, don't I?"

"Why, yes, of course," said Wilbur. "Do they taste good?"

"Delicious. Of course, I don't really eat them. I drink them—drink their blood. I love blood," said Charlotte, and her pleasant, thin voice grew even thinner and more pleasant.

"Don't say that!" groaned Wilbur. "Please don't say things like that!"

"Why not? It's true, and I have to say what is true. I am not entirely happy about my diet of flies and bugs, but it's the way I'm made. A spider has to pick up a living somehow or other, and I happen to be a trapper. I just naturally build a web and trap flies and other insects. My mother was a trapper before me. Her mother was a trapper before her. All our family have been trappers. Way back for thousands and thousands of years we spiders have been laying for flies and bugs."

"It's a miserable inheritance," said Wilbur, gloomily. He was sad because his new friend was so bloodthirsty.

"Yes, it is," agreed Charlotte. "But I can't help it. I don't know how the first spider in the early days of the world happened to think up this fancy idea of spinning a web, but she did, and it was clever of her, too. And since then, all of us spiders have had to work the same trick. It's not a bad pitch, on the whole."

"It's cruel," replied Wilbur, who did not intend to be argued out of his position.

"Well, *you* can't talk," said Charlotte. "*You* have your meals brought to you in a pail. Nobody feeds me. I have to get my own living. I live by my wits. I have to be sharp and clever, lest I go hungry. I have to think things out, catch what I can, take what comes. And it just so happens, my friend, that what comes is flies and insects and bugs. And *further*more," said Charlotte, shaking one of her legs, "do you realize that if I didn't catch bugs and eat them, bugs would increase and multiply and get so numerous that they'd destroy the earth, wipe out everything?"

"Really?" said Wilbur. "I wouldn't want *that* to happen. Perhaps your web is a good thing after all."

The goose had been listening to this conversation and chuckling to herself. "There are a lot of things Wilbur doesn't know about life," she thought. "He's really a very innocent little pig. He doesn't even know what's going to happen to him around Christmastime; he has no idea that Mr. Zuckerman and Lurvy are plotting to kill him." And the goose raised herself a bit and poked her eggs a little further under her so that they would receive the full heat from her warm body and soft feathers.

Charlotte stood quietly over the fly, preparing to eat it. Wilbur lay down and closed his eyes. He was tired from his wakeful night and from the excitement of meeting someone for the first time. A breeze brought him the smell of clover—the sweet-smelling world beyond his fence. "Well," he thought, "I've got a new friend, all right. But what a gamble friendship is! Charlotte is fierce, brutal, scheming, bloodthirsty—everything I don't like. How can I learn to like her, even though she is pretty and, of course, clever?"

Wilbur was merely suffering the doubts and fears

that often go with finding a new friend. In good time he was to discover that he was mistaken about Charlotte. Underneath her rather bold and cruel exterior, she had a kind heart, and she was to prove loyal and true to the very end.

VI

Summer Days

THE EARLY SUMMER DAYS ON A FARM ARE the happiest and fairest days of the year. Lilacs bloom and make the air sweet, and then fade. Apple blossoms come with the lilacs, and the bees visit around among the apple trees. The days grow warm and soft. School ends, and children have time to play and to fish for trouts in the brook. Avery often brought a trout home in his pocket, warm and stiff and ready to be fried for supper.

Now that school was over, Fern visited the barn almost every day, to sit quietly on her stool. The animals treated her as an equal. The sheep lay calmly at her feet.

Around the first of July, the work horses were hitched to the mowing machine, and Mr. Zuckerman climbed into the seat and drove into the field. All morning you could hear the rattle of the machine as it went round and round, while the tall grass fell down behind the cutter bar in long green swathes. Next day, if there was no thunder shower, all hands would help rake and pitch and load, and the hay would be hauled to the barn in the high hay wagon, with Fern and Avery riding at the top of the load. Then the hay would be hoisted, sweet and warm, into the big loft, until the whole barn seemed like a wonderful bed of timothy and clover. It was fine to jump in, and perfect to hide in. And sometimes Avery would find a little grass snake in the hay, and would add it to the other things in his pocket.

Early summer days are a jubilee time for birds. In the fields, around the house, in the barn, in the woods, in the swamp—everywhere love and songs and nests and eggs. From the edge of the woods, the white-throated sparrow (which must come all the way from Boston) calls, "Oh, Peabody, Peabody, Peabody!" On an apple bough, the phoebe teeters and wags its tail and says, "Phoebe, phoe-bee!" The song sparrow, who knows how brief and lovely life is, says, "Sweet, sweet, sweet interlude; sweet, sweet, sweet interlude." If you enter the barn, the swallows swoop down from their nests and scold. "Cheeky, cheeky!" they say.

In early summer there are plenty of things for a child to eat and drink and suck and chew. Dandelion stems are full of milk, clover heads are loaded with nectar, the Frigidaire is full of ice-cold drinks. Everywhere you look is life; even the little ball of spit on the weed stalk, if you poke it apart, has a green worm inside it. And on the under side of the leaf of the potato vine are the bright orange eggs of the potato bug.

It was on a day in early summer that the goose eggs hatched. This was an important event in the barn cellar. Fern was there, sitting on her stool, when it happened.

Except for the goose herself, Charlotte was the first to know that the goslings had at last arrived. The goose knew a day in advance that they were coming—she could hear their weak voices calling from inside the egg. She knew that they were in a desperately cramped position inside the shell and were most anxious to break through and get out. So she sat quite still, and talked less than usual.

When the first gosling poked its grey-green head through the goose's feathers and looked around, Charlotte spied it and made the announcement.

"I am sure," she said, "that every one of us here

will be gratified to learn that after four weeks of unremitting effort and patience on the part of our friend the goose, she now has something to show for it. The goslings have arrived. May I offer my sincere congratulations!"

"Thank you, thank you, thank you!" said the goose, nodding and bowing shamelessly.

"Thank you," said the gander.

"Congratulations!" shouted Wilbur. "How many goslings are there? I can only see one."

"There are seven," said the goose.

"Fine!" said Charlotte. "Seven is a lucky number."

"Luck had nothing to do with this," said the goose. "It was good management and hard work."

At this point, Templeton showed his nose from his hiding place under Wilbur's trough. He glanced at Fern, then crept cautiously toward the goose, keeping close to the wall. Everyone watched him, for he was not well liked, not trusted.

"Look," he began in his sharp voice, "you say you have seven goslings. There were eight eggs. What happened to the other egg? Why didn't it hatch?"

"It's a dud, I guess," said the goose.

"What are you going to do with it?" continued Templeton, his little round beady eyes fixed on the goose.

"You can have it," replied the goose. "Roll it away and add it to that nasty collection of yours." (Templeton had a habit of picking up unusual objects around the farm and storing them in his home. He saved everything.)

"Certainly-ertainly-ertainly," said the gander. "You may have the egg. But I'll tell you one thing, Templeton, if I ever catch you poking-oking-oking your ugly nose around our goslings, I'll give you the worst pounding a rat ever took." And the gander opened his strong wings and beat the air with them to show his power. He was strong and brave, but the truth is, both the goose and the gander were worried about Templeton. And with good reason. The rat had no morals, no conscience, no scruples, no consideration, no decency, no milk of rodent kindness, no compunctions, no higher feeling, no friendliness, no anything. He would kill a gosling if he could get away with it—the goose knew that. Everybody knew it.

With her broad bill the goose pushed the unhatched egg out of the nest, and the entire company watched in disgust while the rat rolled it away. Even Wilbur, who could eat almost anything, was appalled. "Imagine wanting a junky old rotten egg!" he muttered.

"A rat is a rat," said Charlotte. She laughed a tinkling little laugh. "But, my friends, if that ancient egg ever breaks, this barn will be untenable."

"What's that mean?" asked Wilbur.

"It means nobody will be able to live here on account of the smell. A rotten egg is a regular stink bomb."

"I won't break it," snarled Templeton. "I know what I'm doing. I handle stuff like this all the time."

He disappeared into his tunnel, pushing the goose egg in front of him. He pushed and nudged till he succeeded in rolling it to his lair under the trough.

That afternoon, when the wind had died down and the barnyard was quiet and warm, the grey goose led her seven goslings off the nest and out into the world. Mr. Zuckerman spied them when he came with Wilbur's supper.

"Well, hello there!" he said, smiling all over. "Let's see . . . one, two, three, four, five, six, seven. Seven baby geese. Now isn't that lovely!"

VII

Bad News

WILBUR LIKED CHARLOTTE BETTER AND better each day. Her campaign against insects seemed sensible and useful. Hardly anybody around the farm had a good word to say for a fly. Flies spent their time pestering others. The cows hated them. The horses detested them. The sheep loathed them. Mr. and Mrs. Zuckerman were always complaining about them, and putting up screens.

Wilbur admired the way Charlotte managed. He was particularly glad that she always put her victim to sleep before eating it.

"It's real thoughtful of you to do that, Charlotte," he said.

"Yes," she replied in her sweet, musical voice, "I always give them an anaesthetic so they won't feel pain. It's a little service I throw in."

As the days went by, Wilbur grew and grew. He ate three big meals a day. He spent long hours lying on his side, half asleep, dreaming pleasant dreams. He enjoyed good health and he gained a lot of weight. One afternoon, when Fern was sitting on her stool, the oldest sheep walked into the barn, and stopped to pay a call on Wilbur.

"Hello!" she said. "Seems to me you're putting on weight."

"Yes, I guess I am," replied Wilbur. "At my age it's a good idea to keep gaining."

"Just the same, I don't envy you," said the old sheep. "You know why they're fattening you up, don't you?"

"No," said Wilbur.

"Well, I don't like to spread bad news," said the sheep, "but they're fattening you up because they're going to kill you, that's why."

"They're going to *what*?" screamed Wilbur. Fern grew rigid on her stool.

"Kill you. Turn you into smoked bacon and ham," continued the old sheep. "Almost all young pigs get murdered by the farmer as soon as the real cold weather sets in. There's a regular conspiracy around here to kill you at Christmastime. Everybody is in the plot—Lurvy, Zuckerman, even John Arable."

"Mr. Arable?" sobbed Wilbur. "Fern's father?"

"Certainly. When a pig is to be butchered, everybody helps. I'm an old sheep and I see the same thing, same old business, year after year. Arable arrives with his .22, shoots the . . ."

"Stop!" screamed Wilbur. "I don't want to die! Save me, somebody! Save me!" Fern was just about to jump up when a voice was heard.

"Be quiet, Wilbur!" said Charlotte, who had been listening to this awful conversation.

"I can't be quiet," screamed Wilbur, racing up and down. "I don't want to be killed. I don't want to die. Is it true what the old sheep says, Charlotte? Is it true they are going to kill me when the cold weather comes?"

"Well," said the spider, plucking thoughtfully at her web, "the old sheep has been around this barn a long time. She has seen many a spring pig come and go. If she says they plan to kill you, I'm sure it's true. It's also the dirtiest trick I ever heard of. What people don't think of!"

Wilbur burst into tears. "I don't *want* to die," he moaned. "I want to stay alive, right here in my comfortable manure pile with all my friends. I want to breathe the beautiful air and lie in the beautiful sun."

"You're certainly making a beautiful noise," snapped the old sheep.

"I don't want to die!" screamed Wilbur, throwing himself to the ground.

"You shall not die," said Charlotte, briskly.

"What? Really?" cried Wilbur. "Who's going to save me?"

"I am," said Charlotte.

"How?" asked Wilbur.

"That remains to be seen. But I am going to save you, and I want you to quiet down immediately. You're carrying on in a childish way. Stop your crying! I can't stand hysterics."

VIII

A Talk at Home

ON SUNDAY MORNING MR. AND MRS. Arable and Fern were sitting at breakfast in the kitchen. Avery had finished and was upstairs looking for his slingshot.

"Did you know that Uncle Homer's goslings had hatched?" asked Fern.

"How many?" asked Mr. Arable.

"Seven," replied Fern. "There were eight eggs but one egg didn't hatch and the goose told Templeton she didn't want it any more, so he took it away."

"The goose did what?" asked Mrs. Arable, gazing at her daughter with a queer, worried look.

"Told Templeton she didn't want the egg any more," repeated Fern.

"Who is Templeton?" asked Mrs. Arable.

"He's the rat," replied Fern. "None of us like him much."

"Who's 'us'?" asked Mr. Arable.

"Oh, everybody in the barn cellar. Wilbur and the sheep and the lambs and the goose and the gander and the goslings and Charlotte and me."

"Charlotte?" said Mrs. Arable. "Who's Charlotte?"

"She's Wilbur's best friend. She's terribly clever."

"What does she look like?" asked Mrs. Arable.

"Well-l," said Fern, thoughtfully, "she has eight legs. All spiders do, I guess."

"Charlotte is a spider?" asked Fern's mother.

Fern nodded. "A big grey one. She has a web across the top of Wilbur's doorway. She catches flies and sucks their blood. Wilbur adores her."

"Does he really?" said Mrs. Arable, rather vaguely. She was staring at Fern with a worried expression on her face.

"Oh, yes, Wilbur adores Charlotte," said Fern. "Do you know what Charlotte said when the goslings hatched?"

"I haven't the faintest idea," said Mr. Arable. "Tell us."

"Well, when the first gosling stuck its little head

out from under the goose, I was sitting on my stool in the corner and Charlotte was on her web. She made a speech. She said: 'I am sure that every one of us here in the barn cellar will be gratified to learn that after four weeks of unremitting effort and patience on the part of the goose, she now has something to show for it.' Don't you think that was a pleasant thing for her to say?"

"Yes, I do," said Mrs. Arable. "And now, Fern, it's time to get ready for Sunday School. And tell Avery to get ready. And this afternoon you can tell me more about what goes on in Uncle Homer's barn. Aren't you spending quite a lot of time there? You go there almost every afternoon, don't you?"

"I like it there," replied Fern. She wiped her mouth and ran upstairs. After she had left the room, Mrs. Arable spoke in a low voice to her husband.

"I worry about Fern," she said. "Did you hear the way she rambled on about the animals, pretending that they talked?"

Mr. Arable chuckled. "Maybe they do talk," he said. "I've sometimes wondered. At any rate, don't worry about Fern—she's just got a lively imagination. Kids think they hear all sorts of things."

"Just the same, I *do* worry about her," replied Mrs.

Arable. "I think I shall ask Dr. Dorian about her the next time I see him. He loves Fern almost as much as we do, and I want him to know how queerly she is acting about that pig and everything. I don't think it's normal. You know perfectly well animals don't talk."

Mr. Arable grinned. "Maybe our ears aren't as sharp as Fern's," he said.

IX

Wilbur's Boast

A SPIDER'S WEB IS STRONGER THAN IT looks. Although it is made of thin, delicate strands, the web is not easily broken. However, a web gets torn every day by the insects that kick around in it, and a spider must rebuild it when it gets full of holes. Charlotte liked to do her weaving during the late afternoon, and Fern liked to sit nearby and watch. One afternoon she heard a most interesting conversation and witnessed a strange event.

"You have awfully hairy legs, Charlotte," said Wilbur, as the spider busily worked at her task.

"My legs are hairy for a good reason," replied Charlotte. "Furthermore, each leg of mine has seven sections—the coxa, the trochanter, the femur, the patella, the tibia, the metatarsus, and the tarsus."

Wilbur sat bolt upright. "You're kidding," he said.

"No, I'm not, either."

"Say those names again, I didn't catch them the first time."

"Coxa, trochanter, femur, patella, tibia, metatarsus, and tarsus."

"Goodness!" said Wilbur, looking down at his own chubby legs. "I don't think *my* legs have seven sections."

"Well," said Charlotte, "you and I lead different lives. You don't have to spin a web. That takes real leg work."

"I could spin a web if I tried," said Wilbur, boasting. "I've just never tried."

"Let's see you do it," said Charlotte. Fern chuckled softly, and her eyes grew wide with love for the pig.

"O.K.," replied Wilbur. "You coach me and I'll spin one. It must be a lot of fun to spin a web. How do I start?"

"Take a deep breath!" said Charlotte, smiling. Wilbur breathed deeply. "Now climb to the highest place you can get to, like this." Charlotte raced up to the top of the doorway. Wilbur scrambled to the top of the manure pile.

"Very good!" said Charlotte. "Now make an attachment with your spinnerets, hurl yourself into space, and let out a dragline as you go down!"

Wilbur hesitated a moment, then jumped out into the air. He glanced hastily behind to see if a piece of rope was following him to check his fall, but nothing seemed to be happening in his rear, and the next thing he knew he landed with a thump. "Ooomp!" he grunted.

Charlotte laughed so hard her web began to sway.

"What did I do wrong?" asked the pig, when he recovered from his bump.

"Nothing," said Charlotte. "It was a nice try."

"I think I'll try again," said Wilbur, cheerfully. "I believe what I need is a little piece of string to hold me."

The pig walked out to his yard. "You there, Templeton?" he called. The rat poked his head out from under the trough.

"Got a little piece of string I could borrow?" asked Wilbur. "I need it to spin a web."

"Yes, indeed," replied Templeton, who saved string. "No trouble at all. Anything to oblige." He crept down into his hole, pushed the goose egg out of the way, and returned with an old piece of dirty white string. Wilbur examined it.

"That's just the thing," he said. "Tie one end to my tail, will you, Templeton?"

Wilbur crouched low, with his thin, curly tail toward the rat. Templeton seized the string, passed it around the end of the pig's tail, and tied two half hitches. Charlotte watched in delight. Like Fern, she was truly fond of Wilbur, whose smelly pen and stale food attracted the flies that she needed, and she was proud to see that he was not a quitter and was willing to try again to spin a web.

While the rat and the spider and the little girl watched, Wilbur climbed again to the top of the manure pile, full of energy and hope.

"Everybody watch!" he cried. And summoning all his strength, he threw himself into the air, headfirst. The string trailed behind him. But as he had neglected to fasten the other end to anything, it didn't really do any good, and Wilbur landed with a thud, crushed and hurt. Tears came to his eyes. Templeton grinned. Charlotte just sat quietly. After a bit she spoke.

"You can't spin a web, Wilbur, and I advise you to put the idea out of your mind. You lack two things needed for spinning a web."

"What are they?" asked Wilbur, sadly.

"You lack a set of spinnerets, and you lack know-how. But cheer up, you don't need a web. Zuckerman supplies you with three big meals a day. Why should you worry about trapping food?"

Wilbur sighed. "You're ever so much cleverer and brighter than I am, Charlotte. I guess I was just trying to show off. Serves me right."

Templeton untied his string and took it back to his home. Charlotte returned to her weaving.

"You needn't feel too badly, Wilbur," she said. "Not many creatures can spin webs. Even men aren't as good at it as spiders, although they *think* they're pretty good, and they'll *try* anything. Did you ever hear of the Queensborough Bridge?"

Wilbur shook his head. "Is it a web?"

"Sort of," replied Charlotte. "But do you know how long it took men to build it? Eight whole years. My goodness, I would have starved to death waiting that long. I can make a web in a single evening."

"What do people catch in the Queensborough Bridge—bugs?" asked Wilbur.

"No," said Charlotte. "They don't catch anything. They just keep trotting back and forth across the bridge thinking there is something better on the other side. If they'd hang head-down at the top of the thing and wait quietly, maybe something good would come along. But no—with men it's rush, rush, rush, every minute. I'm glad I'm a sedentary spider."

"What does sedentary mean?" asked Wilbur.

"Means I sit still a good part of the time and don't go wandering all over creation. I know a good thing when I see it, and my web is a good thing. I stay put and wait for what comes. Gives me a chance to think."

"Well, I'm sort of sedentary myself, I guess," said the pig. "I have to hang around here whether I want to or not. You know where I'd really like to be this evening?"

"Where?"

"In a forest looking for beechnuts and truffles and delectable roots, pushing leaves aside with my wonderful strong nose, searching and sniffing along the ground, smelling, smelling, smelling . . ."

"You smell just the way you are," remarked a lamb who had just walked in. "I can smell you from here. You're the smelliest creature in the place."

Wilbur hung his head. His eyes grew wet with tears. Charlotte noticed his embarrassment and she spoke sharply to the lamb.

"Let Wilbur alone!" she said. "He has a perfect right to smell, considering his surroundings. You're no bundle of sweet peas yourself. Furthermore, you are interrupting a very pleasant conversation. What were we talking about, Wilbur, when we were so rudely interrupted?"

"Oh, I don't remember," said Wilbur. "It doesn't make any difference. Let's not talk any more for a while, Charlotte. I'm getting sleepy. You go ahead and finish fixing your web and I'll just lie here and watch you. It's a lovely evening." Wilbur stretched out on his side.

Twilight settled over Zuckerman's barn, and a feeling of peace. Fern knew it was almost suppertime but she couldn't bear to leave. Swallows passed on silent wings, in and out of the doorways, bringing food to their young ones. From across the road a bird sang "Whippoorwill, whippoorwill!" Lurvy sat down under an apple tree and lit his pipe; the animals sniffed the familiar smell of strong tobacco. Wilbur heard the trill of the tree toad and the occasional slamming of the kitchen door. All these sounds made him feel comfortable and happy, for he loved life and loved to be a part of the world on a summer evening. But as he lay there he remembered what the old sheep had told him. The thought of death came to him and he began to tremble with fear.

"Charlotte?" he said, softly.

"Yes, Wilbur?"

"I don't want to die."

"Of course you don't," said Charlotte in a comforting voice.

"I just love it here in the barn," said Wilbur. "I love everything about this place."

"Of course you do," said Charlotte. "We all do."

The goose appeared, followed by her seven goslings. They thrust their little necks out and kept up a musical whistling, like a tiny troupe of pipers. Wilbur listened to the sound with love in his heart.

"Charlotte?" he said.

"Yes?" said the spider.

"Were you serious when you promised you would keep them from killing me?"

"I was never more serious in my life. I am not going to let you die, Wilbur."

"How are you going to save me?" asked Wilbur, whose curiosity was very strong on this point.

"Well," said Charlotte, vaguely, "I don't really know. But I'm working on a plan."

"That's wonderful," said Wilbur. "How is the plan coming, Charlotte? Have you got very far with it? Is it coming along pretty well?" Wilbur was trembling again, but Charlotte was cool and collected.

"Oh, it's coming all right," she said, lightly. "The plan is still in its early stages and hasn't completely shaped up yet, but I'm working on it."

"When do you work on it?" begged Wilbur.

"When I'm hanging head-down at the top of my web. That's when I do my thinking, because then all the blood is in my head."

"I'd be only too glad to help in any way I can."

"Oh, I'll work it out alone," said Charlotte. "I can think better if I think alone."

"All right," said Wilbur. "But don't fail to let me know if there's anything I can do to help, no matter how slight."

"Well," replied Charlotte, "you must try to build yourself up. I want you to get plenty of sleep, and stop worrying. Never hurry and never worry! Chew your food thoroughly and eat every bit of it, except you must leave just enough for Templeton. Gain weight and stay well—that's the way you can help. Keep fit, and don't lose your nerve. Do you think you understand?"

"Yes, I understand," said Wilbur.

"Go along to bed, then," said Charlotte. "Sleep is important."

Wilbur trotted over to the darkest corner of his

pen and threw himself down. He closed his eyes. In another minute he spoke.

"Charlotte?" he said.

"Yes, Wilbur?"

"May I go out to my trough and see if I left any of my supper? I think I left just a tiny bit of mashed potato."

"Very well," said Charlotte. "But I want you in bed again without delay."

Wilbur started to race out to his yard.

"Slowly, slowly!" said Charlotte. "Never hurry and never worry!"

Wilbur checked himself and crept slowly to his trough. He found a bit of potato, chewed it carefully, swallowed it, and walked back to bed. He closed his eyes and was silent for a while.

"Charlotte?" he said, in a whisper.

"Yes?"

"May I get a drink of milk? I think there are a few drops of milk left in my trough."

"No, the trough is dry, and I want you to go to sleep. No more talking! Close your eyes and go to sleep!"

Wilbur shut his eyes. Fern got up from her stool and started for home, her mind full of everything she had seen and heard.

"Good night, Charlotte!" said Wilbur.

"Good night, Wilbur!"

There was a pause.

"Good night, Charlotte!"

"Good night, Wilbur!"

"Good night!"

"Good night!"

X

An Explosion

DAY AFTER DAY THE SPIDER WAITED, head-down, for an idea to come to her. Hour by hour she sat motionless, deep in thought. Having promised Wilbur that she would save his life, she was determined to keep her promise.

Charlotte was naturally patient. She knew from experience that if she waited long enough, a fly would come to her web; and she felt sure that if she thought long enough about Wilbur's problem, an idea would come to her mind.

Finally, one morning toward the middle of July, the idea came. "Why, how perfectly simple!" she said to herself. "The way to save Wilbur's life is to play a trick on Zuckerman. If I can fool a bug," thought Charlotte, "I can surely fool a man. People are not as smart as bugs."

Wilbur walked into his yard just at that moment.

"What are you thinking about, Charlotte?" he asked.

"I was just thinking," said the spider, "that people are very gullible."

"What does 'gullible' mean?"

"Easy to fool," said Charlotte.

"That's a mercy," replied Wilbur, and he lay down in the shade of his fence and went fast asleep. The spider, however, stayed wide awake, gazing affectionately at him and making plans for his future. Summer was half gone. She knew she didn't have much time.

That morning, just as Wilbur fell asleep, Avery Arable wandered into the Zuckermans' front yard, followed by Fern. Avery carried a live frog in his hand.

Fern had a crown of daisies in her hair. The children ran for the kitchen.

"Just in time for a piece of blueberry pie," said Mrs. Zuckerman.

"Look at my frog!" said Avery, placing the frog on the drainboard and holding out his hand for pie.

"Take that thing out of here!" said Mrs. Zuckerman.

"He's hot," said Fern. "He's almost dead, that frog."

"He is not," said Avery. "He lets me scratch him between the eyes." The frog jumped and landed in Mrs. Zuckerman's dishpan full of soapy water.

"You're getting your pie on you," said Fern. "Can I look for eggs in the henhouse, Aunt Edith?"

"Run outdoors, both of you! And don't bother the hens!"

"It's getting all over everything," shouted Fern. "His pie is all over his front."

"Come on, frog!" cried Avery. He scooped up his frog. The frog kicked, splashing soapy water onto the blueberry pie.

"Another crisis!" groaned Fern.

"Let's swing in the swing!" said Avery.

The children ran to the barn.

Mr. Zuckerman had the best swing in the county. It was a single long piece of heavy rope tied to the beam over the north doorway. At the bottom end of the rope was a fat knot to sit on. It was arranged so that you could swing without being pushed. You climbed a ladder to the hayloft. Then, holding the rope, you stood at the edge and looked down, and were scared and dizzy. Then you straddled the knot, so that it acted as a seat. Then you got up all your nerve, took a deep breath, and jumped. For a second you seemed to be falling to the barn floor far below, but then suddenly the rope would begin to catch you, and you would sail through the barn door going a mile a minute, with the wind whistling in your eyes and ears and hair. Then you would zoom upward into the sky, and look up at the clouds, and the rope would twist and you would twist and turn with the rope. Then you would drop down, down, down out of the sky and come sailing back into the barn almost into the hayloft, then sail out again (not quite so far this time), then in again (not quite so high), then out again, then in again, then out, then in; and then you'd jump off and fall down and let somebody else try it.

Mothers for miles around worried about Zuckerman's swing. They feared some child would fall off. But no child ever did. Children almost always hang on to things tighter than their parents think they will.

Avery put the frog in his pocket and climbed to the hayloft. "The last time I swang in this swing, I almost crashed into a barn swallow," he yelled.

"Take that frog out!" ordered Fern.

Avery straddled the rope and jumped. He sailed out through the door, frog and all, and into the sky, frog and all. Then he sailed back into the barn.

"Your tongue is purple!" screamed Fern.

"So is yours!" cried Avery, sailing out again with the frog.

"I have hay inside my dress! It itches!" called Fern.

"Scratch it!" yelled Avery, as he sailed back.

"It's my turn," said Fern. "Jump off!"

"Fern's got the itch!" sang Avery.

When he jumped off, he threw the swing up to his sister. She shut her eyes tight and jumped. She felt the dizzy drop, then the supporting lift of the swing. When she opened her eyes she was looking up into the blue sky and was about to fly back through the door.

They took turns for an hour.

When the children grew tired of swinging, they went down toward the pasture and picked wild raspberries and ate them. Their tongues turned from purple to red. Fern bit into a raspberry that had a bad-tasting bug inside it, and got discouraged. Avery found an empty candy box and put his frog in it. The frog seemed tired after his morning in the swing. The children walked slowly up toward the barn. They, too, were tired and hardly had energy enough to walk.

"Let's build a tree house," suggested Avery. "I want

to live in a tree, with my frog."

"I'm going to visit Wilbur," Fern announced.

They climbed the fence into the lane and walked lazily toward the pigpen. Wilbur heard them coming and got up.

Avery noticed the spider's web, and, coming closer, he saw Charlotte.

"Hey, look at that big spider!" he said. "It's tremenjus."

"Leave it alone!" commanded Fern. "You've got a frog—isn't that enough?"

"That's a fine spider and I'm going to capture it," said Avery. He took the cover off the candy box. Then he picked up a stick. "I'm going to knock that ol' spider into this box," he said.

Wilbur's heart almost stopped when he saw what was going on. This might be the end of Charlotte if the boy succeeded in catching her.

"You stop it, Avery!" cried Fern.

Avery put one leg over the fence of the pigpen. He was just about to raise his stick to hit Charlotte when he lost his balance. He swayed and toppled and landed on the edge of Wilbur's trough. The trough tipped up and then came down with a slap. The goose egg was right underneath. There was a dull explosion as the egg broke, and then a horrible smell.

Fern screamed. Avery jumped to his feet. The air was filled with the terrible gases and smells from the rotten egg. Templeton, who had been resting in his home, scuttled away into the barn.

"Good *night*!" screamed Avery. "Good *night*! What a stink! Let's get out of here!"

Fern was crying. She held her nose and ran toward the house. Avery ran after her, holding his nose. Charlotte felt greatly relieved to see him go. It had been a narrow escape.

Later on that morning, the animals came up from the pasture—the sheep, the lambs, the gander, the goose, and the seven goslings. There were many complaints about the awful smell, and Wilbur had to tell the story over and over again, of how the Arable boy had tried to capture Charlotte, and how the smell of the broken egg drove him away just in time. "It was that rotten goose egg that saved Charlotte's life," said Wilbur.

The goose was proud of her share in the adventure. "I'm delighted that the egg never hatched," she gabbled.

Templeton, of course, was miserable over the loss

of his beloved egg. But he couldn't resist boasting. "It pays to save things," he said in his surly voice. "A rat never knows when something is going to come in handy. I never throw anything away."

"Well," said one of the lambs, "this whole business is all well and good for Charlotte, but what about the rest of us? The smell is unbearable. Who wants to live in a barn that is perfumed with rotten egg?"

"Don't worry, you'll get used to it," said Templeton. He sat up and pulled wisely at his long whiskers, then crept away to pay a visit to the dump.

When Lurvy showed up at lunchtime carrying a pail of food for Wilbur, he stopped short a few paces from the pigpen. He sniffed the air and made a face.

"What in thunder?" he said. Setting the pail down, he picked up the stick that Avery had dropped and pried the trough up. "Rats!" he said. "Fhew! I might a' known a rat would make a nest under this trough. How I hate a rat!"

And Lurvy dragged Wilbur's trough across the yard and kicked some dirt into the rat's nest, burying the broken egg and all Templeton's other possessions. Then he picked up the pail. Wilbur stood in the trough, drooling with hunger. Lurvy poured. The slops ran creamily down around the pig's eyes and ears. Wilbur grunted. He gulped and sucked, and sucked and gulped, making swishing and swooshing noises, anxious to get everything at once. It was a delicious meal—skim milk, wheat middlings, left-over pancakes, half a doughnut, the rind of a summer squash, two pieces of stale toast, a third of a ginger-snap, a fish tail, one orange peel, several noodles from a noodle soup, the scum off a cup of cocoa, an ancient jelly roll, a strip of paper from the lining of the garbage pail, and a spoonful of raspberry jello.

Wilbur ate heartily. He planned to leave half a noodle and a few drops of milk for Templeton. Then he remembered that the rat had been useful in saving Charlotte's life, and that Charlotte was trying to save *his* life. So he left a whole noodle, instead of a half.

Now that the broken egg was buried, the air cleared and the barn smelled good again. The afternoon passed, and evening came. Shadows lengthened. The cool and kindly breath of evening entered through doors and windows. Astride her web, Charlotte sat moodily eating a horsefly and thinking about the future. After a while she bestirred herself.

She descended to the center of the web and there she began to cut some of her lines. She worked slowly but steadily while the other creatures drowsed. None of the others, not even the goose, noticed that she was at work. Deep in his soft bed, Wilbur snoozed. Over in their favorite corner, the goslings whistled a night song.

Charlotte tore quite a section out of her web, leaving an open space in the middle. Then she started weaving something to take the place of the threads she had removed. When Templeton got back from the dump, around midnight, the spider was still at work.

XI

The Miracle

THE NEXT DAY WAS FOGGY. EVERYTHING ON the farm was dripping wet. The grass looked like a magic carpet. The asparagus patch looked like a silver forest.

On foggy mornings, Charlotte's web was truly a thing of beauty. This morning each thin strand was decorated with dozens of tiny beads of water. The web glistened in the light and made a pattern of loveliness and mystery, like a delicate veil. Even Lurvy, who wasn't particularly interested in beauty, noticed the web when he came with the pig's breakfast. He noted how clearly it showed up and he noted how big and carefully built it was. And then he took another look and he saw something that made him set his pail down. There, in the center of the web, neatly woven in block letters, was a message. It said:

SOME PIG!

Lurvy felt weak. He brushed his hand across his eyes and stared harder at Charlotte's web.

"I'm seeing things," he whispered. He dropped to his knees and uttered a short prayer. Then, forgetting all about Wilbur's breakfast, he walked back to the house and called Mr. Zuckerman.

"I think you'd better come down to the pigpen," he said.

"What's the trouble?" asked Mr. Zuckerman. "Anything wrong with the pig?"

"N-not exactly," said Lurvy. "Come and see for yourself."

The two men walked silently down to Wilbur's yard. Lurvy pointed to the spider's web. "Do you see what I see?" he asked.

Zuckerman stared at the writing on the web. Then he murmured the words "Some Pig." Then he looked at Lurvy. Then they both began to tremble. Charlotte, sleepy after her night's exertions, smiled as she watched. Wilbur came and stood directly under the web.

"Some pig!" muttered Lurvy in a low voice.

"Some pig!" whispered Mr. Zuckerman. They stared and stared for a long time at Wilbur. Then they stared at Charlotte.

"You don't suppose that that spider . . ." began Mr. Zuckerman—but he shook his head and didn't finish the sentence. Instead, he walked solemnly back up to the house and spoke to his wife. "Edith, something has happened," he said, in a weak voice. He went into the living room and sat down, and Mrs. Zuckerman followed.

"I've got something to tell you, Edith," he said. "You better sit down."

Mrs. Zuckerman sank into a chair. She looked pale and frightened.

"Edith," he said, trying to keep his voice steady, "I think you had best be told that we have a very unusual pig."

A look of complete bewilderment came over Mrs. Zuckerman's face. "Homer Zuckerman, what in the world are you talking about?" she said.

"This is a very serious thing, Edith," he replied. "Our pig is completely out of the ordinary."

"What's unusual about the pig?" asked Mrs. Zuckerman, who was beginning to recover from her scare.

"Well, I don't really know yet," said Mr.

Zuckerman. "But we have received a sign, Edith—a mysterious sign. A miracle has happened on this farm. There is a large spider's web in the doorway of the barn cellar, right over the pigpen, and when Lurvy went to feed the pig this morning, he noticed the web because it was foggy, and you know how a spider's web looks very distinct in a fog. And right spang in the middle of the web there were the words 'Some Pig.' The words were woven right into the web. They were actually part of the web, Edith. I know, because I have been down there and seen them. It says, 'Some Pig,' just as clear as clear can be. There can be no mistake about it. A miracle has happened and a sign has occurred here on earth, right on our farm, and we have no ordinary pig."

"Well," said Mrs. Zuckerman, "it seems to me you're a little off. It seems to me we have no ordinary *spider*."

"Oh, no," said Zuckerman. "It's the pig that's unusual. It says so, right there in the middle of the web."

"Maybe so," said Mrs. Zuckerman. "Just the same, I intend to have a look at that spider."

"It's just a common grey spider," said Zuckerman.

They got up, and together they walked down to

Wilbur's yard. "You see, Edith? It's just a common grey spider."

Wilbur was pleased to receive so much attention. Lurvy was still standing there, and Mr. and Mrs. Zuckerman, all three, stood for about an hour, reading the words on the web over and over, and watching Wilbur.

Charlotte was delighted with the way her trick was working. She sat without moving a muscle, and listened to the conversation of the people. When a small fly blundered into the web, just beyond the word "pig," Charlotte dropped quickly down, rolled the fly up, and carried it out of the way.

After a while the fog lifted. The web dried off and the words didn't show up so plainly. The Zuckermans and Lurvy walked back to the house. Just before they left the pigpen, Mr. Zuckerman took one last look at Wilbur.

"You know," he said, in an important voice, "I've thought all along that that pig of ours was an extra good one. He's a solid pig. That pig is as solid as they come. You notice how solid he is around the shoulders, Lurvy?"

"Sure. Sure I do," said Lurvy. "I've always noticed that pig. He's quite a pig."

"He's long, and he's smooth," said Zuckerman.

"That's right," agreed Lurvy. "He's as smooth as they come. He's some pig."

When Mr. Zuckerman got back to the house, he took off his work clothes and put on his best suit. Then he got into his car and drove to the minister's house. He stayed for an hour and explained to the minister that a miracle had happened on the farm.

"So far," said Zuckerman, "only four people on earth know about this miracle—myself, my wife Edith, my hired man Lurvy, and you."

"Don't tell anybody else," said the minister. "We don't know what it means yet, but perhaps if I give thought to it, I can explain it in my sermon next Sunday. There can be no doubt that you have a most unusual pig. I intend to speak about it in my sermon and point out the fact that this community has been visited with a wondrous animal. By the way, does the pig have a name?"

"Why, yes," said Mr. Zuckerman. "My little niece calls him Wilbur. She's a rather queer child—full of notions. She raised the pig on a bottle and I bought him from her when he was a month old."

He shook hands with the minister, and left.

. . .

Secrets are hard to keep. Long before Sunday came, the news spread all over the county. Everybody knew that a sign had appeared in a spider's web on the Zuckerman place. Everybody knew that the Zuckermans had a wondrous pig. People came from miles around to look at Wilbur and to read the words on Charlotte's web. The Zuckermans' driveway was full of cars and trucks from morning till night—Fords and Chevvies and Buick roadmasters and GMC pickups and Plymouths and Studebakers and Packards and De Sotos with gyromatic transmissions and Oldsmobiles with rocket engines and Jeep station wagons and Pontiacs. The news of the wonderful pig spread clear up into the hills, and farmers came rattling down in buggies and buckboards, to stand hour after hour at Wilbur's pen admiring the miraculous animal. All said they had never seen such a pig before in their lives.

When Fern told her mother that Avery had tried to hit the Zuckermans' spider with a stick, Mrs. Arable was so shocked that she sent Avery to bed without any supper, as punishment.

In the days that followed, Mr. Zuckerman was so busy entertaining visitors that he neglected his farm work. He wore his good clothes all the time now—got right into them when he got up in the morning. Mrs. Zuckerman prepared special meals for Wilbur. Lurvy shaved and got a haircut; and his principal farm duty was to feed the pig while people looked on.

Mr. Zuckerman ordered Lurvy to increase Wilbur's feedings from three meals a day to four meals a day. The Zuckermans were so busy with visitors they forgot about other things on the farm. The blackberries got ripe, and Mrs. Zuckerman failed to put up any blackberry jam. The corn needed hoeing, and Lurvy didn't find time to hoe it.

On Sunday the church was full. The minister explained the miracle. He said that the words on the spider's web proved that human beings must always be on the watch for the coming of wonders.

All in all, the Zuckermans' pigpen was the center of attraction. Fern was happy, for she felt that Charlotte's trick was working and that Wilbur's life would be saved. But she found that the barn was not nearly as pleasant—too many people. She liked it better when she could be all alone with her friends the animals.

XII
A Meeting

One evening, a few days after the writing had appeared in Charlotte's web, the spider called a meeting of all the animals in the barn cellar.

"I shall begin by calling the roll. Wilbur?"

"Here!" said the pig.

"Gander?"

"Here, here, here!" said the gander.

"You sound like three ganders," muttered Charlotte. "Why can't you just say 'here'? Why do you have to repeat everything?"

"It's my idio-idio-idiosyncrasy," replied the gander.

"Goose?" said Charlotte.

"Here, here, here!" said the goose. Charlotte glared at her.

"Goslings, one through seven?"

"Bee-bee-bee!" "Bee-bee-bee!" "Bee-bee-bee!" "Bee-bee-bee!" "Bee-bee-bee!" "Bee-bee-bee!" "Bee-bee-bee!" said the goslings.

"This is getting to be quite a meeting," said Charlotte. "Anybody would think we had three ganders, three geese, and twenty-one goslings. Sheep?"

"He-aa-aa!" answered the sheep all together.

"Lambs?"

"He-aa-aa!" answered the lambs all together.

"Templeton?"

No answer.

"Templeton?"

No answer.

"Well, we are all here except the rat," said Charlotte. "I guess we can proceed without him. Now, all of you must have noticed what's been going on around here the last few days. The message I wrote in my web, praising Wilbur, has been received. The Zuckermans have fallen for it, and so has everybody else. Zuckerman thinks Wilbur is an unusual pig, and therefore he won't want to kill him and eat him. I dare say my trick will work and Wilbur's life can be saved."

"Hurray!" cried everybody.

"Thank you very much," said Charlotte. "Now I

called this meeting in order to get suggestions. I need new ideas for the web. People are already getting sick of reading the words 'Some Pig!' If anybody can think of another message, or remark, I'll be glad to weave it into the web. Any suggestions for a new slogan?"

"How about 'Pig Supreme'?" asked one of the lambs.

"No good," said Charlotte. "It sounds like a rich dessert."

"How about 'Terrific, terrific, terrific'?" asked the goose.

"Cut that down to one 'terrific' and it will do very nicely," said Charlotte. "I think 'terrific' might impress Zuckerman."

"But Charlotte," said Wilbur, "I'm *not* terrific."

"That doesn't make a particle of difference," replied Charlotte. "Not a particle. People believe almost anything they see in print. Does anybody here know how to spell 'terrific'?"

"I think," said the gander, "it's tee double ee double rr double rr double eye double ff double eye double see see see see see."

"What kind of an acrobat do you think I am?" said Charlotte in disgust. "I would have to have St. Vitus's Dance to weave a word like that into my web."

"Sorry, sorry, sorry," said the gander.

Then the oldest sheep spoke up. "I agree that there should be something new written in the web if Wilbur's life is to be saved. And if Charlotte needs help in finding words, I think she can get it from our friend Templeton. The rat visits the dump regularly and has access to old magazines. He can tear out bits of advertisements and bring them up here to the barn cellar, so that Charlotte can have something to copy."

"Good idea," said Charlotte. "But I'm not sure Templeton will be willing to help. You know how he is—always looking out for himself, never thinking of the other fellow."

"I bet I can get him to help," said the old sheep. "I'll appeal to his baser instincts, of which he has plenty. Here he comes now. Everybody keep quiet while I put the matter up to him!"

The rat entered the barn the way he always did—creeping along close to the wall.

"What's up?" he asked, seeing the animals assembled.

"We're holding a directors' meeting," replied the old sheep.

"Well, break it up!" said Templeton. "Meetings

bore me." And the rat began to climb a rope that hung against the wall.

"Look," said the old sheep, "next time you go to the dump, Templeton, bring back a clipping from a magazine. Charlotte needs new ideas so she can write messages in her web and save Wilbur's life."

"Let him die," said the rat. "I should worry."

"You'll worry all right when next winter comes," said the sheep. "You'll worry all right on a zero morning next January when Wilbur is dead and nobody comes down here with a nice pail of warm slops to pour into the trough. Wilbur's leftover food is your chief source of supply, Templeton. *You* know that. Wilbur's food is your food; therefore Wilbur's destiny and your destiny are closely linked. If Wilbur is killed and his trough stands empty day after day, you'll grow so thin we can look right through your stomach and see objects on the other side."

Templeton's whiskers quivered.

"Maybe you're right," he said gruffly. "I'm making a trip to the dump tomorrow afternoon. I'll bring back a magazine clipping if I can find one."

"Thanks," said Charlotte. "The meeting is now adjourned. I have a busy evening ahead of me. I've got to tear my web apart and write 'Terrific.'"

Wilbur blushed. "But I'm *not* terrific, Charlotte. I'm just about average for a pig."

"You're terrific as far as *I'm* concerned," replied Charlotte, sweetly, "and that's what counts. You're my best friend, and *I* think you're sensational. Now stop arguing and go get some sleep!"

XIII

Good Progress

FAR INTO THE NIGHT, WHILE THE OTHER creatures slept, Charlotte worked on her web. First she ripped out a few of the orb lines near the center. She left the radial lines alone, as they were needed for support. As she worked, her eight legs were a great help to her. So were her teeth. She loved to weave and she was an expert at it.

A spider can produce several kinds of thread. She uses a dry, tough thread for foundation lines, and she uses a sticky thread for snare lines—the ones that catch and hold insects. Charlotte decided to use her dry thread for writing the new message.

"If I write the word 'Terrific' with sticky thread," she thought, "every bug that comes along will get stuck in it and spoil the effect.

"Now let's see, the first letter is T."

Charlotte climbed to a point at the top of the left hand side of the web. Swinging her spinnerets into position, she attached her thread and then dropped down. As she dropped, her spinning tubes went into action and she let out thread. At the bottom, she attached the thread. This formed the upright part of the letter T. Charlotte was not satisfied, however. She climbed up and made another attachment, right next to the first. Then she carried the line down, so that she had a double line instead of a single line. "It will show up better if I make the whole thing with double lines."

She climbed back up, moved over about an inch to the left, touched her spinnerets to the web, and then carried a line across to the right, forming the top of the T. She repeated this, making it double. Her eight legs were very busy helping.

"Now for the E!"

Charlotte got so interested in her work, she began to talk to herself, as though to cheer herself on. If you had been sitting quietly in the barn cellar that evening, you would have heard something like this:

"Now for the R! Up we go! Attach! Descend! Pay out line! Whoa! Attach! Good! Up you go! Repeat! Attach! Descend! Pay out line. Whoa, girl! Steady now! Attach! Climb! Attach! Over to the right! Pay out line! Attach! Now right and down and swing that loop and around and around! Now in to the left! Attach! Climb! Repeat! O.K.! Easy, keep those lines together! Now, then, out and down for the leg of the R! Pay out line! Whoa! Attach! Ascend! Repeat! Good girl!"

And so, talking to herself, the spider worked at her difficult task. When it was completed, she felt hungry. She ate a small bug that she had been saving. Then she slept.

Next morning, Wilbur arose and stood beneath the web. He breathed the morning air into his lungs. Drops of dew, catching the sun, made the web stand out clearly. When Lurvy arrived with breakfast, there was the handsome pig, and over him, woven neatly in block letters, was the word TERRIFIC. Another miracle.

Lurvy rushed and called Mr. Zuckerman. Mr. Zuckerman rushed and called Mrs. Zuckerman. Mrs. Zuckerman ran to the phone and called the Arables. The Arables climbed into their truck and hurried over. Everybody stood at the pigpen and stared at the web and read the word, over and over, while Wilbur, who really felt terrific, stood quietly swelling out his chest and swinging his snout from side to side.

"Terrific!" breathed Zuckerman, in joyful admiration. "Edith, you better phone the reporter on the *Weekly Chronicle* and tell him what has happened. He will want to know about this. He may want to bring a photographer. There isn't a pig in the whole state that is as terrific as our pig."

The news spread. People who had journeyed to see Wilbur when he was "some pig" came back again to see him now that he was "terrific."

That afternoon, when Mr. Zuckerman went to milk the cows and clean out the tie-ups, he was still thinking about what a wondrous pig he owned.

"Lurvy!" he called. "There is to be no more cow manure thrown down into that pigpen. I have a terrific pig. I want that pig to have clean, bright straw every day for his bedding. Understand?"

"Yes, sir," said Lurvy.

"Furthermore," said Mr. Zuckerman, "I want you to start building a crate for Wilbur. I have decided to take the pig to the County Fair on September sixth. Make the crate large and paint it green with gold letters!"

"What will the letters say?" asked Lurvy.

"They should say *Zuckerman's Famous Pig*."

Lurvy picked up a pitchfork and walked away to

get some clean straw. Having such an important pig was going to mean plenty of extra work, he could see that.

Below the apple orchard, at the end of a path, was the dump where Mr. Zuckerman threw all sorts of trash and stuff that nobody wanted any more. Here, in a small clearing hidden by young alders and wild raspberry bushes, was an astonishing pile of old bottles and empty tin cans and dirty rags and bits of metal and broken bottles and broken hinges and broken springs and dead batteries and last month's magazines and old discarded dishmops and tattered overalls and rusty spikes and leaky pails and forgotten stoppers and useless junk of all kinds, including a wrong-size crank for a broken ice-cream freezer.

Templeton knew the dump and liked it. There were good hiding places there—excellent cover for a rat. And there was usually a tin can with food still clinging to the inside.

Templeton was down there now, rummaging around. When he returned to the barn, he carried in his mouth an advertisement he had torn from a crumpled magazine.

"How's this?" he asked, showing the ad to

Charlotte. "It says 'Crunchy.' 'Crunchy' would be a good word to write in your web."

"Just the wrong idea," replied Charlotte. "Couldn't be worse. We don't want Zuckerman to think Wilbur is crunchy. He might start thinking about crisp, crunchy bacon and tasty ham. That would put ideas into his head. We must advertise Wilbur's noble qualities, not his tastiness. Go get another word, please, Templeton!"

The rat looked disgusted. But he sneaked away to the dump and was back in a while with a strip of cotton cloth. "How's this?" he asked. "It's a label off an old shirt."

Charlotte examined the label. It said PRE-SHRUNK.

"I'm sorry, Templeton," she said, "but 'Pre-shrunk' is out of the question. We want Zuckerman to think Wilbur is nicely filled out, not all shrunk up. I'll have to ask you to try again."

"What do you think I am, a messenger boy?" grumbled the rat. "I'm not going to spend all my time chasing down to the dump after advertising material."

"Just once more—please!" said Charlotte.

"I'll tell you what I'll do," said Templeton. "I know where there's a package of soap flakes in the woodshed. It has writing on it. I'll bring you a piece of the package."

He climbed the rope that hung on the wall and disappeared through a hole in the ceiling. When he came back he had a strip of blue-and-white cardboard in his teeth.

"There!" he said, triumphantly. "How's that?"

Charlotte read the words: "With New Radiant Action."

"What does it mean?" asked Charlotte, who had never used any soap flakes in her life.

"How should I know?" said Templeton. "You asked for words and I brought them. I suppose the next thing you'll want me to fetch is a dictionary."

Together they studied the soap ad. "'With new radiant action,'" repeated Charlotte, slowly. "Wilbur!" she called.

Wilbur, who was asleep in the straw, jumped up.

"Run around!" commanded Charlotte. "I want to see you in action, to see if you are radiant."

Wilbur raced to the end of his yard.

"Now back again, faster!" said Charlotte.

Wilbur galloped back. His skin shone. His tail had a fine, tight curl in it.

"Jump into the air!" cried Charlotte.

Wilbur jumped as high as he could.

"Keep your knees straight and touch the ground with your ears!" called Charlotte.

Wilbur obeyed.

"Do a back flip with a half twist in it!" cried Charlotte.

Wilbur went over backwards, writhing and twisting as he went.

"O.K., Wilbur," said Charlotte. "You can go back to sleep. O.K., Templeton, the soap ad will do, I guess. I'm not sure Wilbur's action is exactly radiant, but it's interesting."

"Actually," said Wilbur, "I *feel* radiant."

"Do you?" said Charlotte, looking at him with affection. "Well, you're a good little pig, and radiant you shall be. I'm in this thing pretty deep now—I might as well go the limit."

Tired from his romp, Wilbur lay down in the clean straw. He closed his eyes. The straw seemed scratchy—not as comfortable as the cow manure, which was always delightfully soft to lie in. So he pushed the straw to one side and stretched out in the manure. Wilbur sighed. It had been a busy day—his first day of being terrific. Dozens of people had visited his yard during the afternoon, and he had had to stand and pose, looking as terrific as he could. Now he was tired. Fern had arrived and seated herself quietly on her stool in the corner.

"Tell me a story, Charlotte!" said Wilbur, as he lay waiting for sleep to come. "Tell me a story!"

So Charlotte, although she, too, was tired, did what Wilbur wanted.

"Once upon a time," she began, "I had a beautiful cousin who managed to build her web across a small stream. One day a tiny fish leaped into the air and got tangled in the web. My cousin was very much surprised, of course. The fish was thrashing wildly. My cousin hardly dared tackle it. But she did. She swooped down and threw great masses of wrapping material around the fish and fought bravely to capture it."

"Did she succeed?" asked Wilbur.

"It was a never-to-be-forgotten battle," said Charlotte. "There was the fish, caught only by one fin, and its tail wildly thrashing and shining in the sun. There was the web, sagging dangerously under the weight of the fish."

"How much did the fish weigh?" asked Wilbur eagerly.

"I don't know," said Charlotte. "There was my cousin, slipping in, dodging out, beaten mercilessly over the head by the wildly thrashing fish, dancing in, dancing out, throwing her threads and fighting hard. First she threw a left around the tail. The fish lashed back. Then a left to the tail and a right to the midsection. The fish lashed back. Then she dodged to one side and threw a right, and another right to the fin. Then a hard left to the head, while the web swayed and stretched."

"Then what happened?" asked Wilbur.

"Nothing," said Charlotte. "The fish lost the fight. My cousin wrapped it up so tight it couldn't budge."

"Then what happened?" asked Wilbur.

"Nothing," said Charlotte. "My cousin kept the fish for a while, and then, when she got good and ready, she ate it."

"Tell me another story!" begged Wilbur.

So Charlotte told him about another cousin of hers who was an aeronaut.

"What is an aeronaut?" asked Wilbur.

"A balloonist," said Charlotte. "My cousin used to stand on her head and let out enough thread to form a balloon. Then she'd let go and be lifted into the air and carried upward on the warm wind."

"Is that true?" asked Wilbur. "Or are you just making it up?"

"It's true," replied Charlotte. "I have some very

remarkable cousins. And now, Wilbur, it's time you went to sleep."

"Sing something!" begged Wilbur, closing his eyes.

So Charlotte sang a lullaby, while crickets chirped in the grass and the barn grew dark. This was the song she sang.

"Sleep, sleep, my love, my only,
Deep, deep, in the dung and the dark;
Be not afraid and be not lonely!
This is the hour when frogs and thrushes
Praise the world from the woods
and the rushes.
Rest from care, my one and only,
Deep in the dung and the dark!"

But Wilbur was already asleep. When the song ended, Fern got up and went home.

XIV

Dr. Dorian

THE NEXT DAY WAS SATURDAY. FERN STOOD at the kitchen sink drying the breakfast dishes as her mother washed them. Mrs. Arable worked silently. She hoped Fern would go out and play with other children, instead of heading for the Zuckermans' barn to sit and watch animals.

"Charlotte is the best storyteller I ever heard," said Fern, poking her dish towel into a cereal bowl.

"Fern," said her mother sternly, "you must not invent things. You know spiders don't tell stories. Spiders can't talk."

"Charlotte can," replied Fern. "She doesn't talk very loud, but she talks."

"What kind of story did she tell?" asked Mrs. Arable.

"Well," began Fern, "she told us about a cousin

of hers who caught a fish in her web. Don't you think that's fascinating?"

"Fern, dear, how would a fish get in a spider's web?" said Mrs. Arable. "You know it couldn't happen. You're making this up."

"Oh, it happened all right," replied Fern. "Charlotte never fibs. This cousin of hers built a web across a stream. One day she was hanging around on the web and a tiny fish leaped into the air and got tangled in the web. The fish was caught by one fin, Mother; its tail was wildly thrashing and shining in the sun. Can't you just see the web, sagging dangerously under the weight of the fish? Charlotte's cousin kept slipping in, dodging out, and she was beaten mercilessly over the head by the wildly thrashing fish, dancing in, dancing out, throwing . . ."

"Fern!" snapped her mother. "Stop it! Stop inventing these wild tales!"

"I'm not inventing," said Fern. "I'm just telling you the facts."

"What finally happened?" asked her mother, whose curiosity began to get the better of her.

"Charlotte's cousin won. She wrapped the fish up, then she ate him when she got good and ready. Spiders have to eat, the same as the rest of us."

"Yes, I suppose they do," said Mrs. Arable, vaguely.

"Charlotte has another cousin who is a balloonist. She stands on her head, lets out a lot of line, and is carried aloft on the wind. Mother, wouldn't you simply love to do that?"

"Yes, I would, come to think of it," replied Mrs. Arable. "But Fern, darling, I wish you would play outdoors today instead of going to Uncle Homer's barn. Find some of your playmates and do something nice outdoors. You're spending too much time in that barn—it isn't good for you to be alone so much."

"Alone?" said Fern. "Alone? My best friends are in the barn cellar. It is a very sociable place. Not at all lonely."

Fern disappeared after a while, walking down the road toward Zuckermans'. Her mother dusted the sitting room. As she worked she kept thinking about Fern. It didn't seem natural for a little girl to be so interested in animals. Finally Mrs. Arable made up her mind she would pay a call on old Doctor Dorian and ask his advice. She got in the car and drove to his office in the village.

Dr. Dorian had a thick beard. He was glad to see Mrs. Arable and gave her a comfortable chair.

"It's about Fern," she explained. "Fern spends entirely too much time in the Zuckermans' barn. It doesn't seem normal. She sits on a milk stool in a corner of the barn cellar, near the pigpen, and watches animals, hour after hour. She just sits and listens."

Dr. Dorian leaned back and closed his eyes.

"How enchanting!" he said. "It must be real nice and quiet down there. Homer has some sheep, hasn't he?"

"Yes," said Mrs. Arable. "But it all started with that pig we let Fern raise on a bottle. She calls him Wilbur. Homer bought the pig, and ever since it left our place Fern has been going to her uncle's to be near it."

"I've been hearing things about that pig," said Dr. Dorian, opening his eyes. "They say he's quite a pig."

"Have you heard about the words that appeared in the spider's web?" asked Mrs. Arable nervously.

"Yes," replied the doctor.

"Well, do you understand it?" asked Mrs. Arable.

"Understand what?"

"Do you understand how there could be any writing in a spider's web?"

"Oh, no," said Dr. Dorian. "I don't understand it. But for that matter I don't understand how a spider learned to spin a web in the first place. When the words appeared, everyone said they were a miracle. But nobody pointed out that the web itself is a miracle."

"What's miraculous about a spider's web?" said Mrs. Arable. "I don't see why you say a web is a miracle—it's just a web."

"Ever try to spin one?" asked Dr. Dorian.

Mrs. Arable shifted uneasily in her chair. "No," she replied. "But I can crochet a doily and I can knit a sock."

"Sure," said the doctor. "But somebody taught you, didn't they?"

"My mother taught me."

"Well, who taught a spider? A young spider knows how to spin a web without any instructions from anybody. Don't you regard that as a miracle?"

"I suppose so," said Mrs. Arable. "I never looked at it that way before. Still, I don't understand how those words got into the web. I don't understand it, and I don't like what I can't understand."

"None of us do," said Dr. Dorian, sighing. "I'm a doctor. Doctors are supposed to understand everything. But I don't understand everything, and I don't intend to let it worry me."

Mrs. Arable fidgeted. "Fern says the animals talk to each other. Dr. Dorian, do you believe animals talk?"

"I never heard one say anything," he replied. "But that proves nothing. It is quite possible that an animal has spoken civilly to me and that I didn't catch the remark because I wasn't paying attention. Children pay better attention than grownups. If Fern says that the animals in Zuckerman's barn talk, I'm quite ready to believe her. Perhaps if people talked less, animals would talk more. People are incessant talkers—I can give you my word on that."

"Well, I feel better about Fern," said Mrs. Arable. "You don't think I need worry about her?"

"Does she look well?" asked the doctor.

"Oh, yes."

"Appetite good?"

"Oh, yes, she's always hungry."

"Sleep well at night?"

"Oh, yes."

"Then don't worry," said the doctor.

"Do you think she'll ever start thinking about something besides pigs and sheep and geese and spiders?"

"How old is Fern?"

"She's eight."

"Well," said Dr. Dorian, "I think she will always love animals. But I doubt that she spends her entire life in Homer Zuckerman's barn cellar. How about boys—does she know any boys?"

"She knows Henry Fussy," said Mrs. Arable brightly.

Dr. Dorian closed his eyes again and went into deep thought. "Henry Fussy," he mumbled. "Hmm. Remarkable. Well, I don't think you have anything to worry about. Let Fern associate with her friends in the barn if she wants to. I would say, offhand, that spiders and pigs were fully as interesting as Henry Fussy. Yet I predict that the day will come when even Henry will drop some chance remark that catches Fern's attention. It's amazing how children change from year to year. How's Avery?" he asked, opening his eyes wide.

"Oh, Avery," chuckled Mrs. Arable. "Avery is always fine. Of course, he gets into poison ivy and gets stung by wasps and bees and brings frogs and snakes home and breaks everything he lays his hands on. He's fine."

"Good!" said the doctor.

Mrs. Arable said good-bye and thanked Dr. Dorian very much for his advice. She felt greatly relieved.

XV

The Crickets

THE CRICKETS SANG IN THE GRASSES. They sang the song of summer's ending, a sad, monotonous song. "Summer is over and gone," they sang. "Over and gone, over and gone. Summer is dying, dying."

The crickets felt it was their duty to warn everybody that summertime cannot last forever. Even on the most beautiful days in the whole year—the days when summer is changing into fall—the crickets spread the rumor of sadness and change.

Everybody heard the song of the crickets. Avery and Fern Arable heard it as they walked the dusty road. They knew that school would soon begin again. The young geese heard it and knew that they would never be little goslings again. Charlotte heard it and knew that she hadn't much time left. Mrs. Zuckerman, at work in the kitchen, heard the crickets, and a sadness came over her, too. "Another summer gone," she sighed. Lurvy, at work building a crate for Wilbur, heard the song and knew it was time to dig potatoes.

"Summer is over and gone," repeated the crickets. "How many nights till frost?" sang the crickets. "Good-bye, summer, good-bye, good-bye!"

The sheep heard the crickets, and they felt so uneasy they broke a hole in the pasture fence and wandered up into the field across the road. The gander discovered the hole and led his family through, and they walked to the orchard and ate the apples that were lying on the ground. A little maple tree in the swamp heard the cricket song and turned bright red with anxiety.

Wilbur was now the center of attraction on the farm. Good food and regular hours were showing results: Wilbur was a pig any man would be proud of. One day more than a hundred people came to stand at his yard and admire him. Charlotte had written the word RADIANT, and Wilbur really looked radiant as he stood in the golden sunlight. Ever since the spider had befriended him, he had done his best to live up to his reputation. When Charlotte's web said SOME PIG, Wilbur had tried hard to look like some pig. When Charlotte's web said TERRIFIC, Wilbur had tried to look terrific. And now that the web said RADIANT, he did everything possible to make himself glow.

It is not easy to look radiant, but Wilbur threw himself into it with a will. He would turn his head slightly and blink his long eye-lashes. Then he would breathe deeply. And when his audience grew bored, he would spring into the air and do a back flip with a half twist. At this the crowd would yell and cheer. "How's that for a pig?" Mr. Zuckerman would ask, well pleased with himself. "That pig is radiant."

Some of Wilbur's friends in the barn worried for fear all this attention would go to his head and make him stuck up. But it never did. Wilbur was modest; fame did not spoil him. He still worried some about the future, as he could hardly believe that a mere spider would be able to save his life. Sometimes at night he would have a bad dream. He would dream that men were coming to get him with knives and guns. But that was only a dream. In the daytime, Wilbur usually felt happy and confident. No pig ever had truer friends, and he realized that friendship is one of the most satisfying things in the world. Even the song of the crickets did not make Wilbur too sad. He knew it was almost time for the County Fair, and he was looking forward to the trip. If he could distinguish himself at the Fair, and maybe win some prize money, he was sure Zuckerman would let him live.

Charlotte had worries of her own, but she kept quiet about them. One morning Wilbur asked her about the Fair.

"You're going *with* me, aren't you, Charlotte?" he said.

"Well, I don't know," replied Charlotte. "The Fair comes at a bad time for me. I shall find it inconvenient to leave home, even for a few days."

"Why?" asked Wilbur.

"Oh, I just don't feel like leaving my web. Too much going on around here."

"*Please* come with me!" begged Wilbur. "I need you, Charlotte. I can't stand going to the Fair without you. You've just *got* to come."

"No," said Charlotte, "I believe I'd better stay home and see if I can't get some work done."

"What kind of work?" asked Wilbur.

"Egg laying. It's time I made an egg sac and filled it with eggs."

"I didn't know you could lay eggs," said Wilbur in amazement.

"Oh, sure," said the spider. "I'm versatile."

"What does 'versatile' mean—full of eggs?" asked Wilbur.

"Certainly not," said Charlotte. "'Versatile' means I can turn with ease from one thing to another. It means I don't have to limit my activities to spinning and trapping and stunts like that."

"Why don't you come with me to the Fair Grounds and lay your eggs there?" pleaded Wilbur. "It would be wonderful fun."

Charlotte gave her web a twitch and moodily watched it sway. "I'm afraid not," she said. "You don't know the first thing about egg laying, Wilbur. I can't arrange my family duties to suit the management of the County Fair. When I get ready to lay eggs, I have to lay eggs, Fair or no Fair. However, I don't want you to worry about it—you might lose weight. We'll leave it this way: I'll come to the Fair if I possibly can."

"Oh, good!" said Wilbur. "I knew you wouldn't forsake me just when I need you most."

All that day Wilbur stayed inside, taking life easy in the straw. Charlotte rested and ate a grasshopper. She knew that she couldn't help Wilbur much longer. In a few days she would have to drop everything and build the beautiful little sac that would hold her eggs.

XVI

Off to the Fair

THE NIGHT BEFORE THE COUNTY FAIR, everybody went to bed early. Fern and Avery were in bed by eight. Avery lay dreaming that the Ferris wheel had stopped and that he was in the top car. Fern lay dreaming that she was getting sick in the swings.

Lurvy was in bed by eight-thirty. He lay dreaming that he was throwing baseballs at a cloth cat and winning a genuine Navajo blanket. Mr. and Mrs. Zuckerman were in bed by nine. Mrs. Zuckerman lay dreaming about a deep freeze unit. Mr. Zuckerman lay dreaming about Wilbur. He dreamt that Wilbur had grown until he was one hundred and sixteen feet long and ninety-two feet high and that he had won all the prizes at the Fair and was covered with blue ribbons and even had a blue ribbon tied to the end of his tail.

Down in the barn cellar, the animals, too, went to sleep early, all except Charlotte. Tomorrow would be Fair Day. Every creature planned to get up early to see Wilbur off on his great adventure.

When morning came, everybody got up at daylight. The day was hot. Up the road at the Arables' house, Fern lugged a pail of hot water to her room and took a sponge bath. Then she put on her prettiest dress because she knew she would see boys at the Fair. Mrs. Arable scrubbed the back of Avery's neck, and wet his hair, and parted it, and brushed it down hard till it stuck to the top of his head—all but about six hairs that stood straight up. Avery put on clean underwear, clean blue jeans, and a clean shirt. Mr. Arable dressed, ate breakfast, and then went out and polished his truck. He had offered to drive everybody to the Fair, including Wilbur.

Bright and early, Lurvy put clean straw in Wilbur's crate and lifted it into the pigpen. The crate was green. In gold letters it said:

ZUCKERMAN'S FAMOUS PIG

Charlotte had her web looking fine for the occasion. Wilbur ate his breakfast slowly. He tried to look radiant without getting food in his ears.

In the kitchen, Mrs. Zuckerman suddenly made an announcement.

"Homer," she said to her husband, "I am going to give that pig a buttermilk bath."

"A what?" said Mr. Zuckerman.

"A buttermilk bath. My grandmother used to bathe her pig with buttermilk when it got dirty—I just remembered."

"Wilbur's not dirty," said Mr. Zuckerman proudly.

"He's filthy behind the ears," said Mrs. Zuckerman. "Every time Lurvy slops him, the food runs down around the ears. Then it dries and forms a crust. He also has a smudge on one side where he lays in the manure."

"He lays in clean straw," corrected Mr. Zuckerman.

"Well, he's dirty, and he's going to have a bath."

Mr. Zuckerman sat down weakly and ate a doughnut. His wife went to the woodshed. When she returned, she wore rubber boots and an old raincoat, and she carried a bucket of buttermilk and a small wooden paddle.

"Edith, you're crazy," mumbled Zuckerman.

But she paid no attention to him. Together they

walked to the pigpen. Mrs. Zuckerman wasted no time. She climbed in with Wilbur and went to work. Dipping her paddle in the buttermilk, she rubbed him all over. The geese gathered around to see the fun, and so did the sheep and lambs. Even Templeton poked his head out cautiously, to watch Wilbur get a buttermilk bath. Charlotte got so interested, she lowered herself on a dragline so she could see better. Wilbur stood still and closed his eyes. He could feel the buttermilk trickling down his sides. He opened his mouth and some buttermilk ran in. It was delicious. He felt radiant and happy. When Mrs. Zuckerman got through and rubbed him dry, he was the cleanest, prettiest pig you ever saw. He was pure white, pink around the ears and snout, and smooth as silk.

The Zuckermans went up to change into their best clothes. Lurvy went to shave and put on his plaid shirt and his purple necktie. The animals were left to themselves in the barn.

The seven goslings paraded round and round their mother.

"Please, please, please take us to the Fair!" begged a gosling. Then all seven began teasing to go.

"Please, please, please, please, please, please . . . " They made quite a racket.

"Children!" snapped the goose. "We're staying quietly-ietly-ietly at home. Only Wilbur-ilbur-ilbur is going to the Fair."

Just then Charlotte interrupted.

"I shall go, too," she said, softly. "I have decided to go with Wilbur. He may need me. We can't tell what may happen at the Fair Grounds. Somebody's got to go along who knows how to write. And I think Templeton better come, too—I might need somebody to run errands and do general work."

"I'm staying right here," grumbled the rat. "I haven't the slightest interest in fairs."

"That's because you've never been to one," remarked the old sheep. "A fair is a rat's paradise. Everybody spills food at a fair. A rat can creep out late at night and have a feast. In the horse barn you will find oats that the trotters and pacers have spilled. In the trampled grass of the infield you will find old discarded lunch boxes containing the foul remains of peanut butter sandwiches, hard-boiled eggs, cracker crumbs, bits of doughnuts, and particles of cheese. In the hard-packed dirt of the midway, after the glaring lights are out and the people have gone home to bed, you will find a veritable treasure of popcorn fragments, frozen custard dribblings, candied apples abandoned by tired children, sugar fluff crystals, salted almonds, popsicles, partially gnawed ice cream cones, and the wooden sticks of lollypops. Everywhere is loot for a rat—in tents, in booths, in hay lofts—why, a fair has enough disgusting leftover food to satisfy a whole army of rats."

Templeton's eyes were blazing.

"Is this true?" he asked. "Is this appetizing yarn of yours true? I like high living, and what you say tempts me."

"It is true," said the old sheep. "Go to the Fair, Templeton. You will find that the conditions at a fair will surpass your wildest dreams. Buckets with sour mash sticking to them, tin cans containing particles of tuna fish, greasy paper bags stuffed with rotten . . ."

"That's enough!" cried Templeton. "Don't tell me any more. I'm going."

"Good," said Charlotte, winking at the old sheep. "Now then—there is no time to be lost. Wilbur will soon be put into the crate. Templeton and I must get in the crate right now and hide ourselves."

The rat didn't waste a minute. He scampered over to the crate, crawled between the slats, and pulled straw up over him so he was hidden from sight.

"All right," said Charlotte, "I'm next." She sailed into the air, let out a dragline, and dropped gently to the ground. Then she climbed the side of the crate and hid herself inside a knothole in the top board.

The old sheep nodded. "What a cargo!" she said. "That sign ought to say 'Zuckerman's Famous Pig and Two Stowaways.'"

"Look out, the people are coming-oming-oming!" shouted the gander. "Cheese it, cheese it, cheese it!"

The big truck with Mr. Arable at the wheel backed slowly down toward the barnyard. Lurvy and Mr. Zuckerman walked alongside. Fern and Avery were standing in the body of the truck hanging on to the sideboards.

"Listen to me," whispered the old sheep to Wilbur. "When they open the crate and try to put you in, struggle! Don't go without a tussle. Pigs always resist when they are being loaded."

"If I struggle I'll get dirty," said Wilbur.

"Never mind that—do as I say! Struggle! If you were to walk into the crate without resisting, Zuckerman might think you were bewitched. He'd be scared to go to the Fair."

Templeton poked his head up through the straw. "Struggle if you must," said he, "but kindly remember that I'm hiding down here in this crate and I don't want to be stepped on, or kicked in the face, or pummeled, or crushed in any way, or squashed, or buffeted about, or bruised, or lacerated, or scarred, or biffed. Just watch what you're doing, Mr. Radiant, when they get shoving you in!"

"Be quiet, Templeton!" said the sheep. "Pull in your head—they're coming. Look radiant, Wilbur! Lay low, Charlotte! Talk it up, geese!"

The truck backed slowly to the pigpen and stopped. Mr. Arable cut the motor, got out, walked around to the rear, and lowered the tailgate. The geese cheered. Mrs. Arable got out of the truck. Fern and Avery jumped to the ground. Mrs. Zuckerman came walking down from the house. Everybody lined up at the fence and stood for a moment admiring Wilbur and the beautiful green crate. Nobody realized that the crate already contained a rat and a spider.

"That's some pig!" said Mrs. Arable.

"He's terrific," said Lurvy.

"He's very radiant," said Fern, remembering the day he was born.

"Well," said Mrs. Zuckerman, "he's clean, anyway. The buttermilk certainly helped."

Mr. Arable studied Wilbur carefully. "Yes, he's a wonderful pig," he said. "It's hard to believe that he was the runt of the litter. You'll get some extra good ham and bacon, Homer, when it comes time to kill *that* pig."

Wilbur heard these words and his heart almost stopped. "I think I'm going to faint," he whispered to the old sheep, who was watching.

"Kneel down!" whispered the old sheep. "Let the blood rush to your head!"

Wilbur sank to his knees, all radiance gone. His eyes closed.

"Look!" screamed Fern. "He's fading away!"

"Hey, watch me!" yelled Avery, crawling on all fours into the crate. "I'm a pig! I'm a pig!"

Avery's foot touched Templeton under the straw. "What a mess!" thought the rat. "What fantastic creatures boys are! Why did I let myself in for this?"

The geese saw Avery in the crate and cheered.

"Avery, you get out of that crate this instant!" commanded his mother. "What do you think you are?"

"I'm a pig!" cried Avery, tossing handfuls of straw into the air. "Oink, oink, oink!"

"The truck is rolling away, Papa," said Fern.

The truck, with no one at the wheel, had started to roll downhill. Mr. Arable dashed to the driver's seat and pulled on the emergency brake. The truck stopped. The geese cheered. Charlotte crouched and made herself as small as possible in the knot-hole, so Avery wouldn't see her.

"Come out at once!" cried Mrs. Arable. Avery crawled out of the crate on hands and knees, making faces at Wilbur. Wilbur fainted away.

"The pig has passed out," said Mrs. Zuckerman. "Throw water on him!"

"Throw buttermilk!" suggested Avery.

The geese cheered.

Lurvy ran for a pail of water. Fern climbed into the pen and knelt by Wilbur's side.

"It's sunstroke," said Zuckerman. "The heat is too much for him."

"Maybe he's dead," said Avery.

"Come out of that pigpen *immediately*!" cried Mrs. Arable. Avery obeyed his mother and climbed into the back of the truck so he could see better. Lurvy returned with cold water and dashed it on Wilbur.

"Throw some on me!" cried Avery. "I'm hot, too."

"Oh, keep quiet!" hollered Fern. "Keep *qui*-ut!" Her eyes were brimming with tears.

Wilbur, feeling the cold water, came to. He rose

slowly to his feet, while the geese cheered.

"He's up!" said Mr. Arable. "I guess there's nothing wrong with him."

"I'm hungry," said Avery. "I want a candied apple."

"Wilbur's all right now," said Fern. "We can start. I want to take a ride in the Ferris wheel."

Mr. Zuckerman and Mr. Arable and Lurvy grabbed the pig and pushed him headfirst toward the crate. Wilbur began to struggle. The harder the men pushed, the harder he held back. Avery jumped down and joined the men. Wilbur kicked and thrashed and grunted. "Nothing wrong with *this* pig," said Mr. Zuckerman cheerfully, pressing his knee against Wilbur's behind. "All together, now, boys! Shove!"

With a final heave they jammed him into the crate. The geese cheered. Lurvy nailed some boards across the end, so Wilbur couldn't back out. Then, using all their strength, the men picked up the crate and heaved it aboard the truck. They did not know that under the straw was a rat, and inside a knothole was a big grey spider. They saw only a pig.

"Everybody in!" called Mr. Arable. He started the motor. The ladies climbed in beside him. Mr.

Zuckerman and Lurvy and Fern and Avery rode in back, hanging on to the sideboards. The truck began to move ahead. The geese cheered. The children answered their cheer, and away went everybody to the Fair.

XVII

Uncle

WHEN THEY PULLED INTO THE FAIR Grounds, they could hear music and see the Ferris wheel turning in the sky. They could smell the dust of the race track where the sprinkling cart had moistened it; and they could smell hamburgers frying and see balloons aloft. They could hear sheep blatting in their pens. An enormous voice over the loudspeaker said: "Attention, please! Will the owner of a Pontiac car, license number H-2439, please move your car away from the fireworks shed!"

"Can I have some money?" asked Fern.

"Can I, too?" asked Avery.

"I'm going to win a doll by spinning a wheel and it will stop at the right number," said Fern.

"I'm going to steer a jet plane and make it bump into another one."

"Can I have a balloon?" asked Fern.

"Can I have a frozen custard and a cheeseburger and some raspberry soda pop?" asked Avery.

"You children be quiet till we get the pig unloaded," said Mrs. Arable.

"Let's let the children go off by themselves," suggested Mr. Arable. "The Fair only comes once a year." Mr. Arable gave Fern two quarters and two dimes. He gave Avery five dimes and four nickels. "Now run along!" he said. "And remember, the money has to last *all day*. Don't spend it all the first few minutes. And be back here at the truck at noontime so we can all have lunch together. And don't eat a lot of stuff that's going to make you sick to your stomachs."

"And if you go in those swings," said Mrs. Arable, "you hang on tight! You hang on *very* tight. Hear me?"

"And don't get lost!" said Mrs. Zuckerman.

"And don't get dirty!"

"Don't get overheated!" said their mother.

"Watch out for pickpockets!" cautioned their father.

"And don't cross the race track when the horses are coming!" cried Mrs. Zuckerman.

The children grabbed each other by the hand and danced off in the direction of the merry-go-round, toward the wonderful music and the wonderful adventure and the wonderful excitement, into the wonderful midway where there would be no parents to guard them and guide them, and where they could be happy and free and do as they pleased. Mrs. Arable stood quietly and watched them go. Then she sighed. Then she blew her nose.

"Do you really think it's all right?" she asked.

"Well, they've got to grow up some time," said Mr. Arable. "And a fair is a good place to start, I guess."

While Wilbur was being unloaded and taken out of his crate and into his new pigpen, crowds gathered to watch. They stared at the sign ZUCKERMAN'S FAMOUS PIG. Wilbur stared back and tried to look extra good. He was pleased with his new home. The pen was grassy, and it was shaded from the sun by a shed roof.

Charlotte, watching her chance, scrambled out of the crate and climbed a post to the under side of the roof. Nobody noticed her.

Templeton, not wishing to come out in broad daylight, stayed quietly under the straw at the bottom of the crate. Mr. Zuckerman poured some skim milk into Wilbur's trough, pitched clean straw into his pen, and then he and Mrs. Zuckerman and the Arables walked away toward the cattle barn to look at purebred cows and to see the sights. Mr. Zuckerman particularly wanted to look at tractors. Mrs. Zuckerman wanted to see a deep freeze. Lurvy wandered off by himself, hoping to meet friends and have some fun on the midway.

As soon as the people were gone, Charlotte spoke to Wilbur.

"It's a good thing you can't see what *I* see," she said.

"What do you see?" asked Wilbur.

"There's a pig in the next pen and he's enormous. I'm afraid he's much bigger than you are."

"Maybe he's older than I am, and has had more time to grow," suggested Wilbur. Tears began to come to his eyes.

"I'll drop down and have a closer look," Charlotte said. Then she crawled along a beam till she was directly over the next pen. She let herself down on a dragline until she hung in the air just in front of the big pig's snout.

"May I have your name?" she asked, politely.

The pig stared at her. "No name," he said in a big, hearty voice. "Just call me Uncle."

"Very well, Uncle," replied Charlotte. "What is the date of your birth? Are you a spring pig?"

"Sure I'm a spring pig," replied Uncle. "What did you think I was, a spring chicken? Haw, haw—that's a good one, eh, Sister?"

"Mildly funny," said Charlotte. "I've heard funnier ones, though. Glad to have met you, and now I must be going."

She ascended slowly and returned to Wilbur's pen.

"He claims he's a spring pig," reported Charlotte, "and perhaps he is. One thing is certain, he has a most unattractive personality. He is too familiar, too noisy, and he cracks weak jokes. Also, he's not anywhere near as clean as you are, nor as pleasant. I took quite a dislike to him in our brief interview. He's going to be a hard pig to beat, though, Wilbur, on account of his size and weight. But with me helping you, it can be done."

"When are you going to spin a web?" asked Wilbur.

"This afternoon, late, if I'm not too tired," said

Charlotte. "The least thing tires me these days. I don't seem to have the energy I once had. My age, I guess."

Wilbur looked at his friend. She looked rather swollen and she seemed listless.

"I'm awfully sorry to hear that you're feeling poorly, Charlotte," he said. "Perhaps if you spin a web and catch a couple of flies you'll feel better."

"Perhaps," she said, wearily. "But I feel like the end of a long day." Clinging upside down to the ceiling, she settled down for a nap, leaving Wilbur very much worried.

All morning people wandered past Wilbur's pen. Dozens and dozens of strangers stopped to stare at him and to admire his silky white coat, his curly tail, his kind and radiant expression. Then they would move on to the next pen where the bigger pig lay. Wilbur heard several people make favorable remarks about Uncle's great size. He couldn't help overhearing these remarks, and he couldn't help worrying. "And now, with Charlotte not feeling well . . ." he thought. "Oh, dear!"

All morning Templeton slept quietly under the straw. The day grew fiercely hot. At noon the Zuckermans and the Arables returned to the pigpen. Then, a few minutes later, Fern and Avery showed up. Fern had a monkey doll in her arms and was eating Crackerjack. Avery had a balloon tied to his ear and was chewing a candied apple. The children were hot and dirty.

"Isn't it hot?" said Mrs. Zuckerman.

"It's *terribly* hot," said Mrs. Arable, fanning herself with an advertisement of a deep freeze.

One by one they climbed into the truck and opened lunch boxes. The sun beat down on everything. Nobody seemed hungry.

"When are the judges going to decide about Wilbur?" asked Mrs. Zuckerman.

"Not till tomorrow," said Mr. Zuckerman.

Lurvy appeared, carrying an Indian blanket that he had won.

"That's just what we need," said Avery. "A blanket."

"Of course it is," replied Lurvy. And he spread the blanket across the sideboards of the truck so that it was like a little tent. The children sat in the shade, under the blanket, and felt better.

After lunch, they stretched out and fell asleep.

XVIII

The Cool of the Evening

In the cool of the evening, when shadows darkened the Fair Grounds, Templeton crept from the crate and looked around. Wilbur lay asleep in the straw. Charlotte was building a web. Templeton's keen nose detected many fine smells in the air. The rat was hungry and thirsty. He decided to go exploring. Without saying anything to anybody, he started off.

"Bring me back a word!" Charlotte called after him. "I shall be writing tonight for the last time."

The rat mumbled something to himself and disappeared into the shadows. He did not like being treated like a messenger boy.

After the heat of the day, the evening came as a welcome relief to all. The Ferris wheel was lighted now. It went round and round in the sky and seemed twice as high as by day. There were lights on the midway, and you could hear the crackle of the gambling machines and the music of the merry-go-round and the voice of the man in the beano booth calling numbers.

The children felt refreshed after their nap. Fern met her friend Henry Fussy, and he invited her to ride with him in the Ferris wheel. He even bought a ticket for her, so it didn't cost her anything. When Mrs. Arable happened to look up into the starry sky and saw her little daughter sitting with Henry Fussy and going higher and higher into the air, and saw how happy Fern looked, she just shook her head. "My, my!" she said. "Henry Fussy. Think of that!"

Templeton kept out of sight. In the tall grass behind the cattle barn he found a folded newspaper. Inside it were leftovers from somebody's lunch: a deviled ham sandwich, a piece of Swiss cheese, part of a hard-boiled egg, and the core of a wormy apple. The rat crawled in and ate everything. Then he tore a word out of the paper, rolled it up, and started back to Wilbur's pen.

Charlotte had her web almost finished when Templeton returned, carrying the newspaper clipping. She had left a space in the middle of the web. At this hour, no people were around the pigpen, so the rat and the spider and the pig were by themselves.

"I hope you brought a good one," Charlotte said. "It is the last word I shall ever write."

"Here," said Templeton, unrolling the paper.

"What does it say?" asked Charlotte. "You'll have to read it for me."

"It says 'Humble,'" replied the rat.

"Humble?" said Charlotte. "'Humble' has two meanings. It means 'not proud' and it means 'near the ground.' That's Wilbur all over. He's not proud and he's near the ground."

"Well, I hope you're satisfied," sneered the rat. "I'm not going to spend all my time fetching and carrying. I came to this Fair to enjoy myself, not to deliver papers."

"You've been very helpful," Charlotte said. "Run along, if you want to see more of the Fair."

The rat grinned. "I'm going to make a night of it," he said. "The old sheep was right—this Fair is a rat's paradise. What eating! And what drinking! And everywhere good hiding and good hunting. Bye, bye, my humble Wilbur! Fare thee well, Charlotte, you old schemer! This will be a night to remember in a rat's life."

He vanished into the shadows.

Charlotte went back to her work. It was quite dark now. In the distance, fireworks began going off—rockets, scattering fiery balls in the sky. By the time the Arables and the Zuckermans and Lurvy returned from the grandstand, Charlotte had finished her web. The word HUMBLE was woven neatly in the center. Nobody noticed it in the darkness. Everyone was tired and happy.

Fern and Avery climbed into the truck and lay down. They pulled the Indian blanket over them. Lurvy gave Wilbur a forkful of fresh straw. Mr. Arable patted him. "Time for us to go home," he said to the pig. "See you tomorrow."

The grownups climbed slowly into the truck and Wilbur heard the engine start and then heard the truck moving away in low speed. He would have felt lonely and homesick, had Charlotte not been with him. He never felt lonely when she was near. In the distance he could still hear the music of the merry-go-round.

As he was dropping off to sleep he spoke to Charlotte.

"Sing me that song again, about the dung and the dark," he begged.

"Not tonight," she said in a low voice. "I'm too tired." Her voice didn't seem to come from her web.

"Where are you?" asked Wilbur. "I can't see you. Are you on your web?"

"I'm back here," she answered. "Up in this back corner."

"Why aren't you on your web?" asked Wilbur. "You almost *never* leave your web."

"I've left it tonight," she said.

Wilbur closed his eyes. "Charlotte," he said, after a while, "do you really think Zuckerman will let me live and not kill me when the cold weather comes? Do you really think so?"

"Of course," said Charlotte. "You are a famous pig and you are a good pig. Tomorrow you will probably win a prize. The whole world will hear about you. Zuckerman will be proud and happy to own such a pig. You have nothing to fear, Wilbur—nothing to worry about. Maybe you'll live forever—who knows? And now, go to sleep."

For a while there was no sound. Then Wilbur's voice:

"What are you doing up there, Charlotte?"

"Oh, making something," she said. "Making something, as usual."

"Is it something for me?" asked Wilbur.

"No," said Charlotte. "It's something for *me*, for a change."

"Please tell me what it is," begged Wilbur.

"I'll tell you in the morning," she said. "When the first light comes into the sky and the sparrows stir and the cows rattle their chains, when the rooster crows and the stars fade, when early cars whisper along the highway, you look up here and I'll show you something. I will show you my masterpiece."

Before she finished the sentence, Wilbur was asleep. She could tell by the sound of his breathing that he was sleeping peacefully, deep in the straw.

Miles away, at the Arables' house, the men sat around the kitchen table eating a dish of canned peaches and talking over the events of the day. Upstairs, Avery was already in bed and asleep. Mrs. Arable was tucking Fern into bed.

"Did you have a good time at the Fair?" she asked as she kissed her daughter.

Fern nodded. "I had the best time I have ever had anywhere or any time in all of my whole life."

"Well!" said Mrs. Arable. "Isn't that nice!"

XIX

The Egg Sac

NEXT MORNING WHEN THE FIRST LIGHT came into the sky and the sparrows stirred in the trees, when the cows rattled their chains and the rooster crowed and the early automobiles went whispering along the road, Wilbur awoke and looked for Charlotte. He saw her up overhead in a corner near the back of his pen. She was very quiet. Her eight legs were spread wide. She seemed to have shrunk during the night. Next to her, attached to the ceiling, Wilbur saw a curious object. It was a sort of sac, or cocoon. It was peach-colored and looked as though it were made of cotton candy.

"Are you awake, Charlotte?" he said softly.

"Yes," came the answer.

"What is that nifty little thing? Did you make it?"

"I did indeed," replied Charlotte in a weak voice.

"Is it a plaything?"

"Plaything? I should say not. It is my egg sac, my *magnum opus.*"

"I don't know what a magnum opus is," said Wilbur.

"That's Latin," explained Charlotte. "It means 'great work.' This egg sac is my great work—the finest thing I have ever made."

"What's inside it?" asked Wilbur. "Eggs?"

"Five hundred and fourteen of them," she replied.

"Five *hundred* and four*teen*?" said Wilbur. "You're kidding."

"No, I'm not. I counted them. I got started counting, so I kept on—just to keep my mind occupied."

"It's a perfectly beautiful egg sac," said Wilbur, feeling as happy as though he had constructed it himself.

"Yes, it *is* pretty," replied Charlotte, patting the sac with her two front legs. "Anyway, I can guarantee that it is strong. It's made out of the toughest material I have. It is also waterproof. The eggs are inside and will be warm and dry."

"Charlotte," said Wilbur dreamily, "are you really going to have five hundred and fourteen children?"

"If nothing happens, yes," she said. "Of course, they won't show up till next spring." Wilbur noticed that Charlotte's voice sounded sad.

"What makes you sound so down-hearted? I should think you'd be terribly happy about this."

"Oh, don't pay any attention to me," said Charlotte. "I just don't have much pep any more. I guess I feel sad because I won't ever see my children."

"What do you mean you won't see your children! Of *course* you will. We'll *all* see them. It's going to be simply wonderful next spring in the barn cellar with five hundred and fourteen baby spiders running around all over the place. And the geese will have a new set of goslings, and the sheep will have their new lambs . . . "

"Maybe," said Charlotte quietly. "However, I have a feeling I'm not going to see the results of last night's efforts. I don't feel good at all. I think I'm languishing, to tell you the truth."

Wilbur didn't understand the word "languish" and he hated to bother Charlotte by asking her to explain. But he was so worried he felt he had to ask.

"What does 'languishing' mean?"

"It means I'm slowing up, feeling my age. I'm not young any more, Wilbur. But I don't want you to worry about me. This is your big day today. Look at my web—doesn't it show up well with the dew on it?"

Charlotte's web never looked more beautiful than it looked this morning. Each strand held dozens of bright drops of early morning dew. The light from the east struck it and made it all plain and clear. It was a perfect piece of designing and building. In another hour or two, a steady stream of people would pass by, admiring it, and reading it, and looking at Wilbur, and marveling at the miracle.

As Wilbur was studying the web, a pair of whiskers and a sharp face appeared. Slowly Templeton dragged himself across the pen and threw himself down in a corner.

"I'm back," he said in a husky voice. "What a night!"

The rat was swollen to twice his normal size. His stomach was as big around as a jelly jar.

"What a night!" he repeated, hoarsely. "What feasting and carousing! A real gorge! I must have eaten the remains of thirty lunches. Never have I seen such leavings, and everything well-ripened and seasoned with the passage of time and the heat of the day. Oh, it was rich, my friends, rich!"

"You ought to be ashamed of yourself," said Charlotte in disgust. "It would serve you right if you had an acute attack of indigestion."

"Don't worry about my stomach," snarled Templeton. "It can handle anything. And by the way, I've got some bad news. As I came past that pig next door—the one that calls himself Uncle—I noticed a blue tag on the front of his pen. That means he has won first prize. I guess you're licked, Wilbur. You might as well relax—nobody is going to hang any medal on *you*. Furthermore, I wouldn't be surprised if Zuckerman changes his mind about you. Wait till he gets hankering for some fresh pork and smoked ham and crisp bacon! He'll take the knife to you, my boy."

"Be still, Templeton!" said Charlotte. "You're too stuffed and bloated to know what you're saying. Don't pay any attention to him, Wilbur!"

Wilbur tried not to think about what the rat had just said. He decided to change the subject.

"Templeton," said Wilbur, "if you weren't so dopey, you would have noticed that Charlotte has made an egg sac. She is going to become a mother. For your information, there are five hundred and fourteen eggs in that peachy little sac."

"Is this true?" asked the rat, eyeing the sac suspiciously.

"Yes, it's true," sighed Charlotte.

"Congratulations!" murmured Templeton. "This *has* been a night!" He closed his eyes, pulled some straw over himself, and dropped off into a deep sleep. Wilbur and Charlotte were glad to be rid of him for a while.

At nine o'clock, Mr. Arable's truck rolled into the Fair Grounds and came to a stop at Wilbur's pen. Everybody climbed out.

"Look!" cried Fern. "Look at Charlotte's web! Look what it says!"

The grownups and the children joined hands and stood there, studying the new sign.

"'Humble,'" said Mr. Zuckerman. "Now isn't that just the word for Wilbur!"

Everyone rejoiced to find that the miracle of the web had been repeated. Wilbur gazed up lovingly into their faces. He looked very humble and very grateful. Fern winked at Charlotte. Lurvy soon got busy. He poured a bucket of warm slops into the trough, and while Wilbur ate his breakfast Lurvy scratched him gently with a smooth stick.

"Wait a minute!" cried Avery. "Look at this!" He

pointed to the blue tag on Uncle's pen. "This pig has won first prize already."

The Zuckermans and the Arables stared at the tag. Mrs. Zuckerman began to cry. Nobody said a word. They just stared at the tag. Then they stared at Uncle. Then they stared at the tag again. Lurvy took out an enormous handkerchief and blew his nose very loud—so loud, in fact, that the noise was heard by stableboys over at the horse barn.

"Can I have some money?" asked Fern. "I want to go out on the midway."

"You stay right where you are!" said her mother. Tears came to Fern's eyes.

"What's everybody crying about?" asked Mr. Zuckerman. "Let's get busy! Edith, bring the buttermilk!"

Mrs. Zuckerman wiped her eyes with her handkerchief. She went to the truck and came back with a gallon jar of buttermilk.

"Bath time!" said Zuckerman, cheerfully. He and Mrs. Zuckerman and Avery climbed into Wilbur's pen. Avery slowly poured buttermilk on Wilbur's head and back, and as it trickled down his sides and cheeks, Mr. and Mrs. Zuckerman rubbed it into his hair and skin. Passersby stopped to watch.

Pretty soon quite a crowd had gathered. Wilbur grew beautifully white and smooth. The morning sun shone through his pink ears.

"He isn't as big as that pig next door," remarked one bystander, "but he's cleaner. That's what I like."

"So do I," said another man.

"He's humble, too," said a woman, reading the sign on the web.

Everybody who visited the pigpen had a good word to say about Wilbur. Everyone admired the web. And of course nobody noticed Charlotte.

Suddenly a voice was heard on the loud speaker.

"Attention, please!" it said. "Will Mr. Homer Zuckerman bring his famous pig to the judges' booth in front of the grandstand. A special award will be made there in twenty minutes. Everyone is invited to attend. Crate your pig, please, Mr. Zuckerman, and report to the judges' booth promptly!"

For a moment after this announcement, the Arables and the Zuckermans were unable to speak or move. Then Avery picked up a handful of straw and threw it high in the air and gave a loud yell. The straw fluttered down like confetti into Fern's hair. Mr. Zuckerman hugged Mrs. Zuckerman. Mr. Arable kissed Mrs. Arable. Avery kissed Wilbur.

Lurvy shook hands with everybody. Fern hugged her mother. Avery hugged Fern. Mrs. Arable hugged Mrs. Zuckerman.

Up overhead, in the shadows of the ceiling, Charlotte crouched unseen, her front legs encircling her egg sac. Her heart was not beating as strongly as usual and she felt weary and old, but she was sure at last that she had saved Wilbur's life, and she felt peaceful and contented.

"We have no time to lose!" shouted Mr. Zuckerman. "Lurvy, help with the crate!"

"Can I have some money?" asked Fern.

"You *wait*!" said Mrs. Arable. "Can't you see everybody is busy?"

"Put that empty buttermilk jar into the truck!" commanded Mr. Arable. Avery grabbed the jar and rushed to the truck.

"Does my hair look all right?" asked Mrs. Zuckerman.

"Looks fine," snapped Mr. Zuckerman, as he and Lurvy set the crate down in front of Wilbur.

"You didn't even *look* at my hair!" said Mrs. Zuckerman.

"You're all right, Edith," said Mrs. Arable. "Just keep calm."

Templeton, asleep in the straw, heard the

commotion and awoke. He didn't know exactly what was going on, but when he saw the men shoving Wilbur into the crate he made up his mind to go along. He watched his chance and when no one was looking he crept into the crate and buried himself in the straw at the bottom.

"All ready, boys!" cried Mr. Zuckerman. "Let's go!" He and Mr. Arable and Lurvy and Avery grabbed the crate and boosted it over the side of the pen and up into the truck. Fern jumped aboard and sat on top of the crate. She still had straw in her hair and looked very pretty and excited. Mr. Arable started the motor. Everyone climbed in, and off they drove to the judges' booth in front of the grandstand.

As they passed the Ferris wheel, Fern gazed up at it and wished she were in the topmost car with Henry Fussy at her side.

XX

The Hour of Triumph

"SPECIAL ANNOUNCEMENT!" SAID THE loud speaker in a pompous voice. "The management of the Fair takes great pleasure in presenting Mr. Homer L. Zuckerman and his famous pig. The truck bearing this extraordinary animal is now approaching the infield. Kindly stand back and give the truck room to proceed! In a few moments the pig will be unloaded in the special judging ring in front of the grandstand, where a special award will be made. Will the crowd please make way and let the truck pass. Thank you."

Wilbur trembled when he heard this speech. He felt happy but dizzy. The truck crept along slowly in low speed. Crowds of people surrounded it, and Mr. Arable had to drive very carefully in order not to run over anybody. At last he managed to reach the judges' stand. Avery jumped out and lowered the tailgate.

"I'm scared to death," whispered Mrs. Zuckerman. "Hundreds of people are looking at us."

"Cheer up," replied Mrs. Arable, "this is fun."

"Unload your pig, please!" said the loud speaker.

"All together, now, boys!" said Mr. Zuckerman. Several men stepped forward from the crowd to help lift the crate. Avery was the busiest helper of all.

"Tuck your shirt in, Avery!" cried Mrs. Zuckerman. "And tighten your belt. Your pants are coming down."

"Can't you see I'm busy?" replied Avery in disgust.

"Look!" cried Fern, pointing. "There's Henry!"

"Don't shout, Fern!" said her mother. "And don't point!"

"Can't I *please* have some money?" asked Fern. "Henry invited me to go on the Ferris wheel again, only I don't think he has any money left. He ran out of money."

Mrs. Arable opened her handbag. "Here," she said. "Here is forty cents. Now don't get lost! And be back at our regular meeting place by the pigpen very soon!"

Fern raced off, ducking and dodging through

the crowd, in search of Henry.

"The Zuckerman pig is now being taken from his crate," boomed the voice of the loud speaker. "Stand by for an announcement!"

Templeton crouched under the straw at the bottom of the crate. "What a lot of nonsense!" muttered the rat. "What a lot of fuss about nothing!"

Over in the pigpen, silent and alone, Charlotte rested. Her two front legs embraced the egg sac. Charlotte could hear everything that was said on the loud speaker. The words gave her courage. This was her hour of triumph.

As Wilbur came out of the crate, the crowd clapped and cheered. Mr. Zuckerman took off his cap and bowed. Lurvy pulled his big handkerchief from his pocket and wiped the sweat from the back of his neck. Avery knelt in the dirt by Wilbur's side, busily stroking him and showing off. Mrs. Zuckerman and Mrs. Arable stood on the running board of the truck.

"Ladeez and gentlemen," said the loud speaker, "we now present Mr. Homer L. Zuckerman's distinguished pig. The fame of this unique animal has spread to the far corners of the earth, attracting many valuable tourists to our great State. Many of you will recall that never-to-be-forgotten day last summer when the writing appeared mysteriously on the spider's web in Mr. Zuckerman's barn, calling the attention of all and sundry to the fact that this pig was completely out of the ordinary. This miracle has never been fully explained, although learned men have visited the Zuckerman pigpen to study and observe the phenomenon. In the last analysis, we simply know that we are dealing with supernatural forces here, and we should all feel proud and grateful. In the words of the spider's web, ladies and gentlemen, this is some pig."

Wilbur blushed. He stood perfectly still and tried to look his best.

"This magnificent animal," continued the loud speaker, "is truly terrific. Look at him, ladies and gentlemen! Note the smoothness and whiteness of the coat, observe the spotless skin, the healthy pink glow of ears and snout."

"It's the buttermilk," whispered Mrs. Arable to Mrs. Zuckerman.

"Note the general radiance of this animal! Then remember the day when the word 'radiant' appeared clearly on the web. Whence came this mysterious writing? Not from the spider, we can rest assured of that. Spiders are very clever at weaving their webs, but needless to say spiders cannot write."

"Oh, they can't, can't they?" murmured Charlotte to herself.

"Ladeez and gentlemen," continued the loud speaker, "I must not take any more of your valuable time. On behalf of the governors of the Fair, I have the honor of awarding a special prize of twenty-five dollars to Mr. Zuckerman, together with a handsome bronze medal suitably engraved, in token of our appreciation of the part played by this pig—this radiant, this terrific, this humble pig—in attracting so many visitors to our great County Fair."

Wilbur had been feeling dizzier and dizzier through this long, complimentary speech. When he heard the crowd begin to cheer and clap again, he suddenly fainted away. His legs collapsed, his mind went blank, and he fell to the ground, unconscious.

"What's wrong?" asked the loud speaker. "What's going on, Zuckerman? What's the trouble with your pig?"

Avery was kneeling by Wilbur's head, stroking him. Mr. Zuckerman was dancing about, fanning him with his cap.

"He's all right," cried Mr. Zuckerman. "He gets these spells. He's modest and can't stand praise."

"Well, we can't give a prize to a *dead* pig," said the loud speaker. "It's never been done."

"He isn't dead," hollered Zuckerman. "He's fainted. He gets embarrassed easily. Run for some water, Lurvy!"

Lurvy sprang from the judges' ring and disappeared.

Templeton poked his head from the straw. He noticed that the end of Wilbur's tail was within reach. Templeton grinned. "I'll tend to this," he chuckled. He took Wilbur's tail in his mouth and bit it, just as hard as he could bite. The pain revived Wilbur. In a flash he was back on his feet.

"Ouch!" he screamed.

"Hoorray!" yelled the crowd. "He's up! The pig's up! Good work, Zuckerman! That's some pig!" Everyone was delighted. Mr. Zuckerman was the most pleased of all. He sighed with relief. Nobody had seen Templeton. The rat had done his work well.

And now one of the judges climbed into the ring with the prizes. He handed Mr. Zuckerman two ten dollar bills and a five dollar bill. Then he tied the medal around Wilbur's neck. Then he shook hands with Mr. Zuckerman while Wilbur blushed. Avery put out his hand and the judge shook hands with him, too. The crowd cheered. A photographer took Wilbur's picture.

A great feeling of happiness swept over the Zuckermans and the Arables. This was the greatest moment in Mr. Zuckerman's life. It is deeply satisfying to win a prize in front of a lot of people.

As Wilbur was being shoved back into the crate, Lurvy came charging through the crowd carrying a pail of water. His eyes had a wild look. Without hesitating a second, he dashed the water at Wilbur. In his excitement he missed his aim, and the water splashed all over Mr. Zuckerman and Avery. They got soaking wet.

"For goodness' sake!" bellowed Mr. Zuckerman, who was really drenched. "What ails you, Lurvy? Can't you see the pig is all right?"

"You asked for water," said Lurvy meekly.

"I didn't ask for a shower bath," said Mr. Zuckerman. The crowd roared with laughter. Finally Mr. Zuckerman had to laugh, too. And of course Avery was tickled to find himself so wet, and he immediately started to act like a clown. He pretended he was taking a shower bath; he made faces and danced around and rubbed imaginary soap under his armpits. Then he dried himself with an imaginary towel.

"Avery, stop it!" cried his mother. "Stop showing off!"

But the crowd loved it. Avery heard nothing but the applause. He liked being a clown in a ring, with everybody watching, in front of a grandstand. When he discovered there was still a little water left in the bottom of the pail, he raised the pail high in the air and dumped the water on himself and made faces. The children in the grandstand screamed with appreciation.

At last things calmed down. Wilbur was loaded into the truck. Avery was led from the ring by his mother and placed on the seat of the truck to dry off. The truck, driven by Mr. Arable, crawled slowly back to the pigpen. Avery's wet trousers made a big wet spot on the seat.

XXI

Last Day

CHARLOTTE AND WILBUR WERE ALONE. The families had gone to look for Fern. Templeton was asleep. Wilbur lay resting after the excitement and strain of the ceremony. His medal still hung from his neck; by looking out of the corner of his eye he could see it.

"Charlotte," said Wilbur after a while, "why are you so quiet?"

"I like to sit still," she said. "I've always been rather quiet."

"Yes, but you seem specially so today. Do you feel all right?"

"A little tired, perhaps. But I feel peaceful. Your success in the ring this morning was, to a small degree, *my* success. Your future is assured. You will live, secure and safe, Wilbur. Nothing can harm you now. These autumn days will shorten and grow cold. The leaves will shake loose from the trees and fall. Christmas will come, then the snows of winter. You will live to enjoy the beauty of the frozen world, for you mean a great deal to Zuckerman and he will not harm you, ever. Winter will pass, the days will lengthen, the ice will melt in the pasture pond. The song sparrow will return and sing, the frogs will awake, the warm wind will blow again. All these sights and sounds and smells will be yours to enjoy, Wilbur—this lovely world, these precious days . . ."

Charlotte stopped. A moment later a tear came to Wilbur's eye. "Oh, Charlotte," he said. "To think that when I first met you I thought you were cruel and bloodthirsty!"

When he recovered from his emotion, he spoke again.

"Why did you do all this for me?" he asked. "I don't deserve it. I've never done anything for you."

"You have been my friend," replied Charlotte. "That in itself is a tremendous thing. I wove my webs for you because I liked you. After all, what's a life, anyway? We're born, we live a little while, we die. A spider's life can't help being something of a mess, with all this trapping and eating flies. By helping you, perhaps I was trying to lift up my life a trifle. Heaven knows anyone's life can stand a little of that."

"Well," said Wilbur. "I'm no good at making speeches. I haven't got your gift for words. But you have saved me, Charlotte, and I would gladly give my life for you—I really would."

"I'm sure you would. And I thank you for your generous sentiments."

"Charlotte," said Wilbur. "We're all going home today. The Fair is almost over. Won't it be wonderful to be back home in the barn cellar again with the sheep and the geese? Aren't you anxious to get home?"

For a moment Charlotte said nothing. Then she spoke in a voice so low Wilbur could hardly hear the words.

"I will not be going back to the barn," she said.

Wilbur leapt to his feet. "Not going back?" he cried. "Charlotte, what are you talking about?"

"I'm done for," she replied. "In a day or two I'll be dead. I haven't even strength enough to climb down into the crate. I doubt if I have enough silk in my spinnerets to lower me to the ground."

Hearing this, Wilbur threw himself down in an agony of pain and sorrow. Great sobs racked his body. He heaved and grunted with desolation. "Charlotte," he moaned. "Charlotte! My true friend!"

"Come now, let's not make a scene," said the spider. "Be quiet, Wilbur. Stop thrashing about!"

"But I can't *stand* it," shouted Wilbur. "I won't leave you here alone to die. If you're going to stay here I shall stay, too."

"Don't be ridiculous," said Charlotte. "You can't stay here. Zuckerman and Lurvy and John Arable and the others will be back any minute now, and they'll shove you into that crate and away you'll go. Besides, it wouldn't make any sense for you to stay. There would be no one to feed you. The Fair Grounds will soon be empty and deserted."

Wilbur was in a panic. He raced round and round the pen. Suddenly he had an idea—he thought of the egg sac and the five hundred and fourteen little spiders that would hatch in the spring. If Charlotte herself was unable to go home to the barn, at least he must take her children along.

Wilbur rushed to the front of his pen. He put his front feet up on the top board and gazed around. In the distance he saw the Arables and the Zuckermans approaching. He knew he would have to act quickly.

"Where's Templeton?" he demanded.

"He's in that corner, under the straw, asleep," said Charlotte.

Wilbur rushed over, pushed his strong snout under the rat, and tossed him into the air.

"Templeton!" screamed Wilbur. "Pay attention!"

The rat, surprised out of a sound sleep, looked first dazed then disgusted.

"What kind of monkeyshine is this?" he growled. "Can't a rat catch a wink of sleep without being rudely popped into the air?"

"Listen to me!" cried Wilbur. "Charlotte is very ill. She has only a short time to live. She cannot accompany us home, because of her condition. Therefore, it is absolutely necessary that I take her egg sac with me. I can't reach it, and I can't climb. You are the only one that can get it. There's not a second to be lost. The people are coming—they'll be here in no time. Please, please, *please*, Templeton, climb up and get the egg sac."

The rat yawned. He straightened his whiskers. Then he looked up at the egg sac.

"So!" he said, in disgust. "So it's old Templeton to the rescue again, is it? Templeton do this, Templeton do that, Templeton please run down to the dump and get me a magazine clipping, Templeton please lend me a piece of string so I can spin a web."

"Oh, hurry!" said Wilbur. "Hurry up, Templeton!"

But the rat was in no hurry. He began imitating Wilbur's voice.

"So it's 'Hurry up, Templeton,' is it?" he said. "Ho, ho. And what thanks do I ever get for these services, I would like to know? Never a kind word for old Templeton, only abuse and wisecracks and side remarks. Never a kind word for a rat."

"Templeton," said Wilbur in desperation, "if you don't stop talking and get busy, all will be lost, and I will die of a broken heart. Please climb up!"

Templeton lay back in the straw. Lazily he placed his forepaws behind his head and crossed his knees, in an attitude of complete relaxation.

"Die of a broken heart," he mimicked. "How touching! My, my! I notice that it's always me you come to when in trouble. But I've never heard of anyone's heart breaking on *my* account. Oh, no. Who cares anything about old Templeton?"

"Get up!" screamed Wilbur. "Stop acting like a spoiled child!"

Templeton grinned and lay still. "Who made trip after trip to the dump?" he asked. "Why, it was old Templeton! Who saved Charlotte's life by scaring that Arable boy away with a rotten goose egg? Bless my soul, I believe it was old Templeton.

Who bit your tail and got you back on your feet this morning after you had fainted in front of the crowd? Old Templeton. Has it ever occurred to you that I'm sick of running errands and doing favors? What do you think I am, anyway, a rat-of-all-work?"

Wilbur was desperate. The people were coming. And the rat was failing him. Suddenly he remembered Templeton's fondness for food.

"Templeton," he said, "I will make you a solemn promise. Get Charlotte's egg sac for me, and from now on I will let you eat first, when Lurvy slops me. I will let you have your choice of everything in the trough and I won't touch a thing until you're through."

The rat sat up. "You mean that?" he said.

"I promise. I cross my heart."

"All right, it's a deal," said the rat. He walked to the wall and started to climb. His stomach was still swollen from last night's gorge. Groaning and complaining, he pulled himself slowly to the ceiling. He crept along till he reached the egg sac. Charlotte moved aside for him. She was dying, but she still had strength enough to move a little. Then Templeton bared his long ugly teeth and began snipping the threads that fastened the sac to the ceiling. Wilbur watched from below.

"Use extreme care!" he said. "I don't want a single one of those eggs harmed."

"Thith thtuff thticks in my mouth," complained the rat. "It'th worth than caramel candy."

But Templeton worked away at the job, and managed to cut the sac adrift and carry it to the ground, where he dropped it in front of Wilbur. Wilbur heaved a great sigh of relief.

"Thank you, Templeton," he said. "I will never forget this as long as I live."

"Neither will I," said the rat, picking his teeth. "I feel as though I'd eaten a spool of thread. Well, home we go!"

Templeton crept into the crate and buried himself in the straw. He got out of sight just in time. Lurvy and John Arable and Mr. Zuckerman came along at that moment, followed by Mrs. Arable and Mrs. Zuckerman and Avery and Fern. Wilbur had already decided how he would carry the egg sac—there was only one way possible. He carefully took the little bundle in his mouth and held it there on top of his tongue. He remembered what Charlotte had told him—that the sac was waterproof and strong. It felt funny on his tongue and made him drool a bit. And of course he couldn't say anything. But as he was being shoved into the crate, he looked up at Charlotte and gave her a wink. She knew he was saying good-bye in the only way he could. And she knew her children were safe.

"Good-bye!" she whispered. Then she summoned all her strength and waved one of her front legs at him.

She never moved again. Next day, as the Ferris wheel was being taken apart and the race horses were being loaded into vans and the entertainers were packing up their belongings and driving away in their trailers, Charlotte died. The Fair Grounds were soon deserted. The sheds and buildings were empty and forlorn. The infield was littered with bottles and trash. Nobody, of the hundreds of people that had visited the Fair, knew that a grey spider had played the most important part of all. No one was with her when she died.

XXII

A Warm Wind

AND SO WILBUR CAME HOME TO HIS beloved manure pile in the barn cellar. His was a strange homecoming. Around his neck he wore a medal of honor; in his mouth he held a sac of spider's eggs. There is no place like home, Wilbur thought, as he placed Charlotte's five hundred and fourteen unborn children carefully in a safe corner. The barn smelled good. His friends the sheep and the geese were glad to see him back.

The geese gave him a noisy welcome.

"Congratu-congratu-congratulations!" they cried. "Nice work."

Mr. Zuckerman took the medal from Wilbur's neck and hung it on a nail over the pigpen, where visitors could examine it. Wilbur himself could look at it whenever he wanted to.

In the days that followed, he was very happy. He grew to a great size. He no longer worried about being killed, for he knew that Mr. Zuckerman would keep him as long as he lived. Wilbur often thought of Charlotte. A few strands of her old web still hung in the doorway. Every day Wilbur would stand and look at the torn, empty web, and a lump would come to his throat. No one had ever had such a friend—so affectionate, so loyal, and so skillful.

The autumn days grew shorter, Lurvy brought the squashes and pumpkins in from the garden and piled them on the barn floor, where they wouldn't get nipped on frosty nights. The maples and birches turned bright colors and the wind shook them and they dropped their leaves one by one to the ground. Under the wild apple trees in the pasture, the red little apples lay thick on the ground, and the sheep gnawed them and the geese gnawed them and foxes came in the night and sniffed them. One evening, just before Christmas, snow began falling. It covered house and barn and fields and woods. Wilbur had never seen snow before. When morning came he went out and plowed the drifts in his yard, for the fun of it. Fern and Avery arrived, dragging a sled.

They coasted down the lane and out onto the frozen pond in the pasture.

"Coasting is the most fun there is," said Avery.

"The most fun there is," retorted Fern, "is when the Ferris wheel stops and Henry and I are in the top car and Henry makes the car swing and we can see everything for miles and miles and miles."

"Goodness, are you still thinking about that ol' Ferris wheel?" said Avery in disgust. "The Fair was weeks and weeks ago."

"I think about it all the time," said Fern, picking snow from her ear.

After Christmas the thermometer dropped to ten below zero. Cold settled on the world. The pasture was bleak and frozen. The cows stayed in the barn all the time now, except on sunny mornings when they went out and stood in the barnyard in the lee of the straw pile. The sheep stayed near the barn, too, for protection. When they were thirsty they ate snow. The geese hung around the barnyard the way boys hang around a drug store, and Mr. Zuckerman fed them corn and turnips to keep them cheerful.

"Many, many, many thanks!" they always said, when they saw food coming.

Templeton moved indoors when winter came. His ratty home under the pig trough was too chilly, so he fixed himself a cozy nest in the barn behind the grain bins. He lined it with bits of dirty newspapers and rags, and whenever he found a trinket or a keepsake he carried it home and stored it there. He continued to visit Wilbur three times a day, exactly at mealtime, and Wilbur kept the promise he had made. Wilbur let the rat eat first. Then, when Templeton couldn't hold another mouthful, Wilbur would eat. As a result of overeating, Templeton grew bigger and fatter than any rat you ever saw. He was gigantic. He was as big as a young woodchuck.

The old sheep spoke to him about his size one day. "You would live longer," said the old sheep, "if you ate less."

"Who wants to live forever?" sneered the rat. "I am naturally a heavy eater and I get untold satisfaction from the pleasures of the feast." He patted his stomach, grinned at the sheep, and crept upstairs to lie down.

All winter Wilbur watched over Charlotte's egg sac as though he were guarding his own children. He had scooped out a special place in the manure for the sac, next to the board fence. On very cold nights he lay so that his breath would warm it. For Wilbur, nothing in life was so important as this small round object—nothing else mattered. Patiently he awaited the end of winter and the coming of the little spiders. Life is always a rich and steady time when you are waiting for something to happen or to hatch. The winter ended at last.

"I heard the frogs today," said the old sheep one evening. "Listen! You can hear them now."

Wilbur stood still and cocked his ears. From the pond, in shrill chorus, came the voices of hundreds of little frogs.

"Springtime," said the old sheep, thoughtfully. "Another spring." As she walked away, Wilbur saw a new lamb following her. It was only a few hours old.

The snows melted and ran away. The streams and ditches bubbled and chattered with rushing water. A sparrow with a streaky breast arrived and sang. The light strengthened, the mornings came sooner. Almost every morning there was another new lamb in the sheepfold. The goose was sitting on nine eggs. The sky seemed wider and a warm wind blew. The last remaining strands of Charlotte's old web floated away and vanished.

One fine sunny morning, after breakfast, Wilbur stood watching his precious sac. He wasn't thinking of anything much. As he stood there, he noticed something move. He stepped closer and stared. A tiny spider crawled from the sac. It was no bigger than a grain of sand, no bigger than the head of a pin. Its body was grey with a black stripe underneath. Its legs were grey and tan. It looked just like Charlotte.

Wilbur trembled all over when he saw it. The little spider waved at him. Then Wilbur looked more closely. Two more little spiders crawled out and waved. They climbed round and round on the sac, exploring their new world. Then three more little spiders. Then eight. Then ten. Charlotte's children were here at last.

Wilbur's heart pounded. He began to squeal. Then he raced in circles, kicking manure into the air. Then he turned a back flip. Then he planted his front feet and came to a stop in front of Charlotte's children.

"Hello, there!" he said.

The first spider said hello, but its voice was so small Wilbur couldn't hear it.

"I am an old friend of your mother's," said Wilbur. "I'm glad to see you. Are you all right? Is everything all right?"

The little spiders waved their forelegs at him. Wilbur could see by the way they acted that they were glad to see him.

"Is there anything I can get you? Is there anything you need?"

The young spiders just waved. For several days and several nights they crawled here and there, up and down, around and about, waving at Wilbur, trailing tiny draglines behind them, and exploring their home. There were dozens and dozens of them. Wilbur couldn't count them, but he knew that he had a great many new friends. They grew quite rapidly. Soon each was as big as a BB shot. They made tiny webs near the sac.

Then came a quiet morning when Mr. Zuckerman opened a door on the north side. A warm draft of rising air blew softly through the barn cellar. The air smelled of the damp earth, of the spruce woods, of the sweet springtime. The baby spiders felt the warm updraft. One spider climbed to the top of the fence. Then it did something that came as a great surprise to Wilbur. The spider stood on its head, pointed its spinnerets in the air, and let loose a cloud of fine silk. The silk formed a balloon. As Wilbur watched, the spider let go of the fence and rose into the air.

"Good-bye!" it said, as it sailed through the doorway.

"Wait a minute!" screamed Wilbur. "Where do you think you're going?"

But the spider was already out of sight. Then another baby spider crawled to the top of the fence, stood on its head, made a balloon, and sailed away. Then another spider. Then another. The air was soon filled with tiny balloons, each balloon carrying a spider.

Wilbur was frantic. Charlotte's babies were disappearing at a great rate.

"Come back, children!" he cried.

"Good-bye!" they called. "Good-bye, good-bye!"

At last one little spider took time enough to stop and talk to Wilbur before making its balloon.

"We're leaving here on the warm updraft. This is our moment for setting forth. We are aeronauts and we are going out into the world to make webs for ourselves."

"But *where*?" asked Wilbur.

"Wherever the wind takes us. High, low. Near, far. East, west. North, south. We take to the breeze, we go as we please."

"Are *all* of you going?" asked Wilbur. "You can't *all* go. I would be left alone, with no friends. Your mother wouldn't want that to happen, I'm sure."

The air was now so full of balloonists that the barn cellar looked almost as though a mist had gathered. Balloons by the dozen were rising, circling, and drifting away through the door, sailing off on the gentle wind. Cries of "Good-bye, good-bye, good-bye!" came weakly to Wilbur's ears. He couldn't bear to watch any more. In sorrow he sank to the ground and closed his eyes. This seemed like the end of the world, to be deserted by Charlotte's children. Wilbur cried himself to sleep.

When he woke it was late afternoon. He looked at the egg sac. It was empty. He looked into the air. The balloonists were gone. Then he walked drearily to the doorway, where Charlotte's web used to be. He was standing there, thinking of her, when he heard a small voice.

"Salutations!" it said. "I'm up here."

"So am I," said another tiny voice.

"So am I," said a third voice. "Three of us are staying. We like this place, and we like *you*."

Wilbur looked up. At the top of the doorway three small webs were being constructed. On each web, working busily was one of Charlotte's daughters.

"Can I take this to mean," asked Wilbur, "that you have definitely decided to live here in the barn cellar, and that I am going to have *three* friends?"

"You can indeed," said the spiders.

"What are your names, please?" asked Wilbur, trembling with joy.

"I'll tell you my name," replied the first little spider, "if you'll tell me why you are trembling."

"I'm trembling with joy," said Wilbur.

"Then my name is Joy," said the first spider.

"What was my mother's middle initial?" asked the second spider.

"A," said Wilbur.

"Then my name is Aranea," said the spider.

"How about me?" asked the third spider. "Will you just pick out a nice sensible name for me—something not too long, not too fancy, and not too dumb?"

Wilbur thought hard.

"Nellie?" he suggested.

"Fine, I like that very much," said the third spider. "You may call me Nellie." She daintily fastened her orb line to the next spoke of the web.

Wilbur's heart brimmed with happiness. He felt

that he should make a short speech on this very important occasion.

"Joy! Aranea! Nellie!" he began. "Welcome to the barn cellar. You have chosen a hallowed doorway from which to string your webs. I think it is only fair to tell you that I was devoted to your mother. I owe my very life to her. She was brilliant, beautiful, and loyal to the end. I shall always treasure her memory. To you, her daughters, I pledge my friendship, forever and ever."

"I pledge mine," said Joy.

"I do, too," said Aranea.

"And so do I," said Nellie, who had just managed to catch a small gnat.

It was a happy day for Wilbur. And many more happy, tranquil days followed.

As time went on, and the months and years came and went, he was never without friends. Fern did not come regularly to the barn any more. She was growing up, and was careful to avoid childish things, like sitting on a milk stool near a pigpen. But Charlotte's children and grandchildren and great grandchildren, year after year, lived in the doorway. Each spring there were new little spiders hatching out to take the place of the old. Most of them sailed away, on their balloons. But always two or three stayed and set up housekeeping in the doorway.

Mr. Zuckerman took fine care of Wilbur all the rest of his days, and the pig was often visited by friends and admirers, for nobody ever forgot the year of his triumph and the miracle of the web. Life in the barn was very good—night and day, winter and summer, spring and fall, dull days and bright days. It was the best place to be, thought Wilbur, this warm delicious cellar, with the garrulous geese, the changing seasons, the heat of the sun, the passage of swallows, the nearness of rats, the sameness of sheep, the love of spiders, the smell of manure, and the glory of everything.

Wilbur never forgot Charlotte. Although he loved her children and grandchildren dearly, none of the new spiders ever quite took her place in his heart. She was in a class by herself. It is not often that someone comes along who is a true friend and a good writer. Charlotte was both.

Stuart Little

Contents

I

In the Drain

When Mrs. Frederick C. Little's second son arrived, everybody noticed that he was not much bigger than a mouse. The truth of the matter was, the baby looked very much like a mouse in every way. He was only about two inches high; and he had a mouse's sharp nose, a mouse's tail, a mouse's whiskers, and the pleasant, shy manner of a mouse. Before he was many days old he was not only looking like a mouse but acting like one, too—wearing a gray hat and carrying a small cane. Mr. and Mrs. Little named him Stuart, and Mr. Little made him a tiny bed out of four clothespins and a cigarette box.

Unlike most babies, Stuart could walk as soon as he was born. When he was a week old he could climb lamps by shinnying up the cord. Mrs. Little saw right away that the infant clothes she had provided were unsuitable, and she set to work and made him a fine little blue worsted suit with patch pockets in which he could keep his handkerchief, his money, and his keys. Every morning, before Stuart dressed, Mrs. Little went into his room and weighed him on a small scale which was really meant for weighing letters. At birth Stuart could have been sent by first class mail for three cents, but his parents preferred to keep him rather than send him away; and when, at the age of a month, he had gained only a third of an ounce, his mother was so worried she sent for the doctor.

The doctor was delighted with Stuart and said that it was very unusual for an American family to have a mouse. He took Stuart's temperature and found that it was 98.6, which is normal for a mouse. He also examined Stuart's chest and heart and looked into his ears solemnly with a flashlight. (Not every doctor can look into a mouse's ear without laughing.) Everything seemed to be all right, and Mrs. Little was pleased to get such a good report.

"Feed him up!" said the doctor cheerfully, as he left.

. . .

The home of the Little family was a pleasant place near a park in New York City. In the mornings the sun streamed in through the east windows, and all the Littles were up early as a general rule. Stuart was a great help to his parents, and to his older brother George, because of his small size and because he could do things that a mouse can do and was agreeable about doing them. One day when Mrs. Little was washing out the bathtub after Mr. Little had taken a bath, she lost a ring off her finger and was horrified to discover that it had fallen down the drain.

"What had I better do?" she cried, trying to keep the tears back.

"If I were you," said George, "I should bend a hairpin in the shape of a fishhook and tie it onto a piece of string and try to fish the ring out with it." So Mrs. Little found a piece of string and a hairpin, and for about a half-hour she fished for the ring; but it was dark down the drain and the hook always seemed to catch on something before she could get it down to where the ring was.

"What luck?" inquired Mr. Little, coming into the bathroom.

"No luck at all," said Mrs. Little. "The ring is so far down I can't fish it up."

"Why don't we send Stuart down after it?" suggested Mr. Little. "How about it, Stuart, would you like to try?"

"Yes, I would," Stuart replied, "but I think I'd better get into my old pants. I imagine it's wet down there."

"It's all of that," said George, who was a trifle annoyed that his hook idea hadn't worked. So Stuart slipped into his old pants and prepared to go down the drain after the ring. He decided to carry the string along with him, leaving one end in charge of his father. "When I jerk three times on the string, pull me up," he said. And while Mr. Little knelt in the tub, Stuart slid easily down the drain and was lost to view. In a minute or so, there came three quick jerks on the string, and Mr. Little carefully hauled it up. There, at the end, was Stuart, with the ring safely around his neck.

"Oh, my brave little son," said Mrs. Little proudly, as she kissed Stuart and thanked him.

"How was it down there?" asked Mr. Little, who was always curious to know about places he had never been to.

"It was all right," said Stuart.

But the truth was the drain had made him very

slimy, and it was necessary for him to take a bath and sprinkle himself with a bit of his mother's violet water before he felt himself again. Everybody in the family thought he had been awfully good about the whole thing.

II
Home Problems

STUART WAS ALSO HELPFUL WHEN IT came to Ping-pong. The Littles liked Ping-pong, but the balls had a way of rolling under chairs, sofas, and radiators, and this meant that the players were forever stooping down and reaching under things. Stuart soon learned to chase balls, and it was a great sight to see him come out from under a hot radiator, pushing a Ping-pong ball with all his might, the perspiration rolling down his cheeks. The ball, of course, was almost as high as he was, and he had to throw his whole weight against it in order to keep it rolling.

The Littles had a grand piano in their living room, which was all right except that one of the keys was a sticky key and didn't work properly. Mrs. Little said she thought it must be the damp weather, but I don't see how it could be the damp weather, for the key had been sticking for about four years, during which time there had been many bright clear days. But anyway, the key stuck, and was a great inconvenience to anyone trying to play the piano. It bothered George particularly when he was playing the "Scarf Dance," which was rather lively. It was George who had the idea of stationing Stuart inside the piano to push the key up the second it was played. This was no easy job for Stuart, as he had to crouch down between the felt hammers so that he wouldn't get hit on the head. But Stuart liked it just the same: it was exciting inside the piano, dodging about, and the noise was quite terrific. Sometimes after a long session he would emerge quite deaf, as though he had just stepped out of an airplane after a long journey; and it would be some little time before he really felt normal again.

Mr. and Mrs. Little often discussed Stuart quietly between themselves when he wasn't around, for they had never quite recovered from the shock and surprise of having a mouse in the family. He was so very tiny and he presented so many problems to his parents. Mr. Little said that, for one thing, there must be no references to "mice" in their conversation. He made Mrs. Little tear from the nursery songbook the page about the "Three Blind Mice, See How They Run."

"I don't want Stuart to get a lot of notions in his head," said Mr. Little. "I should feel badly to have my son grow up fearing that a farmer's wife was going to cut off his tail with a carving knife. It is such things that make children dream bad dreams when they go to bed at night."

"Yes," replied Mrs. Little, "and I think we had better start thinking about the poem ''Twas the night before Christmas when all through the house not a creature was stirring, not even a mouse.' I think it might embarrass Stuart to hear mice mentioned in such a belittling manner."

"That's right," said her husband, "but what shall we say when we come to that line in the poem? We'll have to say *some*thing. We can't just say ''Twas the night before Christmas when all through the house not a creature was stirring.' That doesn't sound complete; it needs a word to rhyme with house."

"What about louse?" asked Mrs. Little.

"Or grouse," said Mr. Little.

"I suggest souse," remarked George, who had been listening to the conversation from across the room.

It was decided that louse was the best substitute

for mouse, and so when Christmas came around Mrs. Little carefully rubbed out the word mouse from the poem and wrote in the word louse, and Stuart always thought that the poem went this way:

'Twas the night before Christmas when all
through the house
Not a creature was stirring, not even a louse.

The thing that worried Mr. Little most was the mousehole in the pantry. This hole had been made by some mice in the days before the Littles came to live in the house, and nothing had been done about stopping it up. Mr. Little was not at all sure that he understood Stuart's real feeling about a mousehole. He didn't know where the hole led to, and it made him uneasy to think that Stuart might some day feel the desire to venture into it.

"After all, he does look a good deal like a mouse," said Mr. Little to his wife. "And I've never seen a mouse yet that didn't like to go into a hole."

III

Washing Up

STUART WAS AN EARLY RISER: HE WAS almost always the first person up in the morning. He liked the feeling of being the first one stirring; he enjoyed the quiet rooms with the books standing still on the shelves, the pale light coming in through the windows, and the fresh smell of day. In wintertime it would be quite dark when he climbed from his bed made out of the cigarette box, and he sometimes shivered with cold as he stood in his night-gown doing his exercises. (Stuart touched his toes ten times every morning to keep himself in good condition. He had seen his brother George do it, and George had explained that it kept the stomach muscles firm and was a fine abdominal thing to do.)

After exercising, Stuart would slip on his handsome wool wrapper, tie the cord tightly around his waist, and start for the bathroom, creeping silently through the long dark hall past his mother's and father's room, past the hall closet where the carpet sweeper was kept, past George's room, and along by the head of the stairs till he got to the bathroom.

Of course, the bathroom would be dark, too, but Stuart's father had thoughtfully tied a long string to the pull-chain of the light. The string reached clear to the floor. By grasping it as high up as he could and throwing his whole weight on it, Stuart was able to turn on the light. Swinging on the string this way, with his long bathrobe trailing around his ankles, he looked like a little old friar pulling the bellrope in an abbey.

To get to the washbasin, Stuart had to climb a tiny rope ladder which his father had fixed for him. George had promised to build Stuart a small special washbasin only one inch high and with a little rubber tube through which water would flow; but George was always saying that he was going to build something and then forgetting about it. Stuart just went ahead and climbed the rope ladder to the family washbasin every morning to wash his face and hands and brush his teeth. Mrs. Little had provided him with a doll's size toothbrush, a doll's size cake of soap, a doll's size washcloth, and a doll's comb—which he used for combing his whiskers. He carried these things in his bathrobe pocket, and when he reached the top of the ladder he took them out, laid them neatly in a row, and set about the task of turning the water on. For such a small fellow, turning the water on was quite a problem. He had discussed it with his father one day after making several unsuccessful attempts.

"I can get up onto the faucet all right," he explained, "but I can't seem to turn it on, because I have nothing to brace my feet against."

"Yes, I know," his father replied, "that's the whole trouble."

George, who always listened to conversations whenever he could, said that in his opinion they ought to construct a brace for Stuart; and with that he got out some boards, a saw, a hammer, a screw driver, a brad-awl, and some nails, and started to make a terrific fuss in the bathroom, building what he said was going to be a brace for Stuart. But he soon became interested in something else and disappeared, leaving the tools lying around all over the bathroom floor.

Stuart, after examining this mess, turned to his father again. "Maybe I could pound the faucet with something and turn it on that way," he said.

So Stuart's father provided him with a very small, light hammer made of wood; and Stuart found that by swinging it three times around his head and letting it come down with a crash against the handle of the faucet, he could start a thin stream of water flowing—enough to brush his teeth in, anyway, and moisten his washcloth. So every morning, after climbing to the basin, he would seize his hammer and pound the faucet, and the other members of the household, dozing in their beds, would hear the bright sharp *plink plink plink* of Stuart's hammer, like a faraway blacksmith, telling them that day had come and that Stuart was trying to brush his teeth.

IV

Exercise

One fine morning in the month of May when Stuart was three years old, he arose early as was his custom, washed and dressed himself, took his hat and cane, and went downstairs into the living room to see what was doing. Nobody was around but Snowbell, the white cat belonging to Mrs. Little. Snowbell was another early riser, and this morning he was lying on the rug in the middle of the room, thinking about the days when he was just a kitten.

"Good morning," said Stuart.

"Hello," replied Snowbell, sharply. "You're up early, aren't you?"

Stuart looked at his watch. "Yes," he said, "it's only five minutes past six, but I felt good and I thought

I'd come down and get a little exercise."

"I should think you'd get all the exercise you want up there in the bathroom, banging around, waking all the rest of us up trying to get that water started so you can brush your teeth. Your teeth aren't really big enough to brush anyway. Want to see a good set? Look at mine!" Snowbell opened his mouth and showed two rows of gleaming white teeth, sharp as needles.

"Very nice," said Stuart. "But mine are all right, too, even though they're small. As for exercise, I take all I can get. I bet my stomach muscles are firmer than yours."

"I bet they're not," said the cat.

"I bet they are," said Stuart. "They're like iron bands."

"I bet they're not," said the cat.

Stuart glanced around the room to see what he could do to prove to Snowbell what good stomach muscles he had. He spied the drawn window shade on the east window, with its shade cord and ring, like a trapeze, and it gave him an idea. Climbing to the windowsill he took off his hat and laid down his cane.

"You can't do this," he said to the cat. And he ran

and jumped onto the ring, the way acrobats do in a circus, meaning to pull himself up.

A surprising thing happened. Stuart had taken such a hard jump that it started the shade: with a loud snap the shade flew up clear to the top of the window, dragging Stuart along with it and rolling him up inside, so that he couldn't budge.

"Holy mackerel!" said Snowbell, who was almost as surprised as Stuart Little. "I guess that will teach him to show off his muscles."

"Help! Let me out!" cried Stuart, who was frightened and bruised inside the rolled-up shade, and who could hardly breathe. But his voice was so weak that nobody heard. Snowbell just chuckled. He was not fond of Stuart and it didn't bother him at all that Stuart was all wrapped up in a window shade, crying and hurt and unable to get out. Instead of running upstairs and telling Mr. and Mrs. Little about the accident, Snowbell did a very curious thing. He glanced around to see if anybody was looking, then he leapt softly to the windowsill, picked up Stuart's hat and cane in his mouth, carried them to the pantry and laid them down at the entrance to the mouse-hole.

When Mrs. Little came down later and found

them there, she gave a shrill scream which brought everybody on the run.

"It's happened," she cried.

"What has?" asked her husband.

"Stuart's down the mousehole."

V

Rescued

GEORGE WAS IN FAVOR OF RIPPING UP the pantry floor. He ran and got his hammer, his screw driver, and an ice pick.

"I'll have this old floor up in doublequick time," he said, inserting his screw driver under the edge of the first board and giving a good vigorous pry.

"We will *not* rip up this floor till we have had a good search," announced Mr. Little. "That's final, George! You can put that hammer away where you got it."

"Oh, all right," said George. "I see that nobody in this house cares anything about Stuart but me."

Mrs. Little began to cry. "My poor dear little son!" she said. "I know he'll get wedged somewhere."

"Just because *you* can't travel comfortably in a mousehole doesn't mean that it isn't a perfectly suitable place for Stuart," said Mr. Little. "Just don't get yourself all worked up."

"Maybe we ought to lower some food to him," suggested George. "That's what the State Police did when a man got stuck in a cave." George darted into the kitchen and came running back with a dish of applesauce. "We can pour some of this in, and it will run down to where he is." George spooned out a bit of the applesauce and started to poke it into the hole.

"Stop that!" bellowed Mr. Little. "George, will you kindly let *me* handle this situation? Put that applesauce away immediately!"

Mr. Little glared fiercely at George.

"I was just trying to help my own brother," said George, shaking his head as he carried the sauce back to the kitchen.

"Let's all call to Stuart," suggested Mrs. Little. "It is quite possible that the mousehole branches and twists about, and that he has lost his way."

"Very well," said Mr. Little. "I will count three, then we will all call, then we will all keep perfectly quiet for three seconds, listening for the answer." He took out his watch.

Mr. and Mrs. Little and George got down on their hands and knees and put their mouths as close as possible to the mousehole. Then they all called: "Stooooo-art!" And then they all kept perfectly still for three seconds.

Stuart, from his cramped position inside the rolled-up shade, heard them yelling in the pantry and called back, "Here I am!" But he had such a weak voice and was so far inside the shade that the other members of the family did not hear his answering cry.

"Again!" said Mr. Little. "One, two, three—Stooooo-art!"

It was no use. No answer was heard. Mrs. Little went up to her bedroom, lay down, and sobbed. Mr. Little went to the telephone and called up the Bureau of Missing Persons, but when the man asked for a description of Stuart and was told that he was only two inches high, he hung up in disgust. George meantime went down cellar and hunted around to see if he could find the other entrance to the mousehole. He moved a great many trunks, suitcases, flower pots, baskets, boxes, and broken chairs from one end of the cellar to the other in order to get at the section of wall which he thought was likeliest, but found no hole. He did, however, come across an old discarded rowing machine of Mr. Little's, and becoming interested in this, carried it upstairs with some difficulty and spent the rest of the morning rowing.

When lunchtime came (everybody had forgotten about breakfast) all three sat down to a lamb stew which Mrs. Little had prepared, but it was a sad meal, each one trying not to stare at the small empty chair which Stuart always occupied, right next to Mrs. Little's glass of water. No one could eat, so great was the sorrow. George ate a bit of dessert but nothing else. When lunch was over Mrs. Little broke out crying again, and said she thought Stuart must be dead. "Nonsense, nonsense!" growled Mr. Little.

"If he *is* dead," said George, "we ought to pull down the shades all through the house." And he raced to the windows and began pulling down the shades.

"George!" shouted Mr. Little in an exasperated tone, "if you don't stop acting in an idiotic fashion, I will have to punish you. We are having enough trouble today without having to cope with your foolishness."

But George had already run into the living room and had begun to darken it, to show his respect for the dead. He pulled a cord and out dropped Stuart onto the windowsill.

"Well, for the love of Pete," said George. "Look who's here, Mom!"

"It's about time somebody pulled down that shade," remarked Stuart. "That's all I can say." He was quite weak and hungry.

Mrs. Little was so overjoyed to see him that she kept right on crying. Of course, everybody wanted to know how it had happened.

"It was simply an accident that might happen to anybody," said Stuart. "As for my hat and cane being found at the entrance to the mousehole, you can draw your own conclusions."

VI

A Fair Breeze

One morning when the wind was from the west, Stuart put on his sailor suit and his sailor hat, took his spyglass down from the shelf, and set out for a walk, full of the joy of life and the fear of dogs. With a rolling gait he sauntered along toward Fifth Avenue, keeping a sharp lookout.

Whenever he spied a dog through his glass, Stuart would hurry to the nearest doorman, climb his trouser-leg, and hide in the tails of his uniform. And once, when no doorman was handy, he had to crawl into a yesterday's paper and roll himself up in the second section till danger was past.

At the corner of Fifth Avenue there were several people waiting for the uptown bus, and Stuart joined them. Nobody noticed him, because he wasn't tall enough to be noticed.

"I'm not tall enough to be noticed," thought Stuart, "yet I'm tall enough to want to go to Seventy-second Street."

When the bus came into view, all the men waved their canes and brief cases at the driver, and Stuart waved his spyglass. Then, knowing that the step of the bus would be too high for him, Stuart seized hold of the cuff of a gentleman's pants and was swung aboard without any trouble or inconvenience whatever.

Stuart never paid any fare on buses, because he wasn't big enough to carry an ordinary dime. The only time he had ever attempted to carry a dime, he had rolled the coin along like a hoop while he raced along beside it; but it had got away from him on a hill and had been snatched up by an old woman with no teeth. After that experience Stuart contented himself with the tiny coins which his father made for him out of tin foil. They were handsome little things, although rather hard to see without putting on your spectacles.

When the conductor came around to collect the fares, Stuart fished in his purse and pulled out a coin no bigger than the eye of a grasshopper.

"What's that you're offering me?" asked the conductor.

"It's one of my dimes," said Stuart.

"Is it, now?" said the conductor. "Well, I'd have a fine time explaining that to the bus company. Why, you're no bigger than a dime yourself."

"Yes I am," replied Stuart angrily. "I'm more than twice as big as a dime. A dime only comes up to here on me." And Stuart pointed to his hip. "Furthermore," he added, "I didn't come on this bus to be insulted."

"I beg pardon," said the conductor. "You'll have to forgive me, for I had no idea that in all the world there was such a small sailor."

"Live and learn," muttered Stuart, tartly, putting his change purse back in his pocket.

When the bus stopped at Seventy-second Street, Stuart jumped out and hurried across to the sailboat pond in Central Park. Over the pond the west wind blew, and into the teeth of the west wind sailed the sloops and schooners, their rails well down, their wet decks gleaming. The owners, boys and grown men, raced around the cement shores hoping to arrive at the other side in time to keep the boats from bumping. Some of the toy boats were not as small as you might think, for when you got close to them you found that their mainmast was taller than a man's head, and they were beautifully made, with everything shipshape and ready for sea. To Stuart they seemed enormous, and he hoped he would be able to get aboard one of them and sail away to the far corners of the pond. (He was an adventurous little fellow and loved the feel of the breeze in his face and the cry of the gulls overhead and the heave of the great swell under him.)

As he sat cross-legged on the wall that surrounds the pond, gazing out at the ships through his spy-glass, Stuart noticed one boat that seemed to him finer and prouder than any other. Her name was Wasp. She was a big, black schooner flying the American flag. She had a clipper bow, and on her foredeck was mounted a three-inch cannon. She's the ship for me, thought Stuart. And the next time she sailed in, he ran over to where she was being turned around.

"Excuse me, sir," said Stuart to the man who was turning her, "but are you the owner of the schooner Wasp?"

"I am," replied the man, surprised to be addressed by a mouse in a sailor suit.

"I'm looking for a berth in a good ship,"

continued Stuart, "and I thought perhaps you might sign me on. I'm strong and I'm quick."

"Are you sober?" asked the owner of the Wasp.

"I do my work," said Stuart, crisply.

The man looked sharply at him. He couldn't help admiring the trim appearance and bold manner of this diminutive seafaring character.

"Well," he said at length, pointing the prow of the Wasp out toward the center of the pond, "I'll tell you what I'll do with you. You see that big racing sloop out there?"

"I do," said Stuart.

"That's the Lillian B. Womrath," said the man, "and I hate her with all my heart."

"Then so do I," cried Stuart, loyally.

"I hate her because she is always bumping into my boat," continued the man, "and because her owner is a lazy boy who doesn't understand sailing and who hardly knows a squall from a squid."

"Or a jib from a jibe," cried Stuart.

"Or a luff from a leech," bellowed the man.

"Or a deck from a dock," screamed Stuart.

"Or a mast from a mist," yelled the man. "But hold on, now, no more of this! I'll tell you what we'll do. The Lillian B. Womrath has always been able to beat the Wasp sailing, but I believe that if my schooner were properly handled it would be a different story. Nobody knows how I suffer, standing here on shore, helpless, watching the Wasp blunder along, when all she needs is a steady hand on her helm. So, my young friend, I'll let you sail the Wasp across the pond and back, and if you can beat that detestable sloop I'll give you a regular job."

"Aye, aye, sir!" said Stuart, swinging himself aboard the schooner and taking his place at the wheel. "Ready about!"

"One moment," said the man. "Do you mind telling me *how* you propose to beat the other boat?"

"I intend to crack on more sail," said Stuart.

"Not in *my* boat, thank you," replied the man quickly. "I don't want you capsizing in a squall."

"Well, then," said Stuart, "I'll catch the sloop broad on, and rake her with fire from my forward gun."

"Foul means!" said the man. "I want this to be a boat race, not a naval engagement."

"Well, then," said Stuart cheerfully, "I'll sail the Wasp straight and true, and let the Lillian B. Womrath go yawing all over the pond."

"Bravo!" cried the man, "and good luck go with you!" And so saying, he let go of the Wasp's prow. A puff of air bellied out the schooner's headsails and she paid off and filled away on the port tack, heeling gracefully over to the breeze while Stuart twirled her wheel and braced himself against a deck cleat.

"By the by," yelled the man, "you haven't told me your name."

"Name is Stuart Little," called Stuart at the top of his lungs. "I'm the second son of Frederick C. Little, of this city."

"*Bon voyage,* Stuart," hollered his friend, "take care of yourself and bring the Wasp home safe."

"That I will," shouted Stuart. And he was so proud and happy, he let go of the wheel for a second and did a little dance on the sloping deck, never noticing how narrowly he escaped hitting a tramp steamer that was drifting in his path, with her engines disabled and her decks awash.

VII

The Sailboat Race

When the people in Central Park learned that one of the toy sailboats was being steered by a mouse in a sailor suit, they all came running. Soon the shores of the pond were so crowded that a policeman was sent from headquarters to announce that everybody would have to stop pushing, but nobody did. People in New York like to push each other. The most excited person of all was the boy who owned the Lillian B. Womrath. He was a fat, sulky boy of twelve, named LeRoy. He wore a blue serge suit and a white necktie stained with orange juice.

"Come back here!" he called to Stuart. "Come back here and get on *my* boat. I want you to steer *my* boat. I will pay you five dollars a week and you can have every Thursday afternoon off and a radio in your room."

"I thank you for your kind offer," replied Stuart, "but I am happy aboard the Wasp—happier than I have ever been before in all my life." And with that he spun the wheel over smartly and headed his schooner down toward the starting line, where LeRoy was turning his boat around by poking it with a long stick, ready for the start of the race.

"I'll be the referee," said a man in a bright green suit. "Is the Wasp ready?"

"Ready, sir!" shouted Stuart, touching his hat.

"Is the Lillian B. Womrath ready?" asked the referee.

"Sure, I'm ready," said LeRoy.

"To the north end of the pond and back again!" shouted the referee. "On your mark, get set, GO!"

"Go!" cried the people along the shore.

"Go!" cried the owner of the Wasp.

"Go!" yelled the policeman.

And away went the two boats for the north end of the pond, while the seagulls wheeled and cried overhead and the taxicabs tooted and honked from Seventy-second Street and the west wind (which had come halfway across America to get to Central

Park) sang and whistled in the rigging and blew spray across the decks, stinging Stuart's cheeks with tiny fragments of flying peanut shell tossed up from the foamy deep. "This is the life for me!" Stuart murmured to himself. "What a ship! What a day! What a race!"

Before the two boats had gone many feet, however, an accident happened on shore. The people were pushing each other harder and harder in their eagerness to see the sport, and although they really didn't mean to, they pushed the policeman so hard they pushed him right off the concrete wall and into the pond. He hit the water in a sitting position, and got wet clear up to the third button of his jacket. He was soaked.

This particular policeman was not only a big, heavy man, but he had just eaten a big, heavy meal, and the wave he made went curling outward, cresting and billowing, upsetting all manner of small craft and causing every owner of a boat on the pond to scream with delight and consternation.

When Stuart saw the great wave approaching he jumped for the rigging, but he was too late. Towering above the Wasp like a mountain, the wave came crashing and piling along the deck, caught Stuart up and swept him over the side and into the water, where everybody supposed he would drown. Stuart had no intention of drowning. He kicked hard with his feet, and thrashed hard with his tail, and in a minute or two he climbed back aboard the schooner, cold and wet but quite unharmed. As he took his place at the helm, he could hear people cheering for him and calling, "Atta mouse, Stuart! Atta mouse!" He looked over and saw that the wave had capsized the Lillian B. Womrath but that she had righted herself and was sailing on her course, close by. And she stayed close alongside till both boats reached the north end of the pond. Here Stuart put the Wasp about and LeRoy turned the Lillian around with his stick, and away the two boats went for the finish line.

"This race isn't over yet," thought Stuart.

The first warning he had that there was trouble ahead came when he glanced into the Wasp's cabin and observed that the barometer had fallen sharply. That can mean only one thing at sea—dirty weather. Suddenly a dark cloud swept across the sun, blotting it out and leaving the earth in shadow. Stuart shivered in his wet clothes. He turned up his sailor blouse closer around his neck, and when he spied the Wasp's owner among the crowd on shore he waved his hat and called out:

"Dirty weather ahead, sir! Wind backing into the south-west, seas confused, glass falling."

"Never mind the weather!" cried the owner. "Watch out for flotsam dead ahead!"

Stuart peered ahead into the gathering storm, but saw nothing except gray waves with white crests. The world seemed cold and ominous. Stuart glanced behind him. There came the sloop, boiling along fast, rolling up a bow wave and gaining steadily.

"Look out, Stuart! Look out where you're going!"

Stuart strained his eyes, and suddenly, dead ahead, right in the path of the Wasp, he saw an enormous paper bag looming up on the surface of the pond. The bag was empty and riding high, its open end gaping wide like the mouth of a cave. Stuart spun the wheel over but it was too late: the Wasp drove her bowsprit straight into the bag and with a fearful *whooosh* the schooner slowed down and came up into the wind with all sails flapping. Just at this moment Stuart heard a splintering crash, saw the bow of the Lillian plow through his rigging, and felt the whole ship tremble from stem to stern with the force of the collision.

"A collision!" shouted the crowd on shore.

In a jiffy the two boats were in a terrible tangle.

Little boys on shore screamed and danced up and down. Meanwhile the paper bag sprang a leak and began to fill.

The Wasp couldn't move because of the bag. The Lillian B. Womrath couldn't move because her nose was stuck in the Wasp's rigging.

Waving his arms, Stuart ran forward and fired off his gun. Then he heard, above the other voices on shore, the voice of the owner of the Wasp yelling directions and telling him what to do.

"Stuart! Stuart! Down jib! Down staysail!"

Stuart jumped for the halyards, and the jib and the forestaysail came rippling down.

"Cut away all paper bags!" roared the owner.

Stuart whipped out his pocketknife and slashed away bravely at the soggy bag until he had the deck cleared.

"Now back your foresail and give her a full!" screamed the owner of the Wasp.

Stuart grabbed the foresail boom and pulled with all his might. Slowly the schooner paid off and began to gather headway. And as she heeled over to the breeze she rolled her rail out from under the Lillian's nose, shook herself free, and stood away to the southard. A loud cheer went up from the bank. Stuart sprang to the wheel and answered it. Then he looked back, and to his great joy he perceived that the Lillian had gone off in a wild direction and was yawing all over the pond.

Straight and true sailed the Wasp, with Stuart at the helm. After she had crossed the finish line, Stuart brought her alongside the wall, and was taken ashore and highly praised for his fine seamanship and daring. The owner was delighted and said it was the happiest day of his life. He introduced himself to Stuart, said that in private life he was Dr. Paul Carey, a surgeon-dentist. He said model boats were his hobby and that he would be delighted to have Stuart take command of his vessel at any time. Everybody shook hands with Stuart—everybody, that is, except the policeman, who was too wet and mad to shake hands with a mouse.

When Stuart got home that night, his brother George asked him where he had been all day.

"Oh, knocking around town," replied Stuart.

VIII

Margalo

Because he was so small, Stuart was often hard to find around the house. His father and his mother and his brother George seldom could locate him by looking for him—usually they had to call him; and the house often echoed with cries of "Stuart! Stooo-art!" You would come into a room, and he might be curled up in a chair, but you wouldn't see him. Mr. Little was in constant fear of losing him and never finding him again. He even made him a tiny red cap, such as hunters wear, so that he would be easier to see.

One day when he was seven years old, Stuart was in the kitchen watching his mother make tapioca pudding. He was feeling hungry, and when Mrs. Little opened the door of the electric refrigerator to get something, Stuart slipped inside to see if he could find a piece of cheese. He supposed, of course, his mother had seen him, and when the door swung shut and he realized he was locked in, it surprised him greatly.

"Help!" he called. "It's dark in here. It's cold in this refrigerator. Help! Let me out! I'm getting colder by the minute."

But his voice was not strong enough to penetrate the thick wall. In the darkness he stumbled and fell into a saucer of prunes. The juice was cold. Stuart shivered, and his teeth chattered together. It wasn't until half an hour later that Mrs. Little again opened the door and found him standing on a butter plate, beating his arms together to try to keep warm, and blowing on his hands, and hopping up and down.

"Mercy!" she cried. "Stuart, my poor little boy."

"How about a nip of brandy?" said Stuart. "I'm chilled to the bone."

But his mother made him some hot broth instead, and put him to bed in his cigarette box with a doll's hot-water bottle against his feet. Even so, Stuart caught a bad cold, and this turned into bronchitis, and Stuart had to stay in bed for almost two weeks.

During his illness, the other members of the

family were extremely kind to Stuart. Mrs. Little played tick-tack-toe with him. George made him a soap bubble pipe and a bow and arrow. Mr. Little made him a pair of ice skates out of two paper clips.

One cold afternoon Mrs. Little was shaking her dustcloth out of the window when she noticed a small bird lying on the windowsill, apparently dead. She brought it in and put it near the radiator, and in a short while it fluttered its wings and opened its eyes. It was a pretty little hen-bird, brown, with a streak of yellow on her breast. The Littles didn't agree on what kind of bird she was.

"She's a wall-eyed vireo," said George, scientifically.

"I think she's more like a young wren," said Mr. Little. Anyway, they fixed a place for her in the living room, and fed her, and gave her a cup of water. Soon she felt much better and went hopping around the house, examining everything with the greatest care and interest. Presently she hopped upstairs and into Stuart's room where he was lying in bed.

"Hello," said Stuart. "Who are you? Where did you come from?"

"My name is Margalo," said the bird, softly, in a musical voice. "I come from fields once tall with wheat, from pastures deep in fern and thistle; I come from vales of meadowsweet, and I love to whistle."

Stuart sat bolt upright in bed. "Say that again!" he said.

"I can't," replied Margalo. "I have a sore throat."

"So have I," said Stuart. "I've got bronchitis. You better not get too near me, you might catch it."

"I'll stay right here by the door," said Margalo.

"You can use some of my gargle if you want to," said Stuart. "And here are some nose drops, and I have plenty of Kleenex."

"Thank you very much, you are very kind," replied the bird.

"Did they take your temperature?" asked Stuart, who was beginning to be genuinely worried about his new friend's health.

"No," said Margalo, "but I don't think it will be necessary."

"Well, we better make sure," said Stuart, "because I would hate to have anything happen to you. Here. . . ." And he tossed her the thermometer. Margalo put it under her tongue, and she and Stuart sat very still for three minutes. Then she took it out and looked at it, turning it slowly and carefully.

"Normal," she announced. Stuart felt his heart leap for gladness. It seemed to him that he had never seen any creature so beautiful as this tiny bird, and he already loved her.

"I hope," he remarked, "that my parents have fixed you up with a decent place to sleep."

"Oh, yes," Margalo replied. "I'm going to sleep in the Boston fern on the bookshelf in the living room. It's a nice place, for a city location. And now, if you'll excuse me, I think I shall go to bed—I see it's getting dark outside. I always go to bed at sundown. Good night, sir!"

"Please don't call me 'sir,'" cried Stuart. "Call me Stuart."

"Very well," said the bird. "Good night, Stuart!" And she hopped off, with light, bouncing steps.

"Good night, Margalo," called Stuart. "See you in the morning."

Stuart settled back under the bedclothes again. "There's a mighty fine bird," he whispered, and sighed a tender sigh.

When Mrs. Little came in, later, to tuck Stuart in for the night and hear his prayers, Stuart asked her if she thought the bird would be quite safe sleeping down in the living room.

"Quite safe, my dear," replied Mrs. Little.

"What about that cat Snowbell?" asked Stuart, sternly.

"Snowbell won't touch the bird," his mother said. "You go to sleep and forget all about it." Mrs. Little opened the window and turned out the light.

Stuart closed his eyes and lay there in the dark, but he couldn't seem to go to sleep. He tossed and turned, and the bedclothes got all rumpled up. He kept thinking about the bird downstairs asleep in the fern. He kept thinking about Snowbell and about the way Snowbell's eyes gleamed. Finally, unable to stand it any longer, he switched on the light. "There's just something in me that doesn't trust a cat," he muttered. "I can't sleep, knowing that Margalo is in danger."

Pushing the covers back, Stuart climbed out of bed. He put on his wrapper and slippers. Taking his bow and arrow and his flashlight, he tiptoed out into the hall. Everybody had gone to bed and the house was dark. Stuart found his way to the stairs and descended slowly and cautiously into the living room, making no noise. His throat hurt him, and he felt a little bit dizzy.

"Sick as I am," he said to himself, "this has got to be done."

Being careful not to make a sound, he stole across to the lamp by the bookshelf, shinnied up the cord, and climbed out onto the shelf. There was a faint ray of light from the street lamp outside, and Stuart could dimly see Margalo, asleep in the fern, her head tucked under her wing.

"Sleep dwell upon thine eyes, peace in thy breast," he whispered, repeating a speech he had heard in the movies. Then he hid behind a candlestick and waited, listening and watching. For half an hour he saw nothing, heard nothing but the faint ruffle of Margalo's wings when she stirred in dream. The clock struck ten, loudly, and before the sound of the last stroke had died away Stuart saw two gleaming yellow eyes peering out from behind the sofa.

"So!" thought Stuart. "I guess there's going to be something doing after all." He reached for his bow and arrow.

The eyes came nearer. Stuart was frightened, but he was a brave mouse, even when he had a sore throat. He placed the arrow against the cord of the bow and waited. Snowbell crept softly toward the bookshelf and climbed noiselessly up into the chair within easy reach of the Boston fern where Margalo was asleep. Then he crouched, ready to spring. His tail waved back and forth. His eyes gleamed bright.

Stuart decided the time had come. He stepped out from behind the candlestick, knelt down, bent his bow, and took careful aim at Snowbell's left ear—which was the nearest to him.

"This is the finest thing I have ever done," thought Stuart. And he shot the arrow straight into the cat's ear.

Snowbell squealed with pain and jumped down and ran off toward the kitchen.

"A direct hit!" said Stuart. "Thank heaven! Well, there's a good night's work done." And he threw a kiss toward Margalo's sleeping form.

It was a tired little mouse that crawled into bed a few minutes later—tired but ready for sleep at last.

IX

A Narrow Escape

MARGALO LIKED IT SO WELL AT THE Littles' house she decided to stay for a while instead of returning to the open country. She and Stuart became fast friends, and as the days passed it seemed to Stuart that she grew more and more beautiful. He hoped she would never go away from him.

One day when Stuart had recovered from bronchitis he took his new skates and put on his ski pants and went out to look for an ice pond. He didn't get far. The minute he stepped out into the street he saw an Irish terrier, so he had to shinny up an iron gate and jump into a garbage can, where he hid in a grove of celery.

While he was there, waiting for the dog to go away, a garbage truck from the Department of

Sanitation drove up to the curb and two men picked up the can. Stuart felt himself being hoisted high in the air. He peered over the side and saw that in another instant he and everything in the can would be dumped into the big truck.

"If I jump now I'll kill myself," thought Stuart. So he ducked back into the can and waited. The men threw the can with a loud bump into the truck, where another man grabbed it, turned it upside down, and shook everything out. Stuart landed on his head, buried two feet deep in wet slippery garbage. All around him was garbage, smelling strong. Under him, over him, on all four sides of him—garbage. Just an enormous world of garbage and trash and smell. It was a messy spot to be in. He had egg on his trousers, butter on his cap, gravy on his shirt, orange pulp in his ear, and banana peel wrapped around his waist.

Still hanging on to his skates, Stuart tried to make his way up to the surface of the garbage, but the footing was bad. He climbed a pile of coffee grounds, but near the top the grounds gave way under him and he slid down and landed in a pool of leftover rice pudding.

"I bet I'm going to be sick at my stomach before I get out of this," said Stuart.

He was anxious to work his way up to the top of the pile because he was afraid of being squashed by the next can-load of garbage. When at last he did succeed in getting to the surface, tired and smelly, he observed that the truck was not making any more collections but was rumbling rapidly along. Stuart glanced up at the sun. "We're going east," he said to himself. "I wonder what that means."

There was no way for him to get out of the truck, the sides were too high. He just had to wait.

When the truck arrived at the East River, which borders New York City on the east and which is a rather dirty but useful river, the driver drove out onto the pier, backed up to a garbage scow, and dumped his load. Stuart went crashing and slithering along with everything else and hit his head so hard he fainted and lay quite still, as though dead. He lay that way for almost an hour, and when he recovered his senses he looked about him and saw nothing but water. The scow was being towed out to sea.

"Well," thought Stuart, "this is about the worst thing that could happen to anybody. I guess this will be my last ride in *this* world." For he knew that the garbage would be towed twenty miles out and dumped into the Atlantic Ocean. "I guess there's nothing I can do about it," he thought, hopelessly. "I'll just have to sit here bravely and die like a man. But I wish I didn't have to die with egg on my pants and butter on my cap and gravy on my shirt and orange pulp in my ear and banana peel wrapped around my middle."

The thought of death made Stuart sad, and he began to think of his home and of his father and mother and brother and of Margalo and Snowbell and of how he loved them (all but Snowbell) and of what a pleasant place his home was, specially in the early morning with the light just coming in through the curtains and the household stirring and waking. The tears came into his eyes when he realized that he would never see them again. He was still sobbing when a small voice behind him whispered:

"Stuart!"

He looked around, through his tears, and there, sitting on a Brussels sprout, was Margalo.

"Margalo!" cried Stuart. "How did *you* get here?"

"Well," said the bird, "I was looking out the window this morning when you left home and I happened to see you get dumped into the garbage truck, so I flew out the window and followed the truck, thinking you might need help."

"I've never been so glad to see anybody in all my life," said Stuart. "But how are you going to help me?"

"I think that if you'll hang on to my feet," said Margalo, "I can fly ashore with you. It's worth trying anyway. How much do you weigh?"

"Three ounces and a half," said Stuart.

"With your clothes on?" asked Margalo.

"Certainly," replied Stuart, modestly.

"Then I believe I can carry you all right."

"Suppose I get dizzy," said Stuart.

"Don't look down," replied Margalo. "Then you won't get dizzy."

"Suppose I get sick at my stomach."

"You'll just have to *be* sick," the bird replied. "Anything is better than death."

"Yes, that's true," Stuart agreed.

"Hang on, then! We may as well get started."

Stuart tucked his skates into his shirt, stepped gingerly onto a tuft of lettuce, and took a firm grip on Margalo's ankles. "All ready!" he cried.

With a flutter of wings, Margalo rose into the sky, carrying Stuart along, and together they flew out over the ocean and headed toward home.

"Pew!" said Margalo, when they were high in the air, "you smell awful, Stuart."

"I know I do," he replied, gloomily. "I hope it isn't making you feel bad."

"I can hardly breathe," she answered. "And my heart is pounding in my breast. Isn't there something you could drop to make yourself lighter?"

"Well, I could drop these ice skates," said Stuart.

"Goodness me," the little bird cried, "I didn't know you had skates hidden in your shirt. Toss those heavy skates away quickly or we will both come down in the ocean and perish." Stuart threw his skates away and watched them fall down, down, till they disappeared in the gray waves below. "That's better," said Margalo. "Now we're all right. I can already see the towers and chimneys of New York."

Fifteen minutes later, in they flew through the open window of the Littles' living room and landed on the Boston fern. Mrs. Little, who had left the window up when she missed Margalo, was glad to see them back, for she was beginning to worry. When she heard what had happened and how near she had come to losing her son, she took Stuart in her hand, even though his clothes smelled nasty, and kissed him. Then she sent him upstairs to take a bath, and sent George out to take Stuart's clothes to the cleaner.

"What was it like, out there in the Atlantic Ocean?" inquired Mr. Little, who had never been very far from home.

So Stuart and Margalo told all about the ocean, and the gray waves curling with white crests, and the gulls in the sky, and the channel buoys and the ships and the tugs and the wind making a sound in your ears. Mr. Little sighed and said some day he hoped to get away from business long enough to see all those fine things.

Everyone thanked Margalo for saving Stuart's life; and at suppertime Mrs. Little presented her with a tiny cake, which had seeds sprinkled on top.

X

Springtime

SNOWBELL, THE CAT, ENJOYED NIGHTTIME more than daytime. Perhaps it was because his eyes liked the dark. But I think it was because there are always so many worthwhile things going on in New York at night.

Snowbell had several friends in the neighborhood. Some of them were house cats, others were store cats. He knew a Maltese cat in the A & P, a white Persian in the apartment house next door, a tortoise-shell in the delicatessen, a tiger cat in the basement of the branch library, and a beautiful young Angora who had escaped from a cage in a pet shop on Third Avenue and had gone to live a free life of her own in the tool house of the small park near Stuart's home.

One fine spring evening Snowbell had been

calling on the Angora in the park. He started home, late, and it was such a lovely night she said she would walk along with him to keep him company. When they got to Mr. Little's house, the two cats sat down at the foot of a tall vine which ran up the side of the house past George's bedroom. This vine was useful to Snowbell, because he could climb it at night and crawl into the house through George's open window. Snowbell began telling his friend about Margalo and Stuart.

"Goodness," said the Angora cat, "you mean to say you live in the same house with a bird and a mouse and don't do anything about it?"

"That's the situation," replied Snowbell. "But what can I do about it? Please remember that Stuart is a member of the family, and the bird is a permanent guest, like myself."

"Well," said Snowbell's friend, "all I can say is, you've got more self-control than I have."

"Doubtless," said Snowbell. "However, I sometimes think I've got too much self-control for my own good. I've been terribly nervous and upset lately, and I think it's because I'm always holding myself in."

The cats' voices grew louder, and they talked so loudly that they never heard a slight rustling in the vine a few feet above their heads. It was a gray pigeon, who had been asleep there and who had awakened at the sound of cats and begun to listen. "This sounds like an interesting conversation," said the pigeon to himself. "Maybe I'd better stay around and see if I can learn something."

"Look here," he heard the Angora cat say to Snowbell, "I admit that a cat has a duty toward her own people, and that under the circumstances it would be wrong for you to eat Margalo. But *I'm* not a member of your family and there is nothing to stop *me* from eating her, is there?"

"Nothing that I can think of offhand," said Snowbell.

"Then here I go," said the Angora, starting up the vine. The pigeon was wide awake by this time, ready to fly away; but the voices down below continued.

"Wait a minute," said Snowbell, "don't be in such a hurry. I don't think you'd better go in there tonight."

"Why not?" asked the other cat.

"Well, for one thing, you're not supposed to enter our house. It's unlawful entry, and you might get into trouble."

"I won't get into any trouble," said the Angora.

"Please wait till tomorrow night," said Snowbell,

firmly. "Mr. and Mrs. Little will be going out tomorrow night, and you won't be taking such a risk. It's for your own good I'm suggesting this."

"Oh, all right," agreed the Angora. "I guess I can wait. But tell me where I'll find the bird, after I do get in."

"That's simple," said Snowbell. "Climb this vine, enter George's room through the open window, then go downstairs and you'll find the bird asleep in the Boston fern on the bookcase."

"Easy enough," said the Angora, licking her chops. "I'm obliged to you, sir."

"Well, the old thing!" whispered the pigeon to himself, and he flew away quickly to find a piece of writing paper and a pencil. Snowbell said goodnight to his friend and climbed up the vine and went in to bed.

Next morning Margalo found a note on the branch of her fern when she woke. It said: BEWARE OF A STRANGE CAT WHO WILL COME BY NIGHT. It was signed A WELL WISHER. She kept the note under her wing all day long, wondering what she had better do, but she didn't dare show it to anyone—not even to Stuart. She couldn't eat, she was so frightened.

"What had I better do?" she kept saying to herself.

Finally, just before dark, she hopped up to an open window and without saying anything to anybody she flew away. It was springtime, and she flew north, just as fast as she could fly, because something inside her told her that north was the way for a bird to go when spring comes to the land.

XI

The Automobile

For three days everybody hunted all over the house for Margalo without finding so much as a feather.

"I guess she had spring fever," said George. "A normal bird doesn't stay indoors this kind of weather."

"Perhaps she has a husband somewhere and has gone to meet him," suggested Mr. Little.

"She has not!" sobbed Stuart, bitterly. "That's just a lot of nonsense."

"How do *you* know?" asked George.

"Because I asked her one time," cried Stuart. "She told me she was a single bird."

Everybody questioned Snowbell closely, but the cat insisted he knew nothing about Margalo's disappearance. "I don't see why you have to make a pariah out of me just because that disagreeable little chippy flew the coop," said Snowbell, irritably.

Stuart was heartbroken. He had no appetite, refused food, and lost weight. Finally he decided that he would run away from home without telling anybody, and go out into the world and look for Margalo. "While I am about it, I might as well seek my fortune, too," he thought.

Before daybreak next morning he got out his biggest handkerchief and in it he placed his toothbrush, his money, his soap, his comb and brush, a clean suit of underwear, and his pocket compass.

"I ought to take along something to remember my mother by," he thought. So he crept into his mother's bedroom where she was still asleep, climbed the lamp cord to her bureau, and pulled a strand of Mrs. Little's hair from her comb. He rolled the hair up neatly and laid it in the handkerchief with the other things. Then he rolled everything up into a bundle and tied it onto one end of a wooden match. With his gray felt hat cocked jauntily on one side of his head and his pack slung across his shoulder, Stuart stole softly out of the house.

"Good-by, beautiful home," he whispered. "I

wonder if I will ever see you again."

Stuart stood uncertainly for a moment in the street in front of the house. The world was a big place in which to go looking for a lost bird. North, south, east, or west—which way should he go? Stuart decided that he needed advice on such an important matter, so he started uptown to find his friend Dr. Carey, the surgeon-dentist, owner of the schooner Wasp.

The doctor was glad to see Stuart. He took him right into his inner office where he was busy pulling a man's tooth. The man's name was Edward Clydesdale, and he had several wads of gauze in his cheek to hold his mouth open good and wide. The tooth was a hard one to get out, and the Doctor let Stuart sit on his instrument tray so they could talk during the operation.

"This is my friend, Stuart Little," he said to the man with the gauze in his cheek.

"How 'oo oo, Soo'rt," replied the man, as best he could.

"Very well, thank you," replied Stuart.

"Well, what's on your mind, Stuart?" asked Dr. Carey, seizing hold of the man's tooth with a pair of pincers and giving a strong pull.

"I ran away from home this morning," explained Stuart. "I am going out into the world to seek my fortune and to look for a lost bird. Which direction do you think I should start out in?"

Dr. Carey twisted the tooth a bit and racked it back and forth. "What color is the bird?" he asked.

"Brown," said Stuart.

"Better go north," said Dr. Carey. "Don't you think so, Mr. Clydesdale?"

"'ook in 'entral 'ark," said Mr. Clydesdale.

"What?" cried Stuart.

"I 'ay, 'ook in 'entral 'ark," said Mr. Clydesdale.

"He says look in Central Park," explained Dr. Carey, tucking another big wad of gauze into Mr. Clydesdale's cheek. "And it's a good suggestion. Oftentimes people with decayed teeth have sound ideas. Central Park is a favorite place for birds in the spring." Mr. Clydesdale was nodding his head vigorously, and seemed about to speak again.

"If 'oo 'on't 'ocate a 'ird in 'entral 'ark, 'ake a 'ew 'ork 'ew 'aven & 'artford 'ailway 'n 'ook in 'onnecticut."

"What?" cried Stuart, delighted at this new kind of talk. "What say, Mr. Clydesdale?"

"If 'oo 'on't 'ocate a 'ird in 'entral 'ark, 'ake

a 'ew 'ork 'ew 'aven & 'artford 'ailway 'n 'ook in 'onnecticut."

"He says if you can't locate the bird in Central Park, take a New York New Haven & Hartford Railway train and look in Connecticut," said Dr. Carey. Then he removed the rolls of gauze from Mr. Clydesdale's mouth. "Rinse, please!" he said.

Mr. Clydesdale took a glass of mouthwash that was beside the chair and rinsed his mouth out.

"Tell me this, Stuart," said Dr. Carey. "How are you traveling? On foot?"

"Yes, sir," said Stuart.

"Well, I think you'd better have a car. As soon as I get this tooth out, we'll see what can be done about it. Open, please, Mr. Clydesdale."

Dr. Carey grabbed the tooth with the pincers again, and this time he pulled so long and so hard and with such determination that the tooth popped out, which was a great relief to everybody, particularly to Mr. Clydesdale. The Doctor then led Stuart into another room. From a shelf he took a tiny automobile, about six inches long—the most perfect miniature automobile Stuart had ever seen. It was bright yellow with black fenders, a streamlined car of graceful design. "I made this myself," Dr. Carey said. “I enjoy building model cars and boats and other things when I am not extracting teeth. This car has a real gasoline motor in it. It has quite a good deal of power—do you think you can handle it, Stuart?”

“Certainly,” replied Stuart, looking into the driver’s seat and blowing the horn. “But isn’t it going to attract too much attention? Won’t everybody stop and stare at such a small automobile?”

“They would if they could see you,” replied Dr. Carey, “but nobody will be able to see you, or the car.”

“Why not?” asked Stuart.

“Because this automobile is a thoroughly modern car. It’s not only noiseless, it’s invisible. Nobody can see it.”

“*I* can see it,” remarked Stuart.

“Push that little button!” said the Doctor, pointing to a button on the instrument panel. Stuart pushed the button. Instantly the car vanished from sight.

“Now push it again,” said the Doctor.

“How can I push it when I can’t see it?” asked Stuart.

“Feel around for it.”

So Stuart felt around until his hand came in

contact with a button. It seemed like the same button, and Stuart pushed it. He heard a slight grinding noise and felt something slip out from under his hand.

"Hey, watch out!" yelled Dr. Carey. "You pushed the starter button. She's off! There she goes! She's away! She's loose in the room—now we'll never catch her." He grabbed Stuart up and placed him on a table where he wouldn't be hit by a runaway car.

"Oh, mercy! Oh, mercy!" Stuart cried when he realized what he had done. It was a very awkward situation. Neither Dr. Carey nor Stuart could see the little automobile, yet it was rushing all over the room under its own power, bumping into things. First there came a crashing noise over by the fireplace. The hearth broom fell down. Dr. Carey leapt for the spot and pounced on the place where the sound had come from. But though he was quick, he had hardly got his hands on the place when there was another crash over by the wastebasket. The Doctor pounced again. Pounce! Crash! Pounce! Crash! The Doctor was racing all over the room, pouncing and missing. It is almost impossible to catch a speedy invisible model automobile even when one is a skillful dentist.

"Oh, oh," yelled Stuart, jumping up and down. "I'm sorry, Dr. Carey, I'm dreadfully sorry!"

"Get a butterfly net!" shouted the Doctor.

"I can't," said Stuart. "I'm not big enough to carry a butterfly net."

"That's true," said Dr. Carey. "I forgot. My apologies, Stuart."

"The car is bound to stop sometime," said Stuart, "because it will run out of gas."

"That's true, too," said the Doctor. And so he and Stuart sat down and waited patiently until they no longer heard any crashing sounds in the room. Then the Doctor got down on his hands and knees and crawled cautiously all over, feeling here and there, until at last he found the car. It was in the fireplace, buried up to its hubs in wood ashes. The Doctor pressed the proper button and there it stood in plain sight again, its front fenders crumpled, its radiator leaking, its headlights broken, its windshield shattered, its right rear tire punctured, and quite a bit of yellow paint scratched off the hood.

"What a mess!" groaned the Doctor. "Stuart, I hope this will be a lesson to you: never push a button on an automobile unless you are sure of what you are doing."

"Yes, sir," answered Stuart, and his eyes filled with tears, each tear being smaller than a drop of dew. It had been an unhappy morning, and Stuart was already homesick. He was sure that he was never going to see Margalo again.

XII

The Schoolroom

WHILE DR. CAREY WAS MAKING REPAIRS on the car, Stuart went shopping. He decided that, since he was about to take a long motor trip, he should have the proper clothes. He went to a doll's shop, where they had things which were the right size for him, and outfitted himself completely, with new luggage, suits, shirts, and accessories. He charged everything and was well pleased with his purchases. That night he slept at the Doctor's apartment.

The next morning, Stuart started early, to avoid traffic. He thought it would be a good idea to get out on the road before there were too many cars and trucks. He drove through Central Park to One Hundred and Tenth Street, then over to the West Side Highway, then north to the Saw Mill River

Parkway. The car ran beautifully and although people were inclined to stare at him, Stuart didn't mind. He was very careful not to press the button which had caused so much trouble the day before. He made up his mind that he would never use that button again.

Just as the sun was coming up, Stuart saw a man seated in thought by the side of the road. Stuart steered his car alongside, stopped, and put his head out.

"You're worried about something, aren't you?" asked Stuart.

"Yes, I am," said the man, who was tall and mild.

"Can I help you in any way?" asked Stuart in a friendly voice.

The man shook his head. "It's an impossible situation, I guess," he replied. "You see, I'm the Superintendent of Schools in this town."

"That's not an impossible situation," said Stuart. "It's bad, but it's not impossible."

"Well," continued the man, "I've always got problems that I can't solve. Today, for instance, one of my teachers is sick—Miss Gunderson her name is. She teaches Number Seven school. I've got to find a substitute for her, a teacher who will take her place."

"What's the matter with her?" asked Stuart.

"I don't know, exactly. The doctor says she may have rhinestones," replied the Superintendent.

"Can't you find another teacher?" asked Stuart.

"No, that's the trouble. There's nobody in this town who knows anything; no spare teachers, no anything. School is supposed to begin in an hour."

"I will be glad to take Miss Gunderson's place for a day, if you would like," suggested Stuart agreeably.

The Superintendent of Schools looked up.

"Really?"

"Certainly," said Stuart. "Glad to." He opened the door of the little car and stepped out. Walking around to the rear, he opened the baggage compartment and took out his suitcase. "If I'm to conduct a class in a schoolroom, I'd better take off these motoring togs and get into something more suitable," he said. Stuart climbed the bank, went into the bushes, and was back in a few minutes wearing a pepper-and-salt jacket, old striped trousers, a Windsor tie, and spectacles. He folded his other clothes and packed them away in the suitcase.

"Do you think you can maintain discipline?" asked the Superintendent.

"Of course I can," replied Stuart. "I'll make the work interesting and the discipline will take care of itself. Don't worry about me."

The man thanked him and they shook hands.

At quarter before nine the scholars had gathered in School Number Seven. When they missed Miss Gunderson and word got round that there would be a substitute, they were delighted.

"A substitute!" somebody whispered to somebody else. "A substitute, a substitute!"

The news traveled fast, and soon everyone in the schoolroom knew that they were all to have a rest from Miss Gunderson for at least a day and were going to have the wonderful experience of being taught by a strange teacher whom nobody had ever seen before.

Stuart arrived at nine. He parked his car briskly at the door of the school, stalked boldly into the room, found a yardstick leaning against Miss Gunderson's desk, and climbed hand-over-hand to the top. There he found an inkwell, a pointer, some pens and pencils, a bottle of ink, some chalk, a bell, two hairpins, and three or four books in a pile. Stuart scrambled nimbly up to the top of the stack of books and jumped for the button on the bell. His weight was enough to make it ring, and Stuart promptly slid down, walked to the front of the desk, and said:

"Let me have your attention, please!"

The boys and girls crowded around the desk to look at the substitute. Everyone talked at once, and they seemed to be very much pleased. The girls giggled and the boys laughed and everyone's eyes lit up with excitement to see such a small and good-looking teacher, so appropriately dressed.

"Let me have your attention, please!" repeated Stuart. "As you know, Miss Gunderson is sick and I am taking her place."

"What's the matter with her?" asked Roy Hart, eagerly.

"Vitamin trouble," replied Stuart. "She took Vitamin D when she needed A. She took B when she was short of C, and her system became overloaded with riboflavin, thiamine hydrochloride, and even with pyridoxine, the need for which in human nutrition has not been established. Let it be a lesson for all of us!" He glared fiercely at the children and they made no more inquiries about Miss Gunderson.

"Everyone will now take his or her seat!" commanded Stuart. The pupils filed obediently down the aisles and dropped into their seats, and in a moment there was silence in the classroom. Stuart cleared his throat. Seizing a coat lapel in either hand, to make himself look like a professor, Stuart began:

"Anybody absent?"

The scholars shook their heads.

"Anybody late?"

They shook their heads.

"Very well," said Stuart, "what's the first subject you usually take up in the morning?"

"Arithmetic," shouted the children.

"Bother arithmetic!" snapped Stuart. "Let's skip it."

There were wild shouts of enthusiasm at this suggestion. Everyone in the class seemed perfectly willing to skip arithmetic for one morning.

"What next do you study?" asked Stuart.

"Spelling," cried the children.

"Well," said Stuart, "a misspelled word is an abomination in the sight of everyone. I consider it a very fine thing to spell words correctly and I strongly urge every one of you to buy a Webster's Collegiate Dictionary and consult it whenever you are in the slightest doubt. So much for spelling. What's next?"

The scholars were just as pleased to be let out of spelling as they were about arithmetic, and they shouted for joy, and everybody looked at everybody else and laughed and waved handkerchiefs and rulers, and some of the boys threw spit balls at some of the girls. Stuart had to climb onto the pile of books again and dive for the bell to restore order. "What's next?" he repeated.

"Writing," cried the scholars.

"Goodness," said Stuart in disgust, "don't you children know how to write yet?"

"Certainly we do!" yelled one and all.

"So much for that, then," said Stuart.

"Social studies come next," cried Elizabeth Gardner, eagerly.

"Social studies? Never heard of them," said Stuart. "Instead of taking up any special subject this morning, why wouldn't it be a good idea if we just talked about something."

The scholars glanced around at each other in expectancy.

"Could we talk about the way it feels to hold a snake in your hand and then it winds itself around your wrist?" asked Arthur Greenlaw.

"We could, but I'd rather not," replied Stuart.

"Could we talk about sin and vice?" pleaded Lydia Lacey.

"Nope," said Stuart. "Try again."

"Could we talk about the fat woman at the circus

and she had hair all over her chin?" begged Isidor Feinberg, reminiscently.

"No," said Stuart. "I'll tell you, let's talk about the King of the World." He looked all around the room hopefully to see how the children liked that idea.

"There isn't any King of the World," said Harry Jamieson in disgust.

"What's the diff?" said Stuart. "There *ought* to be one."

"Kings are old-fashioned," said Harry.

"Well, all right then, let's talk about the Chairman of the World. The world gets into a lot of trouble because it has no chairman. I would like to be Chairman of the World myself."

"You're too small," said Mary Bendix.

"Oh, fish feathers!" said Stuart. "Size has nothing to do with it. It's temperament and ability that count. The Chairman has to have ability and he must know what's important. How many of you know what's important?"

Up went all the hands.

"Very good," said Stuart, cocking one leg across the other and shoving his hands in the pockets of his jacket. "Henry Rackmeyer, you tell us what is important."

"A shaft of sunlight at the end of a dark afternoon, a note in music, and the way the back of a baby's neck smells if its mother keeps it tidy," answered Henry.

"Correct," said Stuart. "Those are the important things. You forgot one thing, though. Mary Bendix, what did Henry Rackmeyer forget?"

"He forgot ice cream with chocolate sauce on it," said Mary quickly.

"Exactly," said Stuart. "Ice cream is important. Well now, if I'm going to be Chairman of the World this morning, we've got to have some rules, otherwise it will be too confusing, with everyone running every which way and helping himself to things and nobody behaving. We've got to have some laws if we're going to play this game. Can anybody suggest any good laws for the world?"

Albert Fernstrom raised his hand. "Don't eat mushrooms, they might be toadstools," suggested Albert.

"That's not a law," said Stuart, "that's merely a bit of friendly advice. Very good advice, Albert, but advice and law are not the same. Law is much more solemn than advice. Law is extremely solemn. Anybody else think of a law for the world?"

"Nix on swiping anything," suggested John Poldowski, solemnly.

"Very good," said Stuart. "Good law."

"Never poison anything but rats," said Anthony Brendisi.

"That's no good," said Stuart. "It's unfair to rats. A law has to be fair to everybody."

Anthony looked sulky. "But rats are unfair to us," he said. "Rats are objectionable."

"I know they are," said Stuart. "But from a rat's point of view, poison is objectionable. A Chairman has to see all sides to a problem."

"Have you got a rat's point of view?" asked Anthony. "You look a little like a rat."

"No," replied Stuart, "I have more the point of view of a mouse, which is very different. I see things whole. It's obvious to me that rats are underprivileged. They've never been able to get out in the open."

"Rats don't like the open," said Agnes Beretska.

"That's because whenever they come out, somebody socks them. Rats might like the open if they were allowed to use it. Any other ideas for laws?"

Agnes Beretska raised her hand. "There ought to be a law against fighting."

"Impractical," said Stuart. "Men like to fight. But you're getting warm, Agnes."

"No scrapping?" asked Agnes, timidly. Stuart shook his head.

"Absolutely no being mean," suggested Mildred Hoffenstein.

"Very fine law," said Stuart. "When I am Chairman, anybody who is mean to anybody else is going to catch it."

"That won't work," remarked Herbert Prendergast. "Some people are just naturally mean. Albert Fernstrom is always being mean to me."

"I'm not saying it'll work," said Stuart. "It's a good law and we'll give it a try. We'll give it a try right here and now. Somebody do something mean to somebody. Harry Jamieson, you be mean to Katharine Stableford. Wait a minute, now, what's that you've got in your hand, Katharine?"

"It's a little tiny pillow stuffed with sweet balsam."

"Does it say 'For you I pine, for you I balsam' on it?"

"Yes," said Katharine.

"Do you love it very much?" asked Stuart.

"Yes, I do," said Katharine.

"O.K., Harry, grab it, take it away!"

Harry ran over to where Katharine sat, grabbed the little pillow from her hand, and ran back to his seat, while Katharine screamed.

"Now then," said Stuart in a fierce voice, "hold on, my good people, while your Chairman consults the book of rules!" He pretended to thumb through a book. "Here we are. Page 492. 'Absolutely no being mean.' Page 560. 'Nix on swiping anything.' Harry Jamieson has broken two laws—the law against being mean and the law against swiping. Let's get Harry and set him back before he becomes so mean people will hardly recognize him any more! Come on!"

Stuart ran for the yardstick and slid down, like a fireman coming down a pole in a firehouse. He ran toward Harry, and the other children jumped up from their seats and raced up and down the aisles and crowded around Harry while Stuart demanded that he give up the little pillow. Harry looked frightened, although he knew it was just a test. He gave Katharine the pillow.

"There, it worked pretty well," said Stuart. "No being mean is a perfectly good law." He wiped his face with his handkerchief, for he was quite warm from the exertion of being Chairman of the World. It had taken more running and leaping and sliding than he had imagined. Katharine was very much pleased to have her pillow back.

"Let's see that little pillow a minute," said Stuart, whose curiosity was beginning to get the better of him. Katharine showed it to him. It was about as long as Stuart was high, and Stuart suddenly thought what a fine sweet-smelling bed it would make for him. He began to want the pillow himself.

"That's a very pretty thing," said Stuart, trying to hide his eagerness. "You don't want to sell it, do you?"

"Oh, no," replied Katharine. "It was a present to me."

"I suppose it was given you by a boy you met at Lake Hopatcong last summer, and it reminds you of him," murmured Stuart, dreamily.

"Yes, it was," said Katharine, blushing.

"Ah," said Stuart, "summers are wonderful, aren't they, Katharine?"

"Yes, and last summer was the most wonderful summer I have ever had in all my life."

"I can imagine," replied Stuart. "You're sure you wouldn't want to sell that little pillow?"

Katharine shook her head.

"Don't know as I blame you," replied Stuart,

quietly. "Summertime is important. It's like a shaft of sunlight."

"Or a note in music," said Elizabeth Acheson.

"Or the way the back of a baby's neck smells if its mother keeps it tidy," said Marilyn Roberts.

Stuart sighed. "Never forget your summertimes, my dears," he said. "Well, I've got to be getting along. It's been a pleasure to know you all. Class is dismissed!"

Stuart strode rapidly to the door, climbed into the car, and with a final wave of the hand drove off in a northerly direction, while the children raced alongside and screamed "Good-by, good-by, good-by!" They all wished they could have a substitute every day, instead of Miss Gunderson.

XIII

Ames' Crossing

IN THE LOVELIEST TOWN OF ALL, WHERE the houses were white and high and the elm trees were green and higher than the houses, where the front yards were wide and pleasant and the back yards were bushy and worth finding out about, where the streets sloped down to the stream and the stream flowed quietly under the bridge, where the lawns ended in orchards and the orchards ended in fields and the fields ended in pastures and the pastures climbed the hill and disappeared over the top toward the wonderful wide sky, in this loveliest of all towns Stuart stopped to get a drink of sarsaparilla.

Parking his car in front of the general store, he stepped out and the sun felt so good that he sat down on the porch for a few moments to enjoy the feeling of being in a new place on a fine day. This was the most peaceful and beautiful spot he had found in all his travels. It seemed to him a place he would gladly spend the rest of his life in, if it weren't that he might get homesick for the sights of New York and for his family, Mr. and Mrs. Frederick C. Little and George, and if it weren't for the fact that something deep inside him made him want to find Margalo.

After a while the storekeeper came out to smoke a cigarette, and he joined Stuart on the front steps. He started to offer Stuart a cigarette but when he noticed how small he was, he changed his mind.

"Have you any sarsaparilla in your store?" asked Stuart. "I've got a ruinous thirst."

"Certainly," said the storekeeper. "Gallons of it. Sarsaparilla, root beer, birch beer, ginger ale, Moxie, lemon soda, Coca Cola, Pepsi Cola, Dipsi Cola, Pipsi Cola, Popsi Cola, and raspberry cream tonic. Anything you want."

"Let me have a bottle of sarsaparilla, please," said Stuart, "and a paper cup."

The storekeeper went back into the store and returned with the drink. He opened the bottle, poured some out into the cup, and set the cup down on the step below Stuart, who whipped off his cap, lay down on his stomach, and dipped up some of the cool refreshing drink, using his cap as a dipper.

"That's very refreshing," remarked Stuart. "There's nothing like a long, cool drink in the heat of the day, when you're traveling."

"Are you going far?" asked the storekeeper.

"Perhaps *very* far," replied Stuart. "I'm looking for a bird named Margalo. You haven't sighted her, have you?"

"Can't say I have," said the storekeeper. "What does she look like?"

"Perfectly beautiful," replied Stuart, wiping the sarsaparilla off his lips with the corner of his sleeve. "She's a remarkable bird. Anybody would notice her. She comes from a place where there are thistles."

The storekeeper looked at Stuart closely.

"How tall are you?" he asked.

"You mean in my stocking feet?" said Stuart.

"Yes."

"Two inches nothing and a quarter," answered Stuart. "I haven't been measured recently, however. I may have shot up a bit."

"You know," said the storekeeper, thoughtfully, "there's somebody in this town you really ought to meet."

"Who's that?" asked Stuart, yawning.

"Harriet Ames," said the storekeeper. "She's just

your size—maybe a trifle shorter, if anything."

"What's she like?" asked Stuart. "Fair, fat, and forty?"

"No, Harriet is young and she is quite pretty. She is considered one of the best dressed girls in this town, too. All her clothes are tailored specially for her."

"That so?" remarked Stuart.

"Yes. Harriet's quite a girl. Her people, the Ameses, are rather prominent in this town. One of her ancestors used to be the ferryman here in Revolutionary days. He would carry anybody across the stream—he didn't care whether they were British soldiers or American soldiers, as long as they paid their fare. I guess he did pretty well. Anyway, the Ameses have always had plenty of money. They live in a big house with a lot of servants. I know Harriet would be very much interested to meet you."

"That's very kind of you," replied Stuart, "but I'm not much of a society man these days. Too much on the move. I never stay long anywhere—I blow into a town and blow right out again, here today, gone tomorrow, a will o' the wisp. The highways and byways are where you'll find me, always looking for Margalo. Sometimes I feel that I'm quite near to her and that she's just around the turn of the road. Other times I feel that I'll never find her and never hear her voice again. Which reminds me, it's time I was on my way." Stuart paid for his drink, said good-by to the storekeeper, and drove off.

But Ames' Crossing seemed like the finest town he had ever known, and before he reached the end of the main street he swerved sharp left, turned off onto a dirt road, and drove down to a quiet spot on the bank of the river. That afternoon he swam and lay on his back on the mossy bank, his hands crossed under his head, his thoughts returning to the conversation he had had with the storekeeper.

"Harriet Ames," he murmured.

Evening came, and Stuart still lingered by the stream. He ate a light supper of a cheese sandwich and a drink of water, and slept that night in the warm grass with the sound of the stream in his ears.

In the morning the sun rose warm and bright and Stuart slipped into the river again for an early dip. After breakfast he left his car hidden under a skunk cabbage leaf and walked up to the post office. While he was filling his fountain pen from the public inkwell he happened to glance toward the door and what he saw startled him so that he almost lost his balance and fell into the ink. A girl about two inches high had entered and was crossing the floor toward the mail boxes. She wore sports clothes and walked with her head held high. In her hair was a stamen from a flower.

Stuart began to tremble from excitement.

"Must be the Ames girl," he said to himself. And he kept out of sight behind the inkwell as he watched her open her mail box, which was about a quarter of an inch wide, and pull out her letters. The storekeeper had told the truth: Harriet was pretty. And of course she was the only girl Stuart had ever encountered who wasn't miles and miles taller than he was. Stuart figured that if the two of them were to walk along together, her head would come a little higher than his shoulder. The idea filled him with interest. He wanted to slide down to the floor and speak to her, but he didn't dare. All his boldness had left him and he stayed hidden behind the inkwell until Harriet had gone. When he was sure that she was out of sight, he stole out of the post office and slunk down the street to the store, half hoping that he would meet the beautiful little girl, half fearing that he would.

"Have you any engraved stationery?" he asked

the storekeeper. "I'm behind on my correspondence."

The storekeeper helped Stuart up onto the counter and found some letter paper for him—small paper, marked with the initial "L." Stuart whipped out his fountain pen and sat down against a five-cent candy bar and began a letter to Harriet:

"MY DEAR MISS AMES," he wrote. "I am a young person of modest proportions. By birth I am a New Yorker, but at the moment I am traveling on business of a confidential nature. My travels have brought me to your village. Yesterday the keeper of your local store, who has an honest face and an open manner, gave me a most favorable report of your character and appearance."

At this point in the letter Stuart's pen ran dry from the long words and Stuart had to get the storekeeper to lower him head-first into a bottle of ink so that he could refill the pen. Then he went back to letter writing. . . .

"Pray forgive me, Miss Ames," continued Stuart, "for presuming to strike up an acquaintance on so slender an excuse as our physical similarity; but of course the fact is,

as you yourself must know, there are very few people who are only two inches in height. I say 'two inches'—actually I am somewhat taller than that. My only drawback is that I look something like a mouse. I am nicely proportioned, however. Am also muscular beyond my years. Let me be perfectly blunt: my purpose in writing this brief note is to suggest that we meet. I realize that your parents may object to the suddenness and directness of my proposal, as well as to my somewhat mouselike appearance, so I think probably it might be a good idea if you just didn't mention the matter to them. What they don't know won't hurt them. However, you probably understand more about dealing with your father and mother than I do, so I won't attempt to instruct you but will leave everything to your good judgment.

"Being an outdoors person, I am camped by the river in an attractive spot at the foot of Tracy's Lane. Would you care to go for a paddle with me in my canoe? How about tomorrow afternoon toward sundown, when the petty annoyances of the day are behind us and the river seems to flow more quietly in the long shadows of the willows? These tranquil spring evenings are designed by special architects for the enjoyment of boatmen. I love the water, dear Miss Ames, and my canoe is like an old and trusted friend."

Stuart forgot, in the excitement of writing Harriet, that he did not own a canoe.

"If you wish to accept my invitation, be at the river tomorrow about five o'clock. I shall await your arrival with all the eagerness I can muster. And now I must close this offensive letter and catch up with my affairs.

Yours very truly,

STUART LITTLE."

After Stuart had sealed his letter in an envelope, he turned to the storekeeper.

"Where can I get hold of a canoe?" he asked.

"Right here," replied the storekeeper. He walked over to his souvenir counter and took down a little birchbark canoe with the words SUMMER MEMORIES stamped on the side. Stuart examined it closely.

"Does she leak?" asked Stuart.

"It's a nice canoe," replied the storekeeper, bending it gently back into shape with his fingers. "It will cost you seventy-five cents plus a penny tax."

Stuart took out his money and paid the man. Then he looked inside the canoe and noticed that there were no paddles.

"What about paddles?" he said, making his voice

sound businesslike. The storekeeper hunted around among the souvenirs but he couldn't seem to find any paddles, so he went over to the ice cream counter and came back with two little cardboard spoons—the kind you use for eating ice cream on picnics.

"These will work out all right as paddles," he said.

Stuart took the spoons, but he was disgusted with the looks of them.

"They may work out all right," said Stuart, "but I would hate to meet an American Indian while I had one of *these* things in my hand."

The storekeeper carried the canoe and the paddles out in front of the store and set them down in the street. He wondered what this tiny boatman would do next, but Stuart never hesitated. Taking a piece of thread from his pocket, he lashed the paddles to the thwarts, swung the canoe lightly up on his head, and walked off with it as calmly as though he were a Canadian guide. He was very proud of his ability with boats and he liked to show off.

XIV

An Evening on the River

When Stuart arrived at his camp site by the river, he was tired and hot. He put the canoe in the water and was sorry to see that it leaked badly. The birch bark at the stern was held together by a lacing, and the water came in through the seam. In a very few seconds the canoe was half full of water.

"Darn it!" said Stuart, "I've been swindled." He had paid seventy-six cents for a genuine Indian birchbark canoe, only to find that it leaked.

"Darn, darn, darn," he muttered.

Then he bailed out his canoe and hauled it up on the beach for repairs. He knew he couldn't take Harriet out in a leaky boat—she wouldn't like it. Tired though he was, he climbed a spruce tree and found some spruce gum. With this he plugged the seam and stopped the leak. Even so, the canoe turned out to be a cranky little craft. If Stuart had not had plenty of experience on the water, he would have got into serious trouble with it. It was a tippy boat even for a souvenir. Stuart carried stones from the beach down to the water's edge and ballasted the canoe with the stones until it floated evenly and steadily. He made a back rest so that Harriet would be able to lean back and trail her fingers in the water if she wished. He also made a pillow by tying one of his clean handkerchiefs around some moss. Then he went for a paddle to practise his stroke. He was angry that he didn't have anything better than a paper spoon for a paddle, but he decided that there was nothing he could do about it. He wondered whether Harriet would notice that his paddle was really just an ice cream spoon.

All that afternoon Stuart worked on the canoe, adjusting ballast, filling seams, and getting everything shipshape for the morrow. He could think of nothing else but his date with Harriet. At suppertime he took his ax, felled a dandelion, opened a can of deviled ham, and had a light supper of ham and dandelion milk. After supper, he propped himself up against a fern, bit off some spruce gum for a chew, and lay there on the bank dreaming and chewing gum. In his imagination he went over every detail of tomorrow's trip with Harriet. With his eyes shut he seemed to see the whole occasion plainly—how she would look when she came down the path to the water, how calm and peaceful the river was going to be in the twilight, how graceful the canoe would seem, drawn up on the shore. In imagination he lived every minute of their evening together. They would paddle to a large water-lily pad upstream, and he would invite Harriet to step out on the pad and sit awhile. Stuart planned to wear his swimming trunks under his clothes so that he could dive off the lily pad into the cool stream. He would swim the crawl stroke, up and down and all around the lily pad, while Harriet watched, admiring his ability as a swimmer. (Stuart chewed the spruce gum very rapidly as he thought about this part of the episode.)

Suddenly Stuart opened his eyes and sat up. He thought about the letter he had sent and he wondered whether it had ever been delivered. It was an unusually small letter, of course, and might have gone unnoticed in the letterbox. This idea filled him with fears and worries. But soon he let his thoughts return to the river, and as he lay there a whippoorwill began to sing on the opposite shore, darkness spread over the land, and Stuart dropped off to sleep.

The next day dawned cloudy. Stuart had to go up to the village to have the oil changed in his car, so he hid the canoe under some leaves, tied it firmly to a stone, and went off on his errand, still thinking about Harriet and wishing it were a nicer day. The sky looked rainy.

Stuart returned from the village with a headache, but he hoped that it would be better before five o'clock. He felt rather nervous, as he had never taken a girl canoeing before. He spent the afternoon lying around camp, trying on different shirts to see which looked best on him and combing his whiskers. He would no sooner get a clean shirt on than he would discover that it was wet under the arms, from nervous perspiration, and he would have to change it for a dry one. He put on a clean shirt at two o'clock, another at three o'clock, and another at quarter past four. This took up most of the afternoon. As five o'clock drew near, Stuart grew more and more nervous. He kept looking at his watch, glancing up the path, combing his hair, talking to himself, and fidgeting. The day had turned chilly and Stuart was almost sure that there was going to be rain. He couldn't imagine what he would do if it should rain just as Harriet Ames showed up to go canoeing.

At last five o'clock arrived. Stuart heard someone coming down the path. It was Harriet. She had accepted his invitation. Stuart threw himself down against a stump and tried to strike an easy attitude, as though he were accustomed to taking girls out. He waited till Harriet was within a few feet of him, then got up.

"Hello there," he said, trying to keep his voice from trembling.

"Are you Mr. Little?" asked Harriet.

"Yes," said Stuart. "It's nice of you to come."

"Well, it was very good of you to ask me," replied Harriet. She was wearing a white sweater, a tweed skirt, short white wool socks, and sneakers. Her hair was tied with a bright colored handkerchief, and Stuart noticed that she carried a box of peppermints in her hand.

"Not at all, glad to do it," said Stuart. "I only wish we had better weather. Looks rather sticky, don't you think?" Stuart was trying to make his voice sound as though he had an English accent.

Harriet looked at the sky and nodded. "Oh, well," she said, "if it rains, it rains."

"Sure," repeated Stuart, "if it rains, it rains. My canoe is a short distance up the shore. May I help you over the rough places in the path?" Stuart was a courteous mouse by nature, but Harriet said she didn't need any help. She was an active girl and not at all inclined to stumble or fall. Stuart led the way to where he had hidden the canoe, and Harriet followed, but when they reached the spot Stuart was horrified to discover that the canoe was not there. It had disappeared.

Stuart's heart sank. He felt like crying.

"The canoe is gone," he groaned.

Then he began racing wildly up and down the bank, looking everywhere. Harriet joined in the search, and after a while they found the canoe—but it was a mess. Some one had been playing with it. A long piece of heavy string was tied to one end. The ballast rocks were gone. The pillow was gone. The back rest was gone. The spruce gum had come out of the seam. Mud was all over everything, and one of the paddles was all bent and twisted. It was just a mess. It looked just the way a birchbark canoe looks after some big boys are finished playing with it.

Stuart was heartbroken. He did not know what to do. He sat down on a twig and buried his head in his hands. "Oh, gee," he kept saying, "oh, gee whiz."

"What's the trouble?" asked Harriet.

"Miss Ames," said Stuart in a trembling voice, "I assure you I had everything beautifully arranged—

everything. And now look!"

Harriet was for fixing the canoe up and going out on the river anyway, but Stuart couldn't stand that idea.

"It's no use," he said bitterly, "it wouldn't be the same."

"The same as what?" asked Harriet.

"The same as the way it was going to be, when I was thinking about it yesterday. I'm afraid a woman can't understand these things. Look at that string! It's tied on so tight I could never get it off."

"Well," suggested Harriet, "couldn't we just let it hang over in the water and trail along after us?"

Stuart looked at her in despair. "Did you ever see an Indian paddling along some quiet unspoiled river with a great big piece of rope dragging astern?" he asked.

"We could pretend we were fishing," said Harriet, who didn't realize that some people are fussy about boats.

"I don't *want* to pretend I'm fishing," cried Stuart, desperately. "Besides, look at that mud! *Look* at it!" He was screaming now.

Harriet sat down on the twig beside Stuart. She offered him a peppermint but he shook his head.

"Well," she said, "it's starting to rain, and I guess

I'd better be running along if you are not going to take me paddling in your canoe. I don't see why you have to sit here and sulk. Would you like to come up to my house? After dinner you could take me to the dance at the Country Club. It might cheer you up."

"No, thank you," replied Stuart. "I don't know how to dance. Besides, I plan to make an early start in the morning. I'll probably be on the road at daybreak."

"Are you going to sleep out in all this rain?" asked Harriet.

"Certainly," said Stuart. "I'll crawl in under the canoe."

Harriet shrugged her shoulders. "Well," she said, "good-by, Mr. Little."

"Good-by, Miss Ames," said Stuart. "I am sorry our evening on the river had to end like this."

"So am I," said Harriet. And she walked away along the wet path toward Tracy's Lane, leaving Stuart alone with his broken dreams and his damaged canoe.

XV

Heading North

STUART SLEPT UNDER THE CANOE THAT night. He awakened at four to find that the rain had stopped. The day would break clear. Already the birds were beginning to stir and make bright sounds in the branches overhead. Stuart never let a bird pass without looking to see if it was Margalo.

At the edge of the town he found a filling station and stopped to take on some gas.

"Five, please," said Stuart to the attendant.

The man looked at the tiny automobile in amazement.

"Five what?" he asked.

"Five drops," said Stuart. But the man shook his head and said that he couldn't sell such a small amount of gas.

"Why can't you?" demanded Stuart. "You need the money and I need the gas. Why can't we work something out between us?"

The filling station man went inside and came back with a medicine dropper. Stuart unscrewed the cap of the tank and the man put in five drops of gasoline. "I've never done anything like this before," he said.

"Better look at the oil, too," said Stuart.

After everything had been checked and the money had been paid, Stuart climbed in, started the engine, and drove out onto the highway. The sky was growing brighter, and along the river the mists of morning hung in the early light. The village was still asleep. Stuart's car purred along smoothly. Stuart felt refreshed and glad to be on the move again.

Half a mile out of town the road forked. One road seemed to go off toward the west, the other road continued north. Stuart drew up to the side of the northbound road and got out to look the situation over. To his surprise he discovered that there was a man sitting in the ditch, leaning against a signpost. The man wore spurs on his legs. He also wore a heavy leather belt, and Stuart realized that he must be a repairman for the telephone company.

"Good morning," said Stuart in a friendly voice. The repairman raised one hand to his head in a salute. Stuart sat down in the ditch beside him and breathed deeply of the fresh, sweet air. "It's going to be a fine day," he observed.

"Yes," agreed the repairman, "a fine day. I am looking forward to climbing my poles."

"I wish you fair skies and a tight grip," said Stuart. "By the way, do you ever see any birds at the tops of your poles?"

"Yes, I see birds in great numbers," replied the repairman.

"Well, if you ever run across a bird named Margalo," said Stuart, "I'd appreciate it if you would drop me a line. Here's my card."

"Describe the bird," said the repairman, taking out pad and pencil.

"Brown," said Stuart. "Brown, with a streak of yellow on her bosom."

"Know where she comes from?" asked the man.

"She comes from fields once tall with wheat, from pastures deep in fern and thistle; she comes from vales of meadowsweet, and she loves to whistle."

The repairman wrote it all down briefly. "Fields—wheat—pastures, fern & thistle. Vales, meadowsweet.

Enjoys whistling." Then he put the pad back in his pocket, and tucked Stuart's card away in his wallet. "I'll keep my eyes open," he promised.

Stuart thanked him. They sat for a while in silence. Then the man spoke.

"Which direction are you headed?" he asked.

"North," said Stuart.

"North is nice," said the repairman. "I've always enjoyed going north. Of course, south-west is a fine direction, too."

"Yes, I suppose it is," said Stuart, thoughtfully.

"And there's east," continued the repairman. "I once had an interesting experience on an easterly course. Do you want me to tell you about it?"

"No, thanks," said Stuart.

The repairman seemed disappointed, but he kept right on talking. "There's something about north," he said, "something that sets it apart from all other directions. A person who is heading north is not making any mistake, in my opinion."

"That's the way I look at it," said Stuart. "I rather expect that from now on I shall be traveling north until the end of my days."

"Worse things than that could happen to a person," said the repairman.

"Yes, I know," answered Stuart.

"Following a broken telephone line north, I have come upon some wonderful places," continued the repairman. "Swamps where cedars grow and turtles wait on logs but not for anything in particular; fields bordered by crooked fences broken by years of standing still; orchards so old they have forgotten where the farmhouse is. In the north I have eaten my lunch in pastures rank with ferns and junipers, all under fair skies with a wind blowing. My business has taken me into spruce woods on winter nights where the snow lay deep and soft, a perfect place for a carnival of rabbits. I have sat at peace on the freight platforms of railroad junctions in the north, in the warm hours and with the warm smells. I know fresh lakes in the north, undisturbed except by fish and hawk and, of course, by the Telephone Company, which has to follow its nose. I know all these places well. They are a long way from here—don't forget that. And a person who is looking for something doesn't travel very fast."

"That's perfectly true," said Stuart. "Well, I guess I'd better be going. Thank you for your friendly remarks."

"Not at all," said the repairman. "I hope you find that bird."

Stuart rose from the ditch, climbed into his car, and started up the road that led toward the north. The sun was just coming up over the hills on his right. As he peered ahead into the great land that stretched before him, the way seemed long. But the sky was bright, and he somehow felt he was headed in the right direction.

The Trumpet of the Swan

Contents

I

Sam

WALKING BACK TO CAMP THROUGH THE swamp, Sam wondered whether to tell his father what he had seen.

"I know *one* thing," he said to himself. "I'm going back to that little pond again tomorrow. And I'd like to go alone. If I tell my father what I saw today, he will want to go with me. I'm not sure that's a very good idea."

Sam was eleven. His last name was Beaver. He was strong for his age and had black hair and dark eyes like an Indian. Sam walked like an Indian, too, putting one foot straight in front of the other and making very little noise. The swamp through which he was traveling was a wild place—there was no trail, and it was boggy underfoot, which made walking difficult. Every four or five minutes Sam took his compass out of his pocket and checked his course to make sure he was headed in a westerly direction. Canada is a big place. Much of it is wilderness. To get lost in the woods and swamps of western Canada would be a serious matter.

As he trudged on, the boy's mind was full of the wonder of what he had seen. Not many people in the world have seen the nest of a Trumpeter Swan. Sam had found one on the lonely pond on this day in spring. He had seen the two great white birds with their long white necks and black bills. Nothing he had ever seen before in all his life had made him feel quite the way he felt, on that wild little pond, in the presence of those two enormous swans. They were so much bigger than any bird he had ever seen before. The nest was big, too—a mound of sticks and grasses. The female was sitting on eggs; the male glided slowly back and forth, guarding her.

When Sam reached camp, tired and hungry, he found his father frying a couple of fish for lunch.

"Where have *you* been?" asked Mr. Beaver.

"Exploring," replied Sam. "I walked over to a pond about a mile and a half from here. It's the one we see from the air as we're coming in. It isn't much of a place—nowhere near as big as this lake we're on."

"Did you see anything over there?" asked his father.

"Well," said Sam, "it's a swampy pond with a lot of reeds and cattails. I don't think it would be any good for fishing. And it's hard to get to—you have to cross a swamp."

"See anything?" repeated Mr. Beaver.

"I saw a muskrat," said Sam, "and a few Red-winged Blackbirds."

Mr. Beaver looked up from the wood stove, where the fish were sizzling in a pan.

"Sam," he said, "I know you like to go exploring. But don't forget—these woods and marshes are not like the country around home in Montana. If you ever go over to that pond again, be careful you don't get lost. I don't like you crossing swamps. They're treacherous. You could step into a soggy place and get bogged down, and there wouldn't be anybody to pull you out."

"I'll be careful," said Sam. He knew perfectly well he would be going back to the pond where the swans were. And he had no intention of getting lost in the woods. He felt relieved that he had not told his father about seeing the swans, but he felt queer about it, too. Sam was not a sly boy, but he was odd in one respect: he liked to keep things to himself. And he liked being alone, particularly when he was in the woods. He enjoyed the life on his father's cattle ranch in the Sweet Grass country in Montana. He loved his mother. He loved Duke, his cow pony. He loved riding the range. He loved watching guests who came to board at the Beavers' ranch every summer.

But the thing he enjoyed most in life was these camping trips in Canada with his father. Mrs. Beaver didn't care for the woods, so she seldom went along—it was usually just Sam and Mr. Beaver. They would motor to the border and cross into Canada. There Mr. Beaver would hire a bush pilot to fly them to the lake where his camp was, for a few days of fishing and loafing and exploring. Mr. Beaver did most of the fishing and loafing. Sam did the exploring. And then the pilot would return to take them out. His name was Shorty. They would hear the sound of his motor and run out and wave and watch him glide down onto the lake and taxi his plane in to the dock. These were the pleasantest days of Sam's life, these days in the woods, far, far from everywhere—no automobiles, no roads, no people, no noise, no school, no homework, no problems, except the problem of getting lost. And, of course, the problem of what to be when he grew up. Every boy has *that* problem.

After supper that evening, Sam and his father sat for a while on the porch. Sam was reading a bird book.

"Pop," said Sam, "do you think we'll be coming back to camp again about a month from now—I mean, in about thirty-five days or something like that?"

"I guess so," replied Mr. Beaver. "I certainly hope so. But why thirty-five days? What's so special about thirty-five days?"

"Oh, nothing," said Sam. "I just thought it might be very nice around here in thirty-five days."

"That's the craziest thing I ever heard of," said Mr. Beaver. "It's nice here *all* the time."

Sam went indoors. He knew a lot about birds, and he knew it would take a swan about thirty-five days to hatch her eggs. He hoped he could be at the pond to see the young ones when they came out of the eggs.

Sam kept a diary—a daybook about his life. It was just a cheap notebook that was always by his bed. Every night, before he turned in, he would write in the book. He wrote about things he had done, things he had seen, and thoughts he had had. Sometimes he drew a picture. He always ended by asking himself a question so he would have something to think about while falling asleep. On the day he found the swan's nest, this is what Sam wrote in his diary:

> *I saw a pair of trumpeter swans today on a small pond east of camp. The female has a nest with eggs in it. I saw three, but I'm going to put four in the picture—I think she was laying another one. This is the greatest discovery I ever made in my entire life. I did not tell Pop. My bird book says baby swans are called cygnets. I am going back tomorrow to visit the great swans again. I heard a fox bark today. Why does a fox bark? Is it because he is mad, or worried, or hungry, or because he is sending a message to another fox?* Why does a fox bark?

Sam closed his notebook, undressed, crawled into his bunk, and lay there with his eyes closed, wondering why a fox barks. In a few minutes he was asleep.

II

The Pond

THE POND SAM HAD DISCOVERED ON THAT spring morning was seldom visited by any human being. All winter, snow had covered the ice; the pond lay cold and still under its white blanket. Most of the time there wasn't a sound to be heard. The frog was asleep. The chipmunk was asleep. Occasionally a jay would cry out. And sometimes at night the fox would bark—a high, rasping bark. Winter seemed to last forever.

But one day a change came over the woods and the pond. Warm air, soft and kind, blew through the trees. The ice, which had softened during the night, began to melt. Patches of open water appeared. All the creatures that lived in the pond and in the woods were glad to feel the warmth. They heard and felt the breath of spring, and they stirred with new life and hope. There was a good, new smell in the air, a smell of earth waking after its long sleep. The frog, buried in the mud at the bottom of the pond, knew that spring was here. The chickadee knew and was delighted (almost everything delights a chickadee). The vixen, dozing in her den, knew she would soon have kits. Every creature knew that a better, easier time was at hand—warmer days, pleasanter nights. Trees were putting out green buds; the buds were swelling. Birds began arriving from the south. A pair of ducks flew in. The Red-winged Blackbird arrived and scouted the pond for nesting sites. A small sparrow with a white throat arrived and sang, "Oh, sweet Canada, Canada, Canada!"

And if you had been sitting by the pond on that first warm day of spring, suddenly, toward the end of the afternoon, you would have heard a stirring sound high above you in the air—a sound like the sound of trumpets.

"Ko-hoh, ko-hoh!"

And if you had looked up, you would have seen, high overhead, two great white birds. They flew swiftly, their legs stretched out straight behind, their long white necks stretched out ahead, their powerful wings beating steady and strong. "Ko-hoh, ko-hoh, ko-hoh!" A thrilling noise in the sky, the trumpeting of swans.

When the birds spotted the pond, they began circling, looking the place over from the air. Then they glided down and came to rest in the water, folding their long wings neatly along their sides and turning their heads this way and that to study their new surroundings. They were Trumpeter Swans, pure white birds with black bills. They had liked the looks of the swampy pond and had decided to make it their home for a while and raise a family.

The two swans were tired from the long flight. They were glad to be down out of the sky. They paddled slowly about and then began feeding, thrusting their necks into the shallow water and pulling roots and plants from the bottom. Everything about the swans was white except their bills and their feet; these were black. They carried their heads high. The pond seemed a different place because of their arrival.

For the next few days, the swans rested. When they were hungry, they ate. When they were thirsty—which was a great deal of the time—they drank. On the tenth day, the female began looking around to find a place to build her nest.

. . .

In the spring of the year, nest-building is uppermost in a bird's mind: it is the most important thing there is. If she picks a good place, she stands a good chance of hatching her eggs and rearing her young. If she picks a poor place, she may fail to raise a family. The female swan knew this; she knew the decision she was making was extremely important.

The two swans first investigated the upper end of the pond, where a stream flowed slowly in. It was pleasant there, with reeds and bulrushes. Red-winged Blackbirds were busy nesting in this part of the pond, and a pair of Mallard Ducks were courting. Then the swans swam to the lower end of the pond, a marsh with woods on one side and a deer meadow on the other. It was lonely here. From one shore, a point of land extended out into the pond. It was a sandy strip, like a little peninsula. And at the tip of it, a few feet out into the water, was a tiny island, hardly bigger than a dining table. One small tree grew on the island, and there were rocks and ferns and grasses.

"Take a look at this!" exclaimed the female, as she swam round and around.

"Ko-hoh!" replied her husband, who liked to have someone ask his advice.

The swan stepped cautiously out onto the island.

The spot seemed made to order—just right for a nesting place. While the male swan floated close by, watching, she snooped about until she found a pleasant spot on the ground. She sat down, to see how it felt to be sitting there. She decided it was the right size for her body. It was nicely located, a couple of feet from the water's edge. Very convenient. She turned to her husband.

"What do you think?" she said.

"An ideal location!" he replied. "A perfect place! And I will tell you *why* it's a perfect place," he continued, majestically. "If an enemy—a fox or a coon or a coyote or a skunk—wanted to reach this spot with murder in his heart, he'd have to enter the water and get wet. And before he could enter the water, he'd have to walk the whole length of that point of land. And by that time we'd see him or hear him, and I would give him a hard time."

The male stretched out his great wings, eight feet from tip to tip, and gave the water a mighty clout to show his strength. This made him feel better right away. When a Trumpeter Swan hits an enemy with his wing, it is like being hit by a baseball bat. A male swan, by the way, is called a "cob." No one knows why, but that's what he's called. A good many animals have special names: a male goose is called a gander, a male cow is called a bull, a male sheep is called a ram, a male chicken is called a rooster, and so on. Anyway, the thing to remember is that a male swan is called a cob.

The cob's wife pretended not to notice that her husband was showing off, but she saw it, all right, and she was proud of his strength and his courage. As husbands go, he was a good one.

The cob watched his beautiful wife sitting there on the tiny island. To his great joy, he saw her begin to turn slowly round and around, keeping always in the same spot, treading the mud and grass. She was making the first motions of nesting. First she squatted down in the place she had chosen. Then she twisted round and around, tamping the earth with her broad webbed feet, hollowing it out to make it like a saucer. Then she reached out and pulled twigs and grasses toward her and dropped them at her sides and under her tail, shaping the nest to her body.

The cob floated close to his mate. He studied every move she made.

"Now another medium-sized stick, my love," he said. And she poked her splendid long white graceful neck as far as it would go, picked up a stick, and placed it at her side.

"Now another bit of coarse grass," said the cob, with great dignity.

The female reached for grasses, for moss, for twigs—anything that was handy. Slowly, carefully, she built up the nest until she was sitting on a big grassy mound. She worked at the task for a couple of hours, then knocked off for the day and slid into the pond again, to take a drink and have lunch.

"A fine start!" said the cob, as he gazed back at the nest. "A perfect beginning! I don't know how you manage it so cleverly."

"It comes naturally," replied his wife. "There's a lot of work to it, but on the whole it is pleasant work."

"Yes," said the cob. "And when you're done, you have something to show for your trouble—you have a swan's nest, six feet across. What other bird can say that?"

"Well," said his wife, "maybe an eagle can say it."

"Yes, but in that case it wouldn't be a swan's nest, it would be an eagle's nest, and it would be high up in some old dead tree somewhere, instead of right down near the water, with all the conveniences that go with water."

They both laughed at this. Then they began trumpeting and splashing and scooping up water and throwing it on their backs, darting about as though they had suddenly gone crazy with delight.

"Ko-hoh! Ko-hoh! Ko-hoh!" they cried.

Every wild creature within a mile and a half of the pond heard the trumpeting of the swans. The fox heard, the raccoon heard, the skunk heard. One pair of ears heard that did not belong to a wild creature. But the swans did not know that.

III

A Visitor

One day, almost a week later, the swan slipped quietly into her nest and laid an egg. Each day she tried to deposit one egg in the nest. Sometimes she succeeded, sometimes she didn't. There were now three eggs, and she was ready to lay a fourth.

As she sat there, with her husband, the cob, floating gracefully nearby, she had a strange feeling that she was being watched. It made her uneasy. Birds don't like to be stared at. They particularly dislike being stared at when they are on a nest. So the swan twisted and turned and peered everywhere. She gazed intently at the point of land that jutted out into the pond near the nest. With her sharp eyes, she searched the nearby shore for signs of an intruder. What she finally saw gave her the surprise of her life. There, seated on a log on the point of land, was a small boy. He was being very quiet, and he had no gun.

"Do you see what I see?" the swan whispered to her husband.

"*No.* What?"

"Over there. On that log. It's a boy! Now what are we going to do?"

"How did a boy get here?" whispered the cob. "We are deep in the wilds of Canada. There are no human beings for miles around."

"That's what I thought too," she replied. "But if that isn't a boy over there on that log, my name isn't Cygnus Buccinator."

The cob was furious. "I didn't fly all the way north into Canada to get involved with a *boy*," he said. "We came here to this idyllic spot, this remote little hideaway, so we could enjoy some well-deserved privacy."

"Well," said his wife, "I'm sorry to see the boy, too, but I must say he's behaving himself. He sees us, but he's not throwing stones. He's not throwing sticks. He's not messing around. He's simply observing."

"I do not *wish* to be observed," complained the cob. "I did not travel all this immense distance into the heart of Canada to be observed. Furthermore, I don't want *you* to be observed—except by me. You're laying an egg—that is, I *hope* you are—and you are entitled to privacy. It has been my experience that all boys throw stones and sticks—it is their nature. I'm going over and strike that boy with my powerful wing, and he'll think he has been hit with a billy club. I'll knock him cold!"

"Now, just wait a minute!" said the swan. "There's no use starting a fight. This boy is not bothering me at the moment. He's not bothering you either."

"But how did he *get* here?" said the cob, who was no longer talking in a whisper but was beginning to shout. "How did he get here? Boys can't fly, and there are no roads in this part of Canada. We're fifty miles from the nearest highway."

"Maybe he's lost," said the swan. "Maybe he's starving to death. Maybe he wants to rob the nest and eat the eggs, but I doubt it. He doesn't look hungry. Anyway, I've started this nest, and I have three beautiful eggs, and the boy's behaving himself at the moment, and I intend to go right ahead and try for a fourth egg."

"Good luck, my love!" said the cob. "I shall be here at your side to defend you if anything happens. Lay the egg!"

For the next hour, the cob paddled slowly round

and around the tiny island, keeping watch. His wife remained quietly on the nest. Sam sat on his log, hardly moving a muscle. He was spellbound at the sight of the swans. They were the biggest water birds he had ever seen. He had heard their trumpeting and had searched the woods and swamps until he had found the pond and located the nest. Sam knew enough about birds to know that these were Trumpeters. Sam always felt happy when he was in a wild place among wild creatures. Sitting on his log, watching the swans, he had the same good feeling some people get when they are sitting in church.

After he had watched for an hour, Sam got up. He walked slowly and quietly away, putting one foot straight ahead of the other, Indian-fashion, hardly making a sound. The swans watched him go. When the female left the nest, she turned and looked back. There, lying safely in the soft feathers at the bottom of the nest, was the fourth egg. The cob waddled out onto the island and looked in the nest.

"A masterpiece!" he said. "An egg of supreme beauty and perfect proportions. I would say that that egg is almost five inches in length."

His wife was pleased.

. . .

When the swan had laid five eggs, she felt satisfied. She gazed at them proudly. Then she settled herself on the nest to keep her eggs warm. Carefully, she reached down with her bill and poked each egg until it was in just the right spot to receive the heat from her body. The cob cruised around close by, to keep her company and protect her from enemies. He knew that a fox prowled somewhere in the woods; he had heard him barking on nights when the hunting was good.

Days passed, and still the swan sat quietly on the five eggs. Nights passed. She sat and sat, giving her warmth to the eggs. No one disturbed her. The boy was gone—perhaps he would never come back. Inside of each egg, something was happening that she couldn't see: a little swan was taking shape. As the weeks went by, the days grew longer, the nights grew shorter. When a rainy day came, the swan just sat still and let it rain.

"My dear," said her husband, the cob, one afternoon, "do you never find your duties onerous or irksome? Do you never tire of sitting in one place and in one position, covering the eggs, with no diversions, no pleasures, no escapades, or capers?

Do you never suffer from boredom?"

"No," replied his wife. "Not really."

"Isn't it uncomfortable to sit on eggs?"

"Yes, it is," replied the wife. "But I can put up with a certain amount of discomfort for the sake of bringing young swans into the world."

"Do you know how many more days you must sit?" he asked.

"Haven't any idea," she said. "But I notice that the ducks at the other end of the pond have hatched their young ones; I notice that the Red-winged Blackbirds have hatched theirs, and the other evening I saw a Striped Skunk hunting along the shore, and she had four little skunks with her. So I think I must be getting near the end of my time. With any luck, we will soon be able to see our children—our beautiful little cygnets."

"Don't you ever feel the pangs of hunger or suffer the tortures of thirst?" asked the cob.

"Yes, I do," said his mate. "As a matter of fact, I could use a drink right now."

The afternoon was warm; the sun was bright. The swan decided she could safely leave her eggs for a few minutes. She stood up. First she pushed some loose feathers around the eggs, hiding them from view and giving them a warm covering in her absence. Then she stepped off the nest and entered the water. She took several quick drinks. Then she glided over to a shallow place, thrust her head underwater, and pulled up tender greens from the bottom. She next took a bath by tossing water over herself. Then she waddled out onto a grassy bank and stood there, preening her feathers.

The swan felt good. She had no idea that an enemy was near. She failed to notice the Red Fox as he watched her from his hiding place behind a clump of bushes. The fox had been attracted to the pond by the sound of splashing water. He hoped he would find a goose. Now he sniffed the air and smelled the swan. Her back was turned, so he began creeping slowly toward her. She would be too big for him to carry, but he decided he would kill her anyway and get a taste of blood. The cob, her husband, was still floating on the pond. He spied the fox first.

"Look out!" he trumpeted. "Look out for the fox, who is creeping toward you even as I speak, his eyes bright, his bushy tail out straight, his mind lusting for blood, his belly almost touching the ground! You are in grave danger, and we must act immediately."

While the cob was making this elegant speech of warning, something happened that surprised everybody. Just as the fox was about to spring and sink his teeth in the swan's neck, a stick came hurtling through the air. It struck the fox full on the nose, and he turned and ran away. The two swans couldn't imagine what had happened. Then they noticed a movement in the bushes. Out stepped Sam Beaver, the boy who had visited them a month ago. Sam was grinning. In his hand he held another stick, in case the fox should return. But the fox was in no mood to return. He had a very sore nose, and he had lost his appetite for fresh swan.

"Hello," said Sam in a low voice.

"Ko-hoh, ko-hoh!" replied the cob.

"Ko-hoh!" said his wife. The pond rang with the trumpet sounds—sounds of triumph over the fox, sounds of victory and gladness.

Sam was thrilled at the noise of swans, which some people say is like the sound of a French horn. He walked slowly around the shore to the little point of land near the island and sat down on his log. The swans now realized, beyond any doubt, that the boy was their friend. He had saved the swan's life. He had been in the right place at the right time and with the right ammunition. The swans felt grateful. The cob swam over toward Sam, climbed out of the pond, and stood close to the boy, looking at him in a friendly way and arching his neck gracefully. Once, he ran his neck far out, cautiously, and almost touched the boy. Sam never moved a muscle. His heart thumped from excitement and joy.

The female paddled back to her nest and returned to the job of warming the eggs. She felt lucky to be alive.

That night before Sam crawled into his bunk at camp, he got out his notebook and found a pencil. This is what he wrote:

I don't know of anything in the entire world more wonderful to look at than a nest with eggs in it. An egg, because it contains life, is the most perfect thing there is. It is beautiful and mysterious. An egg is a far finer thing than a tennis ball or a cake of soap. A tennis ball will always be just a tennis ball. A cake of soap will always be just a cake of soap—until it gets so small nobody wants it and they throw it away. But an egg will someday be a living creature. A swan's egg will open and out will come a little swan. A nest is almost as wonderful and mysterious as an egg. How does a bird know how to make a nest? Nobody ever taught her. How does a bird know how to build a nest?

Sam closed his notebook, said good night to his father, blew out his lamp, and climbed into his bunk. He lay there wondering how a bird knows how to build a nest. Pretty soon his eyes closed, and he was asleep.

IV

The Cygnets

DURING THE NIGHT, THE SWAN THOUGHT she heard a pipping sound from the eggs. And in the hour just before dawn, she was sure she felt a slight movement under her breast, as though a tiny body were wiggling there. Perhaps the eggs at last were hatching. Eggs, of course, can't wiggle, so the swan decided she must have something under her that wasn't an egg. She sat perfectly still, listening and waiting. The cob floated nearby, keeping watch.

A little swan enclosed in an egg has a hard time getting out. It never *would* get out if Nature had not provided it with two important things: a powerful neck-muscle and a small dagger-tooth on the tip of its bill. This tooth is sharp, and the baby swan uses it to pick a hole in the tough shell of the egg. Once the hole is made, the rest is easy. The cygnet can breathe now; it just keeps wiggling until it wiggles free.

The cob was expecting to become a father any minute now. The idea of fatherhood made him feel poetical and proud. He began to talk to his wife.

"Here I glide, swanlike," he said, "while earth is bathed in wonder and beauty. Now, slowly, the light of day comes into our sky. A mist hangs low over the pond. The mist rises slowly, like steam from a kettle, while I glide, swanlike, while eggs hatch, while young swans come into existence. I glide and glide. The light strengthens. The air becomes warmer. Gradually the mist disappears. I glide, I glide, swanlike. Birds sing their early song. Frogs that have croaked in the night stop croaking and are silent. Still I glide, ceaselessly, like a swan."

"Of course you glide like a swan," said his wife. "How else could you glide? You couldn't glide like a moose, could you?"

"Well, no. That is quite true. Thank you, my dear, for correcting me." The cob felt taken aback by his mate's commonsense remark. He enjoyed speaking in fancy phrases and graceful language, and he liked to think of himself as gliding swanlike. He decided he'd better do more gliding and less talking.

All morning long, the swan heard the pipping of the shells. And every once in a while, she felt something wriggle beneath her in the nest. It was an odd sensation. The eggs had been quiet for so many, many days—thirty-five days in all—and now at last they were stirring with life. She knew that the proper thing to do was to sit still.

Late in the afternoon, the swan was rewarded for her patience. She gazed down, and there, pushing her feathers aside, came a tiny head—the first baby, the first cygnet. It was soft and downy. Unlike its parents, it was gray. Its feet and legs were the color of mustard. Its eyes were bright. On unsteady legs, it pushed its way up until it stood beside its mother, looking around at the world it was seeing for the first time. Its mother spoke softly to it, and it was glad to hear her voice. It was glad to breathe the air, after being cooped up so long inside an egg.

The cob, who had been watching intently all day, saw the little head appear. His heart leapt up with joy. "A cygnet!" he cried. "A cygnet at last! I am a father, with all the pleasant duties and awesome responsibilities of fatherhood. O blessed little son of mine, how good it is to see your face peering through the protecting feathers of your mother's breast, under these fair skies, with the pond so quiet and peaceful in the long light of afternoon!"

"What makes you think it's a son?" inquired his wife. "For all you know, it's a daughter. Anyway, it's a cygnet, and it's alive and healthy. I can feel others under me, too. Perhaps we'll get a good hatch. We may even get all five. We'll know by tomorrow."

"I have every confidence that we will," said the cob.

Next morning very early, Sam Beaver crawled out of his bunk while his father was still asleep. Sam dressed and lit a fire in the stove. He fried a few strips of bacon, toasted two slices of bread, poured a glass of milk, and sat down and ate breakfast. When he was through, he found a pencil and paper and wrote a note.

I have gone for a walk.
Will be back for lunch.

Sam left the note where his father would find it; then he took his field glasses and his compass, fastened his hunting knife to his belt, and set out through the woods and over the swamp to the pond where the swans lived.

He approached the pond cautiously, his field glasses slung over his shoulder. It was still only a little after seven o'clock; the sun was pale, the air was chill. The morning smelled delicious. When he reached his log, Sam sat down and adjusted his glasses. Seen through the glasses, the nesting swan appeared to be only a few feet away. She was sitting very close, not moving. The cob was nearby. Both birds were listening and waiting. Both birds saw Sam, but they didn't mind his being there—in fact, they rather liked it. They *were* surprised at the field glasses, though.

"The boy seems to have very big eyes today," whispered the cob. "His eyes are enormous."

"I think those big eyes are actually a pair of field glasses," replied the swan. "I'm not sure, but I think that when a person looks through field glasses, everything appears closer and bigger."

"Will the boy's glasses make me appear even larger than I am?" asked the cob, hopefully.

"I think so," said the swan.

"Oh, well, I *like* that," said the cob. "I like that very much. Perhaps the boy's glasses will make me appear not only larger than I am but even more graceful than I am. Do you think so?"

"It's possible," said his wife, "but it's not likely.

You'd better not get *too* graceful—it might go to your head. You're quite a vain bird."

"All swans are vain," said the cob. "It is right for swans to feel proud, graceful—that's what swans are for."

Sam could not make out what the swans were saying; he merely knew they were having a conversation, and just hearing them talk stirred his blood. It satisfied him to be keeping company with these two great birds in the wilderness. He was perfectly happy.

In midmorning, when the sun had gained the sky, Sam lifted his glasses again and focused them on the nest. At last he saw what he had come to see: a tiny head, thrusting through the mother's feathers, the head of a baby Trumpeter. The youngster scrambled up onto the edge of the nest. Sam could see its gray head and neck, its body covered with soft down, its yellow legs and feet with their webs for swimming. Soon another cygnet appeared. Then another. Then the first one worked his way down into his mother's feathers again, for warmth. Then one tried to climb up his mother's back, but her feathers were slippery, and he slid off and settled himself neatly at her side. The swan just sat and sat, enjoying her babies, watching them gain the use of their legs.

An hour went by. One of the cygnets, more daring than the others, left the nest and teetered around on the shore of the little island. When this happened, the mother swan stood up. She decided the time had come to lead her children into the water.

"Come on!" she said. "And stay together! Note carefully what I do. Then you do the same. Swimming is easy."

"One, two, three, four, five," Sam counted. "One, two, three, four, five. Five cygnets, just as sure as I'm alive!"

The cob, as he saw his children approach the water, felt that he should act like a father. He began by making a speech.

"Welcome to the pond and the swamp adjacent!" he said. "Welcome to the world that contains this lonely pond, this splendid marsh, unspoiled and wild! Welcome to sunlight and shadow, wind and weather; welcome to water! The water is a swan's particular element, as you will soon discover. Swimming is no problem for a swan. Welcome to danger, which you must guard against—the vile fox with his stealthy tread and sharp teeth, the offensive otter who swims up under you and tries to grab you by the leg, the stinking skunk who hunts by night and blends with the shadows, the coyote who hunts and howls and is bigger than a fox. Beware of lead pellets that lie on the bottom of all ponds, left there by the guns of hunters. Don't eat them—they'll poison you! Be vigilant, be strong, be brave, be graceful, and *always* follow me! I will go first, then you will come along in single file, and your devoted mother will bring up the rear. Enter the water quietly and confidently!"

The mother swan, glad the speech was over, stepped into the water and called her little ones. The cygnets gazed for a second at the water, then tottered forward, gave a jump, and were afloat. The water felt good. Swimming was simple—nothing to it. The water was good to drink. Each baby dipped up a mouthful. Their happy father arched his long graceful neck over and around them, protectively. Then he set off very slowly, with the cygnets following along in single file. Their mother brought up the rear.

"What a sight!" Sam said to himself. "What a terrific sight! Seven Trumpeters all in line, five of them just out of the egg. This is my lucky day." He hardly noticed how stiff he had become from sitting so long on the log.

Like all fathers, the cob wanted to show off his children to somebody. So he led the cygnets to where Sam was. They all stepped out of the water and stood in front of the boy—all but the mother swan. She stayed behind.

"Ko-hoh!" said the cob.

"Hello!" said Sam, who hadn't expected anything like this and hardly dared breathe.

The first cygnet looked at Sam and said, "Beep."

The second cygnet looked at Sam and said, "Beep."

The third cygnet greeted Sam the same way. So did the fourth. The fifth cygnet was different. He opened his mouth but didn't say a thing. He made an effort to say beep, but no sound came. So instead, he stuck his little neck out, took hold of one of Sam's shoelaces, and gave it a pull. He tugged at the lace for a moment. It came untied. Then he let it go. It was like a greeting. Sam grinned.

The cob now looked worried. He ran his long white neck between the cygnets and the boy and guided the babies back to the water and to their mother.

"Follow me!" said the cob. And he led them off, full of grace and bursting with pride.

When the mother thought her young ones had had enough swimming and might be chilly, she stepped out onto a sandy shore and squatted down and called them. They quickly followed her out of the pond and burrowed down under her feathers to get warm. In a moment there wasn't a cygnet in sight.

At noon, Sam got up and walked back to camp, his mind full of what he had seen. Next day, he and his father heard Shorty's motor in the sky and saw the plane approaching. They grabbed their duffel bags. "Good-bye, camp! See you in the fall!" said Mr. Beaver, as he shut the door and gave it a pat. He and Sam climbed into the plane and were soon aloft, on their way home to Montana. Mr. Beaver did not know that his son had seen a Trumpeter Swan bring off her young ones. Sam kept the matter to himself.

"If I live to be a hundred years old," thought Sam, "I'll never forget what it feels like to have my shoelace pulled by a baby swan."

Sam and his father were late arriving home at the ranch, but late as it was, Sam got out his diary before he turned in for the night. He wrote:

There are five cygnets. They are sort of a dirty brownish-gray color, but very cute. Their legs are yellow, like mustard. The old cob led them right up to me. I wasn't expecting this, but I kept very still. Four of the babies said beep. The fifth one tried to, but he couldn't. He took hold of my shoelace as though it was a worm and gave it a tug and untied it. I wonder what I'm going to be when I grow up?

He switched off the light, pulled the sheet up over his head, and fell asleep wondering what he was going to be when he grew up.

V
Louis

ONE EVENING A FEW WEEKS LATER, WHEN the cygnets were asleep, the swan said to the cob, "Have you noticed anything different about one of our children, the one we call Louis?"

"Different?" replied the cob. "In what way is Louis different from his brothers and sisters? Louis looks all right to me. He is growing well; he swims and dives beautifully. He eats well. He will soon have his flight feathers."

"Oh, he *looks* all right," said the swan. "And heaven knows he eats enough. He's healthy and bright and a great swimmer. But have you ever heard Louis make any sound, as the others do? Have you ever heard him use his voice or say anything? Have you ever heard him utter a single beep or a single burble?"

"Come to think of it, I never have," replied the

cob, who was beginning to look worried.

"Have you ever heard Louis say good night to us, as the others do? Have you ever heard him say good morning, as the others do in their charming little way, burbling and beeping?"

"Now that you mention it, I never have," said the cob. "Goodness! What are you getting at? Do you wish me to believe that I have a son who is *defective* in any way? Such a revelation would distress me greatly. I want everything to go smoothly in my family life so that I can glide gracefully and serenely, now in the prime of my life, without being haunted by worry or disappointment. Fatherhood is quite a burden, at best. I do not want the added strain of having a defective child, a child that has something the matter with him."

"Well," said the wife, "I've been watching Louis lately. It is my opinion the little fellow can't talk. I've never heard him make one sound. I think he came into the world lacking a voice. If he had a voice, he'd use it, same as the others do."

"Why, this is terrible!" said the cob. "This is distressing beyond words. This is a very serious matter."

His wife looked at him in amusement. "It's not too serious now," she said. "But it *will* be serious two or three years from now when Louis falls in love, as he will surely do. A young male swan will be greatly handicapped in finding a mate if he is unable to say ko-hoh, ko-hoh, or if he can't utter the usual endearments to the young female of his choice."

"Are you sure?" asked the cob.

"Certainly I'm sure," she replied. "I can remember perfectly well the springtime, years ago, when you fell in love with me and began chasing after me. What a sight you were, and what a lot of noise you made! It was in Montana, remember?"

"Of course I remember," said the cob.

"Well, the thing that attracted me most to you was your voice—your wonderful voice."

"It *was*?" said the cob.

"Yes. You had the finest, most powerful, most resonant voice of any of the young male swans in the Red Rock Lakes National Wildlife Refuge in Montana."

"I *did*?" said the cob.

"Yes, indeed. Every time I heard you say something in that deep voice of yours, I was ready to go anywhere with you."

"You *were*?" said the cob. He was obviously delighted with his wife's praise. It tickled his vanity and made him feel great. He had always fancied himself as having a fine voice, and now to hear it from his wife's own lips was a real thrill. In the pleasure of the moment, he forgot all about Louis and thought entirely of himself. And, of course, he did remember that enchanted springtime on the lake in Montana when he had fallen in love. He remembered how pretty the swan had been, how young and innocent she seemed, how attractive, how desirable. Now he realized fully that he would never have been able to woo her and win her if he had been unable to *say* anything.

"We'll not worry about Louis for the time being," said the swan. "He's still very young. But we must watch him next winter when we are in Montana for the season. We must stay together as a family until we see how Louis makes out."

She walked over to where her sleeping cygnets were and settled down next to them. The night was chill. Carefully, she lifted one wing and covered the cygnets with it. They stirred in their sleep and drew close to her.

The cob stood quietly, thinking about what his wife had just told him. He was a brave, noble bird, and already he was beginning to work out a plan for his little son Louis.

"If it's really true that Louis has no voice," said the cob to himself, "then I shall provide him with a device of some sort, to enable him to make a lot of noise. There must be *some* way out of this difficulty. After all, my son is a Trumpeter Swan; he should have a voice like a trumpet. But first I will test him to make certain that what his mother says is true."

The cob was unable to sleep that night. He stood on one leg, quietly, but sleep never came. Next morning, after everyone had enjoyed a good breakfast, he led Louis apart from the others.

"Louis," he said, "I wish to speak to you alone. Let's just you and I take a swim by ourselves to the other end of the pond, where we can talk privately without being interrupted."

Louis was surprised by this. But he nodded his head and followed his father, swimming strongly in his wake. He did not understand why his father wanted to speak to him alone, without his brothers and sisters.

"Now!" said the cob, when they reached the upper end of the pond. "Here we are, gracefully floating, supremely buoyant, at some distance from the others, in perfect surroundings—a fine morning, with the pond quiet except for the song of the blackbirds, making the air sweet."

"I wish my father would get to the point," thought Louis.

"This is an ideal place for our conference," continued the cob. "There is something I feel I should discuss with you very candidly and openly—something that concerns your future. We need not range over the whole spectrum of bird life but just confine our talk to the one essential thing that is before us on this unusual occasion."

"Oh, I *wish* my father would get to the point," thought Louis, who by this time was getting very nervous.

"It has come to my attention, Louis," continued the cob, "that you rarely *say* anything. In fact, I can't recall ever hearing you utter a sound. I have never heard you speak, or say ko-hoh, or cry out, either in fear or in joy. This is most unusual for a young Trumpeter. It is serious. Louis, let me hear you say beep. Go ahead, say it! Say beep!"

Poor Louis! While his father watched, he took a deep breath, opened his mouth, and let the air out, hoping it would say beep. But there wasn't a sound.

"Try again, Louis!" said his father. "Perhaps you're

not making enough of an effort."

Louis tried again. It was no use. No sound came from his throat. He shook his head, sadly.

"Watch me!" said the cob. He raised his neck to its full height and cried ko-hoh so loud it was heard by every creature for miles around.

"Now let me hear you go beep!" he commanded. "Say beep, Louis—loud and clear!" Louis tried. He couldn't beep.

"Let me hear you burble! Go ahead and burble! Like this: burble, burble, burble."

Louis tried to burble. He couldn't do it. No sound came.

"Well," said the cob, "I guess it's no use. I guess you are dumb."

When he heard the word "dumb," Louis felt like crying. The cob saw that he had hurt Louis's feelings. "You misunderstand me, my son," he said in a comforting voice. "You failed to understand my use of the word 'dumb,' which has two meanings. If I had called you a dumb cluck or a dumb bunny, that would have meant that I had a poor opinion of your intelligence. Actually, I think you are perhaps the brightest, smartest, most intelligent of all my cygnets. Words sometimes have two meanings; the word 'dumb' is such a word. A person who can't see is called blind. A person who can't hear is called deaf. A person who can't speak is called dumb. That simply means he can't say anything. Do you understand?"

Louis nodded his head. He felt better, and he was grateful to his father for explaining that the word had two meanings. He still felt awfully unhappy, though.

"Do not let an unnatural sadness settle over you, Louis," said the cob. "Swans must be cheerful, not sad; graceful, not awkward; brave, not cowardly. Remember that the world is full of youngsters who have some sort of handicap that they must overcome. *You* apparently have a speech defect. I am sure you will overcome it, in time. There may even be some slight advantage, at your age, in not being able to say anything. It compels you to be a good listener. The world is full of talkers, but it is rare to find anyone who listens. And I assure you that you can pick up more information when you are listening than when you are talking."

"My father does quite a lot of talking himself," thought Louis.

"Some people," continued the cob, "go through life chattering and making a lot of noise with their mouth; they never really *listen* to anything—they are too busy expressing their opinions, which are often unsound or based on bad information. Therefore, my son, be of good cheer! Enjoy life; learn to fly! Eat well; drink well! Use your ears; use your eyes! And I promise that someday I will make it possible for you to use your voice. There are mechanical devices that convert air into beautiful sounds. One such device is called a trumpet. I saw a trumpet once, in my travels. I think you may need a trumpet in order to live a full life. I've never *known* a Trumpeter Swan to need a trumpet, but your case is different. I intend to get you what you need. I don't know how I will manage this, but in the fullness of time it shall be accomplished. And now that our talk has come to a close, let us return gracefully to the other end of the pond, where your mother and your brothers and sisters await us!"

The cob turned and swam off. Louis followed. It had been an unhappy morning for him. He felt frightened at being different from his brothers and sisters. It scared him to be different. He couldn't understand why he had come into the world without a voice. Everyone else seemed to have a voice. Why didn't he? "Fate is cruel," he thought. "Fate is cruel to me." Then he remembered that his father had promised to help, and he felt better. Soon they joined the others, and everyone started water games, and Louis joined in, dipping and splashing and diving and twisting. Louis could splash water farther than any of the others, but he couldn't shout while he was doing it. To be able to shout while you are splashing water is half the fun.

VI

Off to Montana

At the end of the summer, the cob gathered his family around him and made an announcement.

"Children," he began, "I have news for you. Summer is drawing to a close. Leaves are turning red, pink, and pale yellow. Soon the leaves will fall. The time has come for us to leave this pond. The time has come for us to go."

"Go?" cried all the cygnets except Louis.

"Certainly," replied their father. "You children are old enough to learn the facts of life, and the principal fact of our life right now is this: we can't stay in this marvelous location much longer."

"Why not?" cried all the cygnets except Louis.

"Because summer is over," said the cob, "and it is the way of swans to leave their nesting site at summer's end and travel south to a milder place where the food supply is good. I know that you are all fond of this pretty pond, this marvelous marsh, these reedy shores and restful retreats. You have found life pleasant and amusing here. You have learned to dive and swim underwater. You have enjoyed our daily recreational trips when we formed in line, myself in front swimming gracefully, like a locomotive, and your charming mother bringing up the rear, like a caboose. Daylong, you have listened and learned. You have avoided the odious otter and the cruel coyote. You have listened to the little owl that says co-co-co-co. You have heard the partridge say kwit-kwit. At night you have dropped off to sleep to the sound of frogs—the voices of the night. But these pleasures and pastimes, these adventures, these games and frolics, these beloved sights and sounds must come to an end. All things come to an end. It is time for us to go."

"Where will we go?" cried all the cygnets except Louis. "Where will we go, ko-hoh, ko-hoh? Where will we go, ko-hoh, ko-hoh?"

"We will fly south to Montana," replied the cob.

"What is Montana?" asked all the cygnets except Louis. "What is Montana—banana, banana? What is Montana—banana, banana?"

"Montana," said their father, "is a state of the Union. And there, in a lovely valley surrounded by high mountains, are the Red Rock Lakes, which nature has designed especially for swans. In these lakes you will enjoy warm water, arising from hidden springs. Here, ice never forms, no matter how cold the nights. In the Red Rock Lakes, you will find other Trumpeter Swans, as well as the lesser waterfowl—the geese and the ducks. There are few enemies. No gunners. Plenty of muskrat houses. Free grain. Games every day. What more can a swan ask, in the long, long cold of winter?"

Louis listened to all this in amazement. He wanted to ask his father how they would learn to fly and how they would find Montana even after they learned to fly. He began to worry about getting lost. But he wasn't able to ask any questions. He just had to listen.

One of his brothers spoke up.

"Father," he said, "you said we would *fly* south. I don't know *how* to fly. I've never been up in the air."

"True," replied the cob. "But flying is largely a matter of having the right attitude—plus, of course, good wing feathers. Flying consists of three parts. First, the takeoff, during which there is a lot of fuss and commotion, a lot of splashing and rapid beating of the wings. Second, the ascent, or gaining of altitude—this requires hard work and fast wing action. Third, the leveling-off, the steady elevated flight, high in air, wings beating slower now, beating strongly and regularly, carrying us swiftly and surely from zone to zone as we cry ko-hoh, ko-hoh, with all the earth stretched out far below."

"It sounds very nice," said the cygnet, "but I'm not sure I can do it. I might get dizzy way up there—if I look down."

"Don't *look* down!" said his father. "Look straight ahead. And don't lose your nerve. Besides, swans do not get dizzy—they feel wonderful in the air. They feel exalted."

"What does 'exalted' mean?" asked the cygnet.

"It means you will feel strong, glad, firm, high, proud, successful, satisfied, powerful, and elevated—as though you had conquered life and had a high purpose."

Louis listened to all this with great attention. The idea of flying frightened him. "I won't be able to say ko-hoh," he thought. "I wonder whether a swan can fly if he has no voice and can't say ko-hoh."

"I think," said the cob, "the best plan is for me to

demonstrate flying to you. I will make a short exhibition flight while you watch. Observe everything I do! Watch me pump my neck up and down before the takeoff! Watch me test the wind by turning my head this way and that! The takeoff must be *into* the wind—it's much easier that way. Listen to the noise I make trumpeting! Watch how I raise my great wings! See how I beat them furiously as I rush through the water with my feet going like mad! This frenzy will last for a couple of hundred feet, at which point I will suddenly be airborne, my wings still chopping the air with terrific force but my feet no longer touching the water! Then watch what I do! Watch how I stretch my long white elegant neck out ahead of me until it has reached its full length! Watch how I retract my feet and allow them to stream out behind, full-length, until they extend beyond my tail! Hear my cries as I gain the upper air and start trumpeting! See how strong and steady my wingbeat has become! Then watch me bank and turn, set my wings, and glide down! And just as I reach the pond again, watch how I shoot my feet out in front of me and use them for the splashdown, as though they were a pair of water skis! Having watched all this, then you can join me, and your mother, too, and we will all make a practice flight together, until you get the hang of it. Then tomorrow we will do it again, and instead of returning to the pond, we will head south to Montana. Are you ready for my exhibition flight?"

"Ready!" cried all the cygnets except Louis.

"Very well, here I go!" cried the cob.

As the others watched, he swam downwind to the end of the pond, turned, tested the wind, pumped his neck up and down, trumpeted, and after a rush of two hundred feet, got into the air and began gaining altitude. His long white neck stretched out ahead. His big black feet stretched out behind. His wings had great power. The beat slowed as he settled into sustained flight. All eyes watched. Louis was more excited than he had ever been. "I wonder if I can really do it?" he thought. "Suppose I fail! Then the others will fly away, and I will be left here all alone on this deserted pond, with winter approaching, with no father, no mother, no sisters, no brothers, and no food to eat when the pond freezes over. I will die of starvation. I'm scared."

In a few minutes, the cob glided down out of the sky and skidded to a stop on the pond. They all cheered. "Ko-hoh, ko-hoh, beep beep, beep beep!"

All but Louis. He had to express his approval simply by beating his wings and splashing water in his father's face.

"All right," said the cob. "You've seen how it's done. Follow me, and we'll give it a try. Extend yourselves to the utmost, do everything in the proper order, never forget for a minute that you are swans and therefore excellent fliers, and I'm sure all will be well."

They all swam downwind to the end of the pond. They pumped their necks up and down. Louis pumped his harder than any of the others. They tested the wind by turning their heads this way and that. Suddenly the cob signaled for the start. There was a tremendous commotion—wings beating, feet racing, water churned to a froth. And presently, wonder of wonders, there were seven swans in the air—two pure white ones and five dirty gray ones. The takeoff was accomplished, and they started gaining altitude.

Louis was the first of the young cygnets to become airborne, ahead of all his brothers and sisters. The minute his feet lifted clear of the water, he knew he could fly. It was a tremendous relief—as well as a splendid sensation.

"Boy!" he said to himself. "I never knew flying

could be such fun. This is great. This is sensational. This is superb. I feel exalted, and I'm not dizzy. I'll be able to get to Montana with the rest of the family. I may be defective, but at least I can fly."

The seven great birds stayed aloft about half an hour, then returned to the pond, the cob still in the lead. They all had a drink to celebrate the successful flight. Next day they were up early. It was a beautiful fall morning, with mist rising from the pond and the trees shining in all colors. Toward the end of the afternoon, as the sun sank low in the sky, the swans took off from the pond and began their journey to Montana. "This way!" cried the cob. He swung to his left and straightened out on a southerly course. The others followed, trumpeting as they went. As they passed over the camp where Sam Beaver was, Sam heard them and ran out. He stood watching as they grew smaller and smaller in the distance and finally disappeared.

"What was it?" asked his father, when Sam returned indoors.

"Swans," replied Sam. "They're headed south."

"We'd better do the same," said Mr. Beaver. "I think Shorty will be here tomorrow to take us out."

Mr. Beaver lay down on his bunk. "What kind of swans were they?" he asked.

"Trumpeters," said Sam.

"That's funny," said Mr. Beaver. "I thought Trumpeter Swans had quit migrating. I thought they spent the whole year on the Red Rock Lakes, where they are protected."

"Most of 'em do," replied Sam. "But not all of 'em."

It was bedtime. Sam got out his diary. This is what he wrote:

I heard the swans tonight. They are headed south. It must be wonderful to fly at night.
I wonder whether I'll ever see one of them again.
How does a bird know how to get
from where he is to where he wants to be?

VII

School Days

A FEW DAYS AFTER THE SWANS ARRIVED AT their winter home on the Red Rock Lakes, Louis had an idea. He decided that since he was unable to use his voice, he should learn to read and write. "If I'm defective in one respect," he said to himself, "I should try and develop myself along other lines. I will learn to read and write. Then I will hang a small slate around my neck and carry a chalk pencil. In that way I will be able to communicate with anybody who can read."

Louis liked company, and he already had many friends on the lakes. The place was a refuge for water birds—swans, geese, ducks, and other waterfowl. They lived there because it was a safe place and because the water stayed warm even in the coldest winter weather. Louis was greatly admired for his ability as a swimmer. He liked to compete with other cygnets to see who could swim underwater the greatest distance and stay down the longest.

When Louis had fully made up his mind about learning to read and write, he decided to visit Sam Beaver and get help from him. "Perhaps," thought Louis, "Sam will let me go to school with him, and the teacher will show me how to write." The idea excited him. He wondered whether a young swan would be accepted in a classroom of children. He wondered whether it was hard to learn to read. Most of all, he wondered whether he could find Sam. Montana is a big state, and he wasn't even sure Sam lived in Montana, but he hoped he did.

Next morning, when his parents were not looking, Louis took off into the air. He flew northeast. When he came to the Yellowstone River, he followed it to the Sweet Grass country. When he saw a town beneath him, he landed next to the schoolhouse and waited for the boys and girls to be let out. Louis looked at every boy, hoping to see Sam. But Sam wasn't there.

"Wrong town, wrong school," thought Louis. "I'll try again." He flew off, found another town, and located the school, but all the boys and girls had gone home for the day.

"I'll just have a look around anyway," thought Louis. He didn't dare walk down the main street, for fear somebody would shoot him. Instead, he took to the air and circled around, flying low and looking carefully at every boy in sight. After about ten minutes, he saw a ranch house where a boy was splitting wood near the kitchen door. The boy had black hair. Louis glided down.

"I'm lucky," he thought. "It's Sam."

When Sam saw the swan, he laid down his ax and stood perfectly still. Louis walked up timidly, then reached down and untied Sam's shoelace.

"Hello!" said Sam in a friendly voice.

Louis tried to say ko-hoh, but not a sound came from his throat.

"I know *you*," said Sam. "You're the one that never said anything and used to pull my shoelaces."

Louis nodded.

"I'm glad to see you," said Sam. "What can I do for you?"

Louis just stared straight ahead.

"Are you hungry?" asked Sam.

Louis shook his head.

"Thirsty?"

Louis shook his head.

"Do you want to stay overnight with us, here at the ranch?" asked Sam.

Louis nodded his head and jumped up and down.

"O.K.," said Sam. "We have plenty of room. It's just a question of getting my father's permission."

Sam picked up his ax, laid a stick of wood on the chopping block, and split the stick neatly down the middle. He looked at Louis.

"There's something wrong with your voice, isn't there?" he asked.

Louis nodded, pumping his neck up and down hard. He knew Sam was his friend, although he didn't know that Sam had once saved his mother's life.

In a few minutes Mr. Beaver rode into the yard on a cow pony. He got off and tied his pony to a rail. "What have you got there?" he asked Sam.

"It's a young Trumpeter Swan," said Sam. "He's only a few months old. Will you let me keep him awhile?"

"Well," said Mr. Beaver, "I think it's against the law to hold one of these wild birds in captivity. But I'll phone the game warden and see what he says. If he says yes, you can keep him."

"Tell the warden the swan has something the matter with him," called Sam as his father started toward the house.

"What's wrong with him?" asked his father.

"He has a speech problem," replied Sam. "Something's wrong with his throat."

"What are you talking about? Who ever heard of a swan with a speech problem?"

"Well," said Sam, "this is a Trumpeter Swan that can't trumpet. He's defective. He can't make a sound."

Mr. Beaver looked at his son as though he didn't know whether to believe him or not. But he went into the house. In a few minutes he came back. "The warden says you can keep the young swan here for a while if you can help him. But sooner or later the bird will have to go back to the Red Rock Lakes, where he belongs. The warden said he wouldn't let just *anybody* have a young swan, but he'd let *you* have one because you understand about birds, and he trusts you. That's quite a compliment, son."

Mr. Beaver looked pleased. Sam looked happy. Louis was greatly relieved. After a while everyone went in to supper in the kitchen of the ranch house. Mrs. Beaver allowed Louis to stand beside Sam's chair. They fed him some corn and some oats, which tasted good. When Sam was ready for bed, he wanted Louis to sleep in his room with him, but Mrs. Beaver said no. "He'll mess up the room. He's no canary; he's enormous. Put the bird out in the barn. He can sleep in one of the empty stalls; the horses won't mind."

Next morning, Sam took Louis to school with him. Sam rode his pony, and Louis flew along. At the schoolhouse, the other children were amazed to see this great bird, with his long neck, bright eyes, and big feet. Sam introduced him to the teacher of the first grade, Mrs. Hammerbotham, who was short and fat. Sam explained that Louis wanted to read and write because he was unable to make any sound with his throat.

Mrs. Hammerbotham stared at Louis. Then she shook her head. "No birds!" she said. "I've got enough trouble."

Sam looked disappointed.

"Please, Mrs. Hammerbotham," he said. "Please let him stand in your class and learn to read and write."

"Why does a bird need to read and write?" replied the teacher. "Only *people* need to communicate with one another."

"That's not quite true, Mrs. Hammerbotham," said

Sam, "if you'll excuse me for saying so. I have watched birds and animals a great deal. All birds and animals talk to one another—they really have to, in order to get along. Mothers have to talk to their young. Males have to talk to females, particularly in the spring of the year when they are in love."

"In *love?*" said Mrs. Hammerbotham, who seemed to perk up at this suggestion. "What do *you* know about love?"

Sam blushed.

"What kind of a bird *is* he?" she asked.

"He's a young Trumpeter Swan," said Sam. "Right now he's sort of a dirty gray color, but in another year he'll be the most beautiful thing you ever saw—pure white, with black bill and black feet. He was hatched last spring in Canada and now lives in the Red Rock Lakes, but he can't say ko-hoh the way the other swans can, and this puts him at a terrible disadvantage."

"Why?" asked the teacher.

"Because it does," said Sam. "If *you* wanted to say ko-hoh and couldn't make a single solitary sound, wouldn't *you* feel worried?"

"I don't *want* to say ko-hoh," replied the teacher. "I don't even know what it means. Anyway, this is all just foolishness, Sam. What makes you think a bird can learn to read and write? It's impossible."

"Give him a chance!" pleaded Sam. "He is well behaved, and he's bright, and he's got this very serious speech defect."

"What's his name?"

"I don't know," replied Sam.

"Well," said Mrs. Hammerbotham, "if he's coming into my class, he's got to have a name. Maybe we can find out what it is." She looked at the bird. "Is your name Joe?"

Louis shook his head.

"Jonathan?"

Louis shook his head.

"Donald?"

Louis shook his head again.

"Is your name Louis?" asked Mrs. Hammerbotham.

Louis nodded his head very hard and jumped up and down and flapped his wings.

"Great Caesar's ghost!" cried the teacher. "Look at those wings! Well, his name is Louis—that's for sure. All right, Louis, you may join the class. Stand right here by the blackboard. And don't mess up the room, either! If you need to go outdoors for any reason, raise one wing."

Louis nodded. The first-graders cheered. They liked the looks of the new pupil and were eager to see what he could do.

"Quiet, children!" said Mrs. Hammerbotham sternly. "We'll start with the letter *A*."

She picked up a piece of chalk and made a big A on the blackboard. "Now you try it, Louis!"

Louis grabbed a piece of chalk in his bill and drew a perfect A right under the one the teacher had drawn.

"You see?" said Sam. "He's an unusual bird."

"Well," said Mrs. Hammerbotham, "A is easy. I'll give him something harder." She wrote cat on the board. "Let's see you write *cat*, Louis!"

Louis wrote cat.

"Well *cat* is easy, too," muttered the teacher. "*Cat* is easy because it is short. Can anyone think of a word that is longer than *cat*?"

"*Catastrophe,*" said Charlie Nelson, who sat in the first row.

"Good!" said Mrs. Hammerbotham. "That's a good hard word. But does anyone know what it means? What *is* a catastrophe?"

"An earthquake," said one of the girls.

"Correct!" replied the teacher. "What else?"

"War is a catastrophe," said Charlie Nelson.

"Correct!" replied Mrs. Hammerbotham. "What else is?"

A very small, redheaded girl named Jennie raised her hand.

"Yes, Jennie? What is a catastrophe?"

In a very small, high voice, Jennie said, "When you get ready to go on a picnic with your father and mother and you make peanut-butter sandwiches and jelly rolls and put them in a thermos box with bananas and an apple and some raisin cookies and paper napkins and some bottles of pop and a few hard-boiled eggs and then you put the thermos box in your car and just as you are starting out it starts to *rain* and your parents say there is no point in having a picnic in the rain, that's a catastrophe."

"Very good, Jennie," said Mrs. Hammerbotham. "It isn't as bad as an earthquake, and it isn't as bad as war. But when a picnic gets called on account of rain, it *is* a catastrophe for a child, I guess. Anyway, *catastrophe* is a good word. No bird can write that word, I'll bet. If I can teach a bird to write *catastrophe*, it'll be big news all over the Sweet Grass country. I'll get my picture in *Life* magazine. I'll be famous."

Thinking of all these things, she stepped to the

blackboard and wrote catastrophe.

"O.K., Louis, let's see you write *that*!"

Louis picked up a fresh piece of chalk in his bill. He was scared. He took a good look at the word. "A long word," he thought, "is really no harder than a short one. I'll just copy one letter at a time, and pretty soon it will be finished. Besides, my life is a catastrophe. It's a catastrophe to be without a voice." Then he began writing. catastrophe, he wrote, making each letter very neatly. When he got to the last letter, the pupils clapped and stamped their feet and banged on their desks, and one boy quickly made a paper airplane and zoomed it into the air. Mrs. Hammerbotham rapped for order.

"Very good, Louis," she said. "Sam, it's time you went to your own classroom—you shouldn't be in my room. Go and join the fifth grade. I'll take care of your friend the swan."

Back in his own room, Sam sat down at his desk, feeling very happy about the way things had turned out. The fifth-graders were having a lesson in arithmetic, and their teacher, Miss Annie Snug, greeted Sam with a question. Miss Snug was young and pretty.

"Sam, if a man can walk three miles in one hour,

how many miles can he walk in four hours?"

"It would depend on how tired he got after the first hour," replied Sam.

The other pupils roared. Miss Snug rapped for order.

"Sam is quite right," she said. "I never looked at the problem that way before. I always supposed that man could walk twelve miles in four hours, but Sam may be right: that man may not feel so spunky after the first hour. He may drag his feet. He may slow up."

Albert Bigelow raised his hand. "My father knew a man who tried to walk twelve miles, and he died of heart failure," said Albert.

"Goodness!" said the teacher. "I suppose *that* could happen, too."

"Anything can happen in four hours," said Sam. "A man might develop a blister on his heel. Or he might find some berries growing along the road and stop to pick them. That would slow him up even if he wasn't tired or didn't have a blister."

"It would indeed," agreed the teacher. "Well, children, I think we have all learned a great deal about arithmetic this morning, thanks to Sam Beaver. And now, here is a problem for one of the girls in the room. If you are feeding a baby from a bottle, and you give the baby eight ounces of milk in one feeding, how many ounces of milk would the baby drink in *two* feedings?"

Linda Staples raised her hand.

"About fifteen ounces," she said.

"Why is that?" asked Miss Snug. "Why wouldn't the baby drink sixteen ounces?"

"Because he spills a little each time," said Linda. "It runs out of the corners of his mouth and gets on his mother's apron."

By this time the class was howling so loudly the arithmetic lesson had to be abandoned. But everyone had learned how careful you have to be when dealing with figures.

VIII

Love

When Louis's father and mother discovered that Louis was missing, they felt awful. No other young swan had disappeared from the lakes—only Louis.

"The question now arises," said the cob to his wife, "whether or not I should go and look for our son. I am disinclined to leave these attractive lakes now, in the fall of the year, with winter coming on. I have, in fact, been looking forward to this time of serenity and peace and the society of other water-fowl. I like the life here."

"There's another little matter to consider besides your personal comfort," said his wife. "Has it occurred to you that we have no idea which direction Louis went when he left? You don't know where he went any more than I do. If you were to start out looking for him, which way would you fly?"

"Well," replied the cob, "in the last analysis, I believe I would go south."

"What do you mean, 'in the last analysis'?" said the swan impatiently. "You haven't analyzed anything. Why do you say 'in the last analysis'? And why do you pick south as the way to go looking for Louis? There are other directions. There's north, and east, and west. There's northeast, southeast, southwest, northwest."

"True," replied the cob. "And there are all those in-between directions: north-northeast, east-southeast, west-southwest. There's north by east, and east by north. There's south-southeast a half east, and there's west by north a half north. The directions a young swan could start off in are almost too numerous to think about."

So it was decided that no search would be made. "We'll just wait here and see what happens," said the cob. "I feel sure Louis will return in the fullness of time."

Months went by. Winter came to the Red Rock Lakes. The nights were long and dark and cold. The days were short and bright and cold. Sometimes the wind blew. But the swans and geese and ducks were safe and happy. The warm springs that fed the lakes kept the ice from covering them—there were always open places. There was plenty of food. Sometimes a man would arrive with a bag of grain and spread the grain where the birds could get it.

Spring followed winter; summer followed spring. A year went by, and it was springtime again. Still no sign of Louis. Then one morning when Louis's grown-up brothers were playing a game of water polo, one of them looked up and saw a swan approaching in the sky.

"Ko-hoh!" cried the cygnet. He rushed to his father and mother. "Look! Look! Look!"

All the waterfowl on the lake turned and gazed up at the approaching swan. The swan circled in the sky.

"It's Louis!" said the cob. "But what is that peculiar little object hanging around his neck by a string? What is that?"

"Wait and see," said his wife. "Maybe it's a gift."

Louis looked down from the sky and spotted what looked like his family. When he was sure, he glided down and skidded to a stop. His mother rushed up and embraced him. His father arched his neck gracefully and raised his wings in greeting.

Everyone shouted "Ko-hoh!" and "Welcome back, Louis!" His family was overjoyed. He had been gone for a year and a half—almost eighteen months. He looked older and handsomer. His feathers were pure white now, instead of a dirty gray. Hanging by a cord around his neck was a small slate. Attached to the slate by a piece of string was a white chalk pencil.

When the family greetings were over, Louis seized the chalk in his bill and wrote "Hi, there!" on the slate. He held the slate out eagerly for all to see.

The cob stared at it. The mother swan stared at it. The cygnets stared at it. They just stared and stared. Words on a slate meant nothing to them. They couldn't read. None of the members of his family had ever seen a slate before, or a piece of chalk. Louis's attempt to greet his family was a failure. He felt as though he had wasted a year and a half by going to school and learning to write. He felt keenly disappointed. And, of course, he was unable to speak. The words on the slate were all he could offer by way of greeting.

Finally his father, the cob, spoke up.

"Louis, my son," he began in his deep, resonant voice, "this is the day we have long awaited—the day of your return to our sanctuary in the Red Rock Lakes. No one can imagine the extent of our joy or the depth of our emotion at seeing you again, you who have been absent from our midst for so long, in lands we know not of, in pursuits we can only guess at. How good it is to see your countenance again! We hope you have enjoyed good health during your long absence, in lands we know not of, in pursuits we can only guess at—"

"You've said that once already," said his wife. "You're repeating yourself. Louis must be tired after his trip, no matter where he's been or what he's been up to."

"Very true," said the cob. "But I must prolong my welcoming remarks a bit longer, for my curiosity is aroused by that odd little object Louis is wearing around his neck and by the strange symbols he has placed upon it by rubbing that white thing up and down and leaving those strange white tracings."

"Well," said Louis's mother, "we're *all* interested in it, naturally. But Louis can't explain it because he is defective and can't talk. So we'll just have to forget our curiosity for the moment and let Louis take a bath and have dinner."

Everyone agreed this was a good idea.

Louis swam to the shore, placed his slate and his chalk pencil under a bush, and took a bath. When he was through, he dipped the end of one wing in the water and sorrowfully rubbed out the words "Hi, there!" Then he hung the slate around his neck again. It felt good to be home with his family. And his family had increased during the months he had spent with Sam Beaver at school. There were now six new cygnets. Louis's father and mother had spent the summer on a trip to Canada, and while there, they had nested and hatched six little cygnets, and in the fall they had all joined up again at the Red Rock Lakes in Montana.

One day, soon after Louis's return, the grain man stopped by with a sack of grain. Louis saw him and swam over. When the man spread the grain on the ground to feed the birds, Louis took off his slate and wrote, "Thank you very much!" He held the slate up to the man, who appeared surprised.

"Say!" said the man. "You're quite a bird! Where did *you* learn to write?"

Louis erased the slate and wrote, "At school."

"School?" said the grain man. "What school?"

"Public school," wrote Louis. "Mrs. Hammerbotham taught me."

"Never heard of her," said the grain man. "But

she must be a darned good teacher."

"She is," wrote Louis. He was overjoyed to be carrying on a conversation with a stranger. He realized that even though the slate was no help with other birds, it *was* going to be a help with people, because people could read. This made him feel a whole lot better. Sam Beaver had given Louis the slate as a good-bye present when he left the ranch. Sam had bought the slate and the chalk pencil with money he had saved. Louis decided he would always carry them with him, no matter where he went in the world.

The grain man wondered whether he had been dreaming or whether he had really seen a swan write words on a slate. He decided to say nothing about it to anyone, for fear people might think he was crazy in the head.

For birds, spring is the time to find a mate. The warm sweet airs of spring stir strange feelings in young swans. The males begin to notice the females. They show off in front of them. The females begin to notice the males, too, but they pretend they are not noticing anything at all. They act very coy.

Louis felt so queer one day, he knew he must be in love. And he knew which bird he was in love with. Whenever he swam past her, he could feel his heart beat faster, and his mind was full of thoughts of love and desire. He thought he had never seen such a beautiful young female swan. She was a trifle smaller than the others, and she seemed to have a more graceful neck and more attractive ways than any of his other friends on the lake. Her name was Serena. He wished he could do something to attract her attention. He wanted her for his mate but was unable to tell her so because he couldn't make a sound. He swam in circles around her and pumped his neck up and down and made a great show of diving and staying down to prove he could hold his breath longer than any other bird. But the little female paid no attention to Louis's antics. She pretended he didn't exist.

When Louis's mother found out that Louis was courting a young female, she hid behind some bulrushes and watched what was going on. She could tell that he was in love by the way he acted, and she saw that he was having no success.

Once, in desperation, Louis swam up to Serena, his beloved, and made a bow. His slate, as usual, was around his neck. Taking the chalk pencil in his mouth, he wrote "I love you" on the slate and showed it to her.

She stared at it for a moment, then swam away. She didn't know how to read, and although she rather liked the looks of a young cob who had something hanging around his neck, she couldn't really get interested in a bird that was unable to *say* anything. A Trumpeter Swan that couldn't trumpet was a bust as far as she was concerned.

When Louis's mother saw this, she went to her husband, the cob.

"I have news for you," she said. "Your son Louis is in love, and the swan of his choice, the female of his desiring, pays no attention to him. It's just as I predicted: Louis won't be able to get a mate because he has no voice. That snippety little female he's chasing after gives me a pain in the neck, the way she acts. But just the same, I'm sorry for Louis. He thinks she's the greatest thing on the lake, and he can't say, 'Ko-hoh, I love you,' and that's what she's waiting to hear."

"Why, this is terrible news," said the cob, "news of the most serious import. I know what it is like to be in love. Well do I remember how painful love can be, how exciting, and, in the event of unsuccess, how disappointing and doleful the days and nights. But I am Louis's father, and I'm not going to take this situation lying down. I shall act. Louis is a

Trumpeter Swan, noblest of all the waterfowl. He is gay, cheerful, strong, powerful, lusty, good, brave, handsome, reliable, trustworthy, a great flier, a tremendous swimmer, fearless, patient, loyal, true, ambitious, desirous—"

"Just a minute," said his wife. "You don't need to tell me all these things. The point is, what are you going to do to help Louis get himself a mate?"

"I'm leading up to that in my own graceful way," replied the cob. "You say that what this young female wants is to hear Louis say, 'Ko-hoh, I love you'?"

"That's right."

"Then she shall hear it!" exclaimed the cob. "There are devices made by men—horns, trumpets, musical instruments of all sorts. These devices are capable of producing sounds similar to the wild sound of our trumpeting. I shall begin a search for such a device, and if I have to go to the ends of the earth to find a trumpet for our young son, I shall find it at last and bring it home to Louis."

"Well, if I may make a suggestion," said his wife, "don't go to the ends of the earth, go to Billings, Montana. It's nearer."

"Very well, I will try Billings. I shall look for a trumpet in Billings. And now, without further ado,

I go. There is no time to lose. Springtime doesn't last forever. Love is fleeting. Every minute counts. I'm leaving this instant for Billings, Montana, a great city teeming with life and with objects made by man. Good-bye, my love! I shall return!"

"What are you going to use for money?" asked his practical wife. "Trumpets cost money."

"Leave that to me," replied the cob. And with that, he took off into the air. He climbed steeply, like a jet plane, then leveled off, flying high and fast toward the northeast. His wife watched him until he was out of sight. "What a swan!" she murmured. "I just hope he knows what he's doing."

IX

The Trumpet

As the cob flew toward Billings on his powerful white wings, all sorts of troublesome thoughts whirled in his head. The cob had never gone looking for a trumpet before. He had no money to pay for a trumpet. He feared he might arrive after the shops had closed for the day. He realized that in the whole continent of North America he was undoubtedly the only Trumpeter Swan who was on his way to a city to get a trumpet.

"This is a queer adventure," he said to himself. "Yet it is a noble quest. I will do anything to help my son Louis—even if I run into real trouble."

Toward the end of the afternoon, the cob looked ahead and in the distance saw the churches and factories and shops and homes of Billings. He decided to act quickly and boldly. He circled the city once, looking for a music store. Suddenly he spied one. It had a very big, wide window, solid glass. The cob flew lower and circled so he could get a better look. He gazed into the store. He saw a drum painted gold. He saw a fancy guitar with an electric cord. He saw a small piano. He saw banjos, horns, violins, mandolins, cymbals, saxophones, marimbaphones, cellos, and many other instruments. Then he saw what he wanted: he saw a brass trumpet hanging by a red cord.

"Now is my time to act!" he said to himself. "Now is my moment for risking everything on one bold move, however shocking it may be to my sensibilities, however offensive it may be to the laws that govern the lives of men. Here I go! May good luck go with me!"

With that, the old cob set his wings for a dive. He aimed straight at the big window. He held his neck straight and stiff, waiting for the crash. He dove swiftly and hit the window going full speed. The glass broke. The noise was terrific. The whole store shook. Musical instruments fell to the floor. Glass flew everywhere. A salesgirl fainted. The cob felt a twinge of pain as a jagged piece of broken glass cut into his shoulder, but he grabbed the trumpet in his beak, turned sharply in the air, flew back through the hole in the window, and began climbing fast over the roofs of Billings. A few drops of blood fell to the ground below. His shoulder hurt. But he had succeeded in getting what he had come for. Held firmly in his bill, its red cord dangling, was a beautiful brass trumpet.

You can imagine the noise in the music store when the cob crashed through the window. At the moment the glass broke, one of the clerks was showing a bass drum to a customer, and the clerk was so startled at seeing a big white bird come flying through the window, he hit the drum a tremendous wallop.

"Bom!" went the drum.

"Crash!" went the splinters of flying glass.

When the salesgirl fainted, she fell against the keys of the piano.

"Rrrongee-rrrongee-rrongee!" went the piano.

The owner of the store grabbed his shotgun, which went off by mistake, blasting a hole in the ceiling and sending down a shower of plaster. Everything was flying around and falling and making a noise.

"Bom!" went the drum.

"Plunk!" went the banjo.

"Rrrongee-rrrongee-rrrongee!" went the piano.

"Ump!" went the bull fiddle.

"Help!" screamed a clerk. "We've been robbed."

"Make way!" shouted the owner. He ran for the door, stepped outside, and fired another shot—*bang!*—at the disappearing bird. His shot was too late. The cob was safe in the sky, beyond the range of gunfire. He was headed home, toward the southwest, high above the roofs and spires of Billings. In his beak was the trumpet. In his heart was the pain of having committed a crime.

"I have robbed a store," he said to himself. "I have become a thief. What a miserable fate for a bird of my excellent character and high ideals! Why did I do this? What led me to commit this awful crime? My past life has been blameless—a model of good behavior and correct conduct. I am by nature law-abiding. Why, oh, why did I do this?"

Then the answer came to him, as he flew steadily on through the evening sky. "I did it to help my son. I did it for love of my son Louis."

Back in Billings, the news spread rapidly. This was the first time a swan had broken into a music store and made off with a trumpet. A lot of people refused to believe it had happened. The editor of the newspaper sent a reporter to the store to look around. The reporter interviewed the owner and wrote an article about the event for the paper. The article was headed:

LARGE BIRD BREAKS INTO MUSIC STORE

White Swan Crashes Through Window and Makes Off With Valuable Trumpet

Everybody in Billings bought a copy of the paper and read all about the extraordinary event. It was talked about all over town. Some people believed it; others said it never could have happened. They said the store owner had just invented it to get some publicity for his store. But the clerks in the store agreed that it had really happened. They pointed to the drops of blood on the floor.

The police came to look over the damage, which was estimated at nine hundred dollars. The police promised they would try to find the thief and arrest him, but the police were sorry to hear that the thief was a bird. "Birds are a special problem," they said. "Birds are hard to deal with."

Back at the Red Rock Lakes, Louis's mother waited anxiously for her husband to return. When he showed up in the night sky, she saw that he had a trumpet with him. It was slung around his neck by its cord.

"Well," she said, as he glided to a stop in the water, "I see you made it."

"I did, my dear," said the cob. "I traveled fast and far, sacrificed my honor, and I have returned. Where is Louis? I want to give him his trumpet right away."

"He's over there sitting on a muskrat house, dreaming about that empty-headed young female he's so crazy about."

The cob swam over to his son and made a presentation speech.

"Louis," he said, "I have been on a journey to the haunts of men. I visited a great city teeming with life and commerce. Whilst there, I picked up a gift for you, which I now bestow upon you with my love and my blessing. Here, Louis, is a trumpet. It will be your voice—a substitute for the voice God failed to give you. Learn to blow it, Louis, and life will be smoother and richer and gayer for you! With the help of this horn, you will be able at last to say ko-hoh, like every other swan. The sound of music will be in our ears. You will be able to attract the attention of desirable young females. Master this trumpet, and you will be able to play love songs for them, filling them with ardor and surprise and longing. I hope it will bring you happiness, Louis, and a new and better life. I procured it at some personal sacrifice to myself and my pride, but we won't go into that now. The long and short of it is, I had no money; I took the trumpet without paying for it. This was deplorable. But the important thing is that you learn to play the instrument."

So saying, the cob removed the trumpet from around his neck and hung it on Louis, alongside the slate and the white chalk pencil.

"Wear it in good health!" he said. "Blow it in happiness! Make the woods and the hills and the marshes echo with the sounds of your youthful desire!"

Louis wanted to thank his father, but he was unable to say a word. And he knew it would do no good to write "Thank you" on the slate, because his father wouldn't be able to read it, never having had an education. So Louis just bobbed his head and waggled his tail and fluttered his wings. The cob knew by these signs that he had found favor in the sight of his son and that the gift of a trumpet was acceptable.

X

Money Trouble

LOUIS WAS THE BEST-LIKED YOUNG MALE swan on Upper Red Rock Lake. He was also the best equipped. He not only had a slate and a chalk pencil around his neck, he had a brass trumpet on a red cord. The young females were beginning to notice him because he looked entirely different from the other cygnets. He stood out in a crowd. None of the others carried anything with them.

Louis was delighted with the new trumpet. All day, the first day he had it, he tried to get it to make a noise. Holding the trumpet was not easy. He tried several different positions, bending his neck and blowing. At first, no sound came out. He blew harder and harder, puffing out his cheeks and getting red in the face.

"This is going to be tough," he thought.

But then he discovered that, by holding his tongue in a certain way, he could get the trumpet to emit a small gasping sound. It wasn't a very pretty noise, but at least it was a noise. It sounded a little like hot air escaping from a radiator.

"Puwoowf, puwoowf," went the trumpet.

Louis kept at it. Finally, on the second day of trying, he got it to play a note—a clear note.

"Ko!" went the trumpet.

Louis's heart skipped a beat when he heard it. A duck, swimming nearby, stopped to listen.

"Ko! Ko ee oo oooph," went the trumpet.

"It will take time," thought Louis. "I'm not going to become a trumpeter in a day, that's for sure. But Rome wasn't built in a day, and I'm going to learn to blow this horn if it takes me all summer."

Louis had other problems besides learning the trumpet. For one thing, he knew that his trumpet wasn't paid for—it had been stolen. He didn't like that at all. For another thing, Serena, the swan he was in love with, had gone away. She had left the lakes with several other young swans and had flown north to the Snake River. Louis was afraid he might never see her again. So he found himself with a broken heart, a stolen trumpet, and no one to give him any lessons.

Whenever Louis was in trouble, his thoughts turned to Sam Beaver. Sam had helped him before; perhaps he could help him again. Besides, springtime was making him restless: he felt an urge to leave the lakes and fly somewhere. So he took off one morning and headed straight for the Bar Nothing Ranch, in the Sweet Grass country, where Sam lived.

Flying was not as easy as it once had been. If you've ever tried to fly with a trumpet dangling from your neck and a slate flapping in the wind and a chalk pencil bouncing around at the end of its string, you know how hard it can be. Louis realized that there were advantages in traveling light and not having too many possessions clinging to you. Nevertheless, he was a strong flier, and the slate and the chalk pencil and the trumpet were important to him.

When he reached the ranch where Sam lived, he circled once, then glided down and walked into the barn. He found Sam grooming his pony.

"Well, look who's here!" exclaimed Sam. "You look like a traveling salesman with all that stuff around your neck. I'm glad to see you."

Louis propped the slate up against the pony's stall. "I'm in trouble," he wrote.

"What's the matter?" asked Sam. "And where did you get the trumpet?"

"That's the trouble," wrote Louis. "My father stole it. He gave it to me because I have no voice. The trumpet hasn't been paid for."

Sam whistled through his teeth. Then he led the pony into his stall, tied him, came out, and sat down on a bale of hay. For a while he just stared at the bird. Finally he said, "You've got a money problem. But that's not unusual. Almost everybody has a money problem. What you need is a job. Then you can save your earnings, and when you get enough money saved up, your father can pay back the man he stole the trumpet from. Can you actually *play* that thing?"

Louis nodded. He raised the trumpet to his beak.

"Ko!" said the trumpet. The pony jumped.

"Hey!" said Sam. "That's pretty good. Do you know any other notes?"

Louis shook his head.

"I've got an idea," said Sam. "I have a job this summer as a junior counselor at a boys' camp in Ontario. That's in Canada. I'll bet I can get you a job as camp bugler if you can learn a few more notes. The camp wants somebody that can blow a horn. The idea is, you blow a lot of loud fast notes in the early morning to wake the boys up. That's called reveille. Then you blow some other notes to call the campers to their meals. That's called the mess call. Then at night when everybody is in bed and the light has faded from the sky and the lake is calm and the mosquitoes are busy in the tents, biting the boys, and the boys are getting sleepy in their beds, you blow some other notes, very soft and sweet and sad. That's called taps. Do you want to go to camp with me and try it?"

"I'll try anything," wrote Louis. "I am desperate for money."

Sam chuckled. "O.K.," he said. "Camp opens in about three weeks. That'll give you time to learn the bugle calls. I'll buy you a music book that tells what the notes are."

And Sam did. He found a book of trumpet calls, such as they use in the Army. He read the instructions to Louis. "Stand erect. Always hold the trumpet straight from the body. Do not point it down toward the ground as this position cramps the lungs and gives the performer a very poor appearance. The instrument should be cleaned once a week to remove the spit."

Every afternoon, when the guests on Mr. Beaver's ranch had gone off on pack trips in the hills, Louis practiced the calls. Pretty soon he could play reveille, mess call, and taps. He particularly liked the sound of taps. Louis was musically inclined and was eager to become a really good trumpeter. "A Trumpeter Swan," he thought, "should blow a good trumpet." He liked the idea of getting a job, too, and earning money. He was just the right age for going to work. He was almost two years old.

On the night before they were to leave for camp, Sam packed all his camping things in a duffel bag. He packed sneakers and moccasins. He packed jerseys that said "Camp Kookooskoos" on the front. He rolled his camera in a towel and packed that. He packed his fishing rod, his toothbrush, his comb and brush, his sweater, his poncho, and his tennis racquet. He packed a pad and pencils and postage stamps and a first-aid kit and a book that told how to identify birds. Before he went to bed, he opened his diary and wrote:

Tomorrow is the last day of June. Pop is going to drive Louis and me to Camp Kookooskoos. I bet it will be the only boys' camp in the world that has a trumpeter swan for the camp bugler. I like having a job. I wish I knew what I was going to be when I am a man. Why does a dog always stretch when he wakes up?

Sam closed his diary, shoved it into the duffel bag with the rest of his stuff, got into bed, turned out the light, and lay there wondering why a dog always stretches when it wakes up. In two minutes he was asleep. Louis, out in the barn, had gone to sleep long ago.

Bright and early next morning, Louis arranged his slate and his chalk pencil and his trumpet neatly around his neck and climbed into the back seat of Mr. Beaver's car. The car was a convertible, so Mr. Beaver put the top down. Sam got in front with his father.

Louis stood tall and white and handsome in the back seat. Mrs. Beaver kissed Sam good-bye. She told him to be a good boy and to take care of himself and not to drown in the lake and not to get into fights with other boys and not to go out in the rain and get sopping wet and then sit around in the chilly air without putting a sweater on, not to get lost in the woods, not to eat too much candy and drink too much pop, not to forget to write letters home every few days, and not to go out in a canoe when it was windy on the lake.

Sam promised.

"O.K.!" cried Mr. Beaver. "Off we go to Ontario, beneath the open sky!" He started the car and tooted the horn.

"Good-bye, Mom!" called Sam.

"Good-bye, son!" called his mother.

The car sped away toward the big main gate of the ranch. Just as it was disappearing from view, Louis turned around in his seat and put his trumpet to his mouth.

"Ko-hoh!" he blew. "Ko-hoh, ko-hoh!"

The sound carried—a wild, clear, stirring call. Everybody back at the ranch heard it and was thrilled by the sound of the trumpet. It was like no other sound they had ever heard. It reminded them of all the wild and wonderful things and places they had ever known: sunsets and moonrises and mountain peaks and valleys and lonely streams and deep woods.

"Ko-hoh! Ko-hoh! Ko-hoh!" called Louis.

The sound of the trumpet died away. The ranchers returned to their breakfast. Louis, on his way to his first job, felt as excited as he had felt on the day he learned to fly.

XI

Camp Kookooskoos

CAMP KOOKOOSKOOS WAS ON A SMALL lake, deep in the woods of Ontario. There were no summer cottages on the lake, no outboard motors, no roads with cars rushing by. It was a wilderness lake, just right for boys. Mr. Beaver left Sam and Louis at the end of a dirt road, and they finished their journey to camp by canoe. Sam sat in the stern and paddled, Louis stood in the bow and looked straight ahead.

The camp consisted of a big log cabin where everybody ate, seven tents where the boys and the counselors slept, a dock out front, and a privy out back. The woods closed in all around, but there was a bare spot that had been made into a tennis court, and there were plenty of canoes in which to take trips to other lakes. There were about forty boys.

When Sam's canoe grounded on the sandy beach next to the camp dock, Louis stepped ashore wearing his slate, his chalk pencil, and his trumpet. About twenty boys rushed down to the landing to see what was going on. They could hardly believe their eyes.

"Hey, look what's here!" one of the boys yelled.

"A bird!" cried another. "Look at the *size* of him!"

Everybody crowded around Louis, wanting to get a close look at the new camper. Sam had to push some of the boys back, to keep Louis from getting crushed.

"Take it easy, will you?" Sam implored.

That evening after supper, the director of the camp, Mr. Brickle, built a big campfire in front of the main lodge. The boys gathered around. They sang songs and toasted marshmallows and swatted mosquitoes. Sometimes you couldn't understand the words of a song because the boys sang with marshmallows in their mouths. Louis did not join the group. He stood by himself at a little distance.

After a while, Mr. Brickle rose to his feet and addressed the boys and the counselors.

"I call your attention," he said, "to a new camper in our midst—Louis the Swan. He is a Trumpeter Swan, a rare bird. We are lucky to have him. I have employed him at the same salary I pay my junior counselors: one hundred dollars for the season. He is gentle and has a speech defect. He came here from Montana with Sam Beaver. Louis is a musician. Like most musicians, he is in need of money. He will wake you at daybreak with his trumpet; he will call you to meals; and at night, when you are dropping off to sleep, he will play taps, and that will bring the day to a close. I caution you to treat him as an equal and to treat him with respect—he packs a terrific wallop with one of those wings. I now introduce, for your listening pleasure, Louis the Swan. Take a bow, Louis!"

Louis was embarrassed, but he came forward and bowed. Then he raised his trumpet to his mouth and blew a long ko. When he finished, from the opposite shore of the lake there came the echo: ko-oo.

The boys clapped. Louis bowed again. Sam Beaver, sitting with the others, his mouth full of marshmallows, was delighted that his plan had succeeded. At the end of the summer, Louis would have a hundred dollars.

A boy named Applegate Skinner stood up.

"Mr. Brickle," he said, "what about me? I don't care for birds. I've never liked birds."

"O.K., Applegate," said Mr. Brickle. "You don't have to like birds. If that's the way you feel about it, just go ahead not-liking birds. Everyone is entitled to his likes and dislikes and to his prejudices. Come to think of it, *I* don't care for pistachio ice cream. I don't know *why* I don't like it, but I don't. Do not forget, however, that Louis is one of your counselors. Whether you like him or not, he must be treated with respect."

One of the new boys who had never been to camp before stood up.

"Mr. Brickle," he said, "why is this camp called Camp Kookooskoos? What does Kookooskoos mean?"

"It's an Indian name for the Great Horned Owl," replied Mr. Brickle.

The new boy thought about this for a minute.

"Then why didn't you just call it Camp Great Horned Owl instead of Camp Kookooskoos?"

"Because," replied Mr. Brickle, "a boys' camp should have a peculiar name; otherwise it doesn't sound interesting. Kookooskoos is a terrific name. It is a long word, but it has only three letters in it. It has two *s*'s, three *k*'s, and six *o*'s. You don't find many names as kooky as that. The queerer the name, the better the camp. Anyway, welcome to Camp Kookooskoos. It rhymes with moose—that's another good thing about it.

"And now it's time for everybody to go to bed. You may take a swim before breakfast tomorrow, and you don't need to wear your swim trunks. Just jump out of bed when you hear the trumpet of the swan, strip off your pajamas, race to the dock, and dive in. I will be there ahead of you to do my celebrated backflip from the diving tower. It freshens me up for the hard day ahead. Good night, Louis! Good night, Sam! Good night, Applegate! Good night, all!"

The light was fading. The boys straggled off to their tents in the darkness. The senior counselors sat together on the porch and smoked one last pipe.

Sam crawled in under his blankets in Tent Three. Louis walked to a high, flat rock by the shore and stood there, waiting. When the lights were all out, he faced the camp, raised his horn to his mouth, and blew taps.

Day is done, gone the sun,
From the lake, from the hills,
From the sky;

All is well, safely rest,
God is nigh.

The last note seemed to linger on the still waters of the lake. From their beds, the boys heard the beautiful sound. They felt sleepy and serene and happy—all but Applegate Skinner, who didn't care for birds at bedtime. But even Applegate was soon asleep, along with the others in his tent. He was asleep, and he was snoring. People who dislike birds often snore.

A deep peace fell over Camp Kookooskoos.

XII
A Rescue

LOUIS LIKED TO SLEEP ON THE LAKE. AT night, after blowing taps, he would waddle down to the sandy beach by the dock. There he removed his slate, his chalk pencil, and his trumpet and hid them under a bush. Then he shoved off into the water. As soon as he was afloat, he would tuck his head under a wing. For a while he would doze and think about home and his parents. Then he would think about Serena—how beautiful she was and how much he loved her. Pretty soon he would be fast asleep. When daylight came, he would swim ashore and eat a light breakfast of water plants. Then he'd put on his things, climb onto the flat rock, and blow reveille. The boys, hearing the trumpet, would wake and rush to the dock to swim before breakfast.

After supper at night the campers would often play volleyball. Louis loved the game. He couldn't hop around as fast as the boys, but he could reach far out with his long neck and poke the ball into the air and over the net. It was very hard to get a ball past Louis—he could return almost any shot. When the boys chose sides at the start of the game, Louis was always the first to be chosen.

The boys loved camp life in Ontario. They learned how to handle a canoe. They learned to swim. Sam Beaver took them on nature walks and taught them to sit quietly on a log and observe wild creatures and birds. He showed them how to walk in the woods without making a lot of noise. Sam showed them where the kingfisher had his nest, in a hole in the bank by a stream. He showed them the partridge and her chicks. When the boys heard a soft *co-co-co-co*, Sam told them they were listening to the Sawwhet Owl, smallest of the owls, no bigger than a man's hand. Sometimes in the middle of the night the whole camp would wake to the scream of a wildcat. Nobody ever *saw* a wildcat during the entire summer, but his scream was heard at night.

One morning when Sam was playing tennis with Applegate Skinner, Sam heard a clanking noise. He looked behind him, and there, coming out of the woods, was a skunk. The skunk's head was stuck in a tin can; he couldn't see where he was going. He kept bumping into trees and rocks, and the can went clank, clank, clank.

"That skunk is in trouble," said Sam, laying down his racquet. "He's been to the dump, looking for food. He poked his head into that empty can, and now he can't get it out."

The word spread quickly through camp that a skunk had arrived. The boys came running to see the fun. Mr. Brickle warned them not to get too close—the skunk might squirt them with perfume. So the boys danced around, keeping their distance and holding their noses.

The big question was how to get the can off the skunk's head without getting squirted.

"He's going to need help," said Sam. "That skunk will starve to death if we don't get that can off."

All the boys had suggestions.

One boy said they should make a bow and arrow, tie a string to the arrow, and shoot the arrow at the can. Then, when they hit the can, they could pull the string and the can would come off the skunk's head. Nobody thought much of *that* suggestion—it sounded like too much work.

Another boy suggested that two boys climb a tree, and one boy could hang by his feet from the other boy's hands, and when the skunk walked under the tree, the boy who was hanging by his feet could reach down and pull the can off, and if the skunk squirted, the perfume wouldn't hit the boy because he would be hanging in the air. Nobody thought much of *that* suggestion. Mr. Brickle didn't like it at all. He said it was extremely impractical and furthermore he wouldn't permit it.

Another boy suggested that they get a block of wood, smear it with glue, and when the skunk knocked against it, the can would stick to the block of wood. Nobody thought much of *that* suggestion. Mr. Brickle said he didn't have any glue anyway.

While everybody was making suggestions, Sam Beaver walked quietly to his tent. He returned in a few minutes with a long pole and a piece of fishline. Sam tied one end of the fishline to the pole. Then he tied a slipknot in the other end of the line and formed a noose. Then he climbed to the roof of the porch and asked the other boys not to get too close to the skunk.

The skunk all this time was blundering around, blindly bumping into things. It was a pitiful sight.

Sam, holding his pole, waited patiently on the roof. He looked like a fisherman waiting for a bite. When the skunk wandered close to the building, Sam reached over, dangled the noose in front of the skunk, slipped the noose around the can, and gave a jerk. The noose tightened, and the can came off. As it did so, the skunk turned around and squirted—right at Mr. Brickle, who jumped back, stumbled, and fell. All the boys danced around, holding their noses. The skunk ran off into the woods. Mr. Brickle got up and dusted himself off. The air smelled strong of skunk. Mr. Brickle smelled, too.

"Congratulations, Sam!" said Mr. Brickle. "You have aided a wild creature and have given Camp Kookooskoos a delicious dash of wild perfume. I'm sure we'll all remember this malodorous event for a long time to come. I don't see how we can very well forget it."

"Ko-hoh!" cried Louis, lifting his trumpet. The lake echoed with the sound. The air was heavy with the rich, musky smell of skunk. The boys danced and danced, holding their noses. Some of them held their stomachs and pretended to throw up. Then Mr. Brickle announced it was time for the morning swim.

"A swim will clear the air," he said, as he walked away toward his cottage to change his clothes.

After lunch each day, the campers went to their tents for a rest period. Some of them read books. Some wrote letters home, telling their parents how bad the food was. Some just lay on their cots and talked. One afternoon during rest period, the boys in Applegate's tent began teasing him about his name.

"Applegate Skinner," said one boy. "Where did you get such a crazy name, Applegate?"

"My parents gave it to me," replied Applegate.

"I know what his name is," said another boy. "*Sour* Applegate. Sour Applegate Skinner." The boys howled at this and began chanting, "Sour Applegate, Sour Applegate, Sour Applegate."

"Quiet!" bellowed the tent leader.

"I don't think it's funny," said Applegate.

"His name isn't Sour Applegate," whispered another boy. "His name is *Wormy* Applegate. Wormy Applegate Skinner." This suggestion was greeted with screams of laughter.

"Quiet!" bellowed the tent leader. "I want quiet in this tent. Leave Applegate alone!"

"Leave *Rotten* Applegate alone!" whispered another boy. And some of the other boys had to pull their pillows over their heads so their snickering couldn't be heard.

Applegate was sore. When the rest period was over, he wandered down to the dock. He didn't like being made fun of, and he wanted to do something to get even. Without saying anything to anybody, he slid a canoe into the water and paddled out into the lake, heading for the opposite shore a mile away. No one noticed him.

Applegate had no business taking a canoe out alone. He had not passed his swimming test. He had not passed his canoe test. He was disobeying a camp rule. When he was a quarter of a mile from shore, in deep water, the wind grew stronger. The waves got higher. The canoe was hard to manage. Applegate got scared. Suddenly, a wave caught the canoe and spun it around. Applegate leaned hard on his paddle. His hand slipped, and he lost his balance. The canoe tipped over. Applegate found himself in the water. His clothes felt terribly soggy and heavy. His shoes dragged him down, and he could barely keep his head above water. Instead of hanging on to the canoe, he started swimming toward shore—which was a crazy thing to do. One wave hit him square in the face, and he got a mouthful of water.

"Help!" he screamed. "Help me! I'm drowning. It'll give the camp a bad name if I drown. Help! Help!"

Counselors sprinted to the waterfront. They jumped into canoes and rowboats and started for the drowning boy. One counselor kicked his moccasins off, dove in, and began swimming toward Applegate. Mr. Brickle raced to the dock, climbed to the diving tower, and directed the rescue operation, shouting through a megaphone.

"Hang on to the canoe, Applegate!" he shouted. "Don't leave the canoe!"

But Applegate had already left the canoe. He was all alone, thrashing about and wasting his strength. He felt sure he would soon go to the bottom and drown. He felt weak and scared. Water had got into his lungs. He couldn't last much longer.

The first boat to get away from the dock was rowed by Sam Beaver, and Sam was pulling hard at the oars, straining every muscle. But things didn't look good for Applegate. The boats were still a long way from the boy.

When the first cry of "Help" was heard in camp, Louis was coming around the corner of the main lodge. He spied Applegate immediately and responded to the call.

"I can't *fly* out there," thought Louis, "because my flight feathers have been falling out lately. But I can certainly make better time than those boats."

Dropping his slate and his chalk pencil and his trumpet, Louis splashed into the water and struck out, beating his wings and kicking with his great webbed feet. A swan, even in summer when he can't fly, can scoot across the water at high speed. Louis's powerful wings beat the air. His feet churned the waves, as though he were running on top of the water. In a moment he had passed all the boats. When he reached Applegate, he quickly dove, pointed his long neck between Applegate's legs, then came to the surface with Applegate sitting on his back.

Cheers came from the people on the shore and in the boats. Applegate clung to Louis's neck. He had been saved in the nick of time. Another minute and he would have gone to the bottom. Water would have filled his lungs. He would have been a goner.

"Thank God!" shouted Mr. Brickle through

his megaphone. "Great work, Louis! Camp Kookooskoos will never forget this day! The reputation of the camp has been saved. Our record for safety is still untarnished."

Louis didn't pay much attention to all the shouting. He swam very carefully over to Sam's boat, and Sam pulled Applegate into the boat and helped him into the stern seat.

"You looked pretty funny, riding a swan," Sam said. "And you're lucky to be alive. You're not supposed to go out alone in a canoe."

But Applegate was too scared and wet to say anything. He just sat and stared straight ahead, spitting water out of his mouth and breathing hard.

At supper that night, Mr. Brickle placed Louis at his right, in the place of honor. When the meal was over, he rose and made a speech.

"We all saw what happened on the lake today. Applegate Skinner broke a camp rule, took a canoe out alone, and upset. He was drowning when Louis the Swan, rapidly outdistancing all other campers, reached his side, held him up, and saved his life. Let us all give Louis a standing ovation!"

The boys and the counselors stood up. They cheered and clapped and beat on tin plates with spoons. Then they sat down. Louis looked embarrassed.

"And now, Applegate," said Mr. Brickle, "I hope the rescue has caused you to change your opinion of birds. The first day you were here in camp, you told us you didn't care for birds. How do you feel now?"

"I feel sick at my stomach," replied Applegate. "It makes you sick at your stomach to almost drown. My stomach still has a lot of lake water in it."

"Yes, but what about birds?" asked Mr. Brickle.

Applegate thought hard for a moment. "Well," he said, "I'm grateful to Louis for saving my life. But I still don't like birds."

"Really?" said Mr. Brickle. "That's quite remarkable. Even though a bird saved you from drowning, you don't care for birds? What have you got *against* birds?"

"Nothing," replied Applegate. "I have nothing against them. I just don't care for them."

"O.K.," said Mr. Brickle. "I guess we'll just have to leave it at that. But the camp is proud of Louis. He is our most distinguished counselor—a great trumpet player, a great bird, a powerful swimmer, and a fine friend. He deserves a medal. In fact, I intend to write a letter recommending that he be given the Lifesaving Medal."

Mr. Brickle did as he promised. He wrote a letter. A few days later, a man arrived from Washington with the Lifesaving Medal, and while all the campers watched, he hung the medal around Louis's neck, alongside the trumpet, the slate, and the chalk pencil.

It was a beautiful medal. Engraved on it were the words:

TO LOUIS THE SWAN, WHO,
WITH OUTSTANDING COURAGE AND
COMPLETE DISREGARD FOR HIS OWN SAFETY,
SAVED THE LIFE OF
APPLEGATE SKINNER

Louis took off his slate and wrote, "Thank you for this medal. It is a great honor."

But he thought to himself, "I'm beginning to get overloaded with stuff around my neck. I've got a trumpet, I've got a slate, I've got a chalk pencil; now I've got a medal. I'm beginning to look like a hippie. I hope I'll still be able to fly when my flight feathers grow in again."

That night when darkness came, Louis blew the most beautiful taps he had ever blown. The man who had brought the medal was listening and watching. He could hardly believe his ears and his eyes. When he returned to the city, he told people what he had seen and heard. Louis's fame was growing. His name was known. People all over were beginning to talk about the swan that could play a trumpet.

XIII

End of Summer

A TRUMPET HAS THREE LITTLE VALVES. They are for the fingers of the player.

By pushing them down in the right order, the player can produce all the notes of the musical scale. Louis had often examined these three little valves on his horn, but he had never been able to use them. He had three front toes on each foot, but, being a water bird, he had webbed feet. The webbing prevented him from using his three toes independently. Luckily, the valves on a trumpet are not needed for bugle calls because bugle calls are just combinations of *do*, *mi*, and *sol*, and a trumpeter can play *do*, *mi*, and *sol* without pressing down any of the valves.

"If I could just work those three valves with my three toes," he said to himself, "I could play all sorts of music, not just bugle calls. I could play jazz. I could play country-and-western. I could play rock. I could play the great music of Bach, Beethoven, Mozart, Sibelius, Gershwin, Irving Berlin, Brahms, everybody. I could really be a trumpet player, not just a camp bugler. I might even get a job with an orchestra." The thought filled him with ambition. Louis loved music, and besides, he was already casting about for ways of making money after camp was over.

Although he enjoyed life at Camp Kookooskoos, Louis often thought of his home on Upper Red Rock Lake in Montana. He thought about his parents, his brothers and sisters, and about Serena. He was terribly in love with Serena, and he often wondered what was happening to her. At night, he would look up at the stars and think about her. In the late evening, when the big bullfrogs were calling *trooonk* across the still lake, he would think of Serena. Sometimes he felt sad, lonely, and homesick. His music, however, was a comfort to him. He loved the sound of his own trumpet.

Summer passed all too quickly. On the last day of camp, Mr. Brickle called his counselors together and paid them what he owed them. Louis received one hundred dollars—the first money he had ever earned. He had no wallet and no pockets, so Mr. Brickle placed the money in a waterproof bag that had a drawstring. He hung this moneybag around Louis's neck, along with the trumpet, the slate, the chalk pencil, and the lifesaving medal.

Louis went to Sam Beaver's tent and found Sam packing his things. Louis took off his slate and pencil.

"I need another job," he wrote. "Where should I go?"

Sam sat down on his bed and thought for a while. Then he said, "Go to Boston. Maybe you can get a job with the Swan Boat."

Louis had never been to Boston, and he had no idea what the Swan Boat was, but he nodded his head. Then on his slate he wrote: "Do me a favor?"

"Sure," said Sam.

"Take a razor blade and slit the web on my right foot, so I can wiggle my toes." He held out his foot.

"Why do you want to wiggle your toes?" asked Sam.

"You'll see," wrote Louis. "I need my toes in my business."

Sam hesitated. Then he borrowed a razor blade from one of the older counselors. He made a long, neat cut between Louis's inner toe and middle toe. Then he made another cut between Louis's middle toe and outer toe.

"Does it hurt?"

Louis shook his head. He lifted his trumpet, placed his toes on the valves, and played *do, re, mi, fa, sol, la, ti, do. Do, ti, la, sol, fa, mi, re, do.* Ko-hoh!

Sam grinned. "The Swan Boat will hire *you,* all right," he said. "You're a real trumpeter now. But with your web cut, swimming will be harder for you. You will have a tendency to swim in circles, because your left foot will push better than your right foot."

"I can manage," wrote Louis. "Thanks very much for the surgery."

Next day, the campers left. The canoes had been hoisted onto racks in the boathouse, the float had been hauled onto the beach, the windows of the lodge had been boarded up against bears and squirrels, mattresses had been packed into zipper bags; everything was snug and ready for the long, silent winter. Of all the campers, only Louis stayed behind. His flight feathers were growing fast, but he still couldn't fly. He made up his mind he would remain at camp, all alone, until he was able to take to the air again, and then he would fly straight to Boston.

The lake was lonely without the boys, but Louis didn't mind being alone. For the next three weeks he took life easy. He grew his flight feathers, dreamed of Serena by day and by night, and practiced his trumpet. He had listened to music all summer—several of the boys had radios and record players—and now he practiced the songs on his trumpet. Every day he got better and better. One day, he composed a love song for Serena and wrote the words and music on his slate:

Oh, ever in the greening spring,
By bank and bough retiring,
For love shall I be sorrowing
And swans of my desiring.

He was really thinking of Serena, but he left her name out of it and kept it impersonal.

His plumage was beautiful now, and he felt great. On the twenty-first of September, he tried his wings. To his great relief, they lifted him. Louis rose into the air. The trumpet banged against the slate, the slate knocked against the money-bag, the life-saving medal clinked against the chalk pencil—but Louis was airborne again. He climbed and climbed and headed for Boston. It was wonderful to be in the sky again.

"Flying is a lot harder than it was before I acquired all these possessions," thought Louis.

"The best way to travel, really, is to travel light. On the other hand, I have to *have* these things. I've got to have the trumpet if I am to win Serena for my wife; I've got to carry this moneybag to hold the money to pay my father's debts; I've got to have the slate and pencil so I can communicate with people; and I ought to wear the medal because I really did save a life, and if I didn't wear it, people might think I was ungrateful."

On and on he flew, toward Boston, which is the capital of Massachusetts, and which is famous for its baked beans, its codfish, its tea parties, its Cabots, its Lowells, its Saltonstalls, and its Swan Boats.

XIV
Boston

LOUIS LIKED BOSTON THE MINUTE HE SAW it from the sky. Far beneath him was a river. Near the river was a park. In the park was a lake. In the lake was an island. On the shore was a dock. Tied to the dock was a boat shaped like a swan. The place looked ideal. There was even a very fine hotel nearby.

Louis circled twice, then glided down and splashed to a stop in the lake. Several ducks swam up to look him over. The park was called the Public Garden. Everybody in Boston knows about it and goes there to sit on benches in the sun, to stroll about, to feed the pigeons and the squirrels, and to ride the Swan Boat. A ride costs twenty-five cents for grown-ups, fifteen cents for children.

After a short rest and a bite to eat, Louis swam over to the dock and climbed out on the shore. The man who was taking tickets for the Swan Boat ride seemed surprised to see an enormous white swan wearing so many things around his neck.

"Hello!" said the Boatman.

Louis lifted his trumpet. "Ko-hoh!" he replied.

At the sound, every bird in the park looked up. The Boatman jumped. Boston residents as far as a mile away looked up and said, "What's *that*?" Nobody in Boston had ever heard a Trumpeter Swan. The sound made a big impression. People eating a late breakfast in the Ritz Hotel on Arlington Street looked up from their food. Waiters and bellboys said, "What's *that*?"

The man in charge of the Swan Boat was probably the most surprised man in Boston. He examined Louis's trumpet, his moneybag, his lifesaving medal, his slate, and his chalk pencil. Then he asked Louis what he wanted. Louis wrote on his slate: "Have trumpet. Need work."

"O.K.," said the Boatman. "You've got yourself a job. A boat leaves here in five minutes for a trip around the lake. Your job will be to swim in front of the boat, leading the way and blowing your horn."

"What salary do I get?" asked Louis on his slate.

"We'll settle that later, when we see how you make out," said the Boatman. "This is just a tryout."

Louis nodded. He arranged his things neatly around his neck, entered the water quietly, took up a position a few yards in front of the boat, and waited. He wondered what would make the boat go. He couldn't see any outboard motor, and there were no oars. In the forward part of the boat were benches for the passengers. In the stern was a structure that was shaped like a swan. It was hollow. Inside of it was a seat, like a bicycle seat. And there were two pedals inside, like the pedals of a bicycle.

When the passengers were all aboard, a young man appeared. He climbed onto the stern of the boat and sat down on the seat inside the hollow swan-shaped structure and began to push the pedals with his feet, as though he were riding a bike. A paddle wheel began to turn. The Boatman cast the lines off, and as the young man pedaled, the Swan Boat slowly moved out into the lake. Louis led the way, swimming with his left foot, holding his trumpet with his right foot.

"Ko-hoh!" said Louis's trumpet. The wild sound rang loud and clear and stirred everyone's blood.

Then, realizing that he should play something appropriate, Louis played a song he had heard the boys sing at camp.

Row, row, row your boat
Gently down the stream;
Merrily, merrily, merrily, merrily,
Life is but a dream.

The Swan Boat passengers were beside themselves with joy and excitement. A real live swan, playing a trumpet! Life was a dream, all right. What a lark! What fun! What pleasure!

"This is real groovy!" cried a boy in the front seat. "That bird is as good as Louis Armstrong, the famous trumpet player. I'm going to call him Louis."

When Louis heard this, he swam alongside the boat, took his chalk pencil in his mouth, and wrote: "That's actually my name."

"Hey, how about that?" yelled the boy. "This swan can *write*, too. Louis can write. Let's give him a cheer!"

The passengers cheered loudly. Louis swam ahead again, leading the way. Slowly and gracefully, the boat circled the island, while Louis played

"Gentle on My Mind" on his trumpet. It was a lovely September morning, hazy and warm. Trees were beginning to show their autumn colors. Louis played "Ol' Man River."

When the Swan Boat docked and the passengers got off, long lines of people were waiting to get aboard for the next ride. Business was booming. Another boat was being made ready, to accommodate the crowds. Everyone wanted to ride the Swan Boats behind a real live swan playing a trumpet. It was the biggest happening in Boston in a long time. People *like* strange events and queer happenings, and the Swan Boat, with Louis out front leading the way, suddenly became the most popular attraction in Boston.

"You're hired," said the Boatman, when Louis climbed out onto the bank. "With you playing the trumpet, I can double my business. I can triple it. I can quadruple it. I can quintuple it. I can . . . I can . . . I can *sextoople* it. Anyway, I'll give you a steady job."

Louis lifted his slate. "What salary?" he asked.

The Boatman gazed around at the crowds waiting to get aboard.

"A hundred dollars a week," he said. "I'll pay you

a hundred dollars every Saturday if you'll swim ahead of the boats and play your horn. Is it a deal?"

Louis nodded his head. The man seemed pleased but puzzled. "If it isn't too much to ask," said the Boatman, "would you mind telling me why you're so interested in money?"

"Everybody is," replied Louis on his slate.

"Yeah, I know," said the Boatman. "Everybody likes money. It's a crazy world. But, I mean, why would a *swan* need money? You can get your meals just by dipping down and pulling up tasty plants at the bottom of the lake. What do you need money for?"

Louis erased his slate. "I'm in debt," he wrote. And he thought about his poor father who had stolen the trumpet and about the poor storekeeper in Billings who had been robbed and whose store had been damaged. Louis knew he must go on earning money until he could pay off what he owed.

"O.K.," said the Boatman, addressing the crowd, "this swan says he's in debt. All aboard for the next ride!" And he began selling tickets. The Boatman owned several boats, all of them shaped like a swan. Pretty soon every boat was full and money was flowing in.

All day long, the Swan Boats circled the lake,

carrying their load of happy people, many of them children. Louis played his trumpet as he had never played it before. He liked the job. He loved to entertain people. And he loved music. The Boatman was just as pleased as he could be.

When the day was over and the boats had made their last trip, the Boatman walked over to Louis, who was standing on shore arranging his things.

"You've done great," said the Boatman. "You're a good swan. I wish I'd had you long ago. And now—where are you planning to spend the night?"

"Here on the lake," Louis wrote.

"Well, I don't know about that," said the man uneasily. "An awful lot of people are curious about you. They might make trouble for you. Bad boys might molest you. I don't trust the people who hang around this park at night. You might get kidnapped. I don't want to lose you. I think I'll take you across to the Ritz Carlton Hotel and get you a room for the night. It's clean, and the food is good. It would be safer. Then I can be sure you'll come to work in the morning."

Louis didn't think much of this idea, but he agreed to go. He thought, "Well, I've never *spent* a night in a hotel—maybe it would be an interesting experience." So he walked along with the Boatman. They left the park and crossed Arlington Street and entered the lobby of the Ritz. It had been a long, tiring day for Louis, but he felt relieved to know that he had a good job and that he could earn money in Boston as a musician.

XV

A Night at the Ritz

WHEN THE DESK CLERK AT THE RITZ Hotel saw the Boatman enter the lobby followed by an enormous snow-white swan with a black beak, the clerk didn't like it at all. The clerk was a carefully-dressed man—very neat, his hair nicely combed. The Boatman stepped boldly up to the desk.

"I'd like a single room for tonight for my friend here," said the Boatman.

The clerk shook his head.

"No birds," he said. "The Ritz doesn't take birds."

"You take celebrities, don't you?" asked the Boatman.

"Certainly," replied the clerk.

"You'd take Richard Burton and Elizabeth Taylor,

wouldn't you, if they wanted to spend the night?"

"Of course," replied the clerk.

"You'd take Queen Elizabeth, wouldn't you?"

"Of course."

"O.K.," said the Boatman. "My friend here is a celebrity. He is a famous musician. He created a sensation in the Public Garden this afternoon. You must have heard the commotion. He's a Trumpeter Swan and plays like the great Armstrong."

The clerk gazed suspiciously at Louis.

"Has he any luggage?" asked the clerk.

"Luggage?" cried the Boatman. "Take a *look* at him! Look at the stuff he's got with him!"

"Well, I don't know," said the clerk, staring at Louis's possessions—his trumpet, his moneybag, his slate, his chalk pencil, his lifesaving medal. "A bird is a bird. How do I know he hasn't got lice? Birds often have lice. The Ritz won't take anybody that has lice."

"Lice?" roared the Boatman. "Did you ever see a cleaner guest in your whole life? Look at him! He's immaculate."

At this, Louis held his slate up to the clerk. "No lice," he wrote.

The clerk stared in amazement. He was beginning to weaken.

"Well, I have to be careful," he said to the Boatman. "You say he's a celebrity. How do *I* know he's famous? You may be just kidding me about that."

Just then, three young girls entered the lobby. They were giggling and squealing. One of them pointed at Louis.

"There he is!" she screamed. "There he is! I'll get his autograph."

The girls rushed up to Louis. The first girl held out a pad and pencil.

"May I have your autograph?" she asked.

Louis took the pencil. Very gracefully, he wrote "Louis" on the pad.

More squeals, more giggles, and the girls rushed away. The clerk watched in silence.

"There!" said the Boatman. "Is he a celebrity or isn't he?"

The clerk hesitated. He was beginning to think he would have to give Louis a room.

At this point, Louis had an idea. He lifted his trumpet and began to play an old song called "There's a Small Hotel."

There's a small hotel with a wishing well.

His tone was beautiful. Guests passing through the lobby paused to listen. The clerk leaned his elbows on the desk and listened attentively. The man behind the newsstand looked up and listened. People sitting upstairs in the lounge put down their cocktails and listened. The bellboys stared and listened. For a few minutes, everything stopped in the lobby while Louis played. He charmed everyone who could hear. Chambermaids in the bedrooms paused in their work to listen to the trumpet. It was a moment of sheer magic. As the song came to an end, people who knew the words sang them softly.

When the steeple bell
Says "Good night, sleep well,"
We'll thank the small hotel, together.

"How about that?" asked the Boatman, grinning at the clerk. "Is this swan a musician or isn't he?"

"He plays a sweet trumpet," the clerk said. "But there is one more question that I hesitate to bring up. What about his personal habits? Will he mess the room all up? Actors are bad enough. Musicians are worse. I can't allow a large bird to occupy one of our beds—it might put us out of business. Other guests might complain."

"I sleep in the bathtub," Louis wrote on his slate. "Will not disturb bed."

The clerk shifted his weight from one foot to the other. "Who's going to pay the bill?" he asked.

"I am," replied the Boatman. "I'll be here early tomorrow morning when Louis checks out."

The clerk couldn't think of any more reasons for not letting the swan have a room.

"Very well," he said. "Sign the register, please!" He handed Louis a pen and a card.

Louis wrote:

LOUIS THE SWAN
UPPER RED ROCK LAKE
MONTANA

The clerk studied it. He seemed satisfied at last. He summoned a bellboy and handed him a key. "Take this gentleman to his room!" he ordered.

Louis removed his medal, his trumpet, his slate, his chalk pencil, and his moneybag and handed them to the bellboy. Together, they walked to the elevators. The Boatman said good-bye.

"Sleep well, Louis!" called the Boatman. "And be ready to come to work promptly in the morning!"

Louis nodded. The elevator door opened. "This way, sir!" said the bellboy. They entered the elevator and waited for the door to close. A rich smell of perfume filled the air. Louis stood very still. Then he felt himself rising. The elevator stopped at the seventh floor, and the bellboy led Louis to a room, unlocked the door, and ushered him in.

"Here you are, sir!" he said. "Would you like a window open?"

The bellboy put Louis's luggage down, snapped on a few lights, opened a window, and laid the room key on the dresser. Then he waited.

"I guess he wants a tip," thought Louis. So he went to his moneybag, loosened the drawstring, and took out a dollar.

"Thank you very much, sir," said the bellboy, taking the dollar. He went out and closed the door softly behind him. Louis was alone at last—alone in a room at the Ritz.

Louis had never spent a night alone in a hotel. First he walked round and around, switching lights on and off, examining everything. In the writing desk, he found a few sheets of letter paper that said:

Ritz Carlton
Boston

He felt mussy and dirty, so he went into the bathroom, climbed into the tub, pulled the shower curtain across, and took a shower bath. It felt good and reminded him of the water fights he used to have with his brothers and sisters. He was careful not to splash any water out of the tub. When he was finished, he stood for a while, admiring the bath mat and preening his feathers. Then he felt hungry.

On the wall of the bedroom, he found a button that said WAITER. Louis put his beak against the button and pressed hard. In a few minutes, there was a knock at the door and a waiter entered. He was nicely dressed and tried not to show surprise at finding a swan in the room.

"May I get you something?" he asked.

Louis picked up his chalk pencil. "Twelve watercress sandwiches, please," he wrote on the slate.

The waiter thought for a moment. "Are you expecting guests?" he asked.

Louis shook his head.

"And you want *twelve* watercress sandwiches?"

Louis nodded.

"Very good, sir," said the waiter. "Do you wish them with mayonnaise?"

Louis didn't know what mayonnaise tasted like, but he thought fast. He cleaned his slate and wrote: "One with. Eleven without."

The waiter bowed and left the room. Half an hour later he was back. He rolled a table into the room, placed a huge platter of watercress sandwiches on it, along with a plate, a knife, a fork, a spoon, salt and pepper, a glass of water, and a linen napkin, nicely folded. There was also a butter dish, with several pieces of butter covered with cracked ice. The waiter arranged everything carefully, then handed Louis a bill to sign. The bill said:

12 w/c sandwiches: $18.00

"Goodness!" thought Louis. "This is an expensive place. I hope the Boatman won't be mad when he sees this supper charge on the bill tomorrow morning."

He borrowed a pencil from the waiter and signed the bill: "Louis the Swan."

The waiter took the bill and stood there, waiting.

"I guess he wants a tip," thought Louis. So he opened his moneybag again, drew out two dollars, and handed it to the waiter, who thanked him, bowed again, and went away.

Because a swan has such a long neck, the table was just the right height for Louis. He didn't need a chair; he ate his supper standing up. He tried the sandwich that had mayonnaise on it and decided he didn't like mayonnaise. Then he carefully pulled each sandwich apart. All he really wanted was the watercress. He piled the slices of bread in two neat piles, scooped the watercress onto his plate, and had a nice supper. He did not touch the butter. When he was thirsty, instead of drinking from the glass of water, he walked into the bathroom, drew a basinful of cold water, and drank that. Then he took his napkin, wiped his beak, and pushed the table out of the way. He felt much better.

To be all alone in a hotel room gives a person a cozy feeling and a feeling of importance. Louis felt great. But soon he began feeling rather lonely, too. He thought of Sam Beaver. He thought of Camp Kookooskoos. He thought of his father and mother and sisters and brothers, back home in Montana. He thought of Serena, the swan he loved, and wondered how she was. The words of the song he had played in the lobby came back to him:

There's a small hotel
With a wishing well;
I wish that we were there, together.

How wonderful it would be, he thought, if Serena could be here at the Ritz to enjoy the hotel with him!

The waiter had left an evening paper on a table. Louis glanced at the front page. To his amazement, he saw a picture of himself on the lake in the Public Garden with the Swan Boat. A big headline said:

BOSTON GOES WILD OVER THE TRUMPET OF THE SWAN

The news story began:

> There's a new bird in town. His name is Louis. He is a Trumpeter Swan that really plays the trumpet. Incredible though it may seem, this rare and beautiful water bird has accepted employment with the Swan Boat management in the Public Garden and is entertaining boat riders with his smooth trumpet. Crowds gathered at the lake this afternoon after his arrival, and the sweet notes of his horn were heard in many parts of Boston. . . .

Louis read the article to the end and then tore it out of the paper. "Sam Beaver ought to know about this," he thought. From the writing desk in his room, Louis took a pen and a sheet of letter paper. This is what he wrote:

Dear Sam:

I am spending the night at the Ritz in fashionable surroundings. You were right about Boston—it is very pleasant. I was able to find work as soon as I arrived. I am associated with the Swan Boat at a salary of $100 a week. You may be interested in the enclosed clipping from today's paper. If all goes well, I'll soon have enough money to pay my father's debt to the music store, and then I will own the trumpet free and clear and will hope that by blowing it passionately I will be able to make a favorable impression on the young female I am in love with. Then everybody will be happy: my father's honor will be restored, the music shop in Billings will be repaid, and I can take a wife. I hope you are well. I miss you. A hotel room, even though it has every convenience, can be a lonely place.

Your friend,
Louis

Louis addressed an envelope to Sam, folded the letter, fitted the newspaper clipping in, and found a six-cent stamp in his moneybag. He sealed the envelope, pasted the stamp on, and dropped the letter in a mail chute outside the door of his room. "Now I'll go to sleep," he thought.

He went into the bathroom, used the toilet, then drew a full tub of cold water in the bathtub. He couldn't get Serena out of his mind. How wonderful it would be if only she were here! Before settling down for the night, he picked up his trumpet and played the song he had composed for her when he was in Ontario:

Oh, ever in the greening spring,
By bank and bough retiring,
For love shall I be sorrowing
And swans of my desiring.

He tried to play softly, but in a minute the phone rang in his room. Louis lifted the receiver and put it to his ear.

"I'm sorry, sir," a voice said, "but I'll have to ask you not to make so much noise. The Ritz does not allow its guests to play brass instruments in the bedrooms."

Louis hung up the phone and put his trumpet away. Then he turned out the lights, climbed into the tub, curved his long neck around to the right, rested his head on his back, tucked his bill under his wing, and lay there, floating on the water, his head cradled softly in his feathers. Soon he was asleep, dreaming of little lakes in the north in the springtime, dreaming of Serena, his true love.

XVI

Philadelphia

Louis worked all the last week of September for the Swan Boat man in the Boston Public Garden. He was a great success and was becoming famous. On Saturday, the Boatman paid him a hundred dollars in cash, which Louis placed carefully in his moneybag. The Boatman, after paying the first night's bill at the Ritz Carlton Hotel, decided to let Louis sleep on the lake instead of in the hotel, and this suited Louis better. He slept with the ducks and geese on the lake, floating gracefully on the surface of the water, his head tucked under his wing.

Louis took good care of his trumpet. He kept it polished, and once a week he cleaned the spit out of it. He learned new songs whenever he could, by listening to people's radios and by attending concerts. He was very good at remembering music he had heard. He was really a natural-born musician—or, in his case, a natural-*hatched* musician.

One song he liked was "Beautiful Dreamer, Wake Unto Me." Whenever he played it, he thought of Serena, and always, when he finished it, the passengers on the Swan Boat clapped loudly and cheered. Louis liked applause. It made him feel lighthearted and gay.

Sometimes, at the end of the afternoon, Louis played "Now the Day Is Over." He made it sound sweet and sad. One afternoon, when he was leading the last trip of the day, he played the "Cradle Song" by Brahms. The passengers sang the words:

Lullaby and good-night,
With roses bedight

A boy in the front seat of the boat pulled an air rifle from under his jacket and began shooting BB shots at Louis's trumpet. Whenever a shot hit the horn, it made a *pinging* sound. So the "Cradle Song" sounded something like this:

Lul-la-by (ping)
and good-night (ping)
With ros-es be-dight (ping)

The children on the boat roared with laughter when they heard this, but the grown-up passengers were angry. One of them seized the boy's rifle. Another went home that night and wrote a letter to *The Boston Globe* urging a stronger gun-control law.

On some afternoons, at the end of the day, people gathered on the shores of the lake to listen while Louis played taps. It was a peaceful scene, a memorable hour. The Swan Boat had never enjoyed such popularity or made such a lot of money for the owner. But Louis knew that the boats would not run all winter. In a few days, the boats would be hauled out for the season, to wait quietly for the arrival of spring.

One day, when Louis was waiting for the boat to take its passengers aboard, a Western Union messenger boy appeared on a bicycle.

"I have a telegram for the swan," he said.

The Boatman seemed surprised, but he took the telegram and handed it to Louis, who opened it promptly. It was from a man in Philadelphia. The message said:

CAN OFFER YOU FIVE HUNDRED DOLLARS A WEEK FOR NIGHTCLUB SPOT. TEN WEEK ENGAGEMENT. PLEASE REPLY.

(SIGNED) ABE ("LUCKY") LUCAS
HOTEL NEMO

Louis did some quick figuring. Five hundred dollars a week for ten weeks—that was five thousand dollars. Five thousand dollars would easily pay his father's debt to the music store.

He took his slate and wrote:

OFFER ACCEPTED. ARRIVE TOMORROW. MEET ME AT BIRD LAKE IN THE ZOO. SPLASHDOWN WILL BE AT FOUR FIFTY-TWO P.M. HOPE THIS WILL BE A CONVENIENT TIME FOR YOU.

Louis showed the message to the Western Union boy, who copied it on a telegraph blank.

"Send it collect!" wrote Louis.

The messenger nodded and rode away. Louis stepped back into the water, the boat's lines were cast off, and Louis led the way. He knew it was his last appearance with the Swan Boat, and he felt a little sad. It was a warm, quiet Sunday afternoon, the last Sunday in September. Louis played all his favorite tunes: "Lazy River," "Beautiful Dreamer," "Oh, Ever in the Greening Spring," "Now the Day Is Over," and then, as the boat neared the dock, he raised his trumpet and blew taps.

The last note echoed from the walls of the Ritz and lingered over the Public Garden. It was a sad farewell. For the people of Boston, it meant the end of summer. For the Boatman, it meant the end of the best week of business he had ever had. For Louis, it meant the end of another chapter in his adventurous life, out in the big world, trying to earn enough money to get his father and himself out of trouble. Louis slept peacefully that night, being very careful that his moneybag was safe. Next day he flew to Philadelphia to keep his appointment with Mr. Lucas, the man who had sent the telegram.

Louis had no trouble finding Philadelphia. Almost anybody can find Philadelphia who tries. Louis simply rose into the air with all his things around his neck, and when he was about a thousand feet high, he followed the railroad tracks to Providence, New London, New Haven, Bridgeport, Stamford, Cos Cob, Greenwich, Port Chester, Rye, Mamaroneck, New Rochelle, Pelham, Mount Vernon, and the Bronx. When he saw the Empire State Building, he veered off to the right, crossed the Hudson River, and followed the railroad tracks to Newark and Trenton and points south. At half past four, he reached the Schuylkill River. Just beyond, he spied the Philadelphia Zoo. Bird Lake looked very attractive from the air. It was crowded with waterfowl of all kinds—ducks and geese mostly. Louis thought he also saw two or three swans.

He circled, picked an open spot, and exactly at four fifty-two he splashed down. His trumpet banged against his slate, his slate knocked against his medal, his medal rapped against his chalk pencil, and his chalk pencil on its string wound itself around his moneybag. All in all, the splashdown caused quite a commotion. The ducks and geese were not expecting anything like this to happen—a big white Trumpeter Swan dropping down out of the sky, loaded with personal possessions.

Louis paid no attention to the other birds. He had a date to keep. He saw a man leaning on the wide railing in front of the Bird House. The man was dressed in a purple suit and wore a Tyrolean hat. His face looked shrewd and wise, as though he knew a great many things, many of them not worth knowing.

"That must be Abe 'Lucky' Lucas," thought Louis.

He swam quickly over.

"Ko-hoh!" he said, through his trumpet.

"My pleasure," replied Mr. Lucas. "You are right on time. The splashdown was sensational. Welcome to the Philadelphia Zoo, which crawls with rare mammals, birds, reptiles, amphibians, and fishes, including sharks, rays, and other fishlike vertebrates. Watch out for wild animals—this place is replete with them: snakes, zebras, monkeys, elephants, lions, tigers, wolves, foxes, bears, hippos, rhinos, woodchucks, skunks, hawks, and owls. I seldom come here; my work confines me to the throbbing heart of the city, among the money changers. I am under great pressure from my work. How was your trip from Boston?"

"Smooth," wrote Louis on his slate. "I made good time. What about my job?"

"A happy question," replied Mr. Lucas. "The job will start on October fifteenth. The contract has been finalized. Your place of employment is a nightclub of great renown, across the river—a place of high fashion and low prices, a jumpy joint. You will be called upon to make appearances each evening except Sunday, and play your trumpet for the happy customers. Once in a while you can join a jazz group: 'Louis the Swan on trumpet.' The pay is very good. My spirits are lifted by thinking about the pay. Wealth and happiness are around the corner for Louis the Swan and Lucky Lucas, the great of heart. My agent's fee is ten percent, a mere bagatelle."

"How do I get to the nightclub?" asked Louis, who only understood about half of what Mr. Lucas was saying.

"In a taxicab," replied Mr. Lucas. "Be at the North Entrance of the Zoo, Girard Avenue and Thirty-fourth Street, at nine o'clock on the evening of October fifteenth, a night that will live in memory. A cab will await your pleasure and will transport you to the club. The driver is a friend of mine. He, too, is under pressure from his work."

"Who's going to pay for the cab?" asked Louis on his slate.

"I am," replied Mr. Lucas. "Lucky Lucas, the generous of heart, pays for the cab for Louis the Swan. And by the way, I see that you are wearing a moneybag and that it is plump with moola. I suggest, from the kindness of my great heart, that you turn this moneybag over to me for safekeeping during your stay in Philadelphia, a place of many thieves and pickpockets."

"No, thank you," wrote Louis. "Will keep moneybag myself."

"Very well," said Mr. Lucas. "And now there is

one other small matter I must bring to your attention. Most of the birds that swim on this luxury lagoon have undergone surgery. Candor compels me to tell you that the tip of one wing is usually removed by the management—a painless operation, popular with zoos the world over. 'Pinioned' is the word for it, I believe. It detains the water bird and prevents him from leaving the narrow confines of this public park and rising into the air, because when one wing is shorter than the other, the balance of the bird is upset. His attempt to take off would be crowned with failure. In short, he can't fly. Sensing in advance the revulsion *you* would feel toward having the tip of one of your powerful wings removed, I approached the Man in Charge of Birds and laid before him a proposition. He has agreed not to clip your wing. It is arranged. He is a man of honor. Your freedom of movement is assured. You will not be pinioned. But in return for this so great favor on the part of the management of the Philadelphia Zoo, you are to give a free concert here at the lake every Sunday afternoon for the people of Philadelphia, the peasantry, who come here to refresh themselves. Is it a deal?"

"Yes," wrote Louis. "Will give Sunday concert."

"Good!" said Mr. Lucas. "Farewell for the nonce! Be at the North Entrance at nine! October fifteen. A cab will await you. Play well, Sweet Swan! You will be the finest thing that has happened to Philadelphia since the Constitutional Convention of 1787."

Louis didn't understand this, but he nodded good-bye to Mr. Lucas and swam off toward the island in the center of the lake. There he stepped ashore, straightened his things, preened his feathers, and rested. He was not sure he was going to like his new job. He was not sure he liked Mr. Lucas. But he needed money badly, and when you need money, you are willing to put up with difficulties and uncertainties. One *good thing* about the whole business was the Zoo itself. It seemed like an extremely nice place in spite of what he had heard about having your wing clipped. Louis had no intention of having a wing clipped.

"I'll sock anybody who tries *that* on me!" he said to himself.

He was pleased to see so many other water birds. There were many kinds of ducks and geese. In the distance, he saw three Trumpeter Swans. They were old residents of the Lake. Their names were

Curiosity, Felicity, and Apathy. Louis decided he would wait a day or two before making their acquaintance.

Bird Lake has a fence around it. When the night came for him to start work, Louis polished his trumpet, put on all his things, flew over the fence, and landed at the North Entrance. He was there promptly at nine. The taxicab was there, waiting, just as Mr. Lucas had promised. Louis got in and was driven away to his new job.

XVII
Serena

DURING THE NEXT TEN WEEKS, LOUIS GOT rich. He went every evening except Sundays to the nightclub and played his trumpet for the customers. He did not like the job at all. The place was big and crowded and noisy. Everyone seemed to be talking too loudly, eating too much, and drinking too much. Most birds like to go to sleep at sundown. They do not want to stay up half the night entertaining people. But Louis was a musician, and musicians can't choose their working hours—they must work when their employer wants them to.

Every Saturday night Louis collected his pay—five hundred dollars. Mr. Lucas was always on hand to receive his agent's fee of ten percent from Louis. After Louis had paid Mr. Lucas, he still had four hundred and fifty dollars left, and he would put this in his moneybag, hop into the waiting taxicab, and return to Bird Lake, arriving at around 3 A.M. His moneybag grew so stuffed with money, Louis was beginning to worry.

On Sunday afternoons, if the weather was good, crowds of people would gather on the shores of Bird Lake, and Louis would stand on the island in the middle of the lake and give a concert. This became a popular event in Philadelphia, where there isn't much going on on Sunday. Louis took the concert very seriously. By playing for the people, he was earning the right to remain free and not have a wing clipped.

He was always at his best on Sundays. Instead of playing jazz and rock and folk and country-and-western, he would play selections from the works of the great composers—Ludwig van Beethoven, Wolfgang Amadeus Mozart, and Johann Sebastian Bach—music he had learned by listening to records at Camp Kookooskoos. Louis also liked the music of George Gershwin and Stephen Foster. When he played "Summertime" from *Porgy and Bess*, the people of Philadelphia felt that it was the most thrilling music they had ever heard. Louis was considered so good on the trumpet he was invited to make a guest appearance with the Philadelphia Symphony Orchestra.

One day, about a week before Christmas, a great storm came up. The sky grew dark. The wind blew a howling gale. It made a whining noise. Windows rattled. Shutters came off their hinges. Old newspapers and candy wrappers were picked up by the wind and scattered like confetti. Many of the creatures in the Zoo became restless and uneasy. Over in the Elephant House, the elephants trumpeted in alarm. Lions roared and paced back and forth. The Great Black Cockatoo screamed. Keepers rushed here and there, shutting doors and windows and making everything secure against the awful force of the gale. The waters of Bird Lake were ruffled by the strong, mighty wind, and for a while the lake looked like a small ocean. Many of the water birds sought protection on the island.

Louis rode out the gale on the lake, in the lee of the island. He faced the wind and kept paddling with his feet, his eyes bright with wonder at the strength of the blast. Suddenly he saw an object in the sky. It was coming down out of the clouds. At first, he couldn't make out what it was.

"Maybe it's a flying saucer," he thought.

Then he realized that it was a large white bird, struggling desperately to come in against the wind. Its wings were beating rapidly. In a moment it splashed down and flopped ashore, where it lay sprawled out, almost as if it were dead. Louis stared and stared and stared. Then he looked again.

"It looks like a swan," he thought.

It *was* a swan.

"It looks like a *Trumpeter* Swan," he thought.

It *was* a Trumpeter Swan.

"My goodness," said Louis to himself, "it looks like Serena. It *is* Serena. She's here at last. My prayers have been answered!"

Louis was right. Serena, the swan of his desiring, had been caught by the fierce storm and blown all the way across America. When she looked down and saw Bird Lake, she ended her flight, almost dead from exhaustion.

Louis was tempted to rush right over. But then he thought, "No, that would be a mistake. She is in no condition at the moment to perceive the depth of my affection and the extent of my love. She is too pooped. I will wait. I will bide my time. I will give her a chance to recover. Then I will renew our acquaintance and make myself known."

Louis did not go to his job that night; the weather was too bad. All night, he stayed awake, keeping watch, at a slight distance from his beloved. When morning came, the wind subsided. The skies cleared. The lake grew calm. The storm was over. Serena stirred and woke. She was still exhausted, and very mussy. Louis stayed away from her.

"I'll just wait," he thought. "When in love, one must take risks. But I'm not going to risk everything with a bird who is too tired to see straight. I won't hurry, and I won't worry. Back home on Upper Red Rock Lake, I was without a voice; she ignored me because I could not tell her of my love. Now, thanks to my brave father, I have my trumpet. Through the power of music, I will impress her with the intensity of my desire and the strength of my devotion. She will hear me say ko-hoh. I'll tell her I love her in a language anybody can understand, the language of music. She will hear the trumpet of the swan, and she will be mine. At least, I *hope* she will."

Usually, if a strange bird appeared on Bird Lake, one of the keepers would report its arrival to the Head Man in Charge of Birds, whose office was in the Bird House. The Head Man would then give the order to have the new bird pinioned—have one of its wings clipped. But today, the keeper who usually tended the waterfowl was sick with the flu and had not come to work. Nobody noticed that a new Trumpeter Swan had arrived. Serena was being very quiet, anyway—she was not attracting any attention. There were now five Trumpeters on the lake. There were the original three captive swans, Curiosity, Felicity, and Apathy. There was, of course, Louis. And now there was the new arrival, Serena, still exhausted but beginning to revive.

Toward the end of the afternoon, Serena roused herself, looked at her surroundings, had a bite to eat, took a bath, then walked out of the water and stood for a long while preening her feathers. She felt distinctly better. And when her feathers were all smoothed out, she looked extremely beautiful—stately, serene, graceful, and very feminine.

Louis trembled when he saw how truly lovely she was. He was again tempted to swim over and say ko-hoh and see if she remembered him. But he had a better idea.

"There is no hurry," he thought. "She's not going to leave Philadelphia tonight. I will go to my job, and when I get back from work, I shall abide near her all through the night. Just at daylight, I'll awaken her with a song of love and desire. She will be drowsy; the sound of my trumpet will enter her sleepy brain and overcome her with emotion. My trumpet will be the first sound she hears. I will be irresistible. I will be the first thing she sees when she opens her eyes, and she will love me from that moment on."

Louis was well satisfied with his plan and began to make preparations. He swam ashore, removed his things, hid them under a bush, then returned to the water, where he fed and bathed. Then he fixed his feathers carefully. He wanted to look his best next morning, when the meeting was to take place. He drifted around for a while, thinking of all the songs he liked and trying to decide which one to play to wake Serena in the morning. He finally decided to play "Beautiful Dreamer, Wake Unto Me." He had always loved that song. It was sad and sweet.

"She will be a beautiful dreamer," thought Louis, "and she will wake unto me. The song fits the situation perfectly."

He was determined to play the song better than he had ever played it before. It was one of his best numbers. He really knew how to play it awfully well. Once, when he played it at one of his Sunday concerts, a music critic from a Philadelphia newspaper heard him, and next morning the paper said: "Some of his notes are like jewels held up to the light. The emotion he transmits is clean and pure and sustained." Louis had memorized that statement. He was proud of it.

Now he was anxious for morning to come, but he still had his job at the nightclub to go to. He knew the night would be long and that he wouldn't be able to sleep.

Louis swam ashore to pick up his things. When he looked under the bush, he received a terrible jolt: his medal was there, his slate and chalk pencil were there, his moneybag was there, but where was the trumpet? His trumpet was gone. Poor Louis! His heart almost stopped. "Oh, no!" he said to himself. "Oh, no!" Without his trumpet, his whole life would be ruined, all his plans for the future would collapse.

He was frantic with anger and fear and dismay. He dashed back into the water and looked up and down the lake. Far off, he saw a small Wood Duck that seemed to have something shiny in its mouth. It was the trumpet, all right! The duck was trying to play it. Louis was furious. He skimmed down the lake, going even faster than he had on the day he had saved Applegate from drowning. He swam straight for the duck, knocked him on the head with a swift blow from his wing, and grabbed the precious trumpet. The duck fainted. Louis wiped the horn, blew the spit out of it, and hung it around his neck, where it belonged.

Now he was ready. "Let the night come! Let the hours pass! Let morning come, when my beautiful dreamer wakes unto me!"

Night came at last. Nine o'clock came. Louis went off to work, riding in the cab. The Zoo quieted down. The visitors had all gone home. Many of the animals slept or snoozed. A few of them—the great cats, the raccoon, the armadillo, the ones that enjoy the nighttime—prowled and became restless. Bird Lake was clothed in darkness. Most of the waterfowl tucked their heads under their wings and slept. At one end of the lake, the three captive swans—Curiosity, Felicity, and Apathy—were already asleep. Near the island, Serena, the beautiful Serena, was fast asleep and dreaming. Her long white neck was folded neatly back; her head rested on soft feathers.

Louis got home from work at two in the morning.

He flew in over the low fence and splashed down near Serena, making as little noise as possible. He did not try to sleep. The night was fair and crisp, as nights often are just before Christmas. Clouds drifted across the sky in endless procession, partially hiding the stars. Louis watched the clouds, watched Serena as she slept, and waited for day to come—hour after hour after hour.

At last, a faint light showed in the east. Soon, creatures would be stirring, morning would be here.

"This is my moment," thought Louis. "The time has come for me to waken my true love."

He placed himself directly in front of Serena. Then he raised the trumpet to his mouth. He tilted his head: the horn pointed slightly upward toward the sky, where the first light was showing.

He began his song.

"Beautiful dreamer," he played, "wake unto me . . ."

The first three or four notes were played softly. Then as the song progressed, the sound increased; the light in the sky grew brighter.

Beautiful dreamer, wake unto me
Starlight and dewdrops are waiting for thee.

Each note was like a jewel held to the light. The sound of Louis's trumpet had never before been heard at this early dawn-hour in the Zoo, and the sound seemed to fill the whole world of buildings and animals and trees and shrubs and paths and dens and cages. Sleepy bears, dozing in their grotto, pricked up their ears. Foxes, hiding in their dens, listened to the sweet and dreamy sound of the horn blown at the coming of light. In the Lion House, the great cats heard. In the Monkey House, the old baboon listened in wonder to the song.

Beau—ti—ful dream—er, wake un—to me . . .

The hippo heard, and the seal in his tank. The gray wolf heard, and the yak in his cage. The badger, the coon, the Ring-tailed Coati, the skunk, the weasel, the otter, the llama, the dromedary, the White-tailed Deer—all heard, listened, pricked up their ears at the song. The kudu heard, and the rabbit. The beaver heard, and the snake, who *has* no ears. The wallaby, the possum, the anteater, the armadillo, the peafowl, the pigeon, the bowerbird, the cockatoo, the flamingo—all heard, all were aware that something out of the ordinary was happening.

Philadelphians, waking from sleep in bedrooms where the windows were open, heard the trumpet. Not one person who heard the song realized that this was the moment of triumph for a young swan who had a speech defect and had conquered it.

Louis was not thinking about his large, unseen audience of animals and people. His mind was not on bears and buffaloes and cassowaries and lizards and hawks and owls and people in bedrooms. His mind was on Serena, the swan of his choice, the beautiful dreamer. He played for her and for her alone.

At the first note from his trumpet, she woke. She raised her head and her neck straightened until her head was held high. What she saw filled her with astonishment. She gazed straight at Louis. At first, she could hardly remember where she was. Directly in front of her, she saw a handsome young male swan, a cob of noble proportions. Held against his mouth was a strange instrument—something she had never seen before. And from this strange instrument came sounds that made her tremble with joy and with love. As the song went on, as the light grew stronger, she fell hopelessly in love with this bold trumpeter who had awakened her from her dreams. The dreams of night were gone. New dreams of day were upon her.

She knew that she was full of sensations she had never had before—feelings of delight and ecstasy and wonder.

She had never seen a finer-looking young cob. She had certainly never seen *any* swan with so many personal possessions around his neck. And she had never been so thrilled by a sound before in her whole life.

"Oh!" she thought. "Oh, oh, oh, oh!"

The song ended. Louis lowered his trumpet and bowed solemnly to Serena. Then he raised his horn again.

"Ko-hoh!" he said.

"Ko-hoh!" replied Serena.

"Ko-hoh, ko-hoh!" said Louis through his trumpet.

"Ko-hoh, ko-hoh!" replied Serena.

Each felt drawn to the other by a mysterious bond of affection.

Louis swam once rapidly around Serena.

Then Serena swam once rapidly around Louis. This seemed to amuse them.

Louis dipped his neck and pumped it back and forth.

Serena dipped her neck and pumped it back and forth.

Louis splashed a little water into the air. Serena

splashed a little water into the air. It was like a game. It was love at long last for Louis; it was love at first sight for Serena.

Then Louis decided to show off. "I'll play her my own composition," he thought. "The one I made up for her last summer at camp." Again he raised his trumpet.

Oh, ever in the greening spring,
By bank and bough retiring,
For love shall I be sorrowing
And swans of my desiring.

The notes were clear and pure. They filled the Zoo with beauty. If Serena had been in any doubt before, she no longer was. She succumbed completely to this charmer, this handsome musician, this rich and talented cob.

Louis knew that his plan had succeeded. His beautiful dreamer had waked, and she had waked unto him. Never again would they be parted. All the rest of their lives they would be together. Thoughts of small quiet lakes in the woods, where canebrakes grew and blackbirds sang, filled Louis's mind. Thoughts of springtime and nesting and little cygnets. Oh, ever in the greening spring!

Louis had been told once by his father what happened to deep-sea divers when they go far, far down into the ocean. At great depths, where the pressure is great and the watery world is strange and mysterious, divers sometimes experience what they call the "rapture of the deep." They feel so completely peaceful and enchanted, they never want to return to the surface. Louis's father had warned him about this. "Always remember, when you dive deep," he had said, "that this feeling of rapture can lead you to your death. No matter how wonderful you feel down there, *don't ever forget to return to the surface*, where you can breathe again!"

Looking at Serena, Louis thought to himself, "I think love is like the rapture of the deep. I feel so good I just want to stay right where I am. I'm experiencing rapture of the deep even though I'm right on top of the water. I have never felt so good, so peaceful, so excited, so happy, so ambitious, so desirous. If love is like this on a cold day in December in the Philadelphia Zoo, imagine what it's going to be like in spring on a remote lake in Canada!"

These were Louis's secret thoughts. He was the happiest bird alive. He was a real Trumpeter Swan at last. His defect of being without a voice had at last been overcome. He felt very grateful to his father.

Cautiously, he placed his head across Serena's long beautiful white neck. It seemed a very daring thing to do, but she seemed to like it. Then he backed away. Serena swam toward him. Cautiously, she placed *her* head across *his* neck. It rested there for a moment; then she swam away.

"What a daring thing!" she thought. "But he seems to like it. How pleasing to know that I have found an acceptable mate—a cob I can love and respect, a cob that appears to be not only musical but also quite wealthy. Look at all those *things*!" said Serena to herself. Her eyes feasted on the trumpet, the slate, the chalk pencil, the moneybag, the lifesaving medal.

"What a gay cob!" she thought. "What a dressy fellow!"

They swam off together toward the other end of the lake, where they could be alone. Then Louis, who was short on sleep, dozed off, while Serena ate her breakfast and fixed herself up.

XVIII
Freedom

THE NEWS OF SERENA'S ARRIVAL ON BIRD Lake had finally reached the Head Man in Charge of Birds. He went out to look at her and was delighted. Then he gave an order to one of his keepers.

"See to it that she is pinioned this morning—right away, before she flies off and leaves us. That swan is a valuable bird. Make sure she doesn't get away!"

Louis was just waking from his nap when he saw two keepers approaching Serena, who was standing on the shore near the ornamental fence. One keeper carried a large net with a long handle. The other carried surgical instruments. They were sneaking up on Serena from behind, very slowly and quietly.

Louis knew right away what they were up to. He

grew hot with rage. If those men succeeded in catching Serena and cutting a wing tip, all his plans would go wrong—she could never fly away to a lonely lake with him; she would have to remain in Philadelphia the rest of her life, a horrible fate.

"This is my moment," thought Louis. "Nobody is going to clip my Love's wing while *I'm* around."

He hustled over to the island and stripped for action. He chucked his trumpet and all his other stuff under a willow tree. Then he returned to the water and waited for the right time to attack.

The keeper holding the net was crawling quietly up on Serena from the rear. She did not notice him—she was just standing there, dreaming of Louis. Slowly, slowly the keeper raised his net. As he did so, Louis went into action. Lowering his long, powerful neck until it pointed straight out in front of him like a lance, he streaked across the water, straight at the keeper, his wings beating the air, his feet beating the water. In a flash, he reached the scene and drove his strong bill straight into the seat of the man's pants. It was a well-aimed jab. The keeper doubled up in pain and dropped the net. The other keeper tried to grab Serena by her throat. Louis beat him over the head with his wings, striking terrific blows and knocking the poor fellow off his feet. Surgical instruments bounced into the air. The net fell into the water. One keeper groaned and held his hand on his behind, where he had been stabbed. The other keeper lay on the ground, almost knocked out.

Serena slipped quickly into the water and glided gracefully away. Louis followed. He motioned for her to stay on the lake. Then he raced back to the island, grabbed his trumpet, his slate, his chalk pencil, his medal, and his moneybag, flew over the balustrade, and walked boldly into the Bird House. He was still mad. He went straight to the office of the Head Man in Charge of Birds. He rapped on the door.

"Come in!" said a voice.

Louis entered. The Head Man was seated at his desk.

"Hello, Louis!" he said.

"Ko-hoh!" replied Louis through his trumpet.

"What's on your mind?" asked the man.

Louis placed his trumpet on the floor and took his slate and chalk pencil from his neck. "I'm in love," he wrote.

The Head Man leaned back in his chair and put his hands behind his head. His face had a faraway look. He gazed out of the window for a moment in silence.

"Well," he said, "it's natural that you're in love. You're young. You're talented. In a couple of months, spring will be here. All birds fall in love in springtime. I suppose you're in love with one of my young swans."

"Serena," wrote Louis. "She arrived the day before yesterday. I used to know her slightly, back in Montana. She loves me, too."

"That doesn't surprise me," said the Head Man. "You're a very unusual young cob. Any young female swan would fall for you. You're a great trumpeter—one of the best. I'm delighted to hear about this love affair, Louis. You and your bride can stay right here on Bird Lake and raise your family in comfort and safety, in the oldest zoo in the United States."

Louis shook his head.

"I have other plans," he wrote. Then he set his slate down and raised his trumpet. "They say that falling in love is wonderful . . ." It was an old song by Irving Berlin. The room was filled with the sound of love. The Head Man had a dreamy look in his eyes.

Louis set his horn down and took up his slate

again. "I am taking Serena away with me in a day or two," he wrote.

"Oh, no you're not!" said the Head Man firmly. "Serena now belongs to the Zoo. She is the property of the people of Philadelphia. She came here because of an act of God."

"It wasn't an act of God," wrote Louis. "It was a high wind."

"Well, anyway," said the Head Man, "she's *my* swan."

"No, she's mine," wrote Louis. "She's mine by reason of the power of love—the greatest force on earth."

The Head Man became thoughtful. "You can't take Serena from the Zoo. She will never fly again. My keepers clipped one of her wings a few minutes ago."

"They tried to," wrote Louis, "but I beat them up."

The Head Man looked surprised. "Was it a good fight?"

"It was a fair fight," replied Louis. "They were sneaking up on her from behind, so I sneaked up on *them* from behind. They hardly knew what hit them."

The Head Man chuckled. "I wish I'd seen it," he said. "But look here, Louis, you've got to realize the position I'm in. I have a duty to the people of Philadelphia. Within the last couple of months, I've acquired *two* rare birds by accident—you and Serena. Two Trumpeter Swans! One arrived here blown by a gale, the other to keep a nightclub engagement. The whole business is most unusual for a zoo. I have my responsibility to the public. It is my duty as Head Man in Charge of Birds to see that Serena stays. You yourself, of course, are free to leave when you want to, because Mr. Lucas insisted that you remain free when we arranged for your Sunday concerts. But in Serena's case . . . well, Louis, she's got to have her left wing tip amputated. The Zoo can't afford to lose a young, beautiful, valuable Trumpeter Swan just because *you* happen to be in love. Besides, I think you're making a great mistake. If you and Serena stay here, you'll be safe. You'll have no enemies. You'll have no worries about your children. No fox, no otter, no coyote will ever attack you with intent to kill. You'll never go hungry. You'll never get shot. You'll never die of lead poisoning from eating the shotgun pellets that are on the bottom of all natural lakes and ponds. Your cygnets will be hatched each spring and will live a long life in perfect ease and comfort.

What more can a young cob ask?"

"Freedom," replied Louis on his slate. "Safety is all well and good: I prefer freedom." With that, he picked up his trumpet and played "Button up your overcoat, when the wind blows free . . ."

The Head Man smiled. He knew just what Louis meant. For a while the two remained silent. Louis put his trumpet aside. Then he wrote: "I ask two favors. First, put off the operation on Serena until after Christmas—I'll guarantee she won't try to escape. Second, let me send a telegram."

"O.K., Louis," replied the Head Man. And he handed Louis a sheet of paper and a pencil. Louis wrote out a telegram to Sam Beaver. It said:

AM IN THE PHILADELPHIA ZOO. THIS IS AN EMERGENCY. COME AT ONCE. I WILL PAY YOUR PLANE FARE. AM NOW WEALTHY.

(Signed) LOUIS

He handed the telegram to the Head Man along with four dollars from his moneybag. The Head Man was astounded. In all his days at the Zoo, this was the first time one of his birds had asked him to send a telegram. And of course he didn't know who Sam Beaver was. But he sent the wire and ordered his keepers to let Serena alone for a few days—which they were glad to do.

Louis thanked him and left. He returned to Serena, and they spent the day happily together, bathing, swimming, eating, drinking, and showing each other in a thousand small ways how much they loved each other.

Sam arrived at the Zoo on the day after Christmas. He was equipped as though he were going into the woods. Under one arm was a sleeping bag, neatly rolled. On his back was a rucksack containing his toothbrush, his comb, a clean shirt, a hand ax, a pocket compass, his notebook, a pencil, and some food. In his belt was a hunting knife. Sam was fourteen now and big for his age. He had never seen a large zoo. He and Louis were overjoyed to see each other again.

Louis introduced Sam to Serena. Then he opened his moneybag and showed Sam his earnings: hundred-dollar bills, fifty-dollar bills, twenty-dollar bills, tens, fives, ones, and some silver coins—a great pile.

"Goodness!" thought Sam. "I hope she's not marrying him for his money."

Louis took his slate and told Sam about the fight with the keepers and about how the Head Man wanted to keep Serena captive by clipping the tip of one wing. He told Sam it would ruin his life if Serena were to lose the power to fly. He explained that as soon as his father's debts were paid and the trumpet honestly belonged to him, he and Serena intended to leave civilization and return to a wild life. "The sky," he wrote on his slate, "is my living room. The woods are my parlor. The lonely lake is my bath. I can't remain behind a fence all my life. Neither can Serena—she's not built that way. Somehow or other we must persuade the Head Man to let Serena go."

Sam stretched out on the shore of Bird Lake and clasped his hands behind his head. He looked up at the great wide sky. It was a clear blue, with small white clouds floating slowly across. Sam knew how Louis felt about freedom. For a long time he lay there, thinking. Ducks and geese swam slowly by, back and forth, an endless procession of captive birds. They seemed happy and well. Curiosity, Felicity, and Apathy—the three Trumpeters—swam by and peered at the strange boy lying on the ground. Finally Sam sat up.

"Listen, Louis," he said. "How's this for an idea?

You and Serena intend to raise a family every year, don't you?"

"Certainly," replied Louis on his slate.

"O.K.," said Sam. "In every family of cygnets, there is always one that needs special care and protection. Bird Lake would be a perfect place for this one little swan that needs extra security. This is a beautiful lake, Louis. This is a great zoo. If I can persuade the Head Man to let Serena remain free, would you be willing to donate one of your cygnets, now and then, if the Zoo needs another swan for the lake? If you agree, I'll go right in and see the Head Man about the matter."

It was now Louis's turn to think and think. After five minutes, he picked up his slate.

"Very well," he wrote. "It's a deal."

Then he picked up his trumpet. "Oh, ever in the greening spring," he played, "By bank and bough retiring . . ."

The waterfowl stopped swimming and listened. The keepers stopped what they were doing and listened. Sam listened. The Head Man in his office in the Bird House laid down his pencil, leaned back in his chair, and listened. The sound of Louis's horn was in the air, and the whole world seemed better and brighter and wilder and freer and happier and dreamier.

"That's a good tune," said Sam. "What is it?"

"Oh, just something I made up myself," wrote Louis on his slate.

XIX

A Talk About Money

IN ALMOST EVERYONE'S LIFE THERE IS ONE event that changes the whole course of his existence. The day Sam Beaver visited the Philadelphia Zoo was the turning point in his life. Up until that day, he had not been able to decide what he wanted to be when he grew up. The minute he saw the Zoo, all his doubts vanished. He knew he wanted to work in a zoo. Sam loved every living thing, and a zoo is a great storehouse of living things—it has just about every creature that creeps or crawls or jumps or runs or flies or hides.

Sam was eager to see them all. But he had Louis's problem to solve first. He must save Serena from captivity. So he picked up his rucksack and his sleeping bag and walked into the Bird House and entered the office. He walked tall and straight, as though he were on a forest trail. The Head Man liked Sam's appearance and noticed that he looked a little like an Indian.

"So you're Sam Beaver," said the Head Man, as Sam advanced on him.

"Why did you come here?" asked the Head Man.

"To defend freedom," replied Sam. "I heard you intended to clip the wing of a swan. I'm here to ask you not to do it."

Sam sat down, and they talked for a whole hour. Sam assured the Head Man that Louis was an old friend. He told about discovering the swan's nest almost three years ago in Canada, about how Louis came into the world lacking a voice, about Louis's attending school in Montana and learning to read and write, about the theft of the trumpet by Louis's father, the old cob, and about Camp Kookooskoos and the Swan Boat in Boston.

The Head Man listened with great attention, but he wasn't sure he believed a word of this strange tale.

Then Sam explained his proposal for allowing Serena to go free instead of making a captive bird out of her. He said he thought it would be a good arrangement for the Zoo, because any time they wanted a young Trumpeter Swan, Louis would give them one of his cygnets. The Head Man was fascinated.

"You mean to say you came all the way to Philadelphia to help a bird?"

"Yes, sir," replied Sam. "I would go anywhere to help a bird. Besides, Louis is special. He's an old friend. We went to the same school. You've got to admit he's quite a bird."

"He sure is," said the Head Man. "His Sunday afternoon concerts have been the biggest attraction the Zoo has ever had. We had a gorilla once named Bamboo—he's dead now. Bamboo was great, but Louis draws even more of a crowd than Bamboo did. We have sea lions that draw big crowds, but nothing to compare with Louis when he plays that horn on Sunday afternoons. People go crazy. And music is good for the animals, too—it soothes them, and they forget the cares of the day. I'm going to miss Louis when he's gone. The whole Zoo will miss him terribly. I wish he'd stay and keep his bride right here—it would be just great."

"Louis would pine away in captivity. He would die," replied Sam. "He needs wild places—little ponds, swamps, cattails, Red-winged Blackbirds in the spring, the chorus of the frogs, the cry of the loon at night. Louis is following a dream. We must all follow a dream. Please let Serena go, sir! Please don't clip her wing!"

The Head Man closed his eyes. He was thinking of little lakes deep in the woods, of the color of bulrushes, of the sounds of night and the chorus of frogs. He was thinking of swans' nests, and eggs, and the hatching of eggs, and the cygnets following their father in single file. He was thinking of dreams he had had as a young man.

"All right," he said, suddenly. "Serena can go. We will not clip her wing. But how can I be sure that Louis will bring me a young Trumpeter Swan when I need one? How do I know he's honest?"

"He's an honorable bird," said Sam. "If he weren't honest and true to his word, he wouldn't have bothered to go out and earn a lot of money to pay the storekeeper back for the trumpet his father swiped."

"How much money has Louis got, anyway?" asked the Head Man.

"He's got four thousand six hundred and ninety-one dollars and sixty-five cents," said Sam. "We just counted it a few minutes ago. He received one hundred dollars from Camp Kookooskoos for playing bugle calls, and all he spent was sixty cents for postage stamps. So he arrived in Boston with ninety-nine dollars and forty cents. Then the Swan Boat man paid him a hundred dollars for one week's work, but he spent three dollars in tips at the hotel where he spent a night. So he had a hundred and ninety-six dollars and forty cents when he got to Philadelphia. The nightclub paid him five hundred dollars a week for ten weeks, which came to five thousand dollars, but he had to pay his agent ten percent of the five thousand dollars, and he also spent seventy-five cents for some new chalk pencils and four dollars to send the telegram to me. So that makes a total of four thousand six hundred and ninety-one dollars and sixty-five cents. It's a lot of money for a bird."

"It sure is," said the Head Man. "It sure is."

"But he is going to pay my airplane fare from Montana to Philadelphia and back again. That will bring the total down to four thousand four hundred and twenty dollars and seventy-eight cents."

The Head Man looked staggered by these figures.

"It's *still* a lot of money for a bird," he said. "What's he going to do with it all?"

"He will give it to his father, the old cob."

"And what's *he* going to do with it?"

"He will fly back to the music store in Billings and give it to the owner, to pay for the stolen trumpet."

"Give *all* of it?"

"Yes."

"But a trumpet isn't worth four thousand four hundred and twenty dollars and seventy-eight cents."

"I know," said Sam. "But there was some damage to the store itself. The old cob was going like the dickens when he crashed through the plate-glass window. He shook things up pretty badly."

"Yes," said the Head Man. "But it *still* wouldn't take all that money to make things right."

"I guess not," said Sam. "But Louis has no use for money anymore, so he's going to turn it all over to the owner of the music store."

The subject of money seemed to interest the Head Man greatly. He thought how pleasant it would be not to have any more use for money. He leaned back in his chair. He found it hard to believe that one of his swans had been able to save more than four thousand dollars and that the money was right out there, hanging around his neck in a moneybag.

"When it comes to money," he said, "birds have it easier than men do. When a bird earns some money, it's almost all clear profit. A bird doesn't have to go to a supermarket and buy a dozen eggs and a pound of butter and two rolls of paper towels and a TV dinner and a can of Ajax and a can of tomato juice and a pound and a half of ground round steak and a can of sliced peaches and two quarts of fat-free milk and a bottle of stuffed olives. A bird doesn't have to pay rent on a house, or interest on a mortgage. A bird doesn't insure its life with an insurance company and then have to pay premiums on the policy. A bird doesn't own a car and buy gas and oil and pay for repairs on the car and take the car to a car wash and pay to get it washed. Animals and birds are lucky. They don't keep acquiring things, the way men do. You can teach a monkey to drive a motorcycle, but I have never known a monkey to go out and *buy* a motorcycle."

"That's right," replied Sam. "But some animals do like to acquire things, even though they don't pay anything for them."

"Such as?" asked the Head Man.

"A rat," said Sam. "A rat will fix up a home for himself, but then he'll bring home all sorts of little objects—trinkets and stuff. Anything he can find that catches his eye."

"You're right," said the Head Man. "You're absolutely right, Sam. You seem to know quite a lot about animals."

"I like animals," said Sam. "I love to watch them."

"Then come with me and we'll explore the Zoo," said the Head Man, getting up from his chair. "I don't feel like working anymore today. I'll show you the Zoo." And away they went, the two of them.

That night Sam slept in the Head Man's office, by special permission. He unrolled his sleeping bag on the floor and crawled in. The plane taking him back home would leave in the morning. Sam's head was full of everything he had seen in the Zoo. And before he turned out the light he took his notebook out of his rucksack and wrote a poem. This is what he wrote:

SAM BEAVER'S POEM

Of all the places on land and sea,
Philadelphia's zoo is the place for me.
There's plenty to eat and a lot to do,
There's a Frigate Bird and a tiny Shrew;
There's a Vesper Rat and a Two-toed Sloth,
And it's fair to say that I like them both.
There's a Canada Goose and a Polar Bear
And things that come from Everywhere.
There are lots of things that you've never seen
Like the Kinkajou and the Wolverine.
You really have to go to the zoo
To see a newborn Wallaroo
Or a Fallow Deer or a White-tailed Gnu.
There are wondrous birds on a beautiful lake,
There's a Timber Wolf and a Hognose Snake.

There are animals with great appeal,
Like the Hummingbird and the Harbor Seal.
There are pony rides, there are birds of prey,
And something happening every day.
There are Wolves and Foxes, Hawks and Owls,
And a great big pit where the Lion prowls.
There are quiet pools and pleasant cages,
Where Reptiles lie and the Tiger rages.
The houses are clean, the keepers are kind,
And one Baboon has a pink behind.
The entire aim of a well-kept zoo
Is to bring the animal world to You.

(Signed) Sam Beaver

Sam left the poem on the Head Man's desk.

Early the next morning, long before the Zoo people came to work, Sam left Philadelphia by plane. Louis and Serena went along with him to the airport. They wanted to wave good-bye. They also planned to leave Philadelphia, right then and there, and fly back to Montana. When the airport officials saw two big white birds out on the airstrip, they raised a terrible fuss. The men in the control tower sent warning messages to the pilots of incoming planes. Members of the ground crew came piling out of buildings and rushed toward Louis and Serena to chase them away. Sam was sitting by a window inside his plane, ready for takeoff, and he saw the whole thing.

Louis grabbed his trumpet.

"Off we go," he played, "into the wild blue yonder!" The notes carried across the airport and startled everyone. "Ko-hoh! Ko-hoh!" called Louis. He put his trumpet away and started racing down the airstrip, with Serena racing after him. Just then, Sam's plane started into the wind for the takeoff. The two swans flew alongside. They were in the air before the plane was, and flying fast. Sam waved from the window. Louis's lifesaving medal gleamed in the morning sun. The plane rose and started to climb. Louis and Serena climbed fast, too.

"Good-bye, Philadelphia!" thought Louis. "Good-bye, Bird Lake! Good-bye, nightclub!"

The plane, with its greater speed, gained on the swans. They began to drop behind. For a little while they headed west, following the plane. Then Louis motioned to Serena that he was going to change course. He banked to the left and swung toward the south.

"We'll go home by the southern route and take our time about it," he said to himself.

And that's what they did. They flew south across

Maryland and Virginia. They flew south across the Carolinas. They spent a night in Yemassee and saw huge oak trees with moss hanging from their branches. They visited the great swamps of Georgia and saw the alligator and listened to the mockingbird. They flew across Florida and spent a few days in a bayou where doves moaned in the cedars and little lizards crawled in the sun. They turned west into Louisiana. Then they turned north toward their home in Upper Red Rock Lake.

What a triumphant return it would be! When he left Montana, Louis had been penniless. Now he was rich. When he left, he had been unknown. Now he was famous. When he left, he had been alone in the world. Now he had his bride by his side—the swan that he loved. His medal was around his neck, his precious trumpet dangled in the breeze, his hard-earned money was in the bag. He had accomplished what he had set out to do. All in a few short months!

Freedom felt so wonderful! Love felt so good!

XX
Billings

ON A BRIGHT CLEAR DAY IN JANUARY, Louis and Serena came home to the Red Rock Lakes. From among the thousands of waterfowl, they quickly found the members of their own families—their fathers and mothers and sisters and brothers. It was a noisy homecoming. Everybody wanted to say hello at once. Ko-hoh, ko-hoh, ko-hoh! The wanderers were home at last.

Louis's father, the old cob, made a graceful speech—rather long, but sincere.

Louis raised his trumpet and played "There's no place like home. Home, home sweet home!" There was a great deal of gossip among the waterfowl about Louis's having persuaded Serena to be his wife. Everybody congratulated the happy couple. And all the brothers and sisters of Louis and Serena gathered around and looked at Louis's possessions. They were much impressed by his worldly goods. They liked the lifesaving medal, they loved the sound of the trumpet, and they were eager to see the money in the moneybag. But Louis did not open the bag. Instead, he took his father and mother to one side. They all three stepped out on shore, where Louis slipped the moneybag off his neck and, with a bow, handed it to the old cob. Four thousand four hundred and twenty dollars and seventy-eight cents.

Then Louis took his slate and wrote a note to the owner of the music store in Billings so his father would have something to show him when he got there. The note said:

To the Storekeeper of Billings:
Enclosed please find $4,420.78.
It will pay you for the trumpet
and the damage to the store.
Sorry about the inconvenience
this has caused you.

The old cob was not able to count money, and he was not able to read, but he took the moneybag and the slate and hung them around his neck. He felt sure he could now pay his debt for the stolen trumpet.

"I shall go," he said to his wife. "I shall redeem my honor. I shall return to Billings, the scene of my crime—a great city, teeming with life—"

"We've heard that before," remarked his wife. "Just take the money and the note and beat it for Billings as fast as you can go. And when you get there, for heavens' sakes be careful! The owner of that music store has a gun. He will remember that the last time he saw a swan coming at him he got robbed. So watch yourself! You're on a dangerous mission."

"Danger!" said the old cob. "Danger! I *welcome* danger and adventure. Danger is my middle name. I would risk my life to redeem my honor and recapture my sense of decency. I shall pay my debt and blot out the foul mark that sullies my good name. I shall rid myself forever of the shame that comes from thievery and wrongdoing. I shall—"

"If you don't stop talking," said his wife, "you won't get to Billings before the stores close."

"You are right, as usual," replied the cob. He adjusted the moneybag and the slate for flight. Then he took off into the air and headed toward the northeast, flying fast and high. His wife and son watched him until he faded from view.

"What a swan!" said his wife. "You have a good father, Louis. I hope nothing happens to him. To tell you the truth, I'm worried."

The old cob flew fast and far. When he spied the churches and factories and shops and homes of Billings, he circled once, then began his downward glide—straight for the music store.

"My hour has come," he said to himself. "My moment of truth is at hand. I shall soon be out of debt, out from under the cloud of shame and dishonor that has cast a shadow over my life for lo these many months."

The cob had been seen already by people down below. One of the salesmen in the music store was standing by the front window, looking out. When he saw the big white bird approaching, he yelled to the storekeeper: "Large bird approaching. Get your gun!"

The storekeeper grabbed his shotgun and raced to the sidewalk. The cob was low in the sky, gliding straight for the store.

The storekeeper raised his gun. He fired both barrels in quick succession. The old cob felt a twinge of pain in his left shoulder. Thoughts of death filled his mind. Looking back, he saw a bright red drop of blood staining his breast. But he kept going, straight for the storekeeper.

"The end is near," he said to himself. "I shall die in the performance of duty. I have only a few moments remaining to live. Man, in his folly, has given me a mortal wound. The red blood flows in a steady trickle from my veins. My strength fails. But even in death's final hour, I shall deliver the money for the trumpet. Good-bye, life! Good-bye, beautiful world! Good-bye, little lakes in the north! Farewell, springtimes I have known, with their passion and ardor! Farewell, loyal wife and loving sons and daughters! I, who am about to die, salute you. I must die gracefully, as only a swan can."

With that, he sank to the sidewalk, held out the moneybag and the slate to the astonished storekeeper, and fainted away at the sight of his own blood. He lay limp on the sidewalk, to all appearances a dying swan.

A crowd quickly gathered.

"What's this?" exclaimed the storekeeper, bending over the bird. "What's going on here?"

He quickly read the note on the slate. Then he tore open the moneybag and began pulling out hundred-dollar bills and fifty-dollar bills.

A policeman hurried to the scene and started to hold the crowd back.

"Stand back!" he shouted. "The swan is wounded. Give him air!"

"He's dead," said a little boy. "The bird is dead."

"He is *not* dead," said the salesman. "He's scared."

"Call an ambulance!" screamed a lady in the crowd.

A small pool of blood formed under the neck of the old cob. He seemed lifeless. Just then a game warden appeared.

"Who shot this bird?" he demanded.

"I did," said the storekeeper.

"Then you're under arrest," said the warden.

"What for?" asked the storekeeper.

"For shooting a Trumpeter Swan. These birds are protected by law. You can't pull a gun on a wild swan."

"Well," replied the storekeeper, "you can't arrest *me*, either. I happen to know this bird. He's a thief. *He's* the one you should arrest. He's been here before, and he stole a trumpet from my store."

"Call an ambulance!" cried the lady.

"What's that you've got in your hand?" asked the policeman. The storekeeper quickly stuffed the money back into the moneybag and held the bag and the slate behind his back.

"Come on, show it to me!" said the cop.

"I want to see it, too," said the warden.

"We *all* want to see it!" cried a fellow in the crowd. "What's in that bag?"

The storekeeper sheepishly handed the money-bag and the slate to the game warden. The warden stood straight, put on his glasses, and read the note in a loud voice: "To the Storekeeper of Billings: Enclosed please find four thousand four hundred and twenty dollars and seventy-eight cents. It will pay you for the trumpet and the damage to the store. Sorry about the inconvenience this has caused you."

At the mention of the sum of money, the crowd gasped. Everyone started talking at once.

"Call an ambulance!" screamed the lady.

"I'll have to take that money to the station house," said the policeman. "This is a complicated case. Anything that involves money is complex. I'll take the money and keep it safe until the matter is decided."

"No, you won't!" said the game warden. "The money is mine."

"Why?" asked the policeman.

"Because," replied the warden.

"Because *what*?" asked the policeman.

"Because the law says the bird is in my custody. The money was on the bird. Therefore, the money goes to me until this is settled."

"Oh, no, you don't!" said the storekeeper, angrily. "The money is mine. It says so right here on this slate. The four thousand four hundred and twenty dollars and seventy-eight cents is mine. Nobody's going to take it away from me."

"Yes, they are!" said the policeman. "*I* am."

"No, *I* am," said the game warden.

"Is there a lawyer in the crowd?" asked the storekeeper. "We'll settle this matter right here and now."

A tall man stepped forward.

"I'm Judge Ricketts," he said. "I'll decide this case. Now then, who saw the bird arrive?"

"I did," said the salesman.

"Call an ambulance!" screamed the lady.

"I saw the bird, too," said a small boy named Alfred Gore.

"O.K.," said the judge. "Describe what happened, exactly as you saw it."

The salesman spoke first. "Well," he said, "I was looking out the window and saw a swan approaching. So I hollered. The boss got his gun and fired, and the bird fell to the sidewalk. There was a drop or two of blood."

"Did you notice anything special about the bird?" asked Judge Ricketts.

"He carried money," replied the salesman. "You don't often see any money on a bird, so I noticed it."

"All right," said the judge. "Now we'll let Alfred Gore tell it as *he* saw it. Describe what you saw, Alfred!"

"Well," said the little boy, "I was very thirsty, and so I wanted to go to a candy store and get something to drink."

"Just tell what you saw, please, Alfred," said the judge. "Never mind how thirsty you were."

"I was coming along the street," continued Alfred, "because I was very thirsty. So I was coming along the street on my way to the candy store to get something to drink, and there, up in the sky, all of a sudden there was a big white bird right over me in the sky and he was sliding down out of the sky like *this.*" Alfred held out his arms and imitated a bird. "And so when I saw the big bird I stopped thinking about how thirsty I was and pretty soon this enormous bird, he was enormous, was on the sidewalk and he was dead and there was blood all over everything and that's what I saw."

"Did you notice anything special about the bird?" asked Judge Ricketts.

"Blood," said Alfred.

"Anything else?"

"No, just blood."

"Did you hear a gun?"

"No, just blood," said Alfred.

"Thank you!" said the judge. "That will be all."

Just then a siren started wailing—woooaw, woooaw, woooaw. An ambulance came screaming down the street. It stopped in front of the crowd. Two men jumped out. They carried a stretcher and set it down next to where the swan lay. The old cob lifted his head and looked around. "I have been at death's door," he thought, "and now I think I am returning to life. I am reviving. I shall live! I shall return on strong wings to the great sky. I shall glide gracefully again on the ponds of the world and hear the frogs and take pleasure in the sounds of night and the coming of day."

As he was thinking these pleasant thoughts, he felt himself being lifted. The ambulance attendants put his slate around his neck, picked him up, laid him gently on the stretcher, and carried him into the ambulance, which had a red light whirling round and around on top of it. One of the men placed an oxygen mask over the old cob's head and gave him some oxygen. And away they drove, making a great deal of noise, to the hospital. There, he was put to bed and given a shot of penicillin. A young doctor came in and examined the wound where the shotgun pellet had hit him. The doctor said the wound was superficial. The old cob didn't know what "superficial" meant, but it sounded serious.

Nurses gathered around. One of them took the swan's blood pressure and wrote something on a chart. The old cob was beginning to feel very well again. It felt good to be in bed, being cared for by nurses—one of whom was quite pretty. The doctor washed the wound and put a Band-Aid on it.

Meantime, back on the sidewalk in front of the music store, the judge was announcing his decision.

"On the basis of the testimony," he said solemnly, "I award the money to the storekeeper, to make up for the loss of the trumpet and damage to the store. I am placing the swan in the custody of the game warden."

"Your Honor," said the warden, "don't forget that the storekeeper is under arrest for shooting a wild swan."

"It was a case of false arrest," said the judge wisely. "The storekeeper fired his gun at the bird because he was afraid his store would be robbed again. He did not know that the swan was bringing money to pay for the trumpet. The gun was fired in self-defense. Everyone is innocent, the swan is honest, the debt is paid, the storekeeper is rich, and the case is dismissed."

A cheer went up from the crowd. The warden looked sulky. The policeman looked glum. But the storekeeper was beaming. He was a happy man. He felt that justice had been done.

"I have an announcement," he said. "I am only going to keep just enough of this money to pay for the stolen trumpet and the repair bills for my store. All the rest of the money will be given to a good cause if I can think of just the right one. Can anyone think of a worthy cause that needs money?"

"The Salvation Army," suggested a woman.

"No," said the storekeeper.

"The Boy Scouts?" suggested a boy.

"No," said the storekeeper.

"The American Civil Liberties Union?" suggested a man.

"Nope," said the storekeeper. "Nobody has

thought of just the right place for me to send this money."

"How about the Audubon Society?" asked a little fellow whose nose looked like the beak of a bird.

"Great! You've got it!" cried the storekeeper. "A bird has been very good to me, and now I want to do something for birds. The Audubon Society is kind to birds. I want this money to be used to help birds. Some birds are in real trouble. They face extinction."

"What's extinction?" asked Alfred Gore. "Does it mean they stink?"

"Certainly not," said the storekeeper. "Extinction is what happens when you're extinct—when you don't exist anymore because there are no others like you. Like the passenger pigeon and the eastern Heath Hen and the Dodo and the Dinosaur."

"The Trumpeter Swan was *almost* extinct," said the game warden. "People kept shooting them, like this crazy storekeeper. But now they are making a comeback."

The storekeeper glared at the warden.

"*I'll* say they're making a comeback," he said. "The swan that was just here *came back* to Billings with four thousand four hundred and twenty dollars and seventy-eight cents and gave it all to me. I call that making a very good comeback. I can't imagine where he *got* all that money. It's a mighty funny thing."

The storekeeper went back into his music store, the policeman went back to the station house, the judge went back to the courthouse, the game warden walked off down the street toward the hospital, and Alfred Gore, who was still thirsty, continued his journey to the candy store. All the rest of the people wandered away.

At the hospital, the old cob lay peacefully in bed thinking beautiful thoughts. He felt thankful to be alive and relieved to be out of debt.

It was getting dark. Many of the patients in the hospital were asleep already. A nurse came into the cob's room to open his window.

When she came back a few minutes later to take the cob's temperature and give him a back rub, the bed was empty—the room was deserted. The cob had jumped out of the window, spread his broad wings, and headed for home through the cold night sky. He flew all night, crossed the mountains, and arrived home soon after daylight, where his wife was waiting for him.

"How did it go?" she asked.

"Very well," he said. "An extraordinary adventure. I was shot at, just as you predicted. The storekeeper pointed a gun at me and fired. I felt an agonizing pain in my left shoulder—which I've always considered the more beautiful of my two shoulders. Blood gushed from my wound in torrents, and I sank gracefully to the sidewalk, where I handed over the money and thus regained my honor and my decency. I was at death's door. A great multitude of people gathered. Blood was everywhere. I became faint and passed out with dignity in front of all. The police arrived—dozens of them. Game wardens flocked to the scene in great numbers, and there was a tremendous argument about the money."

"How did you know all this if you were unconscious?" asked his wife.

"My dear," said the cob, "I wish you wouldn't interrupt me when I am telling the story of my trip. Seeing my grave condition, someone in the crowd summoned an ambulance, and I was taken to the hospital, where I was put to bed. I looked very beautiful lying there, my black bill contrasting with the snowy white sheets. Doctors and nurses attended me and comforted me in my hour of suffering and pain. You can judge how serious my wound was when I tell you that one of the doctors examined it and said it was superficial."

"It doesn't look bad to me," said his wife. "I think you just got nicked. If it had been bad, you couldn't have flown back so soon. Anyway, superficial or not, I'm glad to see you home safe. I always miss you when you're gone. I don't know why, but I do."

And with that, she placed her head across his neck and gave him a slight nudge. Then they had breakfast and went for a swim in an open place in the frozen lake. The cob pulled his Band-Aid off and threw it away.

XXI

The Greening Spring

LOUIS AND SERENA WERE MORE IN LOVE than ever. When spring came, they flew north, Louis wearing his trumpet and his slate and his chalk pencil and his medal, Serena wearing nothing at all. Now that he no longer had to work and earn, Louis felt a great sense of relief. No more would he have to carry a moneybag around his neck.

The two swans flew high and fast, ten thousand feet above the earth. They arrived at last at the little pond in the wilderness where Louis had been hatched. This was his dream—to return with his love to the place in Canada where he had first seen the light of day. He escorted Serena from one end of the pond to the other and back again. He showed her the tiny island where his mother's nest had been. He showed her the log Sam Beaver had been sitting on when Louis had pulled his shoelace because he couldn't say beep. Serena was enchanted. They were in love. It was spring. The frog was waking from his long sleep. The turtle was coming to life again after his nap. The chipmunk felt the warm air, soft and kind, blow through the trees, just as it did in that springtime when Louis's father and mother had visited the pond to nest and raise their young.

The sun shone down, strong and steady. Ice was melting; patches of open water appeared on the pond. Louis and Serena felt the changing world, and they stirred with new life and rapture and hope. There was a smell in the air, a smell of earth waking after its long winter. The trees were putting out tiny green buds, the buds were swelling. A better, easier time was at hand. A pair of Mallard Ducks flew in. A sparrow with a white throat arrived and sang, "Oh, sweet Canada, Canada, Canada!"

Serena chose a muskrat lodge on which to build her nest. It was the right height above the water. The muskrats had built it of mud and sticks. Louis had hoped his wife might decide to make her nest in the same spot where his mother had built hers, but females are full of notions; they want their own way, pretty much, and Serena knew what she was doing. Louis was so delighted when he saw her begin to construct the nest, he didn't really care where it was. He raised his horn to his mouth and played the beginning of an old song called "It's delightful to be married, to be-be-be-be, be-be-be-be married . . ." Then he helped by bringing a few pieces of coarse grass.

Rain or shine, cold or warm, every day was a happy day for the two swans. In time, the eggs were laid and the cygnets were hatched—four of them. The first sound the baby swans heard was the pure, strong sound of their father's trumpet.

"Oh, ever in the greening spring," he played, "By bank and bough retiring . . ."

Life was gay and busy and sweet in the little lonely pond in the north woods. Once in a while Sam Beaver would show up for a visit, and they would have great times together.

Louis never forgot his old jobs, his old friends, or his promise to the Head Man in Charge of Birds in Philadelphia. As the years went by, he and Serena returned each spring to the pond, nested, and had their young. And each year, at the end of summer, when the moult was over and the flight feathers grew back in and the cygnets were ready to try their wings, Louis took his family for a long pleasure trip across America. He led them first to Camp Kookooskoos, where he had saved the life of Applegate Skinner and won his medal. The camp would be closed for the season, but Louis liked to revisit it and wander around, remembering the boys and how he had earned his first hundred dollars as camp bugler.

Then the swans would fly to Boston, where the Swan Boatman always gave them a big welcome. Louis would polish up his horn, blow the spit out of it, and swim in front of the boats again, playing "Row, row, row your boat," and the people of Boston would hear the familiar sound of the trumpet of the swan and would flock to the Public Garden. Then the Boatman would treat Louis and Serena to a night at the Ritz Hotel, while the cygnets spent the night by themselves on the lake, watched over by the Boatman. Serena dearly loved the Ritz. She ate dozens of watercress sandwiches and gazed at herself in the mirror and swam in the bathtub. And while Louis stood and looked out of the window at the Public Garden down below, Serena would walk round and around, turning lights on and off for the fun of it. Then they would both get into the bathtub and go to sleep.

From Boston, Louis would lead his family to the Philadelphia Zoo and show them Bird Lake. Here, he would be greeted warmly by the Head Man in Charge of Birds. If the Zoo needed a young Trumpeter Swan to add to its collection of waterfowl, Louis would donate one of his cygnets, just as he had promised. In later years, Philadelphia was also the place where they would see Sam Beaver. Sam took a job with the Zoo just as soon as he was old enough to go to work. He and Louis always had a great time when they got together. Louis would get out his slate, and they would have a long talk about old times.

After visiting Philadelphia, Louis would fly south with his wife and children so they could see the great savannas where alligators dozed in the swamp water and Turkey Buzzards soared in the sky. And then they would return home to spend the winter in the Red Rock Lakes of Montana, in the lovely, serene Centennial Valley, where all Trumpeter Swans feel safe and unafraid.

The life of a swan must be a very pleasant and interesting life. And of course Louis's life was particularly pleasant because he was a musician. Louis took good care of his trumpet. He kept it clean and spent hours polishing it with the tips of his wing feathers. As long as he lived, he felt grateful to his father, the brave cob who had risked his life in order to give him the trumpet he needed so badly. Every time Louis looked at Serena, he remembered that the sound of the trumpet was what had made her willing to become his mate.

Swans often live to be very old. Year after year, Louis and Serena returned in spring to the same small pond in Canada to raise their family. The days were peaceful. Always, just at the edge of dark, when the young cygnets were getting sleepy, Louis would raise his horn and play taps, just as he used to do at camp long ago. The notes were sad and beautiful as they floated across the still water and up into the night sky.

One summer, when Sam Beaver was about twenty, he and his father were sitting in their camp in Canada. It was after supper. Mr. Beaver was rocking in a chair, resting after a day of fishing. Sam was reading a book.

"Pop," said Sam, "what does 'crepuscular' mean?"

"How should I know?" replied Mr. Beaver. "I never heard the word before."

"It has something to do with rabbits," said Sam. "It says here that a rabbit is a crepuscular animal."

"Probably means timid," said Mr. Beaver. "Or

maybe it means that it can run like the dickens. Or maybe it means stupid. A rabbit will sit right in the middle of the road at night and stare into your headlights and never get out of the way, and that's how a lot of rabbits get run over. They're stupid."

"Well," said Sam, "I guess the only way to find out what 'crepuscular' means is to look it up in the dictionary."

"We haven't got a dictionary here," said Mr. Beaver. "You'll have to wait till we get back to the ranch."

Just then, over at the pond where the swans were, Louis raised his horn and played taps, to let his children know that the day had come to an end. The wind was right, and the sound carried across the swamp.

Mr. Beaver stopped rocking.

"That's funny!" he said. "I thought I heard the sound of a trumpet just then."

"I don't see how you could," replied Sam. "We're alone in these woods."

"I know we are," said Mr. Beaver. "Just the same, I thought I heard a trumpet. Or a bugle."

Sam chuckled. He had never told his father about the swans in the pond nearby. He kept their secret to himself. When he went to the pond, he always went alone. That's the way he liked it. And that's the way the swans liked it.

"What ever happened to your friend Louis?" asked Mr. Beaver. "Louis was a trumpeter. You don't suppose *he's* somewhere around here, do you?"

"He might be," said Sam.

"Have you heard from him recently?" asked Mr. Beaver.

"No," replied Sam. "He doesn't write anymore. He ran out of postage stamps, and he has no money to buy stamps with."

"Oh," said Mr. Beaver. "Well, the whole business about that bird was very queer—I never did fully understand it."

Sam looked across at his father and saw that his eyes had closed. Mr. Beaver was falling asleep. There was hardly a sound to disturb the stillness of the woods.

Sam was tired and sleepy too. He got out his notebook and sat down at the table by the light of the kerosene lamp. This is what he wrote:

Tonight I heard Louis's horn. My father heard it, too. The wind was right, and I could hear the notes of taps, just as darkness fell. There is nothing in all

the world I like better than the trumpet of the swan.
What does "crepuscular" mean?

Sam put his notebook away. He undressed and slid into bed. He lay there, wondering what "crepuscular" meant. In less than three minutes he was fast asleep.

On the pond where the swans were, Louis put his trumpet away. The cygnets crept under their mother's wings. Darkness settled on woods and fields and marsh. A loon called its wild night cry. As Louis relaxed and prepared for sleep, all his thoughts were of how lucky he was to inhabit such a beautiful earth, how lucky he had been to solve his problems with music, and how pleasant it was to look forward to another night of sleep and another day tomorrow, and the fresh morning, and the light that returns with the day.